...ORLD

The Asphodel Meadows

The River of Wailing

The Dragon's Tread

Ashville Grove

Cryptic Falls

Dreadhold

Nevergate

Catterville

The River of Temptation

The Realm of the Nereids

The river of pain

the
...ead

The Bone Court

The Cradle of the Dead

Cave Town

The Elysian Fields

The Outskirts

Vale of Mourning

The Blood Court

Abyssum

Poseidon's Labyrinth

Death

The Compass of Destiny

Doom

Life

Charon

Salvation

THE BONE THIEF SAGA

...one's Story....

AF353077

For my daughter, Valea.
Because I would go to the Underworld and back for you.

The Bone Weaver's Curse

HELEEN DAVIES

THE BONE THIEF SAGA BOOK TWO

PLAYLIST THE BONE WEAVER'S CURSE

CHAPTER ONE — *11 Minutes* by Yungblood feat. Halsey
CHAPTER TWO — *Running Up That Hill* by Loveless
CHAPTER THREE — *I Think I'm Okay* by MGK ft. Yungblood
CHAPTER FOUR — *The Devil Doesn't Bargain* by Alec Benjamin
CHAPTER FIVE — *Worst Case Scenario* by Loveless
CHAPTER SIX — *Someone you loved* by Lewis Capaldi
CHAPTER SEVEN — *War of Hearts* by Ruelle
CHAPTER EIGHT — *Chasing Cars* by Snow Patrol
CHAPTER NINE — *Fall for you* by Secondhand Serenade
CHAPTER TEN — *Hide And Seek* by Imogen Heap
CHAPTER ELEVEN — *Perfect* by Cole Norton
CHAPTER TWELVE — *The Kill* by 30 Seconds to Mars
CHAPTER THIRTEEN — *I Write Sins No Tragedies* by Pan!c at the Disco
CHAPTER FOURTEEN — *Forget Me Too* by Machine Gun Kelly
CHAPTER FIFTEEN — *Young* by The Chainsmokers
CHAPTER SIXTEEN — *Sleeptalk* by Dayseeker
CHAPTER SEVENTEEN — *Bachelor's Death* by Pan!c at the Disco
CHAPTER EIGHTEEN — *Save You* by Simple Plan
CHAPTER NINETEEN — *Decode* by Paramore
CHAPTER TWENTY — *Love To Lose* by Sandro Cavazza, Georgia Ku
CHAPTER TWENTY-ONE — *In the Middle of the Night* by Loveless
CHAPTER TWENTY-TWO — *Enough For You* by Henri Werner
CHAPTER TWENTY-THREE — *In Bloom* by Neck Deep
CHAPTER TWENTY-FOUR — *Til The Day I Die* by The Story of the Year
CHAPTER TWENTY-FIVE — *Don't Blame Me* by Taylor Swift
CHAPTER TWENTY-SIX — *Bad Things* MGK feat. Camilla Cabello
CHAPTER TWENTY-SEVEN — *Run* by Leona Lewis
CHAPTER TWENTY-EIGHT — *Enemy* by Imagine Dragons
CHAPTER TWENTY-NINE — *Scars* by Papa Roach
CHAPTER THIRTY — *Like A Villain* by Bad Omens
CHAPTER THIRTY-ONE — *Bad Blood* by Taylor Swift
CHAPTER THIRTY-TWO — *If I Killed Someone For You* by Alec Benjamin

SCAN ME

TRIGGER WARNINGS

The Bone Thief Saga is a dark fantasy romance set in a brutal, morally grey world and some elements may be triggering for you. Please be careful and take note of the following elements: war, blood, hand-to-hand combat, death, death of a child, graphic language, graphic violence, explicit sexual content, mentioning of cheating, alcohol usage, drug usage, grief.

The Bone Weaver's Curse

HELEEN DAVIES

THE BONE THIEF SAGA BOOK TWO

CHAPTER ONE
LYNNE

"Daddy?" I heard the sweet and innocent voice of Jamie, and my grip on the computer mouse tightened. Quickly, I closed the windows I had opened on the dark web. The fucking deals I was monitoring were suddenly forgotten. My heart sank with guilt and my own promises to keep my work and family separate were ringing in my ears.

I cursed under my breath as I jumped up from my chair, the wheels clattering across the hardwood floor. But it was too late, Jamie had already managed to open the door, and her dark curls were all that I could see. My heart softened immediately, and I smiled tenderly at her.

No matter what happened in my life, she was my angel.

"Jamie, what are you doing here? Where's Mommy?" I asked, trying to remain composed as I wrapped one arm around her. I always felt busted when she caught me working. Damn drug smuggling.

She let go of the door handle, her lower lip quivering as she spoke. "Someone called mommy. The bride wants other flowers, I think. She said I should come to you."

I stroked her cheek and gave her a hug. The sweet, sugary scent of her PAW Patrol shampoo filled my nostrils. "Ah, we can't fight against the Bridezillas... so... how about we go to the playground?" I tried to put a smile on my face, but it felt strained. That guilt. No matter how much I tried to get away from it, it kept me in its grip, smothering any chance of finding peace or redemption. And the worst of it? It was my own fucking fault.

Jamie nodded, her curls bouncing along. "Yes! Will you push me on the swings then?"

I let loose a laugh and ran a hand through my hair. I wanted nothing more than to spend time with Jamie, but those orders on the darknet couldn't wait. With a heavy heart, I said, "Sure, baby, I'll just finish something real quick. Go get your shoes, okay?"

"Okay, but you have to push five minutes longer then!" She giggled and ran off, jumping up and down on the way.

I shook my head, still grinning. I just couldn't believe she was five already. I always thought the saying, that you could tell time by the kids, sucked, but man... it's true. Time did fly.

I went back to the computer to check the last C-WAX order. Something looked strange, and I couldn't take any chances. After all, the importation of the drug was my responsibility, the duty of the drug king of Chicago. Just the thought made me smile proudly as I woke up my computer from standby slumber. I hacked into the darknet again, confirmed the delivery, and suddenly heard Jamie screaming. It wasn't a normal scream. Like the one she gave when she saw a spider or stumbled on something.

No, she screamed in terror.

A cry sliced through me, sinking deep into my marrow and bone, an earthquake of emotion that shattered my very soul,

I pushed myself up against the table, knocked over a mug,

the cold coffee spreading across my keyboard, and ran through the office, right into the hallway.

"Jamie?" I roared and rumbled down the stairs, almost tearing all the photos of my daughter off the wall. But one showing her as a baby in a little toy car fell to the floor no matter what, shards of glass scattering across the glossy staircase as I stepped on them, ignoring the little stings it gave me through my socks. I panted as I tried to see something through our floor to ceiling windows. See anything. See her.

But there was no sign of her.

As cold wind blew past my cheeks, my eyes flicked to the front door.

It was wide open. I ran outside, into the backyard. It had been bright as a spring day a moment ago, but now the sky was darkened, like a veil slowly settling over the sky. In a trance-like state, I navigated towards the playground, my feet plowing through the grass with a sense of urgency. There, before me, stood her play tower. The swing, swaying with eerie silence, danced back and forth, as if moved by an invisible hand, whispering secrets on the wind.

My body involuntarily tensed up as I made my way to the swing, clinging to any surface I could find. As I rounded a hedge, my stomach dropped. Two black figures were bending over something. I needed a span of a moment to realize that that *something* was my baby girl.

"Let go of her," I screamed, my voice as dark as the shadowy creatures before me.

They were not human, neither flesh nor skin. They were shadows with elongated limbs that moved with an unnatural fluidity.

As my gaze fell upon them, one of the shadowy beings slowly lifted its head. Time seemed to freeze, but the creature's lifeless onyx eyes locked onto mine nevertheless. Its mouth creaked open, revealing a cavernous void lined with rows of black, decaying teeth. Each tooth exuded an otherworldly darkness that sent shivers cascading down my spine. Each tooth seemed to ooze a darkness so otherworldly, it made my spine crawl with a chilling terror that gripped me to the core.

My pulse raced but I ran towards them, feeling my heart pound up to my temples.

I had no idea what I would do when I finally reached them, but my will kept pushing me forward.

With a leap, my hands itching to grab hold and unleash pure fury, I was just inches away when a mysterious rustle broke the silence, and they disappeared into thin air. And there, right beneath me, lay Jamie, an unexpected sight that jolted me back to reality.

Her mouth open, her face turned to the side. Utterly lifeless.

My eyes grew heavy as I gripped her small hand that was barely the size of a third of mine.

Five.

She was only five.

This couldn't be true. It just couldn't.

Holding her fragile body close, I let out a bloodcurdling scream that echoed through the air. I felt lost, clueless about what to do next, as I cursed this messed up world we're living in. Every damn day it's getting more dangerous, and I couldn't ignore it anymore.

People had been talking about these dark beings attacking humans, but the media just dismissed them as crazy folks spewing nonsense, calling it all fake news. But ever since Aria showed up, I knew those fuckers were real. And yet, even armed with that knowledge, I couldn't freaking save Jamie.

Refusing to accept the truth, I lifted my baby and buried my head in her neck. "Jamie, it's going to be okay. It's going to be all right, okay?" I said more to myself than to her.

I pulled her up to my lap, rocking back and forth. It couldn't be. This couldn't be real.

One minute. One fucking minute too late.

This was insane. Not possible. No. Within one minute they couldn't have grabbed her and killed her. Within sixty seconds her lively body couldn't just turn into a motionless one. This just couldn't be real. Anyone could die but her.

Tears welled up in my eyes, making them burn, and my breath came out in short, shaky bursts, just like a sad song on repeat. Only that the song was my life now.

Fuck. She didn't even live yet! She just started. Came into this world and gave me joy where there was none. Warmed up my cold hard that turned even colder when Aria took it and ripped it apart.

Why couldn't I turn back time? My grip tightened and I sobbed into her neck.

One fucking minute.

I only had to turn back one minute and then everything would be okay. Everything would be all right again.

I stared at the sky as if someone up there would be capable to help me. What should I do now? What? How the fuck could I undo this? Her little heart wasn't beating. My baby wasn't breathing. Her little chest didn't rise. Someone had to help. Someone had to, some—and that's when the idea came to me.

Aria.

A desperate gasp escaped my throat as I scooped Jamie up in my arms and ran. I could feel the vibrations of her shoes against my body as I raced towards safety. Finally making it inside, I sprinted upstairs and back into my office. Everything around me seemed to blur, and in my mind, Jamie was still smiling happily at me, talking to me, asking me to push the swing.

"I'm going to push the swings for yours, okay?" I promised.

"Just let me fix this." No freaking way was I gonna let this situation slide. My baby, the one who said "daddy" as their first word, couldn't just be dead, not on my watch. No, I would tear this whole world apart if I could save her. I would put up with anything and that's what I was going to do.

With trembling hands, I laid Jamie on the couch.

As my hand gently pulled out from under her head, a hot tear ran down my cheek. No father ever wanted to see his child like this. We were not designed for our children to die before us. No one was supposed to witness something like that. No one.

Her head dropped to her side and I stroked her curls, my fingers trembling. "I'll save you and if it's the last thing I do, I'll save you, baby."

I took a deep breath, inhaling the thick air that felt oppressive and heavy in my lungs.

Rage surged through me, taking hold of every part of my being and tears spilling down my cheeks. All I wanted was to be the one lying on that couch, instead of her. I deserved to be dead. Not her. But thank God I knew exactly what to do.

I unlocked the safe under my desk, having to try it three times to hit the hole since my hand shook like an eel. I shoved the C-Wax away and fumbled all the way to the back, past a gun, and reached for a tiny book. A small electric pulse burst through my body as my sweaty fingers touched the leather strap. I pulled it out and opened it.

Any's diary.

I found it when I was cleaning out his apartment. He left all his possessions to me. I donated the majority of his assets to medical charities and orphanages but kept a few personal items like his private diary and photo albums. In one of those were stories and photos of Aria, needless to say that this one was my favorite. It stirred something inside of me that wanted to find her, to find the tower in the cemetery. But no matter what I did or where I looked, it was all in vain. Ever since she walked out of my life five years ago, I never saw her again.

Then, I read Any's diary, doing all the research to go to the Underworld myself, but I never dared to actually use the spells Any collected.

Until now.

Now I had no choice but to use it.

I cracked open the book, its pages all yellowed and sporting a collection of coffee and wine stains, like battle scars from Any's countless hours of reading and revising. And damn, some pages were torn to shreds, proof that they really went all out with it.

He noted beings that he found, heard about, that he conjured up. Wrote down sayings, legends, gods, spells, something about a stone called the Omphalos stone... There was also a map, and I figured it showed where the damn stone could be found. But some weird shadowy ink-like substance blurred it, so I didn't bother wasting my time with it.

All I wanted back then was to find Aria.

And in the process, I came across something that I would only use in an extreme emergency or when Jamie was grown up and I'd be ready to eventually leave for Aria. I didn't dare to lay my trump card yet. Since I didn't know what would come out of it, who would be summoned. I wanted to see her, to have her with me but I was not a fool and I knew that if I took this step, the possibility that I could never be among the living again would be very likely and I had a daughter I wanted to raise properly.

With determination, I raised my voice and began reading the hastily scribbled words, making sure to capture every intricate detail: *"Isa eat e aleeva nu ave ta Melinoe."*

CHAPTER TWO
RIO

The moment I spoke the last word, a wind came up.

Cold as on the sea, whipping like branches in a storm. My eyes rushed to Jamie and I saw her curls standing on end, dancing like snakes. I reared up in front of her and tried to protect what was still to be protected.

With a resounding thud, the window in front of me burst open, causing me to startle upright. It collided with the bookshelf, sending a few books tumbling to the floor, as another forceful gust of wind rushed into the room.

Before my very eyes, the wind transformed into a sinister black smoke, gradually expanding in size until it consumed my entire office. Now the room was engulfed in an eerie haze, just like the insides of a coal stove.

I pushed myself backward, clutching Jamie's lifeless form tightly against me. Then the smoke formed into a large silhouette, becoming denser until a statue stood before me. Suddenly, I felt a tug right where my heart once was, and I grasped the rough fabric over my chest. Since Aria had touched me there was nothing left inside but stillness. Literally. I had no heart anymore. But now that exact spot where her magic had spread its deadly venom, I felt a tingle and the statue became... human, taking on colors until a woman stood before me.

But not just any woman.

It was the Bone Queen, coming on my demand straight from the Underworld.

She bent her hips lasciviously, delicately resting a hand upon her waist while her eyes locked with mine in a captivating gaze. Damns. Her eyes were like the slits of a snake, but with long lashes just like a frame. While her body seemed to change with every blink, her black hair grew longer until it reached her hips. Her skin was as white as alabaster, the same color as her dress.

The muscles in her jaw strained and she gritted her teeth, realizing that a human had summoned her. I kept a close eye on her as her fingers balled up, gripping her dress. The dim light from above caught the shine of the fabric, adding a little extra flair. The pattern on her skirt, black and white swirls, seemed like a thousand eyes watching me. Staring at me. It looked almost like bones draped over her body.

Her gaze shifted from me and fell onto Jamie, and the anger in her eyes receded like a wave crashing against rocks.

"Why are you bothering me, human?" Her voice was soft, melodic with a definitive undertone as she slowly strode toward me. Something flashed in her pupils and she stopped just in front of me, tilting her head back as if she was contemplating something. "It's you," was all she said but those two words made me stop breathing for a split second.

Why the fuck would she know me?

I stood up from my crouch, my muscles heavy and rigid. "What do you mean? Do you know me?"

She tilted her head to the other side, her eyes narrowing. "Holy hell... it's definitely you."

That's when she started to laugh. She was busting a gut

with laughter! She even had to hold her stomach as she leaned on my bookshelf, supporting herself while my throat tightened. Fuck, anger flared up inside me, brewing like a damn hurricane now.

"I didn't summon you to laugh at me." My knuckles cracked as I clenched my fingers into fists.

"Hell, this is hilarious! How can *you* end up summoning *me*? Please don't tell me you need my help." She wiped a tear of laughter from her eye, scoffing while she straightened her silky dress.

I hardened my expression. Showed her I didn't feel like laughing. In an instant her eyes widened, and the corners of her mouth twitched upward as understanding spread across her face. "You're actually asking me for help, aren't you?"

"I have no idea what's so funny but yes, I summoned you to make a deal. My life for my daughter's." I nodded behind me to Jamie, looking at the floor because I couldn't manage to see her lifeless body any longer. Her little fingers with which she was holding me tightly just half an hour ago, begging me to play with her...

When our eyes met again the lamp above us flickered until the bulb burst and the room was turned pitch black. Now all I could see was her pale skin glowing under the streetlight, and I swear the wound in my heart throbbed even harder.

"Well, well... don't you think it's a bit reckless to speak to a queen like that? From all that I know... you think you're human, so to hell with the demand in your damned voice!" she snarled, and closed the space between us, the silken fabric of her dress shuffling on the floor. "No one calls the queen lightly, *human*." She hissed the last word as if it were synonymous with vermin.

"But I'm willing to pay the price," I said. "*Any* price?"

"Any."

She tilted her head as if considering what price to name but the smirk on her lips told me she already knew it from the moment I summoned her. She played me, or at least she tried to. Fortunately, I wasn't easy to be played.

Slowly, she lifted her hand and caressed my cheek with chilling fingers. The icy sensation sent a shiver down my spine, causing me to involuntarily gasp for breath. As if trying to analyze my scent, she sniffed and suddenly pulled her eyebrows down. "So, the rumors are true, you really were stuck in a human body all this time. I can't believe you are this stupid. You never did anything like that, but well, it's just like I predicted."

I huffed out a dry laugh. "I can't follow."

"Doesn't matter, you'll get the hang of it eventually. So, let's discuss that *deal*." She scoffed once more and started to twist a black curl between her fingertips. I couldn't believe how she thought it was all a big joke. It was anything but a joke for me. "I'll save this kid, but I want three things from you."

Okay, I was already expecting that. It's a tale as old as time that the rulers of the Underworld liked to stick to three conditions. Magical numbers and all.

The queen charged at me then, grabbing my chest and her long fingernails ramming into my skin as the slits in her eyes widened until they were nothing more than two black orbs staring at me— through me. Deep like a void. "You have one chance to save your daughter. Return to the Underworld and bring me a hundred souls, or she will be lost forever. You have no time to spare, and failure is not an option."

She yanked at my shirt, trying to reel me in, but I went against it and grabbed hold of her wrist instead. Then there it was. Only briefly but I saw it. A wince. The queen was scared for a second... but that raised an entirely different question. Why the fuck should she be scared of me?

"Fine. What's the third condition?"

She smiled. "At least your brain wasn't affected much when you let yourself be reborn in that pathetic form."

I tightened my grip on her hand and this time she flinched. I smirked. There was a thing about people with power. Even if you were practically insignificant to them, you had to pretend to be anything but that. "Just tell me your third condition, witch."

"The hundredth soul you have to collect will be the girl you know under the names Lynne or Aria Wadden."

"No."

She clicked her tongue. "I'm afraid, you're in no position to bargain with me in your current form."

"It's not a bargain. I'll do anything you want, but..." I closed the little space between us until her nose was only inches away from mine. "You need to understand something. Something vital. I'm neither a hero nor a good man. I'll do anything to save my beloved, even tear this world apart. I'll bring Lynne to you but if you harm her, I'll do anything in my power to stop you."

She chuckled. "That's nothing new to me... you've always been the villain to my story, *Rio*. But help me out a little, wouldn't you... aren't you afraid I'll take your daughter to the afterlife after all?"

"Try me. Try to hurt her or Lynne and I'm going to find out why you flinched away from me although I should be nothing to you. You said way too much and I'm more than willing to take advantage of it. If you stab me in the back, I'll find a way around your deals. I'm not to be threatened easily."

She paused for a few seconds, blinking away what I'd just said to her.

Of course, I was bluffing.

I had no idea what I'd do against her, but I had always found a way out, and I wouldn't stop now. The fact that she knew me and was afraid of me gave me a strength I could never have dreamed of. Therefore, there had to be something I could do to put her in place. I thought she was going to say something in return, reminding me that she was the all mighty queen and I nothing but a human, maybe something about me having to call her my lady, or your highness, but she did something completely against what I expected. She smiled and grabbed the back of my head with both icy cold hands and... kissed me.

It was like kissing a stone and the moment her lips touched mine, my lips tingled as if I had touched something poisonous. I don't know why but it reminded me of the kiss when I learned about Lynne's origin.

I touched my lips and they burned. Just like back then.

When I flicked my eyes back to her, something in her gaze flickered like fireworks on New Year's Eve. Stifling the urge to wipe my mouth I tried to hide my fear. Poker face it was. "What was that for?"

She shrugged, backing away from me. "To seal our deal."

"Couldn't you have done it any other way?"

The queen twisted her mouth into a playful pout. "Oh, of course, but... let's say I had to make sure of something. I know I won't get that chance ever again." She licked her lip. "Mmm, delicious. I just love when plans work out."

I narrowed my eyes and before I could snarl anything else she said, "Aren't you afraid your little thief gets jealous? As far as I know, you haven't seen each other in a while."

For less than a blink of an eye I lost my composure. It was the second time she had spoken of Aria. She knew that she had been up here and I wondered if she was in trouble because of it. If the Bone Queen had punished her.

"I heard she's having fun with other men and women. I think you're putting your money on the wrong horse. You'd be wiser to just forget about whatever the two of you had and do as I say, capture her and bring her back to me."

"Like agreed, I'll return her to your doorstep."

"Can't wait, she's been on the run for far too long now."

I tried not to screw up my face, but from her smug look, I knew my pain was visible to her. Aria would always trigger something in me. Always. "Is she hurt?" Maybe that's why she didn't come. I've had that thought many times, feared something had happened to her.

"She was captured by my sister, so, I would put it that way, yes. Lynne mistakenly thinks my sister is helping her, she worries that I would hurt her, the silly thing."

I clenched my fingers into fists.

"Well, well." She grinned and reached for my upper arms, gripping them tightly, kneading the muscles I worked out every day. "Mhmm, aren't you such a feast for the eyes? Always were in each form I saw you."

I grasped her hands, my fingers digging into her skin as my heart raced with anger. I forced my voice to remain steady as I looked her deep in the eyes. "We can do this one of two ways," I said through clenched teeth. "Either you stop talking about me or tell me exactly what it is that you think you know about me."

She giggled. Actually fucking giggled. "Oh no, there's no way I'm letting this opportunity pass by. Get ready for a long talk."

I nodded at her hands and said, "Just make sure we both remember what our deal was—no fumbling if I recall correctly."

"Oh, gods. There never will be," she said, her face growing more serious by the moment, but she finally stepped away from me. "You have seven days to spend with your daughter. Prepare to leave this world forever. You shouldn't be here anyway, so it's not likely you will come back. Ever. Once you return to the Underworld, your body will remember. Slowly... but one day you'll wake up and know it all again. And be

Olympia with me, I hope I'm right beside you when you figure it out."

"We agreed on stopping this shit. Speak the truth or stop your boasting."

She rolled her eyes. "If you didn't look like a human rat I could swear it's you talking to me right now, and for the record, I would very much like to spit in your face too but you're right. Let's put an end to this tonight, we'll have many more nights to cherish our reunion."

She snapped her fingers, and I heard Jamie taking a breath.

All the weight suddenly fell from my chest. I wanted to turn around, but the queen grabbed my chin, holding me in place and forcing me to keep looking at her, while she rasped: "Say your goodbyes and then descend through the tower to the Underworld. I will be waiting for you there."

She let go of me and the light came back on. Something flickered in her eyes, something dangerous that I couldn't place right. I opened my mouth but before I could say a word, Jamie's coughing made me turn around and I rushed to her side, kneeling down beside her.

I hugged her, a desperate laughter bubbling up in my throat as she croaked: "Daddy? I think I fell asleep... I was so tired."

"It's all right," I said, forcing the threatening tears to stay in. "Everything is all right. I got you." When I turned around again, the Bone Queen was gone, and I was left with more than just one fucking question.

CHAPTER THREE
LYNNE

"Who peed on your leg?" the queen asked, tilting her head, a wave of red hair settling over her shoulder.

We stood in front of her well as usual and I tried to conjure up some skulling magic. However, also as usual, I failed. Who would have thought that, huh? Without bones, witching just didn't seem to work for me.

"We need to stir emotions in you, my dear," the Blood Queen said, circling me.

Though I had known her for a long time now and was used to certain tics from her, I flinched. That woman's sheer power still got to me, leaving me overwhelmed day in and day out.

She flicked her eyes open and thick, black lashes fluttered up against her rosy cheekbones, "I'm afraid there's only one thing we could try to save this lost cause."

I swallowed, knowing pretty well who she meant with lost cause.

Me. I was the failure.

"It's for the greater good, remember, my dear." Her voice was challenging, quiet but utterly dangerous.

When she lifted a hand to stroke my cheek I had to put my head back to meet her gaze.

"I tried to think about emotions, my queen," I said but she didn't believe me, her expression turning stony, and I could swear the room got colder.

"Oh please, magic isn't about *thinking*. Let me ask you one thing. Do you have to think each word, each sound before you start to

babble?"

I blink several times. "No."

"So it is with yielding magic. There is no such thing as *thinking* before you use your magic. It's all about doing, about working with what the gods granted you. For some reason you're capable of using our world to conjure up your own magic. A strong kind of magic, my dear. A source we need if we want to finally stop my sister's machinations. It's still something you're aiming for, or am I wrong?"

I shook my head, avoiding her gaze once more. "No, My Queen."

"Well, settle for the best of you then, only you can figure out who you are."

I nodded. She told me this over and over again. When she saved me from her sister, she revealed that The Fates themselves told her about my power. An ability we both tried to figure out for what felt like forever. Like I said, a lost cause.

The queen snorted. "Oh, spare me the theatrics, my dear. You don't have to think before using your legs, silly girl. You just do it."

"But—" I clicked my tongue. "Pardon me, but I need more than this, Your Highness. I need something to hold on to. Of course, it is easy for *you*. It's not as easy as walking for me."

"It should be," she snarled, a wrinkle appearing between

her perfectly arched red eyebrows. "And yet I hate that it has come to this. I'm sorry, but we have no other choice than to—" She took a deep breath. "We are doing this in order to save the world, remember this always. Remember what she's done and what she's going to do. I'm trying to help you."

I nodded. She was right.

Ever since I brought back the Book of Silva, The Blood Queen told me everything about what I had done for her evil sister all those years. What a terrible plan she had forged for years, and how she had taken advantage of me. With every bone I stole for her, she prepared the downfall of our worlds, and I had helped the Bone Queen in this.

I was her naive path to power.

A little girl she could form just the way she wanted to. I didn't want to be that girl anymore. I wasn't.

"What if I say a name where I know it's going to dig deep into your heart?" Her voice deepened and I stopped breathing for a short stretch of time. "How about... you think of *Rio*?"

I squeezed my eyes shut, of course... The pain of his name hit me like a ton of bricks, bringing back a flood of emotions. I had managed to get through an entire day without thinking of him, and now here she was, ripping away that moment of peace —a moment of reprieve from the constant onslaught of pain his skulling name brought.

How could she be so cruel? She damn well knew the deep hole I was stuck in because of him. My cheeks burned as I tried to hold back the tears that were threatening to burst forth.

"Remember the promise," she said, her words, though spoken softly, cutting deep into me, "and how each year on Storm Day you went to your grave even though he never came."

I wanted to break away, longing to escape the heartache that I knew was coming. But I couldn't move on. Not really.

Something held me in place with an iron grip. There was this strong tug of our connection, a bond that refused to be broken no matter how hard I tried or how much I wanted it.

"Picture his face." She grabbed my arm, and an electric impulse shook me.

"The blue of his eyes."

"The black of his hair."

"The scent of his body."

My heart pounded up to my temples.

I hated to think of him, hated to remember his touches, hated him. His skulling promises and the way he just left me. The way he never showed up like promised. When I tore open my tear-stained eyes I stared into her merciless face.

She was cold as stone as she said: "*Remember* how he promised to keep your heart forever and how he took it. Crushed it."

The air around me seared, a wave of heat rippling up from my toes. I've spent all these damn years trying to forget him, but all that's left is this burning anger. It's the only thing that reminds me of what we used to be.

"Remember how happy you were in his arms. When he kissed you, touched you—"

"Stop it!" A shrill cry tore from my throat and suddenly my eyes filled with fire, my body wracking with tremors.

I lunged forward to steady myself and stumbled against the queen's well, my fingertips grazing the crimson blood within. The second my finger caught on a droplet of blood, it sent an electric jolt through my arm that caused black smoke to pour from where I touched the surface. In a blink of an eye the entire chamber was shrouded in darkness, encasing the queen like a cocoon ready for her fate.

Oh, no. Oh, skulling no.

My eyes widened in horror as the dark cloud of shadows manifested around us, swirling and churning like a tempest. I could barely breathe, my chest heaving with a mix of terror and awe as cold sweat blanketed my skin. I was rooted to the spot—this was something I'd never even dreamed possible.

Shadows? I never conjured up shadows... ever.

Frantic, I tried to help the queen out, but before I could raise my hands or actually do anything, I heard a deep laugh from within the smoke cone that made my hair rise in unison.

"See?" She laughed and playfully swatted at the smoke as if shooing away a pesky fly. "What a broken heart can do."

The words lingered between us and for a couple of heartbeats I just stared at her. I had the feeling she wanted to say more. That something lay dormant within these words. Another secret she couldn't tell me.

"Oh dear, don't look at me like that. It's good what you've done!" the queen said, tearing me out of my thoughts.

She snapped her fingers and the smoke vanished into thin air. As if I had never conjured it up.

I glanced at the floor, swallowing.

Skull. She shouldn't have used his name against me. Even if Rio finally led to me being able to use magic, I didn't want him to be the reason. He, who taught me what it meant to love, only to drop me like a hot rock. Like all we've been didn't mean anything, although I was the reason for his revenge, for his coup, for his everything. And yet—it was all a lie.

I made a damn oath to myself that this guy wouldn't have any power over me ever again, and now his name compelled me to yield power I wasn't able for months. The queen could have just as easily sprinkled salt into one of my deepest wounds and it would have hurt less.

"Interesting that you can conjure up shadows..." she

mumbled and put a finger under my chin, forcing me to look her in the eyes once again. "We need to learn what you can do. We know nothing about the extent of your magic, my sweet, sweet Lynne. And we'll keep on accomplishing nothing if you continue to know magic only as a term. You must be able to *use* it if we are to save this world from my sister."

I nodded. "I know, My Queen. I'm sorry..."

"You must be exhausted," she said. "You've done a good job. We'll continue at the same time tomorrow, until then I'll try to figure out what these... what the shadows mean."

"Thank you, Your Highness."

I pressed away the threatening tears, something else I had thanks to my stay on Earth. Another vice. Tears. By the Stix, I don't remember how much I had cried over the last few years. I could have filled my own well with them, for sure. Especially at night. When I dreamed about him. When his strong arms grabbed me, his hot lips kissed mine and when he held me tight, whispering sweet nothings into my ear. That's when it was the worst, because it felt so real every damn time. Just as real as the pain when he didn't show up at Englewood Graveyard. When he *never* came, not even once to say goodbye.

I breathed away the lump that was rising in my throat and wanted to turn around just as the queen spoke my name again. "Lynne, one more thing."

I stopped dead in my tracks, my eyebrows shooting up as I looked at her.

"The Bone Weaver is needed tonight."

I swallowed, forcing me to nod. "Of course. How many people are waiting for me?"

"Diggery counted thirty already, just do it like always. Decide who is worth your magic and who isn't. Word will spread no matter what."

I nodded. "Yes, sleep well, Your Highness." I bowed my head and rushed outside.

Once I was out of her study, I let out a deep, deep breath.

I didn't need to lie to myself. Conjuring up shadows almost ate away all my powers, and the very idea that I would have to grant or refuse requests to all the unnecessary beggars again tonight made me want to puke.

But well, I had no choice because one of the many downsides of living in the queen's castle was the etiquette. Every move I made, every word I uttered was carefully scrutinized. I was used to doing whatever I wanted, loitering in my cave and not wearing clothes for weeks at a time if I chose so. Now I had to be careful with who I talked to, what I wore, how I talked or even when I thought I was alone. Or the queen's favor was gone and with it my chance of freedom. Because without the help of the Blood Queen, the Bone Queen would catch me—she didn't have a search warrant open for me for nothing.

My only hope was to master my magic so that I could defend against all these witches and finally find freedom.

Shaking my head in annoyance, I entered a large hallway that connected several of the queen's chambers. The doors were set close but tall windows near the top let some dark red light come in and illuminate the passage.

I pushed open the massive, arched door with a carved rose pattern on, thinking it would lead me out. But before I could even touch the cold brass handle, the door swung open from the other side.

"Hello, my little Bone Thief," he said by the way of greeting, his words knotting my stomach.

Startled, I took a step back, my gaze involuntarily lifting to meet his.

He was dressed in a loose tunic, showcasing his fair complexion, paired with blood-red leather pants. With a confident toss of his head, a wavy blonde curl swirled from one side to the other. The queen's lover.

"Cyril," I said, avoiding his gaze. "What a pleasure..."

There was something ancient sleeping inside him, just like the queen. I couldn't quite figure out what it was, though.

"How was it today?" he casually said, as if it were normal to do small talk with him. I saw how most Blood Courtiers screamed like babies just when they heard his name. He was feared in the castle like monsters in Cave Town.

I held my chin high, trying to tell him that I on the other hand wasn't afraid of him. I had to prove manners with the queen, but I couldn't care less about him but every damn time I laid eyes on him, that weird feeling would creep up on me, and I couldn't stand it. "I managed to actually conjure up some magic."

He smiled. "Oh, how wonderful, so we're getting closer."

Cyril raised a muscular arm and patted me on the back as if I were one of his pets. "There's already a line waiting in front of the dungeon."

"I better hurry up then," I said. "That's my girl."

I reluctantly dipped my head, following the damn protocol, even though every fiber of my being rebelled against it. Whatever. It was his subtle way of telling me to beat it, so he could fuck the queen. I took the chance and made a swift exit.

The word spread around fast that the queen had an apprentice.

A young witch called the Bone Weaver, who could grant them wishes just like the queen. That witch was me. But, I was just separating the wheat from the chaff. Sending her the most promising dealmakers and handling the ones I deemed useless myself. In return, she promised me to finally learn who I am and why I was able to do magic at all. What kind of magic slumbered inside of me. A question that bugged me since day one. A question no one dared to answer for me yet—not even the Bone Queen.

No, for her I was nothing more than a pawn in her game, an instrument she used to achieve what she longed for. She never told me that only magic wielders could sense powers in bones. She made me believe that I had a special skill, that I was something like her little sniffing dog. By the Stix, I was so happy to find magical bones for her—I really wasn't better than a skulling dog.

And the Blood Court slowly but surely became the only place I was safe.

The minute I stepped off these grounds again, I knew the Bone Queen was ready to punish me. I had no idea how she knew about me losing her bone in the human realm but well... she did. I had wronged her, and she wanted to take revenge. The math was simple. Her power was far greater than mine, and I felt helpless against it. Yet I remained safe because of the curse that the gods had imposed upon the queens and the king. The three siblings who ruled the Underworld were known for their cruelty and violence, so they made sure that they couldn't visit each other's kingdoms ever again.

Though I needed the Blood Court's protection, I resented what it meant to live here with all my heart. But I had to stick through a little longer. Just long enough until I could free myself because there was no one going to help me for sure.

I ran down the hallway, noticing the courtiers getting out of my way, and I slowed my pace. I was part of the queen's closest advisors now and accordingly respected. I shouldn't run. So, I raised my head and walked straight, my heels clacking on the red marble.

"The Bone Weaver," one courtier hissed at another.

"Don't look at her, she'll bewitch you."

"I heard she can read your mind."

I rolled my eyes. If I was hated in my past, I was even more so now. The only one who still had enough guts to challenge me was Mal, but he still spent half of the week in Cave Town, the other he worked for the Blood Queen as well. Something I still had to stomach—still couldn't believe. Mal refused to tell me the details of his visits with the queen, but I had a feeling he hid more than it seemed. His healing abilities had always amazed and frightened me. So, of course, I did spy on them. Just a little. Sometimes the queen wasn't feeling well and then soon after he visited her, she would seem almost like she was reborn. I couldn't help but wonder what Mal was really doing. It had to be something big, though. At least we had the chance to kick back, sip on wine, and talk. It felt like old times.

I made my way to the wing where my chambers were located, swung open the grand black double doors, and swiftly secured them behind me. I pressed my back against them and breathed in and out as deeply as I could. I'd show all of them what I could do. One day, I'd be free. Not bound to any of the queens, not bound to a man I believed in loving and not bound to anyone but me. The moment I lifted my head, I felt something stinging in my eyes but there were no tears. No, it felt more like my eyes started to burn. I shook my head, rubbed them and the feeling passed.

Strange.

Shaking away the odd sensation, I entered the room and was met with the sight of the biggest balcony in the castle. It had been a gift from the queen herself. She had always done her best to pamper me. I rushed outside and ran to the stony fence, leaned over it and whistled loudly. When I saw Soothie's curious face poking out of the large cave that showed several cracks with gleaming lava in it, I couldn't help but smile. The sight of his broad muzzle and green eyes made me laugh out loud. I whistled again, louder than before, and he poked farther out of the opening—readying himself to fly.

He took off and just shortly after the air stirred my hair and he landed right next to me.

I fell around his neck. His rough scales brushing against my throat as I put my arms around him. He purred, bending down and resting his head against mine. The taste of fresh air on him drove away the deep ache inside me for a few moments.

"What happened?" I heard a scratchy voice and sighed into Soothie's head. He didn't miss a thing, did he? But well, as long as I had my found family, everything was all right.

"I was able to do magic," I mumbled against Soothie's scales. "What?" Bory cried, tugging at my dress, but I didn't want to let go of Soothie's embrace just yet. I needed it right now.

"Lynne, what happened? Something must be wrong, you're acting like—"

"I wrapped the queen in smoke after she mentioned Rio." I heard Bory gasp, and I finally turned around to face him.

He wanted to say something, but when he saw my glittering eyes, he closed his mouth again, looking up to Soothie instead. I didn't know what they were quietly communicating but it kept Bory from asking more and I was glad about it. I couldn't talk about *him* again. At least not now.

While stroking Soothie's neck, I looked up at the Underworld's sky and all the bones up there. I'd been here for over five years. Five skulling years and never once did she let me touch the blood in her well.

Why now? Why today?

I knew that some magical bones allowed me to use my power but I never tried blood... she never would let me. What if my magic worked similar to the queens' magic? What if I needed a magical resource and just couldn't conjure it up on my own? Despite what the Blood Queen believed in...

Bory cleared his throat. "But, that means we're moving forward, Lynne. That's perfect!"

I glanced down and watched Bory fake a smile for me. Gods, he was so sweet.

"Yeah, it's something. I still must weave tonight, though."

"Are you nervous?"

"Barely."

He laughed. "Come on, let's go inside. What are some more tiny deals for you, eh?"

I took a deep breath, ready to spill the tea. We had this little game where I pretended to be fine and he pretended to not know I wasn't but each time we started it, I felt the worst so it was better to just tell him what was up with me and so I did. "Every skulling deal reminds me of him and you know it."

"We agreed to never speak of that man again, Lynne."

"Tell that to the queen. I just can't believe that it won't stop hurting. When will it stop, Bory?"

"Soon, it's soon getting better," he lied.

I went in and left the door open. Soothie immediately lay down and placed his head right between the door so he could be with us. He was just too big for a castle, for any building to be honest. We had it better in the cave, and I really felt bad, but he insisted on staying with me, so technically his head lived with us, and the other half had to stay outside.

"Something else was weird tonight, though. I managed to... grow shadows out of my fingertips..."

Bory's eyebrows shot up to his forehead. "Shadows?"

I nodded. "Yup."

"But why would you be able to... conjure up shadows of all things possible?"

I threw my hands up into the air. "Bory, honestly, If I knew why I would have told you the minute I saw your fluffy face."

He grunted but didn't answer this time, and I sighed, feeling guilty again. "Bory, I know that this isn't a good sign."

"Not a good sign? You're not understating! This is horrible. Only the Shadow King uses the magic that lurks in the dark..."

I swallowed. "Let's just... stop talking for now. There is another job I need to do."

CHAPTER FOUR
LYNNE

I stood in my dressing room and examined the dress I always put on when bone weaving. It makes me look like a princess. Funny, considering where I was at five years ago. Dressed in nothing but a leather loincloth and top. My skin was constantly covered in dirt and my hair nothing but matted. Today it had been braided by maids, twisted at my temples like the tendrils of roses while thick white curls fell down my back.

Nowadays, my lips are red, my cheeks rosy.

I no longer looked like a thief. I appeared to be noble and yet this image in my mirror didn't match me, especially not with what was going on inside me. I was no longer the girl who foolishly made deals. I was no longer a girl. I was now a woman. A woman who was rightly feared in parts of the country and cried during her sleep.

Because of a skulling man. What a waste of my time.

I brushed off the rush of emotions surging within me, lifted my chin, and let the fiery red fabric wrap snugly around my curves, making a statement that screamed confidence. The corset was tight, squeezing against my pale white skin in a way that made me feel both beautiful and disgusted. I wanted to bask in the beauty of my outfit but couldn't help feeling like I was swimming in a sea of blood.

I sighed. "Well, Bory, let's catch a few more hopeless souls."

"After you, my lady," he said, and we went through my massive chambers, out into the dark hallway.

Some courtiers walked arm in arm down the corridor, chatting about trifles while the candles on the ceiling glowed bright red, splashing their heads with color. I wasn't surprised to see the castle bursting with people again. Every day there was another party in the Blood Queen's castle. So, whenever I left my chambers, there were always people over people over people.

At first, I thought the queen was addicted to attention but at some point I learned that she used the numerous feasts, walks and excursions as a means of reward and punishment— depending on whether she sent invites or not. Realizing that she didn't have enough graces to bestow in order to continually make an impression, she replaced the real rewards with imaginary ones, with the arousal of jealousy, with small everyday favors, and everyone played by her rules. They literally ate out of her hand. And no one was more inventive in this respect than her. She showed such favor every evening to one of the courtiers. That way she made sure everyone did just as she said.

As I tried to make my way downstairs, over several floors, I watched some women passing me. The smile on their faces couldn't be wider. They got another gift from the queen tonight and stupidly cherished it. Because another invention was the skirt privilege: a special skirt with red lapels, red vest, splendid gold and golden embroidery was allowed to be worn only by a few, and their number was fixed. Every time there was a vacancy, a contest was held among the most distinguished of the court as to who the skirts would go to.

I didn't need such a favor, since I already was the queen's

favored, and the courtiers didn't need to be reminded, cause the queen, I and Cyril were the only ones wearing crowns. Well, mine was more or less a tiara, but still, just the glint of its rubies made the courtiers gasp. I greeted a few guards standing to the side walkways and stumbled down the stairs that stretched over six floors. The ceilings were like a vault, alcoves and alcoves at every corner, and in all the side corridors people were cavorting like ants in an anthill. For the first few weeks, I was frightened by the number of courtiers who joined the Blood Queen.

The Bone Queen was exactly the opposite of her sister, she had a tiny court in contrast. She invited only those she trusted and held a ball only once a year. Not as lascivious and brutal as here. The Blood Queen was extreme, in every way. She loved to show off how rich she was, how beautiful, how young, how desirable. She was vain and as soon as someone gave her the feeling she wasn't worshipped enough, they were banned from the court or worse... she loved games and needed people to play them with her.

But the queen not only made sure that the high nobility was present at her court, she also demanded it of the lower nobility. At her lever and coucher, at her meals, in her gardens, she always looked around and noticed everyone when she decided to show herself. She resented the nobles if they didn't take their permanent residence at court, if they came only rarely, and her full disfavor met those who never or rarely showed themselves. If one of these had a request, the queen would only say, "I don't know them," and her judgment was irrevocable, meaning they skulled up. Many of these came to me then, to the Bone Weaver and asked for another chance. Sometimes, very rarely though, when they gave me something I wanted, I granted them another chance. It was just another business the Blood Queen invented. I had to give her that, she was creative.

I walked through the ballroom, knowing all too well that all the courtiers waited for the queen. Soon she would show up for her evening show and it was a show indeed. A good one but I couldn't watch her marveling at herself every night. I was fed up after the first time.

I pushed past some giggling women, wondering why anyone would do this to themselves voluntarily. Most of the people here were good souls, that is, from the cities that lay in the middle of the Underworld, they were not souls to be punished, the noble ones were just dead souls waiting to enter the river of souls and then be resurrected. They didn't have to atone for their sins, like us, who have sinned and therefore lived in the Outskirts or in worse areas like Tartarus, we only lived to be punished.

But now I would deal with souls that had to atone for something, because the noble ones did not come to me. No, it was the scum of this world who came to me. Those who had done something wrong. Like me. When I arrived at a tower I ran down, and down and down until I was in the basement which looked like a huge maw, lit only with dim candles.

Here and there stood guards of the queen, and just as I rounded the corner they straightened up. I would never get used to the cold down here, or the dusty and musty smell. But this place was the only one where the evil souls could find access, because they would never be allowed through the official entrance. Would never even dare to try. So, they came through the sewers and at the end of a long tunnel they entered my realm.

A narrow corridor led me to a stone-built hallway, a round gate with a big wooden door that had an iron ring as a handle. In front of the door stood Illiam, the head of the queen's guard. He was all about wild muscles and tanned skin. His red armor shimmering slightly in the pale candlelight, and the massive breastplates made him even taller and broader than he already was. My eyes involuntarily flitted to his chest, knowing all too well what power lay beneath that metal. What those arms could do. He smiled from the moment my feet touched the stone floor and when he lifted his head by way of greeting, a golden-brown curl fell down to his chin.

"Illiam," I said, my eyebrows shooting up to my forehead. "Isn't it your day off?"

He shrugged. "I don't want a day off when you're at work." I rolled my eyes. "Overprotective much?"

"Where it's needed, yes."

I smiled back and pushed past him, ignoring the casual touch he gave my lower back. I was always nervous before weaving bones, afraid I'd mess something up, that maybe one time it wouldn't work, and I'd be the laughingstock of souls.

I was about to grab the door handle when Illiam touched my arm. Cold armor meeting my heated skin, making me shiver briefly. "Call if you need me."

"Are you afraid for me? I'm the all mighty Bone Weaver, Illiam," I teased, biting my lower lip.

"And I'm your guard. I always worry, no matter what you can do or not."

I raised a hand and tucked the curl behind his ear. "Will I see you tonight?"

His just-serious face turned into a wide grin. "As you wish."

"At least something to look forward to then."

I cleared my throat, the reverberations bouncing off the vaulted stone walls and echoing back to me. My vision adjusted to the candlelight flickering against the walls as I stepped into the catacombs. A black lake filled half of the room, its depths shrouded in darkness. Souls lingered there like rats in shadows, waiting to be heard by me.

"Are you ready to weave bones with me?"

Tonight, I played a role I grew into over the years. The role of a woman that was able to frighten just about anyone with nothing but a blink of her eyes. Just like I did with the old man that sat in front of me right now. I loved to play power games and I truly liked to be feared at times. I don't know what that said about me but the moment the poor soul in front of me stuttered, I grinned with amusement.

"Y-y-yes, Bone Weaver, I have a w-w-wish," the man said.

He was old, copper skinned with a scar all over his face. White hair fell onto his forehead as he tried to word why he was here tonight.

"Everyone has," I said, trying not to roll my eyes. Hell, it was obvious that he *wanted* something of me.

"I wish to be led off by the Bone Queen's first Reaper." My eyebrows shoot up. "You messed with her Reaper?"

I heard that she found a brutal replacement for her deceased first one. Her reapers were famous on their own. Since they were said to know no mercy.

Anyone who had a score to settle with the queen was collected by one of her reapers. They were her bounty hunters, her extended arms. I was on her list as well, but I knew that they would never find me here, because every soul that belonged to the Bone Queen had no access if they wanted to harm the Blood Queen. Souls who asked for the Blood Queen's help would find entrance, but not if they were here to endanger her in any way. Something her reapers would do by hurting me.

"Yes, the queen wants me because I ate food from her pantry. I was one of her cooks and I was hungry, I thought she wouldn't notice a piece of cheese and—"

"—and now the piece got stuck in your throat, huh?"

I propped my head up on my hands and tilted my head, looking at him more closely. It was an old soul, and something told me he hadn't just stolen the piece of cheese. But he was not bad, no, he did not steal for himself.

"Who were you stealing for?"

"For my beloved, she was starving, my lady."

I twisted my lips into a smile. "And since you were sitting at the source, you thought you could help out."

He nodded, looking at his scarred hands in shame. The man was already involved in many conflicts.

"Where is she if you seek shelter here?"

"She's still at the Bone Court but would transfer here if I were granted protection."

"If I redeem you from your pact with the Reaper."

He nodded, his eyes widening as he looked at me pleadingly. I loved that I had the power to either grant him that or not. Which actually depended more on the goods he brought me. Like I learned the hard way today, I really couldn't do anything on my own, and I certainly couldn't do something like release him from a spell. Not from a reaper's spell. Hell, if I could, I would free myself. But I could grant him entry if he paid enough.

"What did you bring me?"

"This," he stammered, searching through his tattered pants pockets. "One moment."

I sighed. I knew why the queen was so eager to have her audience exposed to only filtered desires. Before me, everyone came to her, as if her well was a wishing well. But no one knew what exactly her magic could or couldn't do. Including me.

It was its own mystery.

"Here," he said just as I was getting impatient, and placed four sore bones on the table.

"Hmmm," I said and tapped the bones, separating them so I could analyze how much they were worth. They were living bones, that is, from inhabitants of the Underworld who had not yet been in the flow of souls. They weren't magical bones either, because the dead bones all belonged to the Bone Queen, since they had the most magic in them. Just as all the spilled blood of the world automatically went into my queen's well. The Bone Queen was not allowed to do magic with blood, just as her sister was not allowed to handle bones. Something else I may have to figure out since I could indeed use both...

I looked at the finger bone, then the small part of a hip bone, a dorsal vertebra, and a tiny toe bone. I wondered where he got these, since they were all from different people. But on the other hand... I shouldn't wonder. He paid. That's the only thing that mattered.

So, I placed my fingers over the bones and felt a slight electrical impulse. A dull vibration in my fingertips. The magic was there, weak but it was enough for what he was asking me to do. Okay, I could even do it for free. All it took me was to open that damn door for him, but I had to get the magic out of the bones first. That was my bread and butter.

"I will weave it," I said, and the man exhaled in relief, his gaze sliding upward as if to thank the gods for it.

I suppressed a snort. As if the gods had their fingers in the pie here. No, they stayed very far away from the Underworld. Our gods were the Bone, the Blood and the Shadow King and these were more than enough.

I put my fingers over the bones and felt the vibration, the life in them, which I took with my touch. The difference between people who could transform magic and those who could not was that they felt it, saw it, smelled it. All senses had to be activated. If this was not the case, the magic could not be taken and used. Nobody had magic just like that, we all took it from our world in some way.

"I," the man began, but I hissed and he immediately fell silent. "Don't speak while I'm weaving, or do you want me to accidentally witch you into a rat?" I grumbled and got set to work.

I extracted the magic and imagined how I would weave the bones together like threads, connecting their magic so that I could set it free to claim it. I wove and wove and wove, my fingers trembling over the bone, until I heard a dull sound. The bones shook as if in an earthquake and connected with each other. Like pieces of a puzzle they joined together, weaving themselves into one, big bone. Until all the magic that had just been in them got squeezed out and flowed into me. Became mine.

I heard the man sigh and grinned. This was just the beginning of what the Blood Queen taught me. I would soon be able to do even more, soon become stronger and collect more magic.

"Now, give me your hand," I whispered, my eyes still shut tight as I extended my palm towards the stranger. He firmly grasped it, his weathered skin telling tales of scars and time. I clung onto his roughness, tracing the lines and indentations etched upon it. "Now, envision the bond you long to sever."

And from one moment to the next, something inside me loosened. I felt the spell being taken from him, as if a ribbon were being pulled from my stomach. I exhaled strained, my eyes opened, and I stared into two glittering eyes.

"Thank you, Bone Weaver. I am beyond grateful."

I shook myself off, still buzzing with a bit of leftover magic that I could play around with later. But instead of the usual grateful smiles and endless thanks, the guy suddenly glanced down at his hands, shivering like crazy.

Something didn't seem right.

I narrowed my eyes at him. "What's up with you?"

"I-I-I," he stammered and stood up, his knees buckling. "May I now seek asylum with the queen?"

I waited, eyeing him up and checking my surroundings.

"Of course, go through that door," I nodded behind me, "a guard is waiting for you there and will tell you the desired time you can speak with the queen."

"Th-thank you." He lowered his head and looked down at the sewers. Then he ran upstairs, stopped with his hand on the door handle, and cold sweat ran down my back as his hollow eyes pierced mine. "I-I'm sorry," he said, and walked through the door.

CHAPTER FIVE
LYNNE

I opened my mouth to call for Illiam when a dark figure appeared from behind the sewers.

At first, my eyes flicked to his black boots, to the long, dirty cloak swaying against his heels. I tilted my head, checking if the guards did let him through, if he was just another one seeking my help... but they must have since there was no other possibility to get past them.

Since everything *seemed* normal, I tried to cool down my nerves. Maybe the old guy was just a bit... emotional. Yeah, that had to be it. I watched the man approach me, slowly. He was tall and his walk so confident, not making me feel any better since the souls that usually came to me weren't confident.

"Lynne, are you all right?" I heard Bory whisper in my dress pocket, he climbed up to peek at the man, little feet scratching at my rigid skin.

"I guess..." I stammered, still fixing the stranger with my gaze. "I'm not so sure, though."

My inner warning system was on high alert, and I snatched the dagger I had stashed under the table. Just in case, I told myself, as he inched closer. Something about him gave me the creeps, and I couldn't help but wonder what shady deal he had up his sleeve.

With a nonchalant air, he had his hands casually stuffed into the pockets of his coat, probably feigning interest in his surroundings. His gaze swept over the spiderwebs dangling from the ceiling, the rows of wine barrels lining the room, my cluttered desk, and finally, landed on me. The hood cast such a deep shadow on his face that I couldn't see his face, but I felt his stare on me. It was like he undressed me. Slowly but intensely, making me hold my breath for several split seconds. Sighing deeply, my eyes flicked to his tunic. It was half open, showing tanned, dense muscles. The man didn't fit anywhere in my pattern at all.

"Take a seat," I said, gripping the handle of my dagger.

"Thank you," he said in a deep voice that made all my hair on my nape stand up at once.

Was he disguising his voice or was it naturally that deep? I couldn't figure it out.

As he settled into the seat, I instinctively edged back until the backrest pressed into my spine.

"Are you ready to... weave bones with me?" I said but this time my voice didn't come out half as confident as it did earlier. I pinched Bory slightly. A sign for him to run for Illiam in case things got worse.

The man leaned casually in the chair across from me and I saw white teeth flashing under his hood. "I'm afraid I have a bone to pick with *you*."

I swallowed. "In what way?"

He leaned forward, a musky scent I couldn't place invading my nose. "Tell me why you are doing all of this?"

"Have you ever heard of a job?"

"Bone weaving is not a job, you're robbing souls of their time and steal their magic for nothing. You didn't even spill the beans to the guy about what you made him give up in order to waltz into the castle. So, I want to know why. Whether you're being blackmailed."

I narrowed my eyes. Who the skull was this man?

Technically speaking, he was right but only the queen's closest advisors knew that we did steal time. All her deals, and therefore mine, robbed the souls of a little of their penitential time. Time that they had already spent, either to atone for sins or to wait until the hour was ripe to send them into the flow of souls. With each deal that period became longer and the stolen time then went to the queen's youth. She became younger and more beautiful with each bargain. Similar to her sister, both were very vain. One of the few things they had in common. However, the Bone Queen witched herself young, while the Blood Queen stole her youth.

He huffed out a bitter laugh. "You don't even deny it?"

"What for, you seem to know all about me."

He shrugged and ran a finger over the wooden armrest.

I squinted at him and cringed when I spotted a fancy ring on his finger. It was all gold and blinged out with a bunch of sparkly diamonds. Talk about being out of place around here.

A memory flashed up in the back of my mind, in those forgotten nooks I'd rather keep locked away. I squeezed the dagger tighter, my knuckles turning white, as if I could ward off the memory by sheer force.

"Well, I don't know all about it, I don't know *your* side of things."

"Curiosity killed the cat, didn't it?" I retorted, mustering a brave facade despite the chill creeping up my spine. With a futile attempt, I tried to catch a glimpse beneath his hood, only to be met with impenetrable darkness. "Why should I share anything with you?"

He let out a low chuckle, his voice carrying an air of

mystery. "Ah, but that's precisely why I want to hear your side of the story first."

"That costs."

A smile showed under his hood. Beautiful white teeth... "I could offer you a kiss."

My throat bobbed with a dry swallow. What? "That's nothing I'd want. Come up with something else before I think you're trying to offend me."

He laughed again. A sweet sound that stung my heart. He then pulled out a roll of parchment from under his coat, unrolled it right before my eyes—slowly and deliberately—and slapped it in the middle of the table, his fingers spreading out in a fan over it. "An order from the queen."

My heart skipped a beat, and I leaned closer to the letter, my eyes devouring every word, especially my name and the unexpected request. A bounty of immense amount to anyone who helped bring me back to the queen. As if on cue, my eyes darted to the canalization and caught a fingertip. It was barely visible, but it was there. Skull.

How could I've missed it? He had killed the guards. That's how he got in.

But how in the world was that possible? No one found entrance who wanted to harm the queen. And in harming me he attacked her.

I rushed up to my feet, pointing the dagger right at him and gritting my teeth. My heart beating up to my throat now. "You are the Bone Queen's Reaper."

"Indeed." He stood up as well, not appearing to be threatened by my weapon at all.

I wanted to round the table, run away but before I could even lift a foot, he grabbed my arm that clasped the dagger. He held me so tight that I didn't have a chance to dodge it and there was this sting. This otherworldly ache. His touch was like holding onto burning coals, and I couldn't help but cry out in pain. I desperately tried to fight back, flailing my other hand, but he effortlessly snatched it too. As his hood slipped off, revealing his face, I felt my breath catch in my throat.

This couldn't be true.

"My lady," Illiam yelled, the door bursting open with a loud thud, hitting the stone wall.

But my eyes, however, didn't leave *him*. Never left Rio for even a second. I couldn't believe what I saw. Couldn't believe that my mind wasn't tricking me.

Rio stood in front of me. Rio.

I felt like I was shattered into a thousand pieces, looking at his hands on mine. At his touch. At the ring on his finger. At his tunic... looked back up to his face, his eyes, his damn sapphire eyes that haunted me in the night. Every damn night.

"Rio," I said, but my voice was nothing more than a whisper in the night.

His intense gaze softened for a fleeting moment before he abruptly released my hands. With swift and fluid movements, he drew a sword from under his cloak, engaging in a deadly duel with Illiam.

A surge of heat washed over me, mingled with dizziness and a sickening sensation in my stomach. My mouth watered, and I feared I might throw up, but I took a deep breath, waiting until the feeling passed. Just then, I caught something on my hand. His touch still lingered there like a memory's ghost. But instead of a memory he left something real there. A mark. It had to be the mark of the Bone Queen's Reaper. I was now bound to him. No matter where he went, I had to go with him until we reached the Bone Court.

"What do you want?" Illiam cried, dodging another blow from Rio.

"Her," he said, and I cringed.

Three letters and they went straight through my flesh right at where it hurt the most. I touched my chest, breathing against the rising lump in there. I felt so sick. So skulling sick. I didn't know what to do, but luckily Bory screamed at that moment and got me out of my stupor. "Is that Rio?"

I nodded, watching the two of them fight like a damsel in distress. Nothing fit, nothing at all. Rio could fight like a legionnaire. Rio was *here*. Rio was in the Underworld and hadn't aged a day since I'd seen him.

"Did he hurt you?" asked Illiam, lashing out at Rio, but I couldn't answer. My mind went through every possibility there was of how this could have happened. Nothing made sense. Nothing at all. He couldn't be in the Underworld. He couldn't be the Bone Queen's FIRST Reaper, her most powerful man. How? How could—

"Lynne! Did he hurt you!" Illiam parried Rio again, but he cut off one of his curls with a mischievous glint in his eyes.

"Whoops. Pretty boy not so pretty anymore," Rio said and danced around him as if Illiam was nothing but a child to him.

"Yeah, no, I mean, STOP IT!" I cried, slowly coming to my senses. "Get up there, run into the castle," Illiam yelled. "Please."

Rio's smug face twisted in a haughty sneer as he blocked Illiam's way with his foot, daring him to make another move. In fury, I stepped forward and roared, my veins thrumming with an unbridled intensity that burned like a wildfire. All of my rage from years of betrayal surged forward and threatened to consume me entirely, replacing every single thought and emotion until nothing remained but the urge to make him pay.

"*He's* the new reaper?" Bory stammered.

"Yes," I said, flicking his little shoulder and causing him to fall back into the pocket of my dress. I didn't want him to get hurt by any means. "Stay ducked, Bory!"

Illiam took a swing and Rio deflected the blow with his sword.

I tensed up, wishing I could do something to help Illiam, but all I actually did was stand there and watch as he unleashed a flurry of punches on Rio. I panicked and just threw my dagger at Rio. For a moment it seemed that Illiam had gained the upper hand, but then

Rio spun away from Illiam's grasp, catching my dagger in mid-air and sending chills down my spine. My emotions were torn between fear and admiration as I watched him swiftly dodge every blow that Illiam threw at him, yet I knew that I had to act fast if I wanted to protect Illiam. No clue why but Rio was strong. Really strong. In a way he shouldn't be since he should be... just a human. With a deep breath, I scanned the room, trying to figure out what else I could try.

What was he thinking? Showing up like that after five skulling years and then trying to kill my guard? The only one who helped me through the nights? I chewed on the inside of my cheeks and grabbed the chair Rio's skulling ass sat on just mere minutes ago.

I hurled it right into his direction, swearing like a sailor. But instead of blocking Rio, Illiam fell over it. I sucked in the air between my gritted teeth, damn my bad luck. Illiam rolled off easily though and I wanted to thank the gods already—but it was too late. Rio stood on one of his arms, looming over him with the sword tip pressed against Illiam's throat.

"Your last words will decide whether I let you live or not. So, how will you enlighten me?" Rio said.

"You won't get her," Illiam said.

"Wrong choice of words." Rio laughed, flipping him upside down and lifted him up into the air with a single arm. My breath got caught in my throat, disbelief sweeping through me like a wave. Illiam was wearing armor that weighed tons, yet Rio had lifted him as if he were made of nothing but air. Bory tried to talk to me, but I just couldn't focus on anything other than what was happening right before my eyes. Rio was human... Rio couldn't fight the queen's best man like this. How... he only knew how to do fist or gunfights...

I shouted at them, begging them to just stop fighting.

Illiam groaned, his eyes tearing up as Rio whirled him around by the neck and held him in a chokehold. But Rio didn't even so much as flinch as he showed me Illiam's face and my guard stared at me, his eyes wide and fearful as Rio clasped his hands around his throat. My stomach lurched as I watched Illiam try to pry himself from Rio's grip, digging his nails into Rio's arms.

"Lynne! What are you doing? Use your damn magic!" I heard Bory and I wanted to lift my hands to use the little mana I had stolen from the old man and turn it into something, but I just couldn't. I was like rooted to the ground.

"Lynne!"

"I—I don't know—"

Bory climbed up to my shoulders and patted my cheeks. All I could see was his blue fur moving up and down in the corner of my eyes. "I think you're in a shock... please forgive me but I have to do it—"

He didn't even finish his sentence when his first blow hit me, followed by another. I tore my eyes open and looked straight into Bory's guilty expression. "I'm sorry, Lynne! I heard this helps and you can't just stand there and do nothing—"

"Look at her," Rio suddenly growled, snatching back my attention with a ferocity that set my heart racing even faster. "She belongs to me, and any claim you might have had on her is nothing but a distant memory."

His eyes, as blue and turbulent as the sea, blazed with an

unyielding determination as he tightened his grip on Illiam, who wriggled in protest like a worm on a hook.

I felt the weight of Bory on my back as he climbed down and prayed that he was alerting the guards. I could only hope that there were any guards left.

"Lynne, run," Illiam said and my gaze snapped back at him. "Please, run. You're not his property. I'm fine, don't waste your time on me."

Rio let out a sharp, cold laugh, and I knew then that he was done talking to him. "Night, Goldilocks," he said, slamming his sword against Illiam's head with a force that made him crumble to the ground.

My breath hitched, and I struggled to catch it as my heart pounded relentlessly in my chest.

I glared at Rio with a fierce anger that burned within me, feeling the heat rise up to my face. It took everything in me to steady my voice and speak: "Thank you, Bory," I said, my voice barely above a whisper. "I really needed that skulling slap."

I turned my attention to Rio and finally charged toward him. "Yours?" I growled, my voice laced with fury. "You think you have any claim over me? You lost that right long ago, hiding from me like the coward you are!"

"Hiding?" Rio's voice dripped with sarcasm, and I could practically taste the bitterness in his words. "I haven't been *hiding* from you. You're the one who vanished without a trace."

"You knew where I was, where I waited for you year after year like the fool I am."

He tilted his head to the side, a devilish smirk tugging at the corners of his lips. "Well, I came after you eventually, didn't I? Only to find you had already moved on."

He simply nodded down at Illiam and heat rushed through me, wakening up every nerve ending.

"Moved on? From what, exactly? I was never yours to begin

with. And what is this?" I snarled, stepping over Illiam. "You actually have the audacity to show up here and think you have any claim over me? Unbelievable!" I stopped right in front of him, our bodies just inches apart.

Rio's laughter echoed through the empty alley. "Oh, darling, you're wrong. You're mine. Always have been, even if you think you have to be angry with me right now." His eyes glittered with a dark amusement. "And I'm done arguing. It's time to leave. I have a little deal with... the Bone Queen."

I didn't flinch. I refused to show him any sign of weakness, not now, not ever. "Hell no, I ain't going anywhere," I spat. "You can't just come back, taking what you want, hurting people for fun. It's sick."

Rio's expression darkened as he leaned into my space. "Oh, you don't get to judge me. Not after you refused to show up at the cemetery just to sleep with this asshole at my feet."

I held his gaze, not backing down. "I waited for you at the cemetery. It's you who didn't show up, so naturally, I stopped waiting. It was over between us."

"Over?" Rio's voice was mocking. "You think it's that easy? You think you can just walk away from me, and everything will be fine?"

"Yes," I said, my voice unwavering. "I do."

"Oh, you'll live and learn, darling. There's no way out of this, we're bound together, if you like it or not, never wondered why you kept searching for me? Visiting me on Earth? There's a reason."

I bristled at his words, my heart pounding in my chest. The actual nerve he had! "You're delusional," I spat. "I belong to no one but myself."

Rio's eyes flashed with something dangerous. I couldn't help and retreated. My heart jumped against my ribcage as he followed, and before I could act, he backed me up against the cold stone wall. His

hand tightened around my throat, while the other rested beside my head.

"You may belong to yourself, but your heart belongs to me," he whispered, his breath hot against my lips. "Also, I know a queen or two who believes in owning you. That's why I'm taking you with me now. We have to sort this out."

I struggled against his grip, but it was no use. Rio was stronger than me, and I was clearly at his mercy. So odd, since I was stronger than him on Earth...

"You don't understand," he said, his glance suddenly softening. "I'm doing this to protect you."

"Protect me?" I spat, struggling to pry his grip from my throat. "From what? Your lies? Your deceit? Your damn hand squeezing the life out of me?"

Rio's expression darkened, and I could feel the tension radiating off him in waves. But he finally released his grip, and I could swear I caught a glimpse of guilt flickering in his eyes. Perhaps he was as taken aback by his outburst as I was.

"I had no choice," he said through gritted teeth. "The Bone Queen is powerful. She would have taken you anyway. At least this way, you're under my protection."

I scoffed. "You call that protection? You put a reaper spell on me and want to sell me to the Bone Queen. How is that protecting me?"

"This spell... it's..." Rio's voice trailed off, his expression now betraying a mix of confusion and concern. "I... look, you're safer with her than out here with the Blood Queen. Just trust me."

I laughed bitterly, shaking my head. "Safer with the Bone Queen... right. You've gotta be kidding, or did you suddenly turn into a complete idiot?"

"Not kidding," Rio said firmly. "I know I messed up. I know I hurt you. But I'm trying to make it right. Let me take you to the Bone Queen and I'll explain it all to you. It's the only way to keep you safe for now."

"That's the story she's been spoon-feeding you, huh? That woman is a walking lie, and so are you," I shot back, sidestepping to catch my breath. "Just like you've always been."

"I'm not lying," he protested, grabbing my elbow to stop me in my tracks. "I'm trying to keep you safe. You just have to trust me." He reached out for my hand, but I swiftly pulled away.

"Let me go. I won't let you sell me to the Bone Queen."

"I can't," he whispered. "You're mine, now and forever."

A shiver ran down my spine as I realized the truth in his words. I really was bound to Rio, whether I wanted to be or not —that reaper spell made sure of it. His eyes flicked to my lips and all the memories came back like an unwanted weave at the shore. Wrapping me up. Choking me. He wasn't the same man anymore.

Something had happened. Something big.

I nudged my chin forward, having to tip my head back to meet his gaze.

"What did she promise you? What are you gaining from this?" I asked, my voice filled with suspicion.

"Can't spill the beans yet, sweetheart."

"Liar."

"Not lying. I'm just keeping some secrets to myself."

"That's lying by omission," I fumed, my fists clenching in frustration.

Rio's eyes flitted over my body then. There was a fire in his eyes, a fire I couldn't place and when he still didn't answer me, I raised my hand to hit him.

I just didn't know what else to do. I was nothing but a hot mess of emotions, caught between wanting to rip him apart, kiss him senseless, cry my heart out in his embrace, or just scream my lungs out. The hurt he caused me was like a knife twisting in my chest. Seeing him standing there, claiming me, while knowing he just wanted to dump me back with the queen because he's already married, was beyond infuriating.

Rio grasped my wrist before I could actually hit him, pulling me even closer.

My eyes fell onto the ring on his finger again. "Did something happen to the one you're married to?" I said, coldly. "I bet she's happy that you're wandering the Underworld for her and claiming other women like they're your properties."

Rio's grip on my wrist tightened, his eyes darkening. "Don't talk about things you know nothing about."

"Then enlighten me," I challenged.

"Not now. We have guards approaching, and this is no place for explanations." His fingers found their way to my elbow, and against my better judgment, I allowed his touch to linger.

"Convenient, isn't it? Suddenly you care about my safety. But you're easy to read. I'm just another conquest for your ego, another pawn in your game, right, Mr. Drug King of Chicago?"

"You know it's not like that," he said, his voice filled with urgency as the approaching footsteps grew louder. "I did what I had to do to protect you."

"Oh, yeah, I'm sure you're just going to deliver me perfectly safe and sound to your precious queen," I retorted. "But here's some news for you: I don't need you making decisions for me. I'm not anyone's property, and I was perfectly fine before you showed up. Actually, I felt incredible. You're the only concern I have right now, so if you truly want me to feel safe, then do us both a favor and go. Vanish to wherever you—"

"Aria," he interrupted, his expression frantic as he reached out his hands to cup my cheeks. "I know." His voice was barely above a whisper now. "It must look strange. Believe me, I know but I never wanted any of this for you. I had no other choice. We have to catch up and—"

I pulled away from his touch once more, my own resolve hardening. "There's always a choice. And you made yours. Now it's time for me to make mine. This is over. It should have been clear for you but whatever you're seeking here, it's not going to work."

My fingers curled into fists, my toes digging into my shoes as I waited for the guards to arrive. I wouldn't be fooled by his sweet words or soft touches again. Not when everything he said was a lie.

He had a point, though. There was definitely something fishy going on, and I was determined to get to the bottom of it. He'd already deceived me once, pretending to be van der Volt, and I wasn't going to fall for his tricks again. Who knew what schemes he had cooking up now, what dark alliances he'd forged, and why he was so hellbent on coming after me after five long years of silence.

Fact was, I *knew* that he hadn't shown up. I'd waited for hours, scouring the graveyard for any sign of him, but he was nowhere to be found. He was definitely lying, and I was going to uncover the truth, no matter who he was working for or what his motives were.

"Aria..." Rio started again but suddenly Bory's scream made us flinch and turn towards the door.

"Guards are coming, Lynne!" Bory said as he hopped into the room, running towards me as if the tide was coming in behind him.

I closed my eyes, and rubbed the bridge of my nose, reminding myself that I needed to tell him he shouldn't tell villains that someone was coming to kick their butts. Of course, Rio didn't let any time pass, whirled me around, and tossed me over his shoulders.

"He's taking me through the sewers!" I shouted at the top of my lungs, hoping anyone could hear me and send some guards my way. "Shut it now. We're in a tight spot since you dragged your feet," he muttered, wincing as my blows landed on his back.

"You're the one who got us into this mess!" I yelled, my frustration reaching its peak. "If I make it out alive, I swear I'll kill you all by myself."

He chuckled, stepping into the water canal as he hastily escaped from the castle with me. "Oh, so now we're embracing our inner murderers, huh? As much as I enjoy that side of you, darling, let me remind you of something. If you're following through, we'll go down together because that lovely mark on your skin binds us, in life and death."

CHAPTER SIX
RIO

I held her tight while she lolled like a worm on my shoulders. Fuck, it was anything but easy to hold her right up there. As I waded through the water, I tried to forget the expression on her lover's face, jealousy threatening to take over. I heard that it was a guard, and I silently cursed the bastard ever since.

But it almost took my breath away. Seeing her again. Seeing the man who had touched her in my absence.

Everything I heard about her at the Bone Court seemed to be true and I just couldn't believe my eyes. Couldn't believe she was this grown up now, not one inch of her was the girl I'd known. Her features were sharper, her eyes determined, her gestures calculating, and she handled souls like a boss. She sat there, dominated the room without speaking, and the souls asked for a chance, asked for her help, and she played them. I would expect that from myself—but not from Aria. And by the gods, her beauty. Fuck. Fucking fuck.

Her unfathomable beauty just left me speechless.

At first, I didn't do anything but watch her. I knocked off the guards easily, they weren't used to fighting back and certainly weren't used to someone like me. The Horsemen had trained me well over the past years, taught me what I'd forgotten and to save Jamie and Aria I was willing to do anything. But well, for Aria, this wasn't exactly what she would call a rescue. Deep down I had hoped that she was coerced into stealing the souls' time. That she was compelled to assist the Blood Queen. I had hoped she longed to be rescued from the queen, that she didn't come here willingly but... she never used those words.

No. She was voluntarily a Blood Court member.

From all that I'd learned, saw and what I'd fought against... it filled me with disgust. How could she aid that blood bitch? How could she not know that she was using her to work with the Book of Silva?

"Put me down!" she yelled, tearing me out of my thoughts again. I grumbled. "Quiet." I looked up as if some of these fucking gods could see me and lend me some nerves. She just *had* to be quiet. After all, the queen's guards were on their way thanks to Bory and I didn't want to take more lives than necessary. Admittedly, stealing one of the Blood Queen's most important members wasn't easy. But we didn't come here with a simple plan. It was a bloody path from the start and would be bloodier soon.

I got a fist in the spine.

Grunting, I grabbed her ass tighter, hurrying, my feet splashing the black water to all sides. While running, I tried to forget that guard's shitty face. Forget what some courtiers told me about the Bone Weaver's whereabouts. About whom she fucked. I bit away the jealousy that Aria's look at him triggered in me and was glad when we reached the end of the tunnel.

"Now!" I yelled, and the moment I jumped out of the sewers with Aria, Any lit two fuses, which we had prepared just before I went to assassinate the guards. I watched it burn, fast as a snake creeping forward and ducked behind a rock. With a gentle movement, I carefully lowered into a seated position, guiding her onto my lap. Aria's legs instinctively curled around my waist as an explosion erupted with a loud bang that scared away the mist before us.

"What—" she screamed but before the sound could fully escape her lips, another explosion tore through the night sky. The blast shook the ground beneath us, sending tremors through the air and scattering debris in all directions. In a split second it walled up the sewers.

I rolled off Aria, shielding her body with mine as another pressure wave knocked us both to the ground. The explosion hit me like a punch, filling the air with a foul odor and swirling debris. As I pushed myself up on my elbows, memories of a different kind of fun flooded my mind. But there was nothing fun about this. Not when Aria was sprawled beneath me, her skin covered in grime and soot because I fucking blew up the Blood Queen's sewer system.

"Are you insane?" She coughed, the thick clouds of smoke and dust swirling around us like the ghosts of our past. "Gods, you must be."

She frantically checked on Bory, pulling up her dress pocket to reveal a disheveled little blue head covered in a puff of dust. He let out a comical sneeze, creating a mini-tornado of debris, and she promptly scooped him out to give him a good dust-off. Once he assured her, he was fine, she carefully nestled him back into his pocket, and glared back at me. "Get off of me!"

Despite her protests, I couldn't bring myself to let her go just yet. Pinning her to the ground, I gazed deeply into her captivating features—from the adorable point of her nose to the high rise of her cheekbones, and those luscious lips that begged to be kissed. I drank it all in as if I had to make sure that everything was still in its rightful place.

Our eyes locked in a moment of realization that we had

finally been reunited. After being separated for years, it felt like yesterday when I claimed those rosy lips as mine. How could fate keep pulling us apart, time and time again? If she only knew what we've been through and what's about to come... what we still have to fight for...

"I said, get off me," she growled again, pushing against my chest. "Apparently, you've gained weight and it hurts."

I couldn't help but grin at her fiery attitude. Damn, I've missed her. "I haven't gained anything, sweetheart. And I have a feeling you like the memory of lying on your back under my body," I teased, lowering myself until our noses were touching. We were so close that I could feel the heat of her body against mine. There was a tension between us, a pull that had been growing for what felt like forever and fuck, I knew that we were both acutely aware of it.

Her gaze flicked to my lips, and I could tell that she was thinking about kissing me. I leaned in, ready to brush my lips against hers, but she turned away, saying: "So, you kidnapped me and decided to host a spontaneous barbecue. What's next? Campfire songs?"

"Well, not quite. Our next move is to make a run for it. Trust me, if there were any alternative options, I wouldn't have resorted to kidnapping," I explained, my words carrying a genuine tone despite the absurdity of the situation.

"Isn't this just the perfect fairytale? Kidnapping, fleeing, and a romantic dungeon getaway waiting for me... Do they offer room service in those cells you'll lock me up?"

A mischievous grin tugged at my lips. Two could definitely play this game. "Ah, the ambiance of a dimly lit dungeon, and the comforting sound of rats scurrying by. It's going to be the perfect love nest for us, darling."

Suddenly, Any emerged from the shadows, leading our white horses by the reins.

"Nice that you're back to your usual bickering," he remarked, a hint of urgency in his voice. "But we really need to get a move on. They'll figure out how to cross the lava and follow us in no time. We have to reach the neutral borders before they do."

"Not you too," Aria groaned, exasperation evident in her tone. I sighed and finally pulled her up with me.

Once I came to a stand, I gave her the coat and said: "Come on, get on the horse."

She glanced behind me and took in the two horses. They were stocky with thick fur on their hooves, long, bushy tails, and white saddles showing the banner of the Bone Queen, three bones intertwined, resembling a snake with green, gleaming eyes.

"I won't ride with you," she said, cold eyes meeting mine as she covered herself with my coat. I was glad that I couldn't glare at her boobs any longer. If she was in the game, my sanity was in question.

"Then with me," Any said, grabbing her by the arm. "Out of the question," she said, wriggling out of his grip.

Fine. I was about done being nice now. "His horse or mine. If needed I'll tie you to my horse."

She hit her silky red dress with a fist and at that, something beeped and she widened her eyes. "Oh, Bory! Oh gods, I'm so sorry, I forgot you're here."

"Of course, I'm here!" he said, crawling out of one of her pockets, glaring wickedly at me as well. "I ain't going anywhere without you."

"Hi, Bory, good to see you again," Any said, grinning as he spat on the ground in front of us.

"Skull off, you two rogues," he said.

Alright, it would take us a bit to get warm again too. So, I nodded to the snorting horses. "His or mine horse? The clock is ticking." Aria sighed and stomped sourly to Any's horse. Before she climbed up, she gave me one last evil look. "Don't ever call me *yours* again. Never again, do you understand?" She grabbed the saddle and threw herself onto the animal's back, nodding to Any. "I hate you too but a little less than that one."

Any grinned. "Good to know, nice to see you again too, little sister."

She snorted and looked forward in a huff as Any sat down behind her. "And my name is Lynne."

"Not really," Any mumbled, shooting me a sad look but I ignored him, breathing away the punches that her words granted me.

Don't call me yours again. Never again.

Bory was still glaring at me as well. Without missing a beat, I flashed him a cheeky wink, swung myself up onto my horse, and nudged it forward. They'll come around. Once we have the chance to talk properly, they'll understand that things aren't always what they seem. At least that's what I was telling myself...

WE RODE along a narrow black path high into the mountains, and as always in this world we saw nothing, nothing at all except a thick veil of smoke. Couldn't really say I've missed it. I was now used to the Topworld and many things were just better there, even if I had never thought so before. Just thinking about the world up there made me all sentimental. Especially when it came to Jamie.

I wondered how she was doing and if I'd ever get to see her again, and how old she'd be by then. It hurt knowing I was missing out on her growing up. Man, I never thought I could love a human this much…

I took a deep breath, attempting to shove the thought of her to the farthest corners of my mind, as I always did. It wasn't a walk in the park, but I couldn't afford to crumble because I missed her. I had to keep my composure or all of us were lost.

I increased my speed, galloping over a ledge. On either side, the rock formations revealed cracks, with molten lava seeping through, its red-hot core shimmering with an intense glow. I glanced over my shoulders a couple of times and noticed Aria checking the mountain. She was certainly up to something. She always was. With her, you never knew and we had to be very alert. The thought made me smile as I rode along against the wind, a white arrow shooting through the darkness.

All the while I overheard Any's several attempts to strike up a conversation with her, but she remained tight-lipped, refusing to utter a single word. And hell, I could feel her glare burning a hole through my back. I wondered if she despised my company or simply the fact that I had kidnapped her. If the tables were turned, I certainly wouldn't be thrilled about being abducted but circumstances forced my hand. Desperate times call for desperate measures, and all.

But we'd arrive at camp soon, and all we needed was time. Time to talk. Not that I could tell her what's going on thanks to the fucking curse but… I'd find a way to ease it. A way to make her trust me.

As we reached the top of the hill, a sudden, high-pitched scream pierced the night sky. I reined in my horse and turned to Any, who was still making his way up the steep incline, his mount weighed down by the both of them. A quick glance at Aria told me that she was ahead of us though. The mischievous glint in her eyes was a warning sign that she wasn't going to just play along. Well, fuck it, I was in trouble.

Before I could even blink, she flung herself off the cliff, eyes sparkling with pure adrenaline. The wind caught hold of her, playing with her white-blonde hair. Any's hand reached out, trying to snatch her, but he missed by a hair's breadth, wincing in frustration. She spun and twirled, like a rebellious dancer defying gravity's rules. My heart pounded up to my temples as I dismounted from my horse and ran to the edge of the cliff, watching in horror as she plummeted downward. But then, something massive swooped in beneath her. Something *monstrous*, casting a shadow that swallowed the faint red light surrounding us and the air quivered with a deep, ominous rumble, causing an unsettling knot to form in the pit of my stomach.

Any gasped in amazement behind me. "A Sircha," he said, fear written all over his face.

I opened my mouth to say something, but I heard a hard impact, and my eyes flew back to Aria landing on that beast's back. She laughed, stroked its head and zoomed past us. The air whooshed and roared as the dragon's wings flapped.

In an instant, Any reached for his saddlebag and took out his crossbow, but I raised a hand, signaling him to stop whatever he'd had in mind. "No, it's her dragon. She'd never forgive us," I said, slowly returning to my horse. "She won't get far. Just wait." If we'd hurt her dragon, she'd hate us both forever. I knew that it was like family to her.

So, I crossed my arms and watched her fly away, waiting for the magic to happen.

"She's getting away, Rio," Any said, his voice wavered, betraying the nervousness he was trying to hide.

"*Just wait,*" I repeated, my eyes glued to her.

She looked so small on this monster and the fear crept in that maybe the spell I put on her wouldn't work, that I'd really lose her again. I fisted my fingers as she flew over black mountain tips, her white hair flying in the wind like a flag.

But then she flinched, grabbing her chest.

I sighed deeply but soon the fear she'd get away got replaced with another. She could fall off her dragon and I tensed up. Turned still like a corpse.

Eyes wide open, she looked at me over her shoulder. Her breath got caught and she patted the beast's head as it suddenly turned, its wings flapping restlessly now.

The spell started to work. And it hurt her.

My stomach churned and I took a step forward, although there was nothing I could do to help her from down here. I checked the surroundings, tried to find just something that would stop her pain. The dragon flew at top speed. Its wings were like the pulse of an ocean wave, pushing another breath of wind and dust over Any and me. I stopped short when it reached us, a shadow darkening my sight even more.

I had only seen a handful of dragons so far, but it was impressive.

Each time.

I tipped my head back and looked at the scales on his stomach, glittering in the dim light that came from the lava cracks. He was massive and Aria sat on top of it as if it were normal to ride such a monster. A Sircha... but something was off about her dragon. Its facial expression was worried—not evil, not bloody.

The dragon swooped down, growling before it touched down on the charcoal earth with a thunderous braking. The ground shook beneath us and the dragon rammed its talons into the earth, tearing up four deep gorges. Aria barely clung to its back, while I felt a pang of guilt for putting her in danger. Her skin had turned an alarming shade of pale now, and I let out a deep sigh of relief when the dragon finally came to a stop.

She was back and she was alive.

With a graceful movement, the dragon arched its neck back and delicately plucked Aria's dress with its teeth, ensuring that she didn't fall off. I watched in fascination as it carefully lifted her down and laid her on the ground, its movements gentle and precise.

"I've never seen anything like that," Any murmured next to me, clearly as awestruck as I was.

"Neither have I," I replied, still staring.

"Sirchas are known to be aggressive, to be death incarnate. I've never heard of anyone *riding* on them," Any continued.

As we watched in silence, the dragon caressed Aria with a tender touch of his nostrils, its gaze filled with horror and its eyes watery as it sniffed her over, whimpering softly.

"Seems like this one has feelings..." I murmured. "It's just odd..."

When I started to jog towards them, something shifted in the dragon's eyes and it bared its teeth, warning me to stay back. Fuck. I was an idiot. The dragon wasn't weak or anything, he simply had a unique connection with her. There were different rules for me. So, I slowed down, raising both hands in a sign of peace and cautiously made my way towards them.

"You don't want to hurt me," I tried.

The dragon's eyes gleamed with fire as he cocked his head. "Be careful," Any said, slowly stepping behind me.

"Without me, she'll die. We need to be together, neither she nor I can go far from each other." The moment she'd venture too far from me, an intangible shackle would ensnare her, making it effortless for me to retrieve her. There was no way she could escape my grasp. No one could, not if I willed it to be so.

It was like the dragon could read my mind. The slits of his eyes narrowed to such a thin strip that they were almost no longer visible, and he let out a growl.

"She's dying," I said, nodding at Aria and trying not to look too closely because the state she was in hurt me more than anything.

The dragon's low growl reverberated through the air, tendrils of smoke curling from its flared nostrils. But to my surprise, it allowed me to draw closer to Aria, as though it comprehended the gravity of separating her from me.

But I knew he despised me with a ferocity that was palpable in his gaze. I couldn't shake off the feeling that it knew exactly who— and what—I was. Luckily, the dragon couldn't articulate its thoughts to Aria, for we needed time. Enough time for her to grasp the truth, to come to terms with it all. It was far too soon for her to learn the reality of our world, of us.

I approached Aria with caution, taking measured steps as I closed the distance between us. Her eyes flickered open as she sensed my presence. With each inhale and exhale, her chest rose and fell, a tangible reminder of the fragile state the gods put her in.

"It's okay," she whispered to her dragon, trembling as she tried to prop herself up, her arms shaking so badly. With another whimper, the dragon nudged her back a little, getting Aria to sit up. It's then when Bory hopped from the dragon's back as well, cursing under his breath as he took Aria in.

"You could have said a thing or two about that skulling invisible leash," he snarled at me as feather-like paws scurried over her skin, checking if my spell hurt her physically but no. It just made her faint. *Just...*

When Aria's gaze met mine, her features hardened. "Yeah, just one little hint would have been wonderful."

I tried to remain composed and act as if her pain didn't affect me, but in the depths of my heart, I felt my world crumbling. All I wanted was to hold her tight, kiss her and never let go of her again. Despite it all, I shrugged, hiding the torment that was stirring inside me. "You should have known a reaper wouldn't simply let his prey slip away," I stated matter-of-factly.

"What else could I have done? I can't just return to the Bone Queen," she spat, her words laced with unmistakable fear. "Have you forgotten what we once meant to each other? Do you hate me so much now that you're willing to sacrifice me to her? Don't you even care that you're sending me to my death?"

Hell, I would never send her to death. Never. Wincing, I longed to close the distance between us, wanting to comfort her and making amends for the wrongs I'd committed. But her dragon rose up behind her, its eyes narrowed and its mouth open in a warning hiss, sending a cloud of smoke my way. His piercing gaze told me to feel fortunate that it hadn't already scorched me to ashes. *Up to here and no farther.*

"I wouldn't be taking you to her if that were the case," I tried.

"Is that so?" She pointed to her wrist, to the mark of our bond. "Then what is this? An accident?"

"Aria—"

"Don't call me that."

"It's your name."

"My name is Lynne, I have no clue why you keep on holding onto that woman. This version of me is dead. Stop pining after her and stop lying right into my face, *Reaper*. I won't just follow you into my death. I will always fight."

I fisted my fingers. "Just because you have lost your memories doesn't mean they aren't a part of you. They will resurface in due time. And no—" I finally closed the space, ignoring the warning hiss of her dragon and crouched down before her. He wouldn't hurt me, because he would never injure her. "You must hear me out. I have no idea why the heck you're with the Blood Queen, but she is the one lying to you."

"Oh, please," she hissed. "I'm pretty sure you're the one

who's being lied to. Of course, the Bone Queen wants me back, the minute I stepped through the veil into this world again, I had a choice and the Blood Queen offered me freedom. Something I would never get from the Bone Queen. She wants me dead, Rio. She's still full of rage since I lost that skulling bone and made a deal with her sister."

"And what about her sister?" I asked, trying to keep my cool. "Don't you give a damn about what she's done? She's trying to destroy the worlds with the damn book you gave her."

"What?" Aria snorted bitterly. "She's not. The Blood Queen needed that book because *your* skulling queen is the real threat here!"

"She's not *my* queen."

"But she's manipulating you as if she were."

"Yeah, because that makes perfect sense," I muttered sarcastically, my voice dripping with disbelief. I was wondering if she was playing a joke on me. But the look on her face told me she was dead serious. "You actually believe the garbage The Blood Queen's feeding you... and you really let yourself be swayed by that wicked witch? I thought you're smarter than this. Of course, she's trying to keep you on her side, to use your fucking skills, Aria. So that's why you never showed up on The Day of the Dead because she told you so, am I right?"

Aria was so close now that our noses nearly touched. "What do you mean I never showed up? I was there. Every damn year, I waited for you, and no one told me to stop. I eventually stopped perfectly on my own since you chose another woman."

"Aria... you weren't there," I retorted, gripping her shoulders.

Both Bory and her dragon hissed. "I would have seen you."

"This is—no. You know what? I'm done with it. Your lies. I've had enough, this is just ridiculous." She tried to stand up, and her knees buckled.

I reached out to help, but she clung to her dragon's neck instead, struggling to stand on her own. Bory tried to push her up from behind but instead he ended up glaring at me while shoving a bit at her shoes.

I folded my arms and stepped back, giving them some space. How could one be this stubborn. After some deep breaths I tried again: "Have you ever thought that maybe your queen messed with your mind? That she sent you to the Topworld at the wrong time because she wanted you to hate me? That it wasn't even Stormday?"

"Um, you hear the skull you talk, right?" Aria grunted, still leaning onto Soothie. "I know it was Stormday. I know when it starts and ends, and I don't need anyone to tell me that. I think your queen messed with you."

"The Bone Queen isn't *my* queen," I repeated. "But yes, maybe she had a hand in this too. Something's not right, so maybe we should focus on that instead of yelling at each other."

"I like yelling at you," Aria said.

"I do too," Bory chimed in.

"Fine," I sighed, feeling defeated and agreeing with the fact that my efforts apparently had been for nothing. "We'll discuss this later then."

"Fine."

I turned away. "Get on the horse. Mine this time."

"No," Aria said, overtaking me, seemingly all better now.

I rolled my eyes. Why couldn't she just agree to one fucking thing? Just one? This woman was going to be the end of me.

"Go ahead," I said, stopping dead in my tracks and earning an annoyed look from Any. "If you faint, at least I can drag you along without a fight."

She halted. "That sounds so awfully wrong."

"Aria," Any said calmly, approaching her with his horse in tow. "Come on. We can explain everything to you later, once we've calmed down a bit. You'll see that everything makes sense."

"Don't call me that," Aria said, and I swear her eyes sparked a

bit.

"Get on," Any tried again, nodding at his horse. "Please."

"No, she's riding with me," I said, pulling my horse in by the reins as well. "She's lost the privilege of choosing."

"Seems like someone's feeling a bit possessive today." Aria stopped right before me, laying a hand on the saddle. "But you know," she suddenly purred, while swinging herself on my horse. "I don't mind a little bit of control."

She lowered herself then and ran her hand down my chest, making my breath catch in my throat. That fucking woman.

I looked up at her, feeling unwanted heat rising in my body. "Is that so?"

"Mhmm," she hummed, her lips hovering dangerously close to mine. "How about you ask my guard. Unlike you, he ought to remember what I like."

My jaw tightened, jealousy burning just beneath the surface as she seized the reins. Before I could snap back at her, she teasingly tried to ride away, tempting me with her wicked grin. In a flash, I lunged onto the horse behind her, wrapping my arms around her waist possessively. I held her tightly, struggling to contain my urge to crush her against me in fury. Fuck. She had a point. I was indeed manipulated. But guess who was pulling the strings here? Her all along. She was playing with my emotions like a master puppeteer.

"Don't test me, one more snarky remark like that—" I warned, gripping her tightly by the hips. The feel of her curves against my rough skin already sent a shiver down my spine, and I couldn't resist nuzzling her neck. "—and you will get to know my true self."

"Oh, I fear you're all bark and no bite," she taunted. "But just to remind you, I don't submit to anyone except in the bedroom, and even then, it's on my terms."

I gritted my teeth, my grip even tighter now. "You're playing with fire. And you might get burned."

She snorted. "Go on. Burn me."

CHAPTER SEVEN
LYNNE

The heat radiating off of him was intense. I mean, it was freezing outside with the wind howling like crazy, but Rio had me boiling up. It was like all these forgotten sensations were resurfacing, making my stomach knot up and my head spin every time he looked at me.

I skulling hated how he made my body react to just anything he did or said. I tried to play it cool, even acted like I was up to pissing him off, but honestly, I just felt vulnerable inside. This situation was beyond hopeless, and I had no clue how to get myself out of it.

Any rode in front of us. He was busy answering Bory's questions. I think he had made it his own mission to find out more about our situation and started with Any. All the while, I stared at the back of his head, just so I wouldn't look at Rio's hands around my waist, at the skulling ring on his finger.

I wished I could ask Soothie to incinerate it and turn it into a pool of molten goo. Just as the thought crossed my mind, I glanced up at him, feeling a pang of sadness as he soared overhead. The glow from the skulls in the sky cast a haunting pattern on his dark scales, tempting me to climb onto his back once more. I was locked up in that damn castle for way too long. But alas, the stubborn prick behind me adamantly denied my request to ride on my dragon again.

His massive arms encircled me like a barrier as we journeyed through the treacherous lands of the Blood Queen. But riding on a horse through the Underworld wasn't exactly something I was accustomed to. Most souls here didn't have the means for a horse, and those who did often had them stolen or eaten.

But these horses were different.

They were well-trained, able to navigate these dangerous lands with ease. When I stroked its hair, I realized it was a monster, created by the Bone Queen herself. In this world, she could only create creatures and monsters, not humans or animals, as they came to our world with the dead souls. Here, the rules were different. Souls couldn't be inserted into bodies, they had to swim with the soul stream and enter the Topworld where spirit and body could connect. Many beasts down here were not dead, but rather creations of the Bone Queen. It wasn't until I returned to the Topworld that I realized how much the two queens clung to human customs and tried to imitate them. But everything created in this world was far from what was seen in the light of day above. These horses looked like real ones but as soon as we took off the spell, they could take on any form we could think of. Morph into whatever the Bone Queen desired them to be.

"Don't feel like insulting me any longer?" Rio said after we rode in silence for what felt like an eternity. His deep baritone sent shivers down my spine, but I refused to give him the satisfaction of acknowledging it.

"Insulting you is the only thing keeping me sane right now," I retorted, biting my lip to hide the effect his words had on me.

It had been so long since I'd seen him, since I'd felt his touch, and yet the wounds he left still felt fresh.

My eyes couldn't help but wander to the damn ring on his finger once again, a constant reminder of what I couldn't have. "A wife, huh?" I said, picking up the topic to finally discuss it. Or at least I tried. Couldn't hide my bitter tone though.

"Yeah, we've already been through that, haven't we?" His words stung, fueling a surge of jealousy within me.

"No, not really. It's surprisingly hard for me to get past the fact that you're a cheater. I never expected that from you, but I guess I never truly knew you, did I?" I said.

He moved in closer, his chest pressed tightly against my back, and I could feel his warm breath tickling my ear. Oh, I was so brutally aware of every move. "I never cheated on you, sweetheart," he whispered, and I could feel my resolve crumbling, even though I liked that resolve. No, I loved it.

I opened my mouth to argue, but the words died on my lips.

The truth was, I didn't want to fight with him. Not really. I just wanted to feel his lips on mine, his hands on my damn body. I needed him to say sorry, to tell me that he just fooled me, and he never had another woman. That I was the love of his life and that he entered the Underworld to be with me. But I knew it would never happen. Not now, not ever. This was just me. Forever lost in the fairy tale my mind had created to punish me. For whatever reason.

"Cheating is never okay, and don't think I'd help you with that. I just feel sorry for your wife."

"You don't have to, she'd be happy for me."

"What?" I said, my gaze jumping to his. "What are you not telling me?"

"It's more about what can't I tell you, Aria."

"Is she dead?"

"Yes."

"Oh... I'm sorry," I whispered. "I mean... gods. I don't want to know anything about your women but—Let's just ride. No talking."

"Fine," he said, his unspoken words hanging in the air.

I knew he wanted to say something else—just like me—but didn't as well and so we rode in silence again, the tension between us palpable.

The Underworld was a desolate place, but even it seemed to come alive with the electricity between us. And as the sun from the Topworld began to rise behind the skulls, shining through the tiny cracks—just a bit—I couldn't help but wonder where we were going, and what would happen when we got there. Why he chose to betray me. To deliver me to the Bone Queen. Why he—Okay, no, I couldn't simply sit here in silence and ignore it.

"WHAT DID SHE PROMISE YOU?" I asked. "She knew you had a strong impact on me and—" I bit my lip. Just don't say anything wrong. "That not just anyone would be able to get me out of the Blood Castle."

"I thought you didn't want to talk anymore?" I growled. "Fine, have it your way."

He tightened his grip on the reins, coaxing the horse to the right as his body leaned into the turn. But his command over the horse was nothing compared to the commanding presence he had over me. His breath, hot against my ear, sent delicious shivers down my spine as he leaned in closer and closer. The tight grip on the reins betrayed the raw intensity of his emotions, and I couldn't resist the magnetic pull between us.

Our bodies pressed together, every touch demanding my full attention.

But I wasn't about to let my guard down, no matter how tempting it was to surrender to his touch. The battle between my heart and my head raged on, desire and fear clashing within me. Yet, even amidst the inner turmoil, I craved more of him.

So, what did it say about me?

That I was ridiculously stupid. Stupid as hell.

"Okay, did you screw up something in the gang and have to save your *kingdom*?" I hissed the last part of the sentence, barely hiding my irony. "Or did you die too, and this is your unique way of suffering?"

"Well, look who's interested in talking after all," he said, the muscles of his thighs flexing against my own. I suppressed one grunt after another. This was my own Tartarus.

"I wish Soothie would tear your head off."

"Good thing I protected myself with the bond, huh?"

His horse sped up and I fell a little to the side because I refused to hold onto him.

"I'm sorry but we have to arrive at our destination before nightfall." His voice rasped against my ear, while his hand found its place on my waist once more, keeping me in place.

Oh, memories were a pain in the ass.

All these pictures that came up in my head the minute his lips touched my ears. Briefly. A split second at the most but it was enough to remind me when he used to whisper sweet nothings against it. What he'd whispered while he'd touched me...

"And my gang is doing great, my life couldn't have gone any better and I didn't technically die either."

Stitch after stitch after stitch. *His life was great without me.*

He took a deep breath, his words heavy with emotion. "But

then my daughter was attacked by Shadowslaves and everything changed."

My heart skipped a beat. His daughter? I couldn't ignore the pang of jealousy that rose in me, but I pushed it down, reminding myself of the bigger picture.

"I had no choice but to make a deal with the Bone Queen to save her," he said.

So, he risked everything for his daughter. It was both admirable and heartbreaking. Not because he had saved her, but because it meant that he hadn't come here for me. It was painful to admit, selfish even, but a small part of me just kept on holding onto the damn hope that he had come to the Underworld *for* me. That he still had feelings for me. But now that hope was gone, and with it, any chance that Rio and I could ever rekindle what we once had.

He had a daughter. He was married.

He wasn't mine anymore.

"Then she forced you to become her Reaper..."

"To save Jamie, yes."

I nodded, asking something I probably shouldn't have. Again. "A-And how long have you been here?"

"I honestly can't tell you, time here goes differently as you know, but when I arrived here, I hadn't seen you for five years."

"Yeah, because you didn't come to the cemetery."

"And here we go again. I was there," he said, and I rolled my eyes as he slowed down the horse. "Each year I waited for you, Aria."

"Could you at least stop calling me that." I turned a little, but accidentally looked into his damn eyes and cursed under my breath. I shouldn't look into his eyes... he had the most beautiful eyes for skull's sake. The most handsome face, too.

"You'll always be Aria for me."

"Aria *died*." I didn't mention that it was because of him

killing me... her... since that was another delicate issue between us. Technically, I was in the Underworld because of him, and he kept on making things worse for me. Great. My choice of men was just *great*.

"It's Aria or darling. You can choose."

"Did The Bone Queen damage your brain?" I stared ahead again, trying to forget all his body parts that touched mine. Calling me darling was even worse than Aria. I bet he called his other woman darling too. What a cheap trick.

"How's your... daughter doing now?" I asked, steering the conversation in a different direction, though this one wasn't really any better. By the gods, I think I lost the ability to speak... maybe I should just knock him off the horse, get my anger out of the system.

"She's alive, that's all I know," he said, suddenly hesitating.

When he took a deep breath, I turned around and glanced into teary eyes. I quickly pivoted back again and planned on delaying to punch him. It was evident that he was wounded already, unmistakably so...

Rio cleared his throat. "I'm doing everything to keep it that way. I'm thinking about her every day but it hurts... to never see her again."

A hushed stillness lingered in the air, tugging at the fragile threads connecting us, and damn it, he knew exactly how to make me feel guilty. He deserved another punch, but he was my damn weak point. Something the Bone Queen most definitely knew and took advantage of. No one but him could have done the job and kidnap me. No one could paralyze my senses like he did.

We rode in silence for a while, but then he took another deep breath, and it seemed like he wanted to lighten the mood when he said: "Do you think your guard is up already?"

A shiver danced across my skin. This wasn't how I imagined our chat would go on. Well, two could play at this game.

"I hope so," I snapped back.

He leaned into my space again, whispering: "He was the worst guard ever." His stubbly cheek touched mine and I arched my back, pressing it against his core and feeling a wave of energy surge through me.

"He's the best guard ever," I challenged him, half-closing my eyes as I leaned into him as well.

"Liar."

"Maybe I am."

I ran my fingers through his hair, pulling him closer after I checked that neither Bory nor Any noticed anything. When his lips touched my neck, I gasped in response, and my head fell back as pleasure shot through me. He held onto the reins with one hand, while the other one trailed down my waist, stretching out against my pelvis, his touch mere centimeters from my most sensitive spot. Thank the Stix I wore underpants.

My heart was pounding as his fingers trailed over the smooth fabric of my dress. His breath hot against my ear as he kept on whispering: "Quit feeding me that line about wanting to escape from me. I see right through your act. I know what you truly want."

His palm slowly traveled up my thigh, and I gasped in surprise. But before he could go any further, I sunk my teeth into his arm, causing him to curse and release me. "When did you become a mind reader?"

"I'm not."

"Then stop making stupid assumptions. All I want is to be free." I inhaled deeply, attempting to calm myself. "Unless you can give me a rock-solid guarantee that you won't sell me out to the Bone Queen, you can forget about having any piece of me."

One of his hands rested on my hip again. "To fulfill my deal,

I must bring you to the Bone Queen, but you have my word, nothing will happen to you. I'll make sure of—"

I pushed his hand away and said, "Let's just ride then. And keep your hands off me, or I'll show you what the Blood Queen taught me."

Admittedly, I was just bluffing since I couldn't reveal my skills just now. He'd report it back to the Bone Queen, and I couldn't afford to let my enemies know what I was capable of. I closed my eyes and focused on the rhythm of the horse underneath me, swaying with its movements. Rio demanded the impossible from me—to trust him.

And there was one thing Rio had proven to me time and time again: there simply was no trusting him.

CHAPTER EIGHT
LYNNE

After riding for hours, we finally burst out of the abyss into an eerie glow, casting flickering light on a camp in front of us. Among several tents that were black as the night, a jumbled pile of bones stood, like a monument to the deceased.

It wasn't until that moment that Rio spoke to me again. "Hold your tongue, now," he said, his voice low and urgent. "The other five reapers aren't as taken with you as I am."

I turned to face him. "Excuse me?"

"We set up camp here before Any and I left to get you," he said, his gaze flickering toward the tents before us. "But it's still a long way to go, and they're here to make sure we'll arrive safely."

I swallowed hard, my mind racing. He was right, of course. There were dangers lurking in every shadow, waiting to ensnare us. He could have asked me to fly to the Bone Queen, but I guess he knew that I would fly anywhere but there and Soothie would just follow my lead since he'd never listen to Rio.

"Shall we leave right away? Wake the others?" Any rode up beside us, his eyes darting nervously around the camp.

Rio shook his head. "No," he said, his tone final. "We'll wait until daylight. It's safer."

Any nodded, and we dismounted from our horses.

As I gazed around at the tents, hastily thrown up and barely holding together, I couldn't help but wonder when Rio had learned all of this. Why his knowledge was this vast, but I had no time to ponder for long as one of the seven tents opened.

A woman with two long dark braids emerged. Her attire was all black, emblazoned with the symbol of the Bone Queen across her chest. Her dark brown cheeks were streaked with dust, a telltale sign that they had been out here for quite some time, where dusty clouds hung over the land even during the day.

I didn't intend to, but the way the woman's gaze lingered on Rio made my stomach churn, and I found myself unintentionally dazzling her with my own gaze.

"Volt?" she said, and a grunt escaped me. Of course, that's what he would call himself. He welcomed this woman with... a hug.

"Gods... you guys are so lucky that nothing happened to you!" she said.

"Why would the Blood Queen be a threat to me," he said, and the woman chuckled, leaving me to wonder why she wouldn't be a threat to him. The queen is a threat to everyone...

She wrapped her arms around Rio, and I stared into her satisfied smile as she rested her head on his shoulder. Suddenly, I felt like so lost in this place and turned away.

Rio broke away from the embrace. "Are you on night watch again?"

She shrugged. "I lost to Ash yesterday."

"He probably cheated," Rio grinned, and I hated the way he looked at her.

"For sure," she said.

Gods. I hated the way she made me feel. She was so beautiful, tall, and athletic and another reaper of the Bone Queen. I looked like a little kid next to her and glanced down at my feet.

Maybe tonight I would cut off her stupid pretty hair. "Is that *her*?"

My gaze jumped up to her as she sized me up, trying to know why he was putting himself in danger to get someone like me.

I just stood there, jutting my chin and challenging her with my gaze. Yes, I would definitely cut her braids. "If you're asking whether I'm the Bone Weaver, then yes. That's me." I put extra emphasis on my title because it was feared throughout the country, and I wore it proudly.

But the name didn't do anything to her, she simply raised a black eyebrow and didn't answer me, instead she looked at Rio again and

I came up with a thousand ideas how to torture her with my magic at that moment. Not ideal. Especially considering that my arts weren't really reliable yet and were mostly guided by emotions.

I took one deep breath in and out and tried to calm down again. No need to make a fuss. I would be able to escape them eventually, but before I could manage it, I had to figure out how to break this skulling connection with Rio. I wasn't sure if I would be able to get back to the Blood Queen with him. Therefore, I had to get rid of him first, break the bond.

"I imagined her... more grown-up," she said, and I hissed at her comment but before I could snap something back, Any put a hand on my shoulder.

"I warned you about bringing these two together. So good luck," he whispered to Rio and walked straight to a tent that was probably his. "I'm gonna study the route we're taking tomorrow, don't bite your heads off, guys." He ducked into his tent and my focus went back to Rio.

"Ebony," he said, holding her casually by the arm as if it were normal to be touchy like this. "Be nice, okay? You know what she means to me."

"Yeah, we all do…"

Ebony looked up at him and in that very moment, something scared her, whatever she just saw in his gaze, because she backed away and nodded. I narrowed my eyes. Why would a reaper who had been in the service of the Bone Queen for years be afraid of a human? It gave me the creeps. Something was wrong and Rio was hiding essential things from me again. There was no way that he could be respected or feared by anyone we met. He must have somehow managed to gain strength right before he ventured into the Underworld. But what did he do? By the Hellhounds. My curiosity almost killed me.

And yet. Did I explain to him what I had seen at the Blood Court? No, because we were both in the service of another queen. If someone had told me that yesterday, I would have spit in his face laughing.

There was a tug at my dress, and I looked down at Bory and picked him up, leaving Rio and Ebony some space. It seemed like they had *things* to discuss.

"Do you know where we are?" Bory said, squinting his little eyes.

"Somewhere near Catterville," I said.

It was a hamlet right on the Black Sea, where the Neirides wreaked havoc.

I didn't know if Rio and his new gang knew this, but the Neirides were not to be trifled with. From now on, we would pass the outlets of the black sea and everywhere where the black water splashed, they could be lurking.

They were the 50 daughters of Nereus. Nymphs who protected castaways and entertained sailors with games but wreaked havoc with everyone else. They lived in caves at the bottom of the Black Sea, apparently also had access to all waters of the Topworld and wanted to pull everyone into the abyss with them, make them part of theirs.

"Catterville is no good," Bory said, and I nodded, "hopefully he knows we should avoid the water."

"I have a feeling he knows more than us," I said, watching him continue to talk to Ebony.

He whispered something sharply in her ear and I wrinkled my nose without meaning to.

"You're jealous," Bory blurted out, and I blinked. "What?"

"You're jealous. You have a dysfunctional relationship with love, you know that?"

"Like you know anything about love," I said, moving closer to Rio again, hoping Bory would stop slapping the truth in my face. Sometimes I wished he wasn't this honest... just sometimes...

"She's sleeping in my tent," I heard Rio say, while I squeezed in between Ebony and him.

"No," I said, noticing Ebony's eyes widen as if no one would dare talk to him like that. "Only over my dead body."

Ebony gasped. "You have to punish her, she's not allowed to be like that with—"

"Shht," he interrupted her, and Ebony immediately shut her mouth. "Continue the night watch, we leave early tomorrow. She will sleep with me. I'm not repeating myself, Eb."

Ebony nodded and then went into her tent after giving me one last evil look and I was alone with him again.

"Get in." Rio nodded toward the tent. "And what if I don't want to?"

I watched as he pressed his lips together in a firm line,

and wondered if his attempt at intimidation was really worth it. But exhaustion won out, and I decided to let him think he had the upper hand. He always liked to believe he was the one in control but not with me. Usually. Tonight, I let him have his moment. At least until I saw the tent and its small size.

I jerked to a halt in front of the tent. "No," I said firmly. "You can sleep with Any. I don't feel like squeezing in there with you."

A low growl rumbled in his throat.

I couldn't bring myself to share that cramped space with him! It reminded me too much of the times we had spent entwined, promising each other the world...

"Go. In."

"I don't want to."

"It's not a question of wanting, it's a question of safety. I'm certainly not leaving you out here alone."

I rolled my eyes. "Do you know how many countless nights I've been *alone*? I know the Underworld like the back of my hand."

He approached me and all of a sudden, I felt that strange power emanating from him again, I didn't want to, but I took a step back, nevertheless. It was as if some kind of magnetic field was emanating from him. The moment he saw me stagger back, he grabbed my arm, took a deep breath in and out, and pulled me into the tent.

I was so perplexed that I said nothing and just stumbled along. But Bory's whisper rang out a split second later. "What the actual skull was that? Did you see his eyes?"

"Not now, Bory," I said, figuring it was smarter to chat about Rio and his mysterious powers when he wasn't within earshot.

Rio closed the tent behind us and it was pitch black now. I

couldn't even see his outline anymore. Nothing at all and my heart started pounding like crazy.

"Lie down, there's only this one cot and I'm not up to argue any longer with you," he said.

I plopped myself onto the cot, blindly patting around in the dark, hoping to avoid falling flat on my face. But at least the cot was broad enough for both of us, although the whole situation was just too much for me. I haven't seen him for ages and now I should just cuddle up with him?

This was so wrong on so many levels.

As he sat down beside me, I couldn't help but feel my heart racing in my chest. Rio and I would be sharing the cot for the night, and this forced proximity was making my head spin. I closed my eyes and inhaled deeply, trying to calm myself down. It was just sleeping. All good.

It had been so long since I had slept properly and the thought of him lying next to me actually sounded perfect... too perfect. My mind played me, since this was a scenario, I imagined over a hundred of times while I tried to fall asleep...

But as he began to shed his armor next to me, my heart skipped a beat. The rustling sound was almost too much to bear.

I took a deep breath.

"I'm planning to sleep, and I'm certainly not sleeping in armor," he said, as if reading my mind. "So yes, I have to strip."

I swallowed hard and listened as he took of his shoes, his tunic... And then, as he drew closer, his intoxicating scent enveloped me like a warm embrace, leaving me weak in the knees. It was intoxicating, despite the fact that he had been living in the wilderness for weeks. I turned away, biting my tongue. This was madness.

My body couldn't handle this.

As he lay down beside me, the cot creaked under his weight

but when his arm brushed against my back, it sent shivers down my spine. We both breathed heavily, the tension between us thick enough to cut with a knife but I couldn't focus on anything other than his barely clothed body next to mine.

I clung to the rough blanket, desperate for some kind of barrier between us. But it was no use. He shifted, and the warmth of his bare back seared against mine.

I peered into the darkness, my fingers aching to touch his skin and re-explore every inch of his body. Did he still feel the same way about me as he used to? Did he still crave me as I craved him?

The nights were always the hardest, when memories of him haunted me relentlessly. Memories of our battles, our kisses, and now, here he was, an entirely new person. Just like last time, I knew nothing about him.

Restless, I tossed and turned, debating whether to tuck my feet under the blanket or leave them out in the frigid air. I let out a sigh, feeling completely torn.

Shit, I couldn't sleep like that. Was it the same for him?

I rolled onto my back, trying to ignore the overwhelming scent of him that surrounded me. His shoulder rose and fell in a steady rhythm, tempting me to reach out and touch him. But I stopped myself, questioning why I still craved him after all he had done. Maybe Bory was right, maybe there was something wrong with me and my idea of love. He had rejected me, despite his words, and yet here I was, still yearning for him with an intensity that defied reason.

Could it be some kind of magic that kept pulling me back to him, through death and across time? Was it the residual Aria within me that longed for him, missing the way things used to be? I couldn't make sense of it.

At some point I woke up, and watched him sleep.

I knew I had to act now. Sleep was impossible for me

anyway, and since he had dozed off before me, I might just have a chance to slip away unnoticed. So, I rose from the cot and quietly made my way out of the tent, hoping to escape his spell once and for all.

I slipped out of camp, rounded the campfire and stopped.

How far would I be able to go? I just needed a bit of space... I peeked into my pocket. Bory slept like a little baby in there. I just tucked him in and snugly placed him in there. He had such a deep sleep. I think he'd even sleep through an earthquake. If my scheme played out as intended, we'd make a swift escape to Soothie and he wouldn't even notice.

I shook my head and was glad that the lava cracks gave me some light. It was always dark here anyway but at night it was the worst, during the day it looked like it was dawning in Topworld. But at night it was just dark. I decided to walk a few steps farther and hid at the bottom of the mountain behind a large rock. Closing my eyes,

I prayed that it would work. But the bones I got from bone weaving still gave me enough magic, so it just had to.

As I knelt before the rock, my fingers brushed over its rough surface.

The truth was, I had no clue how my magic worked—it was an enigma even to myself. With a touch, I could breathe life into things or take it away. It was a power that left me both awed and scared.

The Underworld was full of all sorts of magic. There were those who relied on spells, with anchors such as bones, blood, or herbs. And then there were those who wielded ancient heirlooms, imbued with potent magic. But there were also some who possessed their own unique brand of magic. Apparently, I was one of those.

My arcane abilities were linked to life—a force that both fascinated and terrified me because magic could be used for good but also bad. It was a reminder of the Deathwalkers I had created in the Topworld, a mistake that I couldn't seem to shake from my mind. But I refused to let it consume me, pushing the guilt and regret far back where they belonged.

The stone got warm under my grip, and I tried to imagine that I could talk to *her*. That I needed her.

Give me the Blood Queen.

Bring her here.

Make this stone alive.

I focused on the Old Language, and then I felt the gift inside me leave my body with only a little bit remaining.

I relied heavily on my anchor to access the source of energies—also known as mana—that allowed me to wield my power. So technically, the old man who wanted me to bone weave for him, gave me the mana I was using now. I wasn't proud since he really paid with some years of his life, but without stealing mana from bones or souls, I couldn't do anything. Without bones, blood, or some other anchor, it was nearly impossible for me to tap into my talents. The Blood Queen had warned me that it could take years to master this skill...

As I tried to channel more power into the stone, the heat became almost unbearable.

I gritted my teeth, trying to hold on, but it got too hot. I forced myself to hold onto its surface for a moment longer before I pulled away. It was clear that I still had much to learn about my magic, and the power it held. But for now, I would have to be content with taking things slow, until I could master that damn power.

Unfortunately, it took way too long and just as I had begun to lose hope, the stone suddenly stirred. Gods... it vibrated! A shiver ran down my spine as I watched in awe, hardly daring to believe what I was seeing.

Could it be possible that my magic had worked?

As the stone continued to glow, I held my breath, scarcely daring to breathe. And then, as if in confirmation of my success, the edges of the stone became blurred, almost as if it was coming to life before my very eyes. I couldn't help but suck in a sharp breath, my teeth biting into my lip in excitement. It worked!

Right before my eyes, the stone morphed into a small Blood Queen right before me.

She coughed and glared angrily at me from below.

"I mean," she said, fixing her long hair, "I'm glad you were able to use your magic at all, but why am I a fairy?"

"It had to be small," I whispered, casting a quick glance at the camp behind me. Rio never slept deeply, and I didn't want to risk waking him up. "I don't have enough mana in me to morph you into something bigger," I added, hoping she would understand the gravity of the situation.

"Very well," she murmured. "Small it is, then. Where are you?"

"Near Catterville."

"By the bloody depths of damnation!" she exclaimed, wrinkling her delicate nose as she settled onto a nearby tree stump, as if standing for too long was beneath her. "I cannot reach you there, nor can my magic."

My stomach dropped. That meant she couldn't help me, and I had to forget about running away tonight. But we had to do something...

"How did he manage to infiltrate my castle?" the queen

interrupted my train of thoughts, "I already turned several guards into Shadowslaves. Worthless creatures."

I sucked in a breath, trying to ignore the fact that she punished them because of me. Sometimes I forgot just how merciless she could be.

"Illiam too?"

"No, he was the only one with the guts to go after that bastard and try to take him down. The rest of them were just wasting my air."

"But, my lady, we need a plan. Something we can do about this situation?"

The queen nodded. "Yes, we need a plan indeed... but there's not a lot we can do. I fear you must guide them to a neutral ground. I need to be able to use my powers and my range is very limited. So, we need you to return as quickly as possible."

"I know. I'm so sorry for what happened..." I avoided her gaze, looking at my feet. This was such a mess. We didn't have much time to begin with, and now I managed to push us into another agonizing situation that will be difficult to get out of— even with the help of the Blood Queen herself. I knew that I had to return and open that damned book before her sister unleashed chaos upon this world. Since I brought the book back, it was on me to open the seven sigils and I still didn't have enough power to do so. "I shouldn't have—"

The Blood Queen silenced me with a raised finger. "It's of no consequence now. We will be able to use Rio in some way, but first, we must get you to a safe place where I can yield my powers and rescue you."

I considered her words, weighing the options. "What about Cave Town? It's not far from here."

She raised a brow. "Ah, of course. That insignificant little town. Yes, guide them there, it's considered a neutral area since no one actually reigns over it. I will see if my demons can block your path, so it will appear as a necessary detour. However, my hands are tied. Thanks to the Shadow King's the gods forbid me from intervening too much. I'm trapped within my kingdom."

She spat out the last sentence with venom, and I knew just how much she loathed her brother. It was the one thing both queens shared, aside from their unquenchable thirst for power.

"I'll take them there," I said, glancing around as I heard footsteps approaching. "But what do I do once we arrive?"

"We'll overpower the reapers," she said cryptically, a sly smile playing on her lips. "One last question: your dragon is with you, isn't it?"

I nodded.

"Tell him to fly back to me. I'll send you my best soldiers and they'll wait for you at Cave Town."

"I will. Thank you, My Queen."

My heart was jumping on one side that help was coming but I also felt bad towards Rio, a totally stupid thought. Why should I feel bad? Rio had no claim over me. None. And he was the one who kidnapped. I shook off whatever feelings he provoked in me, focusing on the task at hand. The fate of the world rested on my shoulders, and I couldn't let my personal feelings cloud my judgment. Not when all of this was my fault.

It wasn't just luck that brought me to the Bone Queen. She knew exactly how to lure me in, tapping into my restless nature and my lack of concern for the consequences. I had been easy prey, and now I was paying the price. For years, I had been aiding her in her search for the bones, unaware of whose bones they really were. That was until the Blood Queen intervened and enlightened me. They were the bones of Zeus, the once mighty ruler of the gods. After he was overthrown, his bones were torn apart and mixed with those of mortals, scattered across the sky to ensure he could never return to power.

But the Bone Queen had other plans.

She needed someone with the power to bring life to the dead, and that someone was me. With my help, she was one step closer to bringing back her beloved ruler. It was a dangerous game, but I was in too deep to back out now, so I agreed to whatever the Blood Queen said. Because she was right.

"I have another problem," I confessed and showed her my wrist. "Rio marked me. When he dies, so will I."

The queen closed her eyes and sighed. "Oh, I forgot about that...

mark."

A feeling of dread settled in my stomach. Did this mean she didn't know how to break the bond between me and Rio?

"As I told you I can't do anything from here, but I'll see if the blood I got from the harvest can help me," she continued. "We'll have to get you home first, so I have enough time to remove the mark. I can only do it from my realm, not from this far away."

I knew what she was getting at. There was no way I could carry this mark forever, it had to go. "All right," I agreed. "Then we'll take Rio with us."

I was about to ask more when I heard someone clearing up his throat. I rustled up and saw Rio's silhouette. Rigid as a statue itself. I bent down slightly, touched the little Blood Queen, and just like that, the stone was nothing else but a stone again.

I wouldn't be able to contact her for a long time, because I didn't have nearly enough mana left in me to summon dust.

"What in the ever-loving hell are you up to?" he growled, his steps heavy and serious as he stormed towards me.

I quickly got up from my crouch and straightened my dress. "Oh, just engaging in a little bladder liberation. Got a problem with that? Number one is a universal task, you know?"

He squinted his eyes, coming to a sudden stop right in front of me, his exposed chest shamelessly teasing and tempting my senses once again. "You're supposed to stay with me. It's too dangerous out here."

"Don't talk to me about danger, Rio," I scoffed and started walking towards the tent, but he grabbed my arm and I winced. "What? I just want to go back to sleep."

"Who were you talking to?"

"No one," I retorted, trying to tug my arm free. He pulled me closer, and I held my breath.

"She is using you. Can't you see that, Aria?"

I wanted to protest, since he said my name again, but suddenly I wasn't feeling so well anymore. My knees buckled, and I think I uttered his name instead.

It sounded like a strangled cry.

He caught me before I hit the ground, and the world went black.

CHAPTER NINE
ARIA

I dashed into the classroom, making a beeline for my seat and carelessly dropping my school bag onto the polished marble floor. Tina was already perched in her spot, her dark eyes fixed on me as if I were a fascinating spectacle. Her gaze roved over my short uniform skirt and the nonchalantly tucked-in white shirt.

I raised an eyebrow in response, silently questioning what the hell was up with her. In a playful exchange, she shrugged back at me, her fiery red hair illuminated by the soft glow seeping through the grand Victorian windows. I planted my ass on the chair next to her, wishing I could sit somewhere else. There were five rows of six desks, and I knew there was plenty of space left but since I was forced to sit here, I was fucked.

Stupid rules. Stupid teachers.

Tina and I used to be friends, but now all I longed for was to steer clear of her. Determined to avoid her, I focused my gaze on the teacher's desk positioned in front of us. With nothing particularly captivating about it, my eyes then darted to the vibrant green bulletin board adorning the wall just behind it. There was still some teacher's work featured from last French class. But there was a glitch. It's *la soirée du dimanche* not *le soirée du dimanche.*

Tina sighed and I flicked my hair, the vibrant strands of chinlength blonde cascading around my face, as I flashed a confident grin in response. Bite me, bitch. "Tina, is something wrong?" Except with her, of course.

"I wanted to ask you something..."

I knew it. God help me. "Then shoot." I took out my pencil and some class books, ready to stick my nose in there just so that I didn't have to look at her anymore.

"I heard there's a party at Sam's this Friday and I didn't get invited..."

"That's called Karma, Tina, and it's spelled: fuck you, bitch," I growled and caught Any, who turned around once he heard my swearing. I made a face at him. I'm defending him right here, so how about he acted a bit more grateful?

Tina wrinkled her nose and moved farther away. She hated sitting next to me as much as I hated sitting next to her. Since she'd cheated on my brother, I was done. Done with trust, done with friendship, and most of all, done with her contacting my brother. Any was about to come to me when I hinted with my gaze alone that he could stay where he was, because over my dead body would he ever be allowed to talk to that bitch next to me again. And there was no need for him to come to her rescue.

"I'm fine with you ignoring me but you don't have to exclude me from all the parties, Aria."

I scoffed. "I didn't exclude you from anywhere. Sam is Any's friend, it was his very own idea to not invite you. Maybe it's time to understand that you dug your own social grave."

Yeah, it was more likely that hell froze over than the both of us to ever talk like normal people again. My brother meant everything to me and anyone messing with him would have to deal with me. He's always been the kind one and I learned to fight for both of us.

Of course, our teachers caught on right away that hell was hot between Tina and I and believed that a new seating arrangement would be the best solution. They thought that if I just sat next to her long enough, everything would be *fine* soon again. That we would get along. That we would no longer burden the whole class with our arguments.

Fine, my ass.

I would make her regret. Because my brother certainly wouldn't. Any shook his head and sat down in his seat again, two rows in front of us. No one sat next to him, simply because Any talked to everyone and teachers wanted it to be quiet. I don't know how many times I advised him not to get involved with Tina. Hundreds of times, I'm sure, but he never listened to me and—

"Good morning," Mr. Callaghan greeted, leaving the door ajar behind him.

My curiosity piqued, I cast a quick glance at the partially open door, catching sight of a lurking shadow beyond. A tinge of anticipation tingled within me. Was there an esteemed guest speaker scheduled for today? Had I overlooked an important announcement?

I watched Mr. Callaghan put his bag on the table, run his hands through his golden hair, and smooth out his suit. Like us, the teachers had to dress formally. We wore the Hathenways school uniform, blue plaid skirts for the girls with equally blue blazers and blue suits for the boys as well as teachers.

"We have a new student," he announced, gesturing towards the door. The room fell silent as we all turned to see who it was. The door creaked open and in walked a guy. My breath hitched as my eyes landed on him. He was older than us, with tanned skin and piercing blue eyes that seemed to stare right through me. And boy he was tall. Really tall. I felt myself stiffen involuntarily, but when he finally tore his gaze away from me, I let out a deep breath.

"Fuck he is hot," Tina said.

"Stop talking to me." I nervously tucked a strand of my hair behind my ear. She was right, though. He was incredibly hot.

"Meet Rio Rènero, he won a scholarship to our school and..."

Mr. Callaghan kept talking, but I knew exactly why he was here. Any had been drinking alcohol on school grounds last semester with his friends from college and was discovered. Another reason he was sitting alone. Father had to pay the school a lot of money, so they brought in some kind of scholarship that gave a poor student free education. I guess Rio was the one who won then.

I couldn't help but be impressed by his intelligence, from what I knew the assessment test was pretty hard. However, as expected, a few of our classmates were already struggling to cope with his mere presence. The uprising waves of jealousy were unmistakable. Perhaps it was his towering height or his irresistible good looks that intimidated them. And as it happened with Hathenways, envy was quicker to surface than admiration for his achievements.

I overheard the first whispers, "Look, one from the ghetto."

Another called him Italian trash, and I couldn't help but inhale sharply. I spun around, scanning for the source of the filth. It was William, laughing with Daniel. Mr. Callaghan was still talking about the "great" project, but here, as always, the rich used the poor for their own gain. "Look how we help the poor, we are great, we use the money to make the world better."

Ladies and gents, capitalism in all its glory.

"I wonder if he hustles to afford the uniform?" Daniel snickered, and the pencil in my hand cracked.

"Rio comes from Englewood and had the highest test score

we've ever had. I'm looking forward to a great school year with you," Callaghan said, finally letting Rio sit down beside Any. Before sitting, Rio looked at me again, causing my cheeks to flame.

"He's mine," Tina declared, and my stomach turned.

"He's not a possession. Shut up," I chided, but deep down, I felt possessive too. I wanted to call him mine the minute I saw him. I had never felt something like that, and it felt rather strange... unnatural... but fuck, he was so damn hot.

I stared at Rio's thick, wavy brown hair for the entire English class, unable to focus on anything else. For the first time, I didn't care if I missed something important. I had to find out what Rio was whispering to Any instead. I had to know and oh God, I had to look into those eyes again.

So, as soon as the bell rang, Rio rushed out of the classroom. "Wow what a day—" Tina started but even before she could finish her sentence, I sprang into action, determined to catch a fleeting glimpse of him before he vanished from view.

"Hey, Rio!" I called out, chasing after him like a complete idiot. Just when I had accepted that he had taken off, he stopped.

Fuck. My heart skipped a beat because I hadn't really thought about what I wanted to say to him. All I knew was that I wanted to talk with him. About something. Anything.

Once I caught up to him, I had a hundred different ways to start the conversation playing in my head. But when Rio flashed that smile again, it lit up his whole face and sent my heart into a frenzy. Damn, now I had no clue what to do next. I was so fucking stupid.

"You're Aria, right?" he said, a hint of excitement in his deep voice.

"Yeah," I replied, trying not to let my nerves get the best of me. I wanted to ask how he knew my name, but he beat me to it.

"Your brother spilled the beans in class, so don't think I'm some creepy stalker or anything," he blurted out, his cheeks turning a cute shade of red. It made me smile in return.

"The pleasure's all mine," I croaked. "Quite the accomplishment you've made there. Top score. Some of the classmates are already green with envy." At least that was a real conversation.

"Well, don't worry, I've had my fair share of dealing with jerks," he added with a wink, an actual wink.

Just as I was trying to figure out what I wanted to ask him next, Any swooped in and playfully wrapped an arm around Rio, giving me a chance to catch my breath.

"So, you guys have already met? That's awesome. He's coming home with us by the way, Sis," Any said.

"Um," I stuttered, feeling my cheeks flush with heat. "What do you mean he's coming home with us?"

"We're just giving him a little introduction, helping him get settled," Any explained casually, as if it were the most normal thing in the world. "You don't mind, do you?"

I wanted to say no, that it was totally fine, but my voice seemed to be stuck in my throat again, so I just shook my head in the most stupid way.

"Thanks, guys," Rio said, his voice warm and deep. "I have no clue how this school app works or actually anything here…"

In that fleeting moment, his piercing blue eyes locked onto mine, and I knew I was in trouble, but there was nothing I could do to stop it.

CHAPTER TEN
RIO

"What have you done?" Bory hissed again, his eyes boring into me.

I did my best to ignore him as I held the smelling salts near her nose, hoping she'd breathe them in. The lousy lamp I lit didn't provide much light, making it harder to see her response.

"Bory, I get your point, but her passing out has nothing to do with our bond," I muttered under my breath. I hoped it was true.

After a few deep breaths of the smelling salts, she suddenly shot up, her eyes wide open. Bory and I both flinched, inhaling sharply. She looked around frantically, her features contorted in fear, but her expression gradually softened as she recognised us—Bory on her left and me on her right.

"My father," she whispered urgently.

"Your what?" I asked, surprised. I hadn't heard her mention that man in years.

She grabbed onto my arm tightly, her grip almost painful. "Something my father did...and Aria...I mean I did something..." She groaned and ran her hand over her face. "I saw you. You visited our house and Any, he was there too, and we helped you but my father, he did something, and I can't remember. Rio, why can't I remember?"

"Okay, I think I understand what's going on here," I said, taking her hands in mine. "You start to remember parts of your previous life."

She nodded, her eyes still wide open.

"That's what happens to some souls when the barrier between their different lives starts to break down," I explained.

"What do you mean?" grumbled Bory.

Well, I had to be smart about this. Talking about that stuff out here in the open wasn't the best plan, especially after she chose to sneak off and blabber to the Blood Queen. So, I looked down at her face and said: "I'll give you the answer once you stop sneaking off in the night and tell me who you've been talking to."

Aria narrowed her eyes but didn't say a word. I waited.

After seemingly fighting some inner battle, she glanced to the side, and I knew she wouldn't tell me. There was no trust between us anymore...

Bory intervened. "But what exactly did you see, Lynne? You need to be more precise," he said.

Aria waved her hands in front of her face, struggling to find the words.

"I think I saw *us* meet," she said, gesturing between us, "but then my memories jumped and all of a sudden we were kissing in the garden and—" she swallowed as if the memory had hurt her deeply and I reached out to hold her hand. This time, she let me. "—and I saw a light and my father showing up out of nowhere. Then something happened, but I don't know anymore... it was so odd."

Aria's frustration grew. "These memories... it makes it all seem so useless. All I had known and—"

"Shhh," Bory said, placing a comforting hand on her shoulder. "That's exactly why your body protects you from remembering... the more lives you lived the more memories fight to come to light. It's exhausting but we'll find out, Lynne, we'll get to know the truth, but you need to calm down first. This isn't doing you any good."

Bory was right.

So, I added, "We don't know anything about your father. I think he has his hand in this too since he's really angry with me but—"

I winced as my heart pounded against my chest. Fuck. I already had said too much. Fuck that curse.

Aria noticed my discomfort, her hand squeezing mine tighter. "What's wrong with you?"

"Nothing," I replied, forcing a smile. "It's all good, just a little... back pain." But it wasn't. Nothing was good. However, Aria's memories were the start of everything. If she could piece together the puzzle on her own, maybe we could fight back. Maybe we could end all of this shit.

Aria sighed in disbelief. "It just doesn't make any sense. I was afraid, really afraid of my father... Rio."

I nodded in agreement. "He's keeping things."

"You all are keeping *things*," she said, and she was right. I would love to tell her everything I knew, but I had to be sure she was ready to break the curse once and for all. If we didn't, I couldn't tell her anything without consequences. And in the Underworld consequences meant dying.

Her eyes, dark as the night sky, searched mine for answers that I couldn't give her. I knew she was hurting, confused, and scared, but if I tried to form the words, the curse would kill me. That's why we needed to hurry. Hurry home.

I pulled away and sat up, running my hands through my

hair. "We have to keep moving. The Bone Queen is waiting for us, and we need to finish the job."

Aria sat up too, her eyes narrowing in anger. "This is nerve-racking, Rio. You say it like I don't matter at all, *finishing* a job. I get that you need to save your daughter, but you could have tried to find another solution, I'm sure the Blood Queen would have helped you without killing me."

I sighed heavily, feeling the weight of the world on my shoulders. She didn't understand. Of course, she thought it was simple but hell, our love story was anything but simple. "It's complicated, Aria. I can't lose Jamie, and I can't lose you. I did my best and tried to find the best solution and once we're with the Bone Court, I promise to explain more. I just need to end that fucking contract with the queen first."

She swayed a little, exhaustion etched deep in the lines of her face. I think I had pushed her too far, too fast, but we needed those memories back. Without them, we were lost. Every one of us, her, Jamie, our friends, family, the world... we all needed her to finish the puzzle.

Gently, I placed a hand on her delicate shoulder, coaxing her back onto the cot. Aria hesitated, but I knew that we couldn't push too hard—her memories were fragile, like a glass figurine on the brink of shattering. "It's time to let your mind rest," I whispered, my voice soft.

Aria nodded, her eyes clouded with doubt, and I could sense the weight of responsibility settling heavily on my own shoulders. But I couldn't falter now. We had come too far to give up.

I turned to Bory, his expression puzzled as he watched us. "Get some rest too," I murmured to him. He grumbled and shuffled off to his own corner of the room.

As I blew out the flickering candle, the room plunged into darkness, and I settled down next to her, my arm wrapping protectively around her slim frame. At first, she tensed, but I coaxed her closer, aware of the heat emanating from my bare chest. I needed her close, needed her to know that I wouldn't let them take her away from me again. Not without a fight.

I resisted the temptation to caress her body and instead whis pered against her ear, "It's a safety precaution, so you don't run away again. Try it and I'll lay on top of you."

When Aria pressed herself closer to me and her warmth seeped into my skin, I knew she was up for another fight. She wasn't giving up as well.

"No guilty conscience because of your wife at all?" she whispered, her voice like honey on a summer breeze.

I tightened my hold on her, knowing that this was dangerous territory. "We're just sleeping," I replied, my voice strained with desire. She laughed softly, the sound sending shivers down my spine. "Do you hold all your prisoners like this?" She spun around, and I found myself face to face with her. Her pretty face hovered just inches from mine. As her fingers trailed languidly over my chest, I fought to maintain my cool. "What happened to you all those years you hid from me?"

I tensed, feeling her hot breath on my lips. "I know what you're up to," I growled, my voice rough with emotion. "You're trying to cloud my mind, but I'm not going to back down. I can't tell you what you want to know."

Aria rubbed her thighs against my dick, her breath hot on my neck. "Don't you care? Don't you think about her at all when I touch you?" she whispered, her fingers trailing lower, inching closer to the waistband of my pants. "I'm sorry, but I need to understand the person you've become. You can't just lecture me about right and wrong and then act like I belong to you. It's like those five years never happened. So, tell me, what happens when I touch you here?"

My control slipped. "Stop it," I growled, holding her hand in place before it could go any farther. "I know you're angry and no, I won't fuck you. Not like this. Not when you're out to hurt me, not when you're this exhausted and not when you're this angry. You need to sleep and never mention my wife like this ever again."

She grinned, undeterred. "Then make me stop," she said and placed her hand on my throbbing dick.

That was when I knew I had to act.

With a sudden burst of strength, I grabbed her and held her tightly, feeling her struggles fade as I whispered: "*Sala te doreme.*" The ancient words that would send her into a deep sleep.

Resting my forehead against hers, I took a deep breath and tried to quell the turmoil within me. This was supposed to be a simple mission, but everything had spiraled out of control.

I closed my eyes, trying to find the strength to face the consequences of my actions.

But for now, all I could do was hold her close and hope that we would both make it out of this alive.

"WHO ARE WE AFTER THIS TIME?" Ebony inquired as we gathered around the campfire with Any and the others. Aria was still sleeping, and I had insisted that we wait until she awoke on her own. Our preparations were nearly complete, with only our tent left to be packed up. The horses were saddled, and the rest of the camp was ready to be left behind. But there was something bothering me. Bory had vanished since morning and so had Soothie.

I wondered what business he had with the dragon, but I knew better than to expect answers from Aria's helpers. Still, they were up to something. So, my speech didn't convince her, and I had to think of something else to get her on my side.

"Alec Counterharden," I replied firmly.

"Why don't we just go straight to the queen?" Ash chimed in, prompting me to roll my eyes. He was our warrior, always playing the big, hotheaded and merciless man.

"She's our last stop, mate," I reminded him. "The queen wanted her to be the 100th."

Ash averted his gaze, while the others smirked at him. "Right, right. Got it," he muttered.

"We've got one more soul to capture, and then it's off to see the queen, job's as good as done," I announced.

Ebony nodded in agreement. "As long as you keep your end of the deal. Just don't let her looks cloud you."

I knew she was referring to last night. So, I've been right. She was listening. "Of course, I will, Eb. I won't endanger my daughter."

Ebony sighed. "Funny how much you've changed on Earth…"

As I opened my mouth to speak, a sudden rustling caught our attention, and all heads turned to my tent. Aria emerged, donning my clothes in place of her dress. It was a wise decision, given the arduous journey ahead of us. Yet the garments hung loosely on her lithe frame, giving her the appearance of a rap star. I couldn't help but chuckle at the sight, earning an amused glance from Ebony.

It was funny how easily such human thoughts still crossed my mind.

"Did you sleep well?" I asked, and she nodded. "Strangely well."

She didn't know, thankfully, that I was able to force her to sleep, make her do what I wanted and that was for the best. I couldn't risk her wrath if she found out. Ash wasted no time in dismantling our tent, and I was grateful for the efficiency of our group as they prepared to ride out.

"You said we're off to Catterville? What's our business there?" Aria asked, her eyes curious.

"We've got a job to do," Ebony replied, nodding towards my horse. "You should saddle up too. We have a long ride ahead of us."

"We have to fetch another soul there," Ash said.

"That's Ash, by the way," I continued, indicating the muscular man with the red scar on his face. "He's our master spy. You already know Ebony and Any. This is Isix and Briz."

Isix, a bald girl with tribal tattoos all over her face, nodded back at me before turning her attention to extinguishing the fire.

Briz, on the other hand, was the youngest of our group. Despite his youth, he was a force to be reckoned with. His umber skin was complemented by fiery red hair, which seemed to glow in the light of the dying fire. He stood tall and proud, with a fierce determination in his eyes that belied his age.

Aria's gaze swept over our group, filled with contempt and distrust. In her eyes, we were no better than kidnappers, intent on doing her harm. It pained me to see her so wary of us, but I understood her hesitation. After all, she didn't know the truth about the Blood Queen and her minions.

"How did *you* become one of them? A skulling reaper?" Aria asked Any out of the blue while she watched Ash securing my tent to my horse.

"The spot was open," he replied nonchalantly, shrugging.

Aria scoffed, her disbelief evident on her face. "Sure, I've heard of the queen making people with no skills her henchmen."

Any raised an eyebrow, and everyone turned dead quiet. "I

never said I have no powers," he replied, leaving Aria speechless.

She turned to me, and I couldn't resist the urge to grin wider. Yes, Any had powers too, just like her. They shared the same father, after all. But explaining that to her was like trying to tame a wild animal. It had to be done slowly and carefully since she always wanted more.

"He'll show you his gifts in Catterville. Now, get on your horse, we have to finish this job quickly and return to the queen," I instructed, hoping to avoid any more unnecessary questions.

But, of course, Aria remained stubbornly rooted in place, her arms crossed and a defiant glare in her eyes. "And what, pray tell, will you do if I refuse? I will not be sent to fetch another innocent soul for you and your puppets," she challenged.

"That soul hardly is innocent," Ebony retorted, her own eyes flashing with anger. "You will do as Volt says. Get on the horse."

I stepped forward, placing a calming hand on Ebony's shoulder. "Let's not resort to violence," I said softly, turning to Aria. "We only wish to protect you. It would be easier for all of us if you could do as we say."

Aria snorted, her eyes flickering between me and Ebony. "Oh, I understand perfectly well," she said. "You're using me, just like everyone else has. Once a pawn, forever a pawn, huh?"

I drew myself up to my full height, meeting her gaze with a steely resolve. "You are not a pawn," I said firmly. "You are a valuable asset to our cause, yes. We need you. But if you choose to fight against us, then know this—you will not win. We will do whatever it takes to protect you, protect my daughter and our people."

Aria hesitated for a moment, her expression conflicted.

Ebony's gaze jumped up to mine and I knew that she needed to hear that as well.

"You may not believe it now, but we're on the same side," I said, my tone firm. I took hold of Aria's arm and led her away from the others. My people were already wary of her, and I didn't want to fuel their suspicion any further.

So, I leaned in close to her ear and whispered, "Whatever you and Bory have planned, it's not going to work. You're fighting against your own will right now. It's better to play along, the sooner you grasp that, the easier for all of us."

Aria's expression softened for a moment before hardening once again with her characteristic stubbornness. I could have sworn she was up for another verbal sparring but with a heavy sigh, she climbed onto the horse, her movements begrudging but compliant.

"Good girl," I said and swiftly lifted myself onto the saddle behind her.

Giving the horse a gentle nudge with my heels, we finally set off towards Catterville.

CHAPTER ELEVEN
LYNNE

The fog hung low over Catterville, as if shrouding the city in a cloak of secrecy. The moon cast an eerie glow over the ancient walls, and the rain fell heavily, as if trying to wash away the sins of those who wandered its streets. And in Catterville, there were plenty of sinners to be found. It was a haven for those who operated outside the laws of the warring kingdoms that surrounded it, and they flocked to its shelter, seeking refuge from those who would hunt them down.

To be honest, the thought of making this place my home had crossed my mind more times than I cared to admit. So, I knew I wasn't any better than the rest of the sinners that called this place home. In fact, I might have been worse.

As we rode through the city, the weight of Rio's gaze on me was horrible. Plus, my mind was flooded with a whirlwind of questions. Why was he here? Why did he have such power? Was it something the queen had promised him? Or did he have another motive?

I could see the reluctance in his eyes as we trotted through the rain-soaked streets. The thought of being the queen's butcher for the criminals of this city didn't sit well with him.

And yet, he led us on this search, determined to find the soul the queen was looking for. I knew why he brought me along to hunt the soul down. He wanted to send a message, to show me exactly what would happen if I continued to act against him. The silence between us was heavy, thick with unspoken words and tension and I knew I had to be careful, one wrong move and I could end up like the soul we were after. He was done playing lover with me.

The Horsemen flanked us, their horses snorting and pawing as we made our way through the empty alleyways of Catterville. The sound of their hooves echoed against the walls, blending with the patter of raindrops on the rooftops above. My heart raced as I felt the weight of twelve watchful eyes upon me.

I needed a good plan to get away from them, even for just a moment. After I led them to Cave Town, I had to disable Rio somehow, and that wasn't possible without enough mana. Which is why I had to take the chance because as luck would have it, Catterville was just the place to find what I needed to get free.

We left our horses at a stable and left for a tavern. Rio never strayed from my side, moving through the alleys with the confidence of a king. He seemed unafraid of the shadows that lurked in the corners, and I couldn't help but frown. I had worked hard to instill fear in the Underworld, but this man seemed to have stumbled in and effortlessly gained the same level of respect.

I just wished to understand who he truly was. I was certain that he had a life here before me or before we met as Aria and Rio in the Topworld... and I was dying to find out what kind of life. If I had heard of him before... As we made our way past the rowdy taverns, the hood that Rio had lent me barely concealed my face from the curious eyes that followed us. The clacking of my shoes on the cobblestones seemed to echo through the empty alleyways, drawing the attention of maids who stood in the doorways of the inns and offered us drinks and lodging.

Behind the stained windows, I glimpsed men hanging on the necks of women, lost in a drunken haze. It was a reminder of the sinful underbelly of Catterville, a place where anything could happen. I just had to look for a weak soul, who was willing to lend me some time to weave it into mana.

"Stay close," Rio said, his arm snaking around my back protectively as his crew trailed behind us, ever watchful.

"Don't baby me," I grumbled. "I'm no damsel in distress, and I know how to handle myself in these parts."

"I just want to make sure you're safe. The shadows here can be dangerous, and I won't let them touch you."

"I wasn't born yesterday," I retorted, rolling my eyes at Rio's protective stance. "I know the danger of a single touch. I've known it since my drop. And others touching me is none of your business."

The stories of Catterville were ingrained in me since forever, tales of demons who tempted and ensnared souls, leading them to sin and trapping them in the Underworld for eternity. The price for one's transgressions was steep, and those who dared to challenge the Bone Queen's rule were doomed to suffer for all eternity.

But I wasn't one to back down from a challenge, and I wasn't about to let Rio or anyone else tell me what to do. I also knew that most demons listened to the Blood Queen these days, so they wouldn't hurt me. Never. They were her pets, since they fed on blood. And honestly, my queen's barrels in the cellar were not filled with wine, but with blood. So, we had more than enough for them and the upper hand in here.

"I'd have to kill anyone who touches you, so I'd say it's pretty damn much my business," Rio said, nodding toward a wooden stand that showed Catterville's executioner's platform.

Three men had been impaled on stakes and their pale eyes stared back at us. Their jaws were cramped, open, and black. Like gorges. Flies buzzed around them and flew into their open mouths.

I cringed and tried not to smell the acrid scent of decomposing corpses that polluted the entire district. I held an arm over my nose, but it didn't help much.

My eyes were glued to the dead bodies and I wondered where their souls were now. Of course, they wouldn't die just because someone hung them. They lost their body, but their soul wasn't finished yet. If they would have suffered enough, there was a chance of redemption. But let's be honest, this was Catterville, so hanging souls here meant they dropped somewhere again, somewhere worse than last time.

They would suffer even more now and their flesh was nothing but a feast to the demons.

Rio bent down and surveyed the area, his gaze darting back and forth. Without warning, he reached for the ground and grasped onto an unremarkable ring, tugging it upwards. As the trap door creaked open, he looked at me with a raised eyebrow, inviting me to follow him down. With a deep breath, I peered into the darkness below, shrouded in a thick blanket of fog.

Rio leapt down first, the sound of his landing echoing through the cavernous space.

"Jump, darling," he said with a smug smirk, and I gritted my teeth, resisting the urge to plant a kick right into his chiseled jaw. His stupid pet names were grating on my nerves.

Just then, a warm hand landed on my shoulder, and I turned to find Ebony giving me a knowing grin. "You heard Volt. Didn't you?"

"I—"

"Enough, Aria," Ebony said, cutting me off with a sharp tone. "You're not the only one who didn't want to be here. But we have a job to do, and we can't do it if you keep acting like a spoiled child."

I bristled at her words, but before I could retort, Rio cleared his throat and that was enough for Ebony to just throw me down the pit. I had no time to scream or anything because from one moment to the other I found myself in Rio's arms. Something I wanted to avoid at all costs because my damn body wasn't to be trusted when it came to this man.

"Let me down," I snapped. "Behave and I will."

"You know," I said as Rio stepped to the side with me in his arms while the others climbed down like the good little dogs they were. "You can play the hero card as much as you want but the truth is, you're no hero—"

"Oh," a deep chuckle escaped him. "I never said I'd be."

I blinked. Several times caught off guard by his unexpected admission.

"Maybe I'm the villain, well I certainly am but, you know what?" He marched into the depths of the corridor, his lower hand dangerously near to my butt. "I'm not *your* villain, I guess everybody else's and all I'm doing right now is waiting until you realize it too."

"And what makes you think I'll ever see it your way?"

He smirked, his eyes glinting with something dark and dangerous. "Because, you're already drawn to the darkness. I can see it in the way you look at me."

I swallowed, feeling a shiver run down my spine. He was right, damn him.

I lifted my chin defiantly. "That doesn't mean I'm going to let you win."

His smile widened, and he leaned in closer, his breath hot against my ear. "I don't aim to just claim victory. I want to seize it all, leaving nothing in my wake."

A shiver ran down my spine as I craved to dig deeper and

squeeze out more details from him, but the others caught up to us. No way he'd spill the beans with their ears all perked up, damn it. He let me down, but then yanked my arm like a leash, treating me like one of his mutts. I scowled, wishing he could see the ice in my glare, like Medusa's snakes freezing him on the spot.

Oh, I loved Medusa.

Step by step, we reached a large, round door. On the walls were torches showing its dilapidated wood. Rio knocked. Exactly three times and a hatch opened. I peeked over my shoulder to see the Horsemen standing there as if this was normal. As if they were used to waiting for Rio. As if they knew him for decades—not months, nor years.

Before my mind could wander any further, a cone of light filtered through a small opening, illuminating musty limestone walls. A green eye peeked through the hole, blinking as it took us all in. Then, his somber voice asked, "Password?"

"*Sitaenae*," Rio replied without hesitation. I gazed up at him, my mind reeling. The Old Language... it was impossible for any mere mortal to have knowledge of such a tongue.

The man blinked, shut the hatch, and I heard the sound of keys rustling. He unlocked the door and Rio led me into a secret inn. The air reeked of stale beer, and as the horseman pushed me inside, I noticed the round, beer-bellied, bald man frowning at me from below.

His gaze locked onto mine as we walked past occupied tables, and we were soon surrounded by drinking, drooling, farting men who watched our every move. I glanced at them from under my hood as they laughed loudly, shoved each other, and spilled more beer than they drank. But when they noticed us, they abruptly fell silent.

I couldn't help but wonder why they were giving me those strange looks, but right at that moment, I felt Bory making his way up my leg and plopping himself back into the pocket of my dress.

"Oh, Bory! You're back!" I whispered excitedly, letting Rio tug me along.

"Yeah, it was a real struggle, you know," Bory sighed dramatically, munching on a cracker that was almost as big as him.

I narrowed my eyes. "Struggle, huh? Looks like you found time to snack."

He grinned mischievously, crumbs falling from his mouth. "Well, a hero's gotta eat, you know. It's survival out there."

"I'mjustgladyou'rebackinonepiece.Andwhatabout Soothie?"

"All good. The little guy's got his own adventures going on, he's pretty proud."

I couldn't help but chuckle. My boys were amazing.

The man led us past faded tiles and creaking beams, the musty scent of age permeating the air. We entered another room with a cluster of doors, each one more nondescript than the last. But one door, forged of iron and as sturdy as a fortress wall, captured my attention.

The man stopped short, turning to me as he spoke, "Well, well, if it isn't Mi—"

"Aster," Rio interrupted sharply, cutting off the man midsentence.

His gaze faltered briefly before he regained his composure, nodding in understanding. "Of course. Forgive me, I assumed you were coming straight to the usual spot."

"As you know, I can't," Rio replied coolly, nodding towards the staircase leading to the upper floors. I followed his gaze and noted a number of rooms leading off the landing. "We'll need a room."

"For how long?" the man asked, a hint of suspicion in his voice. "Depends on how long it takes us to find what we need."

"Of course." The man swallowed and beads of sweat formed on his forehead. "Follow me, please."

He led the way quickly and scurried up the stairs, offering us a glimpse of his back full of sweat. I stomped after Rio, but then I noticed that the Horsemen didn't follow us.

I stopped dead in my tracks and looked down at Any standing next to the others like he was rooted to the ground. "Aren't you coming?"

"We... have plans," he simply said, earning a nasty glance from Ebony.

I rolled my eyes. Fine, he'd just keep it from me then. Let him. I was doing my own thing anyway.

The bulky man stopped and pointed to a door. He opened his mouth, but just when Rio shook his head, he closed it shut again, and left.

"Why is he acting so strange?" I checked my hood. He seemed to have recognized me... maybe as the Bone Weaver?

Rio shrugged and turned an iron key already stuck in the door, letting us in. "Maybe he has weak nerves."

"He doesn't seem so."

We entered the room and I found myself in a very simple bedroom. It was nothing special, a bed, a box, a desk, wooden floorboards and planks. Typical for Catterville. When my gaze swept to the bed, a tiny one, Rio's hand clasped my waist, swiftly spinning me until our faces were mere inches apart.

"Rio..." I breathed.

"Always Volt down here, please."

Gods. I hated that name, and with good reason.

He leaned in so close that our breaths mingled, and I could feel the heat emanating from his body. As his forehead touched mine, my heart started pounding so hard that I feared it would burst out of my chest. He took a deep breath and closed his eyes, as if he too wanted to memorize this moment. Memorize us not fighting for once.

My longing for him was more than just a feeling, it was a tangible ache that throbbed through every inch of my body. And to make matters worse, my little mind game from last night only served to make things even more messed up. It seems my plan has completely backfired, leaving me in an even needier position than before. I knew I'd kick myself later, but damn if that was gonna stop me from craving him even harder.

I tugged him close, his body trapping me between the wall and his muscled body. When he flung his eyes open, piercing me with his gaze, I was struck by the beauty of them. As always. I just can't help it. They were like sparkling sapphires, reflecting the depths of a crystal-clear ocean. I lifted my hand and traced the softness of his lips with my thumb. One second he playfully nibbled on my finger and the next his mouth was on mine, sending my heart into a frenzy.

The kiss was like a wildfire, raging out of control and consuming everything in its path. It was a connection that bound us together, two souls intertwined in a dance of fire and desire, and I knew deep down that all the time I spent trying to forget him, to push him out of my heart and mind, had been in vain. No matter how hard I tried to convince myself otherwise, my love for him never truly died. It was still there, burning bright and fierce, even though I knew I shouldn't feel this way but damn it. I still loved him.

I grabbed his vest, pulling him closer as his tongue slid along mine. We're all tangled up, our tongues and teeth clashing, lips pressing urgently, and hands roaming eagerly. By the Stix, I've missed this. Missed him.

But just as swiftly as his lips had claimed mine, he pulled away, leaving me breathless and dizzy.

Without a word, he took a step back, opening the door. My heart plummeted as I realized what was happening.

Then, with a final, heartbreaking glance, he said: "I'd rather you didn't fall back into those patterns where you lie to me and make plans behind my back, but—" He reached for the door-knob. "I don't think we're past that behavior just yet. So, I have to lock you up. Get some rest, I'll be right back, darling," and with that he slammed the door shut right in my face.

Gasping, I reached for the handle, but he already turned the key in the lock!

I couldn't help but feel helpless and stupid. How dare he do this to me? That bastard.

"But the bond," I yelled, grasping for some semblance of control. "I've got it covered, don't worry," he said through the door before he disappeared.

Bory grumbled from inside my coat pocket, and I set him free, only to be greeted by a disgruntled face that resembled a grumpy crumb-covered tumbleweed. Cracker crumbs clung to his fur like a misguided attempt at camouflage.

"I really have to complain, could you please let me out of your coat pocket when you're necking? This is so weird," he said. In a comical flurry, he furiously brushed and pawed at his fur, determined to rid himself of the pesky crumbs that had somehow become lodged in his fur during our little wall encounter. Oops.

"It's not like I planned on kissing him," I protested, watching him shudder, as if he needed to rid himself of the image of Rio and I.

"Still very weird." Bory pretended to retch, and I rolled my eyes. "You know what? Next time, bite him. He'd deserve it. Skulling asshole."

CHAPTER TWELVE
RIO

"So, how mad is she?" Any called out to me as I rattled down the stairs.

"Very, means we need to hurry up and hear these fuckers out before she comes up with something to get back at me."

"Not sure if we can be this quick." Any smirked.

I stopped when I touched the brass handle, glancing at my Horsemen. "Ebony and Ash, you go to Haven and look for Axter there. My spies said he'd be hanging around with a guy that wears feathers in his hair."

"We're not talking about raven feathers, are we?" Ebony said, raising her eyebrows.

"We are," I said. "That motherfucker."

"He's yours once you get the intel."

"Deal," she said and yanked Ash outside.

I looked at Briz and Isix, "You two are checking the brothels." Briz grinned, the dimples in his cheeks flashing like beacons, belying his youthfulness. Perhaps no more than sixteen, fuck, he was far too young to be a henchman.

"I said checking."

"Come on, dude…" He rolled his green eyes, but Isix pushed him outside.

"Let's go, and don't call *him* dude." The sight before me was almost comical—Isix, a pint-sized girl, and Briz, a teenage giant who could have passed as a member of a human boy band.

We all shared a common bond, though: we lived on the dark side of life. And so, we banded together, our alliance forged over countless years of working side by side.

Any's frustration practically radiated from him as he stood by my side. "What about us?" he said, his arms crossed tightly across his chest.

"We'll drink mead and gather intel on Axter here," I replied smoothly, knowing that Any was itching to go on a hunt too.

"Or we could bring her along and go out," Any suggested, a glint in his green eyes.

"No. I don't trust her," I confessed. "She's convinced that the Blood Queen has our backs. She'll only lead us down the wrong path. And I can't risk exposing us."

Any finally relented, nodding in agreement. "Fine. Then let's have some fun tonight. And let the others do the dirty work."

"Exactly."

I pushed open the door of the dimly lit tavern, stepping into a swirling haze of smoke and lively chatter. This hidden sanctuary attracted all sorts of folks seeking refuge from the chaos of everyday life. Well, it's been that way since the damn day it opened.

It was like returning to a comforting embrace, a place where I felt like I truly belonged. Despite the passage of time, the tavern retained its dark and secretive ambiance, but the flickering candlelight cast a warm and inviting glow, promising more than just a hiding spot. The antique furnishings added character to the space, and the mingling scents of sweat and wine filled the air, grounding me in the present moment.

But amidst the changes in the world, it was a relief to see that some things had stayed the same. My gaze swept across the room, taking in the row of ale barrels and the long, weathered counter that stretched out before me. In one corner, a group of men huddled together, their voices murmuring in hushed tones as they engaged in a tense card game.

"Are we doing what I think we are?" Any asked. "Of course."

Without further explanation, Any and I headed to the men that played cards and got a nod as we sat down. I didn't have to look at their cards to know what they played. Crooks and Cats, a game of runes. They had to guess symbols and who had a pair in their hand and who didn't. It was more luck than logic, so, of course I found it irrelevant. I cleared my throat and waited for the men to spare me a second.

"Men, can I have a word with you?" I said and one looked up from his cards.

He was young and looked like he'd been through some kind of trauma. His body was twisted and disfigured, his face contorted, as if there was some agony and rage he'd tried to hide.

"Who is asking?" he said, and I twisted my lips into a crooked smile.

I loved it when they didn't know.

"Just a traveler, no one that's going to get you into trouble."

"Whatever you want, I'm only interested in coins," he grunted and looked down at his cards again. He didn't have to say it out loud, it was more than clear he didn't mean just *any* coins, but Bloodcoins.

The other two men chuckled, and I glanced at Any, who curled a hand into a fist under the table. I shook my head. They weren't worth it, and we needed news, something we wouldn't get with threats. The smallest of the men took a card from the bigger one next to me and placed it face down on the table.

The last pair. Game over.

"We can talk about coins as soon as I get what I want," I said, and the big boy finally turned toward me.

"Why should I believe anything you'd say?" Big boy bristled, showing me yellowed and blackened teeth.

Any nudged me with his knee and pointed at the smaller man who started to shuffle the cards.

He probably was in his early fifties, his face thinning and his hair gray. The only thing that gave him away was the wrinkles on his forehead. He knew who I was, what I wanted, and he was wise enough to not speak up. Any was right, he was the one we had to go for.

"I wouldn't believe anything I'd say either, but actually, it's not you I want to talk to," I clarified, shifting my focus to the man sitting before me.

He stopped shuffling the cards and placed them on the table, resting his scarred hands next to them.

"Then fuck off," the man beside me spat, but the fire in my eyes silenced him in an instant. I hated resorting to intimidation, but he left me with no choice. As the room fell into a hush, the elder man at the table fixed me with a knowing stare. I quickly glanced over to Any and made them stiff like pillars.

"You're searching for Axter?" The old man glanced at his friends, both in a frozen state now.

"Just a little... trick," I said with a sly grin on my face, thanking Any with a simple nod, "you know. I don't like rude souls."

When I cleared my throat, he was quick to speak: "He slept in the Gauntled Inn and he's close..." The sound of his voice had taken on an eerie quality, it seemed to echo off the walls and it had a strange cadence to it, as if something was living inside of him, controlling the words he uttered. I smirked. I knew who controlled him. It was me and it was an amazing feeling.

"How close?" I said, as calm as I could. One soul. Only one soul and I would be free again, ready to unleash all I got.

The man's eyes turned milky, and I knew I had to break the spell or someone would notice it—notice me. I sighed deeply once he spit out the words I needed: "It's the man the woman is approaching."

But when I fully understood what his words meant, I caught my breath for a split second and turned around. Woman. He said woman and we both knew that this bar was no place for women so it only could be—

Aria.

I couldn't believe it.

She had somehow managed to break free and *summon* Axter within minutes. He was nowhere in sight when Any and I entered the bar.

I was seething with anger and disbelief, ready to explode. And to top it all off, she had the nerve to ditch her coat and strut around in her fucking skin-baring dress. Her presence was messing with my focus, making the guys at my table antsy and whispering to each other. I had to keep it together, not let my frustration show, but it was getting harder by the second.

I turned toward the man at our table again, breathed out and black smoke came out of my mouth, it sneaked its way into their noses and within the blink of an eye they started playing cards as if nothing had happened—ignoring Any and me again. Both of us checked the surroundings but everything was fine.

"Thanks, Any," I sighed. Without him, hiding my magic wouldn't have been this easy and I would have been discovered a long time ago. What I just did with the men at the table, he had done with the patrons. With all of them. Yes, he was that powerful.

He waved it off and nodded at Aria. "Want me to do something about her?"

I followed his train of sight and shook my head again. "Let's wait, I want to see what she's up to. I love it when she thinks she has the upper hand."

"The two of you have strange foreplay."

"You have no idea."

My eyes followed her as she sauntered to the bar toward a man with broad shoulders and dark, wavy hair. Before she touched his arm, she looked over her shoulders and grinned at me, teasingly and fucking sexy as always. She wanted to make me pay because I had shut the door right into her face. Very well. Play as long as you can.

Any was joking about our foreplay but, unfortunately, he wasn't wrong here. I couldn't help but look at her swaying hips as she grinned lasciviously at Axter. I just hoped she knew what she was doing. And I hoped I could behave myself, because I hated it when she flirted with other men. Hated it when she did it to provoke me like she used to on Earth. How will it be for me down here? Where everything was stronger... all my feelings... all my flaws...

My muscles coiled tight as I watched her whisper something in his ear, and he nodded in agreement. When she took a seat next to him, he leaned forward with his elbows on the table, his fingers laced together. Her giggles grated on my nerves, and I couldn't help but muster fucking Axter. He stole from the queen. I didn't know what but since he messed with her rules, he has been a walking dead man ever since.

He was looking at her with an air of authority, as if he was used to the attention. He had a strong jaw line and a slightly crooked nose, suggesting he may have been in a couple of fights before. I had to suppress the thought that I wanted to be his next one.

Aria's laughter filled the air as she tilted her head back in pure delight. The sight of her joy was enough to make him grin, his eyes pinned on her like a magnet. Meanwhile, I clenched my fists, trying to ignore the overwhelming urge to possess her. Damn, she was hot, with her long white locks cascading down her back, and those curves that hugged her petite frame in all the right ways.

But I couldn't keep obsessing over how she looked underneath that freaking dress.

No, I had to focus on the present, on fixing what was broken between us. She had to understand that she was mine, and mine alone. Loyalty was non-negotiable, and I needed her to prove herself before I could put my trust in her again.

A faint frown tugged at the corners of my lips as she sprang to her feet and grabbed the man's wrist, pulling him away from my presence. I watched them vanish into the distance, a wave of uncertainty crashing over me.

"Follow?" Any questioned.

I wasted no time and leaped to my feet, eagerly following her lead.

I tried to convince myself that it was just our bond compelling me to keep her in my line of sight, but deep down, I knew it was my fucking nature rearing its ugly head. It was a trait I despised yet found impossible to ignore. Since discovering what love truly meant, I became frantic in my need to hold onto it. Fuck. It was easier when I thought I could never love anyone. But now, I had *her*. And Jamie. And Cherry. And all of my friends.

Too much to lose.

As she weaved through the throngs of patrons, I watched from a distance, my blood boiling with envy as the man followed her every step. They eventually reached the back of the bar, where a roaring fireplace illuminated a cozy alcove. A single table made of cherry wood and two chairs. I leaned against an opposite wall, perfect to watch and listen.

As they took their seats, Axter had his back to me, while Aria faced me. She flashed me a mischievous glance before leaning forward to speak to him.

"Are you ready to weave bones with me?" she said, her voice cold.

CHAPTER THIRTEEN
LYNNE

The man pulled his lips into a crooked smile when I repeated the words I'd said hundreds of times before. But the moment I withdrew the bones from my dress pocket, I was filled with dread. The man's eyes had a cold and calculating expression that made my pulse miss a beat and I hoped he wouldn't notice.

He was a little hunched over, with deep creases etched into his weathered face. His once strong frame had become frail and thin, as if he were slowly fading away.

But there was only one way for me to play my part, and that was to act like I was cold—just as Rio had always done.

I took a deep breath. I could do this.

I was the Bone Weaver.

"Before we start," I said, placing the bones carefully in the middle of the table. "You must grant me something in return. I would normally ask for bones, but since you don't have any, I will take a higher price."

"What will it cost me?" His voice was low and gravelly. I shrugged. "Depends on what you wish for."

What he didn't realize was that saying yes to this bargain

meant he was going to die and although I wanted this to leave me all cold and unbothered—it didn't. But I had to because I needed his mana to fight against Rio.

I jumped at the chance when Bory suggested summoning Axter to butter up Rio by helping him with his job. And since Axter was a bad soul at heart, it was easy to compel him to come to me. I just needed a grain of mana. A little bit and oh, for skull's sake... it was so easy. He didn't just want to come—he *needed* to. That was the beauty of souls: their insatiable hunger for power made them flock to me, like snakes to a charmer's flute.

"I need a minute," he said, leaning back into his chair.

It was then when I heard a deep sigh that I glanced behind Axter and met Rio's gaze. His eyes were wide with interest, and I smirked at him. He glowered at Axter as if all it took was one wrong word and he'd crush his head. I'd be lying if I said this didn't please me— hell it did. But right now, I was killing two birds with one stone.

I tore my eyes from Rio and focused on Axter again. "What's your heart's desire?" I asked, twirling the bones in my hand. The magic in them crackled against my skin, but I kept my cool. "Anything you want, just name it." I grinned at him, watching as he hesitated. It was clear that he had never been given such an opportunity before.

He closed his eyes and swallowed hard as if the following were the hardest words he ever said: "I... I wish for love."

I frowned and for a split second my gaze met Rio's again and the insides of my stomach twisted. Well, that was unexpected. "Why?"

He shrugged. "I've never been truly loved. Do you think I would have let you seduce me to bargain with you if I were happy?"

I let out an exasperated sigh.

Of course he wouldn't wish for something worthwhile. "I could grant you love," I said, my tone laced with irritation. Such a foolish desire. I took a deep breath, knowing that what I was about to do would bring both pleasure and pain. Love was a tricky thing, and I had learned that the hard way. And yet, he had asked for it, so I was going to deliver. It was foolish of me to think that I could grant his wish immediately.

If he had asked for wealth or power, I could have easily conjured an illusion. But love? That required some more time, but I'd come up with something to make it sound reasonable to Rio.

For now, I had to concentrate on creating an illusion. I was still mastering the ancient language, and without full fluency, I could only cast simple spells. Thankfully, the Blood Queen had taught me the word *Ternetae*. It allowed for self-deception. All I had to do was whisper the word and then weave the desired illusion.

Elirath. Love.

"What do I have to do for it?" he asked, his voice trembling with excitement.

I casually slipped my hand under my dress, pulling out a gleaming dagger, secured tightly in a hidden garter. With a flick of my wrist, I presented it to him, watching as his eyes widened in surprise.

"I just need a drop of blood, drip it on the bones on the table and we're ready."

Axter paused, eyeing the dagger with caution before accepting it from my outstretched hand. He drew the sharp blade across his palm, leaving a thin red line in its wake. He hissed, but held the hand over the bones and we watched the blood drip, coating them red. If I didn't get bones, I had to draw the mana from him directly. Simple math.

He swallowed. "How does it... work?"

"You'll leave this bar and meet a girl. As soon as you lay eyes on each other, you'll fall hopelessly in love," I lied, twirling the bones in my fingers and calculating how long my spell would last. "After that, all you have to do is return to this bar and ask for a man named Volt and pay for the spell to last from then on." Or rather, pay with your life.

"That's it?" he asked, sounding surprised.

"That's it," I confirmed. I briefly considered adding some more details to persuade him to agree, but before I could speak, he said, "Fine."

"Now, touch the bones. They'll draw some mana from your soul, which I'll use to weave to initiate your wish," I said.

He swallowed nervously but reached for the bones nonetheless. I saw his eyes widen as he felt their pull. The unavoidable strength that drained his limbs of mana. I kept a close eye on him as the pain visibly shot through him. He shuddered slightly and I wanted to grab the bones, see how strong his mana was. Each soul was different, and I figured when he managed to run away from the Bone Queen this long, he wasn't just anyone. He must have had a good mana flow. And I needed a lot of it to make Rio unconscious so that Soothie could fly us home.

We all had mana in us, because it was what held us together.

A person without mana lacked life. It was the breath we needed so that the heart beat. The stone that started life rolling, activated the soul. Magic. And right now, I took as much as I could without killing him, leaving just enough mana for him to survive another day. I tried to tell myself that it's fine because he was going to die anyway but hell, I knew this would haunt me. Just like all the other times I've done it before.

I wanted to grasp the bones when the mana flowed out of him, but I had to save it for later. My lower lip quivered as I thought about what I could do with all that power. I could possibly transform two of Rio's Horsemen into Deathwalkers, but the others would simply overwhelm me.

So, sticking to the other idea it was. Waiting for an interruption and taking advantage of it.

I stopped Axter before he lost it all, and took the bones under his hands, my fingers twitched over them as I claimed them. He gasped and fell back into his chair, his eyes frantically pinning me.

When I started to weave, I felt the bone's power in my fingertips. A crackling like a living flame. It felt so good to finally have an anchor again. The bones jolted open and began to link with one another. They came together like jigsaw pieces, twisting themselves into one large bone. Until all of the magic that had just been in them was transferred to me.

Once I finished, the bone shattered into tiny pieces, which I carefully gathered and returned to my bag. Each time I used the same bones to weave, there came less mana back. It was like recycling. I knew humans recycled things in the Topworld, and even there the pieces shrunk. Just like my bones. Now I only had four left, three less. That's why I needed more bones or blood. Why the queens were in constant need. I wondered what it was like to be able to cast without an anchor. It had to be amazing, because you never needed anything. Just yourself.

"What are you—" he started, but I quickly touched his arm and whispered: "*Ternetae Elirath*" and with that the spell was cast. Like a puppet, he stood up and found his way through the crowd, strolling to the door where he'd meet the love of his life.

I smiled at the thought that at least his last hours would be fun.

Rio plopped down in Axter's chair and wheezed, "You've gone and made the guy I was supposed to fetch disappear."

I folded my arms. "No, I helped you."

"He's gone. How is this helping?"

"He would have been long gone if I hadn't compelled him to come to this bar. You would have lost him," I explained, hoping to convince him.

Rio's tone was sardonic as he replied, "Is that so," as if he wasn't going to believe a word I said. He was too clever for that.

"Well, he'll be back tomorrow and ready to be returned to the Bone Queen."

He casually draped his arms behind his neck. "So, we have some time. Why don't you tell me how you compelled him and broke out of your room then?"

CHAPTER FOURTEEN
RIO

"I'd be a fool to spill my secrets to my enemy," Aria said, and her words pricked at my heart.

"I'm not your enemy—"

"—but you're still selling me to the Bone Queen, aren't you?"

"Like I said, I can't tell you what I know or don't know."

"What if you're wrong about your queen's intentions?" I asked, my gaze fixing on her delicate features.

Her face was still youthful and innocent, glowing with a natural radiance without a trace of makeup—but she had changed, nonetheless. Something dark now flickered in her eyes, something that even I was beginning to fear. But her eyes were still gold flecks in a sea of emerald, reminding me of a forest during a hurricane. Oh, how I wished I could tell her the truth...

"I'm not wrong," she countered.

I smirked, unable to resist another retort. "Darling, this isn't helping. But I must say, your determination is quite admirable."

With a huff, she rose from her seat, her eyes flashing with

defiance now. "It's simple. If you won't share your secrets with me, then neither will I."

As she took a step closer, she suddenly halted, positioned right between my legs. In that instant, my instincts kicked in, causing me to lean into her. For a fleeting moment, our eyes locked, and a weighty silence stretched in the narrow gap between us. It felt as if years of missed opportunities, past wrongdoings, and misunderstandings loomed over us like the Sword of Damocles, waiting to be addressed and resolved.

Briefly, her features softened, as if she forgot her anger for a moment and I lifted my hand to grab her waist. Fuck, I've missed her. Gently, my fingers caressed the delicate curve of her hip, feeling the satin fabric's softness against my skin.

Her gaze softened for a split second but hardened in the next. "Your queen is going to kill me. I can't believe you're fine with that. I wanted to show you that you can trust me and help you to capture that soul, but I don't know anymore. Maybe I was just wasting my time."

With that she left, and I watched her go, her hair lit by golden lighting as she sauntered through the men. Her measured steps carried her slowly through the dingy atmosphere, over old wooden floors and chipped paint. My eyes followed her every step until she slipped out of sight.

Sighing deeply, I rubbed the bridge of my nose with my thumb and index finger. Why did everything have to be this hard? I knew she had to leave to calm down, take a break, and try to work it out. I felt the same. I wasn't even angry with her. I'd been angry at my own insecurities and fear that I'd let it get out of hand. I knew she needed clarity, honesty. But that's something I just couldn't give her for now.

I didn't notice the strange looks I was getting. The men at the bar were probably wondering why I was so enthralled by an empty chair in front of me, I'd even forgotten they were there. I raised my glass of whiskey to my mouth and drank it in a single gulp, then let out a sigh just as shaky as my hands. I had to fix this. Somehow.

"Stop that shit!" I heard Aria yell.

I rushed up and pushed my way through the crowd to her, my heart pounding up to my temple. Whoever touched her would be dead soon. Once I pushed myself through the crowd, I saw one of Axter's friends holding her by the elbow. He was tall, broad-shouldered with a balding head and a craggy face. His clothes were slightly tattered.

Any was already standing next to them and fixed the man, one of his hands on his dagger, which put me on alert. Any was never quick to defend. He was more of a pacifist than anything else, which meant this guy had already done what he shouldn't have. I pushed a man in front of me, didn't care if it was gentle, if he fell on his face, or whatever—I had to get to Aria. For a brief second, Any's eyes met mine and his startled face told me my eyes probably had a black shadow by now. Whatever. Everyone around us would soon forget they were here anyway. So, I shrugged at Any and grabbed the guy holding Aria by the head and turned him to face me.

"Let go of her," I said, my voice carrying the veiled threat of what would happen if he didn't. Once he lifted his dark brown eyes, they widened so much his irises were edged in white. Finally, he grasped who I was and recoiled in fear. "Nothing! N-nothing! She tripped and fell, that's it! I was just helping her get up!"

"He's telling the truth," Any said. "It's the other one who's making trouble. Sly is here."

I narrowed my eyes but released my grip on him. The man stepped away, looking visibly shaken as his hands flew up in surrender. I remained standing in front of Aria, my chest heaving, and my fists clenched as I saw Sly. Like back then, he had dark, wavy hair that fell around his angular face, framed by his pale complexion. His cheeks were slightly flushed while his skin shone milky white in the light as he stared Aria down.

Ignoring the shivering guy from before I turned and gripped Aria by the waist, telling the other man exactly who's here with her. Sly looked at me but wasn't scared, he smirked even.

"I see," he said, appraising and judging with a single glance. "You two found each other again."

"What do you mean?" Aria said and my hand gripped her even tighter.

He shrugged. His eyes were the same color as the night sky, and filled with a deep, cold anger. He was an old acquaintance.

"It's not my place to tell you, milady. But you should be careful." I felt my eyes burning and as if he did too, he looked up at me. "I imagine you must be very angry, milord, but playing with fire always comes with burns."

I opened my mouth to say something, but Aria suddenly pushed me away.

"Could you please stop being so overprotective? I can protect myself."

"It's in his nature," Sly said, and I warned him with my eyes not to say a single word, as I knew he wouldn't last the night.

"I don't see why a Reaper would care about his victims, after all, all he has to do is bring the heart all the way to the principal." She pursed her lips in a big white slash.

"Reaper, huh?" Sly said, and the corners of his mouth tipped upward.

"What are you doing here, anyway," I interrupted him before he said anything stupid.

"As I told *your henchman*," he nodded to Any, "I'm looking for something for *the* lord, if you know what I mean."

"For the lord," I said, knowing it could only be the Shadow

King, since Sly was one of his closest confidants. Not the smartest but you couldn't always choose your people.

He nodded.

"What do you mean we found each other again? How do you know we've met before?"

"Weaver," I said, careful to whom I revealed her true name, "let's go."

I put my hand on her lower back, but she resisted again. "How many times, do I have to tell you, that I can decide for myself?" She turned to me and suddenly her eyes glowed white. It took my breath away. A sense of foreboding started to loom like a dark cloud, creeping through the room with a chill and a heavy silence. All the drinking men were glued to their seats, tensing up with every passing second. Fuck, we started to stand out.

"Slow down," I growled, noticing how the mark on my forearm burned.

Her power awakened something in me that I didn't want. I looked around, slowly everyone murmured, whispered until it got louder and louder. I had to act before they started a mass panic. If they knew who we were, they would run away in fear and spread rumors.

I didn't need that, not until I had everything ready. "Slow down," I repeated.

I grabbed her shoulders with both hands, but it seemed like her magic was getting the better of her. There was a flash in her eyes as if the biggest storm was coming. An uneasy silence blanketed the room as everyone held their breath, waiting for something—anything—to break the tension. The only sound that could be heard was faint and far away an ominous rumble that seemed to be growing louder with each passing second and it was then when the barkeeper touched Aria's shoulder, saying: "Milord, I think you should leave

—"

"No! Watch out," I said, but it was too late. We all knew that no one should touch her when her eyes turned white. Expect him apparently. And he dropped dead.

I bit my lips, closing my eyes before the uproar would start. Her magic was like a cold chill, making the hairs on the back of everyone's necks stand up. It was like a dark, oppressive fog that had descended upon the room, blocking out the light and making it difficult to breathe.

"Volt," Any said and I opened my eyes to utter chaos.

Chairs scraped back hastily, and drinks were knocked over as all the men rushed to their feet at once, pushing and shoving each other towards the door in a desperate attempt to escape. The smell of fear was palpable in the air, sharp and acidic, like sweat and adrenaline. Shouts of alarm pierced the air, the nervous gibberish of people trying to convince themselves that everything was okay and that there was nothing to fear.

As if on cue, my eyes flicked to Aria and her jaw hung slightly open as she took in the unexpected sight before her, stiffening up as she struggled to comprehend what she did. Bory climbed out of her pocket, his frantic eyes taking in the mess before us.

"I never—this doesn't work down here—only in the Topworld, I

—"

"Volt!" Any said again, tearing me out of my stupor.

"Fuck," I rasped. I almost messed up. If only one managed to escape, we were all fucked. Jamie would be. Cherry. Punchy. Everyone. I clenched my fingers into fists. All I could do now was to make everyone forget.

I knew my eyes were a bottomless abyss as I lifted my hands

and spread my palms forward. From this simple gesture, a mist of black fog surged forth, covering all in my path as if some unseen force were driving it onwards. The fog was thick and roiling like dark storm clouds with an eerie luminescence that seemed to cling to the air. It coiled around the patrons, crawling up their limbs like snakes until they were completely enveloped.

My magic wouldn't save them, but Any's would.

Finally, the smoke found its way to Aria while she perceived everything as if in a trance.

"What are you doing?" she breathed, her eyes darting back and forth between me and Any. "Why don't you cloud *him*? What is this?"

She tried to shake the smoke away, but it clung to her like a second skin. The fog was different with her though, slower. It moved as if it wanted to caress her—kiss her even.

"Because you need to forget what happened here," Any said, looking at me, asking if I was okay.

"All good, Any." I turned to Aria again. "It's better this way, you wouldn't let up to find out what I really am and you're not ready yet to know."

"What does that even mean, Rio?"

"That you still need time."

I fully covered her with smoke now and let Any make everyone forget. Her eyelids flickered slightly before she fell over. I took her in my arms. She should have stayed in her room.

Now, both Any's and my magic would need days to recover. Fuck that fucking deal.

Fuck those witches.

CHAPTER FIFTEEN
RIO, 20 YEARS AGO

I was walking down the hallway of Any's rich ass mansion, searching for a bathroom in the middle of the night. I was lost in my own thoughts, trying to remember the way to the nearest one, when suddenly, I heard footsteps approaching from the opposite direction. I glanced down the long and wide hallway with gleaming marble floors and walls adorned with intricate murals and paintings. The soft glow of several lamps that lined the walls cast a warm, golden light over everything, creating an atmosphere of pure luxury.

Still lost in thought I rounded the corner and Aria stood there. For a moment, we kept frozen in place, our eyes locked in an intense gaze. Then, we both started walking towards each other, drawn by an irresistible force.

I looked down at her, my heart racing as I saw her wearing nothing but a silk dress that didn't hide anything. Her gaze swept over my bare chest with a faint smile on her lips and I nervously tucked up my pajama pants, cursing myself for not wearing a t-shirt when I slept over. I just hoped her mother didn't wake up and see us like this. I bet I wouldn't ever be allowed to walk these floors again.

"Hi," she said softly, her voice barely audible.

"Hi," I replied, feeling my heart skip a beat. "What are you doing?"

"I could ask you the same thing," she said with a chuckle. "I was going to the bathroom."

"Me too," I said, feeling a rush of relief that we had such a mundane excuse for running into each other. We both knew deep down that the bathroom was just an excuse to stop us from knocking on each other's doors.

And yet, we walked together in silence, our footsteps echoing down the empty hallway. Man, it felt like we were the only two people in the world.

When we reached the bathroom, we hesitated for a moment, unsure of what to do next. None of us wanted to admit that we didn't actually need to go to the bathroom. But on the other hand, we didn't want to leave either. Didn't want to waste any more time we could spend together instead. The mischievous grin on her lips made it clear that she had no intention of leaving or using the bathroom as intended. In an instant, our unspoken agreement led us down a different path... far away from the confines of the bathroom.

"Aria," I said, a warning undertone in my voice.

"What?" she smirked.

"We can't go in there together."

She playfully flung the bathroom door open. "Why not?"

I grinned, rolling my eyes. Man, she was my ultimate weakness. "If your mom catches us like this, I'm gonna be banned from your place."

"Hey, good news, I couldn't care less about what my mom thinks," she retorted, tugging me inside anyway and swiftly locking the door behind her.

I raised an eyebrow, teasingly. "And I have no idea what I'll do if she catches us half-naked in your freaking expensive bathroom."

It was a sight to behold, no doubt about it. The moment I stepped into her bathroom my eyes widened in awe. The glistening marble floor spanned the entire space, like a lavish runway fit for royalty. But the true centerpiece was the grandiose bathtub, carved from a single block of pristine white marble, adorned with exquisite gold inlay along its edges. And to top it all off, a sleek modern sink with gleaming gold fixtures added the final touch.

"Let's not talk about my mother now, okay?" she purred and placed both of her hands against my chest, and I knew that all I wanted was to be near her.

Since we kissed the last time, all I could think about was her. Staying here for the night was like torture. Playing videogames with Any was torture. Because I knew she was in the room next door. Because I heard her talking outside of his room. Because she came in, casually throwing herself onto his couch, pretending to be into the game so that she could be with me.

We liked each other for quite some time now. And both of us knew it.

But I couldn't tell Any I fell for his sister. I couldn't tell her mom because it would be better for Aria to throw me out anyway. I was the ghetto boy, like I was called in school by now, the only reason I wasn't beaten was because the most popular kids counted me as their friend.

I couldn't mess this up. It was all I had.

"You're different since we kissed," she said, her toes touching mine as she stopped right in front of me.

"The two of us being together is dangerous, Aria. I thought maybe if I stayed away... that it would be better for the both of us," I said and tucked away a loosened strand of white-blonde hair.

She waited a couple of seconds to answer but the moment she did her eyes were full of fire again. "What if I like dangerous?"

I smirked, if she only knew what I did to afford all the rich clothes for school. I bet she wouldn't use these words. "You don't. No one from here does, because being in the danger zone means there's a chance of losing, Aria. And if things go south, I could end up losing everything. It's different for you. We're not the same."

"But what's the worst that could happen? I can handle my mother," she insisted confidently.

I shook my head, a hint of worry in my eyes. She was so used to being privileged that she couldn't see it clearly. "Listen, it's not just about handling your mother. What if I mess this up? Have you thought about the consequences then? If things go downhill, it's not just about losing the school, it's about losing everything. My home, my friends, and even you... It would mean my siblings losing all the hope we're desperately holding onto right now."

I stroked her cheek with the back of my hand, her skin so soft and warm against the roughness of mine. It felt so wrong to touch her. Someone so precious like Aria. Someone like me shouldn't be allowed to be near her. Someone who deals with drugs, gets into shootings every other weekend. Lives in a place where water leaks into the rooms, where people sniffed cocaine from CDs and yet—I felt a fiery heat course through my veins as I beheld the raw desire in her gaze.

Fuck, she was so beautiful.

Without warning, she surged forward and our lips crashed together in a forbidden kiss.

The heat of our passionate embrace filled the room,

banishing all doubt from my mind and my heart. I tasted the sweetness of her lips, felt the soft curves of her body pressed against mine. We staggered backward, and in doing so, my back brushed against the water tap. As we kissed the gentle rushing of the water from the sink provided a soothing backdrop to our searing intensity. I cupped her face and forced myself to stop the kiss. Her look was frantic as her gaze pinned mine, trying to understand why I broke away.

"Wait a second. I need to take this in, need to remember you just the way you are right now. With this dress. With the tangled hair. I need to remember this forever."

I took her in, not telling her why I was so adamant about remembering this moment. There was this fear that this moment wouldn't last. That one day I'd wake up without her. I was a lost cause and not made for a happy ending.

So, I tried my best to fully embrace the moment, taking in every exquisite detail. Her untamed mane of sun-kissed hair that tumbled down her back—a cascade of soft, unruly locks. I relished the touch of her smooth, porcelain-like skin as my thumbs traced circles upon it. Memories of her heart-shaped face and her inviting, full lips flooded my mind.

However, it was her captivating eyes that truly held me prisoner—big and round like those of a doll, with fluttering lashes resembling the wings of a delicate bird. God, her beauty was undeniable, but there was also something else in her gaze. A sense of fragility as if she could be shattered at any moment.

"I love you," she breathed.

But as her words hung in the air, a flicker of frantic uncertainty danced in her eyes. It was as if she feared my response, worried that she had revealed her love too soon. Breathing heavily, she wanted to pull away, but I held her head tenderly between my hands, not allowing her to move an inch.

I bent down to her lips and whispered: "I love you too. Every inch of me belongs to you since the day we met."

"And every part of me is yours, Rio."

Our lips crashed down on each other with an intensity that defied reason. Aria tugged at my shorts, her fingers fumbling with the buttons in a hurry to explore the skin beneath. Each passing second only fueled our urgency, the longing mirroring in the intensity of our kisses. My shorts dropped to the floor, leaving me standing there in nothing but my boxers. Without hesitation, I lifted her up, my hands firmly gripping her delicious curves as her legs wrapped around my waist. Spinning around, I seated her on the bathroom sink, the cool surface forgotten in the heat of the moment.

My hands traced a path across her body, my fingertips exploring every inch of the territory she had promised to me. Every contour and curve, every secret and sacred spot, was mine to discover and cherish. She belonged to me, and in that moment, it felt like the most incredible possession I could ever hold.

But then, out of nowhere, a loud crack pierced through the air, disrupting the moment entirely. It was as if the world came to a screeching halt, freezing us in place with hearts pounding restlessly in our chests. For a split second we exchanged wide-eyed glances, the unspoken tension thick between us and then, we pulled apart.

"It's coming from the storage room," Aria whispered, nodding to another door opposite from the one we entered. "But that's odd. No one ever uses that room."

"Whoever it is, let's go," I said, yanking her down from the sink and quickly fixing her dress, as if her mom could somehow count the wrinkles and figure out how many times I'd gotten a little too touchy.

"No, wait," she interrupted, stopping me with a hand on my chest. "I want to check who's there."

"Are you insane? It's probably your mother, searching for something."

Aria shook her head. "No, Mom takes sleeping pills, she sleeps like the dead. It's not her."

She turned away from me and I struggled since I had no idea how the hell I should act now. Follow her? Run?

Fuck. This was such a mess. "Aria, we really shouldn't—"

"Shhh," she said and slowly opened the door. A blinding light hit our eyes, and we both instinctively turned away, trying to shield ourselves from its brightness.

"Fuck," I croaked, bringing an arm up to my face. "What the fuck is that?"

"To save her," a voice whispered.

I strained my ears, the faint murmurs of their hushed conversation reaching me from the shadows.

"I can't," another one said, sounding a lot like Any. "I can't do it.

He's my friend."

"You have to, they're trying to get her downstairs again, boy. It's the only way to save her."

"Okay, I... I'll do it. But how long will you be gone this time?"

"A couple of weeks. Athena holds another meeting and I need the gods to wait until she knows how to close the worlds again."

"She doesn't know?"

"No one does. Keep a close eye on *him* and watch your sister."

I heard the door shutting and suddenly Aria rammed me. "Out. Out of here," she whisper-screamed and pushed me out of the bathroom in my boxers.

CHAPTER SIXTEEN
LYNNE

When I opened my eyes, the sun was beaming at me and I shot up, my heart immediately beating in chord again.

"Bory?"

"Here!" he called, hopping to the foot of my bed. "Man, you slept late."

"I feel like I got hit by a troll." I groaned, my head pounding with a vengeance.

Everything around me seemed hazy and indistinct, as if reality itself was trying to hide from me. My memories of last night were a jumbled mess, like pieces of a puzzle that refused to fit together. I rubbed my temples, trying to shake off the confusion.

"How did I get back in here, Bory?"

Bory's eyes darted away from mine, his expression guarded. "Well, Rio didn't say much when he came back with you," he muttered. "Just that you needed some rest."

I raised an eyebrow. "Rest? That doesn't sound like me. Tell me what happened, Bory!"

He shifted uncomfortably. "It's a bit complicated," he

hedged. "Bory, you know I don't have time for your games. What did Rio
do?"

He took a deep breath. "He brought you in here yesterday. You were out cold. Again."

I frowned, trying to piece together what had happened. "But I didn't drink too much," I protested.

"Well, it wouldn't be your first escapade…"

I rolled my eyes. "Bory, then what did he do? Did he say anything? Gave you a hint why I was unconscious?"

He shook his head. "No, but look, I was asleep because you know whenever I'm nervous I need to sleep."

"I'm not mad you didn't come downstairs, you wouldn't have liked it at all. It stank of smoke and alcohol and man sweat and—"

Suddenly I almost choked on blue feathers because Bory actually dared to hold my mouth shut. "Lynne, listen to me, I'm trying to tell you something. So, I felt bad because I didn't want to go downstairs with you and when I got up I had this *funny* feeling."

I mumbled something against his hand, and he pulled it away. "What did you say?" he said.

"That I'd listen better if you didn't put feathers into my mouth!"

"Fine. But look, I'm dead serious, this isn't good. It think someone put a forgetting spell on you."

I stared at him, feeling a wave of panic wash over me. "What?
Who would be strong enough to do that?"

Bory raised his arms in mock defense. "Who knows? Maybe it was Rio, maybe it was Any, or perhaps both of them. Either way, it's definitely a red flag. We've got to unravel this mystery before it bcomes a ticking time bomb. Oh, and by the way, you really need to stop fainting!"

I gasped. "I didn't faint, he knocked me out!"

"Or maybe you're just too hypnotized by his enchanting charm. Wouldn't be the first time! Watch out for those swoon-inducing looks, they're dangerous!"

"You're not actually taking a jab at me, are you?" I raised an eyebrow, trying to hide the amusement in my voice.

Bory shrugged, his puffy arms flailing in the air. "Well, you do need a reality check. That guy is running rampant because you've got the hots for him."

I shot him a pointed look. "Better watch that mouth of yours, or I might change my mind about having you for a snack. Burlacks are considered tasty, remember that."

"We can't trust him for sure, though, Lynne. He's always been... mysterious."

"True, but Rio can't cast spells as strong as that—he's human," I said, my voice wavering slightly. At least that's what I wanted him to be.

Bory's eyebrows furrowed, forming dark little bars on his forehead. "Really? You really think he's human?"

"No." I rolled my eyes. "But a reaper can't do magic besides hunting down souls. So, this means, he's neither human, nor a reaper. This is just insane. He can't be several creatures in one. Maybe it was Any? Rio said something about him having powers too..."

Bory looked uncomfortable. "You didn't smell like Any, that's the problem... your scent smelled like drowned in Rio. It's what makes me think he put the spell on you, but this shouldn't be surprising. He's not exactly forthcoming with information. And he's got a lot of secrets. Always."

I chewed on my lip, trying to make sense of everything. "Oh skull... Bory... do you think I did this to him? Back then when I touched him and killed him? Do you think he changed into...

into a mystical creature with powers and that's why the Bone Queen got interested in him?"

My heart slammed against my ribcage like it was desperate to escape. Everything inside of me was wound tight like a spring, ready to unleash at any moment. What if I made him into this...

Bory tilted his head, his expression determined. "It could be, yes. Something big is happening for sure and we need to investigate. We have to talk to Rio and find out what's going on. There's still the possibility that the Bone Queen changed him into a monster..."

"Why? Just so he could get me?" I threw myself back in frustration and glared at the wooden ceiling above me. Of course, Rio wasn't human, that much was clear, but something about him just didn't add up. People feared him and avoided him like the plague, yet he could effortlessly stroll into the Blood Queen's castle, and many claimed to know him. Maybe no one turned him into something... what if he's always been more than human...

Bory sighed. "He's always one step ahead of us, and I don't understand why... He just dropped from Earth, so how can he already be pulling the strings on things down here?"

I grinned, feeling my own surge of anger. "He's damn good at it.

But that doesn't mean we can't beat him at his own game."

"Oh, you're scheming!" Bory smirked mischievously. "Hold on a second. I'm not sure if your plotting is an improvement over Rio's plotting or just a different kind of trouble."

"It will be all fine, Bory. Hear me out. Since he's so convinced that the Bone Queen only wants the best for him, we will make sure he's wrong. You know what's next to Cave Town? The oracle of the Dead. And it never lies. So, I say it's time to hit him with the truth."

Bory gasped. "The Necromantion? Are you out of your mind? You can't rely on an oracle, Lynne. It could tell you something you don't even want to know! What if it doesn't go our way? We could be worse off than before! By the Dead."

Well, Bory might've been partially right, but there was no way I was going to cower and surrender. The oracle may hold the key to our predicament, but I had a plan, a glimmer of hope that we had to cling onto. Rio, that slippery snake, was keeping his lips sealed shut, leaving us with no choice but to seek out the oracle. It's simple as that.

"We have to find out Rio's true intentions and warn him about the Bone Queen's plan," I urged, my voice firm with conviction. "We can't afford to wait for Rio to make a move. We have to take the initiative and outsmart him. Think about it, Bory," I clasped his shoulders, hoping to convey my urgency, "what if the oracle advises Rio to align with the Blood Queen? We'd be safe. If the Bone Queen captures me, she'll stop at nothing to resurrect the Olympians. That's the end of the worlds."

My gaze settled on Bory's wavering expression.

"We have to seize this chance, Bory. It's a risk we simply have to take. If not, we'll be forced to steal the missing bones to revive Zeus. And that maniac can't set foot on Earth ever again."

Bory's eyes widened in alarm as my words echoed in the silence. I could see the weight of our situation settling on him. It was up to us to save the world, and we couldn't let anything stand in our way, not even Rio or a cryptic oracle.

Bory sighed heavily. "I know, but I really dread dealing with oracles..."

"Same with witches but we simply have no time. What if Rio has more hidden qualities? What if the Blood Queen's army is no threat to him? We'd do better if he'd come with us willingly and maybe the oracle can show him—show us—the truth. Win win."

Bory nodded reluctantly. "Well, okay, okay, let's convince him to go to the oracle then. Cave Town is close by too, so at least our little detour doesn't look suspicious then."

As I stood up, I noticed strange clothes on my body. I was wearing trousers and a buttoned-up blouse that covered every inch of my skin. A nun was nothing compared to me. "Um, Bory... why am I wearing this? I had my Bone Weaver dress on," I glanced around, and it had disappeared without a trace, "and hadn't put on something else. What the skull?"

Bory nervously scratched his head as his hands trembled. "Um yeah... Rio changed your clothes."

"I'm going to kill him."

Bory shook his head. "Be careful, I'm not sure which one of you has more power honestly, but well of course I'm talking to myself right now because she doesn't listen anymore..."

I rummaged through my bag of bones and pulled out the key I had weaved yesterday. If he was trying to keep me locked away, he should have taken more time to figure out how I kept escaping.

"Was it... weird? Did he seem to... like it?" My cheeks burned as I realized what I had asked.

Bory narrowed his eyes. "Unclothing you?" I nodded.

"No, he was more worried than anything else. He didn't really look."

I let out a low growl. "Which means he looked, so now I really have to kill him."

I searched the room for my dress and found it under the bed. The idiot. As if I wouldn't look there. I quickly changed and when I gripped my door's handle Bory asked, "What are you doing? Don't leave, you won't earn his trust if you escape again."

"I just want to sneak up on him, find out what he's up to and maybe find a way to strangle him without—"

As I swung open the door, Ebony quickly rose from her chair, and I shut my mouth closed. Her hair cascaded down her shoulders in tousled waves, and since I saw her in a brightly lit room for the first time my gaze unwillingly dropped to her attire.

Hell, she was beautiful. And her dress... oh, her dress. It was a deep, regal shade of blue that hugged every one of her curves, almost like it had been tailored just for her. A gilded sash cinched her waist tightly, drawing attention to the sliver of dark skin that was revealed above it. The heavy fabric of the dress was adorned with intricate crimson swirls that seemed to dance across it, highlighting every gorgeous detail of her figure. And here I was, wearing the ugliest turtleneck.

"Ebony," I said, my voice trembling. "What are you doing in front of my door?"

"Babysitting, since it looks like you can't stay in bed," she said with a smirk, eyeing me up and down.

Bory stopped in his tracks at my feet and looked up at me. "Lynne, what—oh no."

"Oh no, very well," Ebony said and sent a shiver up my spine.

I arched an eyebrow, sizing up Ebony. "Listen up, girl. You might want to watch your back."

"Or what?" she taunted, her dark curls bouncing as she tossed her head. "Are you going to run to Volt like a scared little mouse?"

My fists clenched at my sides, but I refused to back down. "I don't need a man to fight my battles for me."

She smirked at me, a wicked twist to her lips. "Sure didn't seem like that some hours ago," she drawled, making a show of looking around for Rio. "Bad news, he's not here to come to your rescue."

I ground my teeth together, trying to come up with a scathing retort. But then Any's voice echoed up from below. "Food's ready, ladies. Ebony, let her out."

I shot Ebony a venomous glare as she grinned and gestured for me to follow her.

"Let me out. Like a dog," I muttered under my breath, my cheeks burning with embarrassment.

She laughed out loud, the sound like tinkling glass. "You're a feisty one, aren't you? I wonder what Volt will do when I tell him you tried to sneak out again…"

My face grew redder than ever as I realized how close she was to rattling me out. "Oops… you wouldn't like that, huh? Wanted to sneak away in private…" she said with a knowing smile.

"Ebony? You okay?" said Any, and I stiffened. "Don't…" I tried. "Please. Don't tell him."

Her expression darkened and she grabbed my shoulder where Bory sat, shaking him along. "I want a wish."

I nearly choked on that. "A wish. Of course…"

"Give me a wish, a small one and I won't say anything."

Any sighed. "Okay. I'll come up. What the fuck happened this time…"

"Fine," I said. "A very small one!"

Ebony rushed to the banister, leaned over it and yelled, "By all the Hellhounds, stop pushing drama. It's all fine, we're just having a little… girl's talk."

"Nice as ever," Any grumbled but stopped and stomped back to where he came from. We waited a few seconds and when the door closed again, I sighed. "Thanks."

Ebony started plucking her fingernails. "What were you thinking breaking out, anyway? You knew there'd be trouble."

"Yeah, but I was going to take a look around and maybe find... *Volt* alone..."

"For what?" she asked, leaning casually in the doorway again. "Stuff."

"Mmm. I get it, I wouldn't want to reveal anything either. So, look, I'll think of how to phrase it correctly and come see you once I'm sure. I can't waste this."

There was a brief moment between us, and I thought I'd seen something very sincere in her glance. She really had a wish. For a long time and the fact that she didn't even slightly grin this time told me it wasn't fun at all.

I nodded, wondering what a woman like her could wish for. "Deal."

"Deal. Now be a good girl and give me that key." She gave a subtle nod, her eyes fixated on the key clutched tightly in my hand. Reluctantly, I extended my palm, surrendering it to her. "Perfect. Let's eat, I'm hungry as a Chimera."

CHAPTER SEVENTEEN
RIO

As we sat at the corner table in the bar, waiting for Axter to arrive, my heart was thumping with anticipation. Soon, Aria's soul would be the only thing standing between me and my freedom, and they'd all regret underestimating me. I'm making them pay.

The other patrons gave us a wide berth, probably still feeling the after-effects of my unleashed magic from the night before.

"You could have given us some intel." Ash grumbled through a mouthful of porridge. "We were out there searching for Axter all night while you were here, sipping whiskey and waiting for your girl to tramp him."

I forced a smile. "Patience, Ash," I said, my tone calm and measured. "This will be good practice for all of us." I hoped my words would encourage him to focus on the task at hand. He was always too impulsive, too eager for a fight. A trait that had gotten us into trouble more times than I could count.

Ash slammed the tip of his knife into the table. Of course, he wouldn't focus on what's important. "We've been fighting tooth and nail, while you've been off *gallivanting*," he spat, his words biting with resentment.

"Be careful with your words, Ash," Isix cautioned, her voice steelier than a blade.

Briz looked between us all, clearly uneasy with the tension in the air. I gave him an understanding smile, hoping to alleviate his discomfort. "We're just a little stressed, Briz. Don't worry about it."

With a roll of his eyes, Ash took the knife out of the table and got back to his porridge. "You've been gone for decades, so obviously working together again won't be easy."

Isix glanced at me with concern, but I simply waved it off and spoke over Ash, "It's normal that there will be a few people unhappy with how things have gone."

"Unhappy is an understatement, asshole," Ash mumbled.

Just then, Any came over and plopped down in his seat. "Are we being bitchy again?" he asked.

"Careful," Isix grinned. "He's on his period."

I sighed. "Aren't you guys ever going to act like adults? At least once?" I said.

Ash lifted his gaze and a strange darkness passed through his eyes. "If you could once act like—"

"Ash," I said firmly, sufficient to stop him from finishing his fucking sentence.

Isix cleared her throat. As usual, she was hardly eating anything. Her expression told me she had some bone to pick with me as well, but it seemed like all my people did. Isix never talked much but her look was enough to let me know I had a lot of work ahead of me. The Horsemen were my best friends once...

Just then, Aria and Ebony entered the room, laughing and seemingly in good spirits with each other. I cocked my eyebrows. That was strange, yet somehow fitting. Both of them were stubborn by nature, and if you crossed them, they would be angry for eternity.

The two sat down across from me and Aria smiled slyly. "Did you have a good night's sleep, or were you too busy playing dressup with my wardrobe?"

I returned her grin, knowing that was the one thing that got under her skin. "Slept like a baby in your arms, darling."

She clenched her fist around the spoon, her knuckles whitening with tension.

"Did she snore? I think I heard snoring from your room," Ebony teased.

"Massively," I replied, flashing a wide grin.

Just as Aria was about to launch that spoon my way, Maurus appeared out of thin air and plopped porridge into our bowls, making her crinkle her nose in disgust.

"Are we used to better food by now?" I asked mockingly.

Aria scoffed. "No, just manners."

She started to eat then while Ebony smacked away hungrily, her black hair nearly getting mixed up with the food as she wolfed it down.

After a while, Ebony glanced at Ash, a mischievous glint in her eyes. "Cat got your tongue? I'm not used to such silence when you're around. Why don't you confront her about your aimless wandering in Catterville's alleys yesterday? You talked my ear off about it."

Ash raised an eyebrow, pointing the tip of his knife in my direction. "Well, that one," he nodded towards me, "would wring my neck. Can't go mocking his sweetheart, right?"

The Horsemen erupted in laughter, their hearty guffaws filling the space. Aria, usually composed, seemed visibly uncomfortable, squirming in her seat and scratching the back of her neck.

"Guys," I tried to diffuse the situation, but Ash just smacked his lips and leaned back in his chair. Yeah he was still really pissed at me... "Look," I said calmly, although I wanted to remind him that he wasn't the one calling the shots here, but I knew Aria was getting uncomfortable, and before she could get herself into trouble with all of them, I quickly changed the subject. "Axter should be arriving soon, and then we can make our way to the Bone Queen without another stop, okay? It will all be over soon."

Aria's body was tense as I spoke. I could tell she wanted to fight me on this again, but there never seemed to be a moment when we could talk without interruption, and when we were alone, I didn't know if I could resist the temptation of something else entirely.

I avoided her glance and then the door suddenly opened, crashing against the wall with a loud bang that made everyone including me jump. I glanced up from my porridge and saw Axter standing there—his face blank and expressionless. Behind him, I noticed a woman, tears streaming down her face as she cried out, "Stay with me, don't go!"

Aria caught her breath, her lower lip trembling as she watched the woman frantically clawing at Axter's back, begging him.

I got up and headed over to Axter, reaching out my hand to him.

Ash and Isix quickly jumped in, trying to hold back the woman as she fought them off with loud, fierce screams that echoed all around. After a struggle, they finally managed to drag her out of the inn. Once the woman's cries had faded away, Axter stood before me and I placed my hand on his forehead, speaking softly, "You have sinned."

All eyes in the inn were fixed on us now, with bated breath. Axter's hands trembled as he held onto my arms, but he stood his ground. His face ashen and his expression wide with fear, but he remained determined to face whatever lay ahead. He knew he had to fight, no matter how frightened he was, and I couldn't help but admire his courage.

"Tell me your name and you will be redeemed," I said.

He hesitated, his face contorted with fear at the thought of revealing his true identity.

I clenched my fists in anticipation as he finally uttered a name, "Ephraim."

I felt a wave of relief sweep through me since only the real name of a soul could be used to bring it back to the Bone Queen. I closed my eyes, my hand vibrating on his forehead as I felt his soul travel back to the Bone Queen. Not every soul knew their real name—the first ever given name of a soul before it was reincarnated several times. But when the soul was ready to be reincarnated, it spoke of itself. This was the most difficult part of the harvesting.

Not every soul was ready to accept the sins and so they would never tell me their real name and I had to torture it out of them. That was my least favorite part. In that sense, Aria had made this job way easier for me and I wondered if she knew about that... if her using her magic was a way to ease the pain for me. But I guess not. She was up to something, and I feared it had nothing to do with making me feel better.

Axter heaved a sigh of relief and the power dissipated from my hand as his soul was sucked away in an instant. Aria caught my eye and scowled. I knew what kind of thoughts swept through her mind right now. I could have done the same to her the minute we met, and she was right. She was a wanted soul too. But her case was different from his. The Bone Queen wanted her alive and she didn't want her very essence, the innermost part of herself—she wanted her as a whole. And our deal meant that until Aria entered her castle I wasn't free. There was a flash of understanding between us and I knew that it only meant one thing: she knew the deal was still on and she hated me for it.

As Axter vanished, Aria hurled the napkin into her still-full porridge bowl.

"You're a skulling prick," she said and stormed off, leaving me stunned.

I closed my mouth and watched her leave.

A threatening tension lingered in the air as Ash and Isix returned to the inn, glancing around the room in search of answers. The patrons, however, remained fixated on their meals, studiously avoiding any interaction with any of us. The silence was deafening, and it was almost as if the air itself was waiting for someone to break it.

"Women, huh?" Ash said, smirking.

I sighed and wanted to steer after Aria, but Any beat me to it. "Let me talk to my sister first."

CHAPTER EIGHTEEN
LYNNE

"He's terrible." I clenched my teeth as I grabbed Bory from my dress pocket and placed him onto my shoulder. He had managed to swipe a spoonful of porridge and was happily slurping it like a lollipop from Topworld. As I continued my rant, he nodded along, savoring the stolen treat all the way up to our room. "Did you see how powerful he is? He can kill innocent people with just one flick of his skulling wrist!"

"I mean, Axter was far from innocent and Rio's always been a criminal, so, why stop now," Bory cut in, taking another slurp, seemingly unfazed by the chaos around us.

"I don't care about his human years," I snarled. "It's the power he holds in the Underworld that freaks me out. Sure, some humans might think they have a bit of influence, but down here? It's a whole different story. You can't just stroll in and start bossing everyone around like you own the place. That's not how things work in the Underworld."

"You know, I hate to say this, but you are the one who keeps on running into his arms like a magnet drawn to rusty nails... or no, wait, that simile doesn't fit quite well. You are more like a moth that keeps on being attracted to the wrong flam—"

I flicked him down on the floor and he groaned in despair as his spoon, still clinging to its last remnants of porridge, went flying across the corridor. "Sometimes, Bory, you need to learn to shut up." He gave me a glare that could have melted ice, but I couldn't waste any more time on arguments. All I wanted was for him to gossip with me. I wanted to loosen-up a little, Stix damn it, instead of listening to another lecture. But just when I was about to grasp the doorknob, a hand clasped onto my arm, pulling me back gently.

"Aria, hold on," said the voice behind me.

"Oh no, not you," I sighed, spinning around to face my treacherous *brother*. "Can you at least call me Lynne?"

He hesitated before nodding, and a faint smile tugged at the corners of his lips. As I took in his adorable face, a pang of guilt washed over me, remembering all he had done for me recently. But every time I looked at him, all I could think of was his desire to kill Rio. In retrospect, it was something he did for me, as he had been investigating the murder from my past life, only to find out it was his longtime crush. Maybe I should cut him some slack.

"Gonna be hard for me, but I'll try," Any added.

My breathing hitched as I remembered how he used to look at me with so much love in his eyes. I had broken his heart when I chose to join the Blood Queen. I knew that all he wanted was to keep me safe, and it must have hurt him so badly that I decided to side against him, but it wasn't too late for him to side with me. It wasn't too late for Rio either.

"Aren't you a little glad we got you out?" Any said. "I was so afraid of you... alone with the Blood Queen. I couldn't wait for us to finally save you..."

I tried to look at him as intensely as I could, touching his arm, "Any, I don't know what that crazy woman has been telling you, but you guys didn't save me. In fact, if you really want to save me, you'll have to bring me back to the Blood Court. Now."

He shook his head. "The Bone Queen won't hurt you," he said determinedly.

I sighed and my grip on his arm softened. "She manipulated you guys. Coincidentally, her best ability. Why don't you let me explain what I saw? I have proof that she'll bring doom to all our worlds."

"Aria, I—"

Just then, we heard the sound of shattering glass.

"That came from your room, Lynne," Bory said, and my heart sunk in my chest.

I was ready to dash forward but Any shoved me aside and charged into my room instead. Squeezing in right behind, I came to an abrupt halt. When I saw who had broken in, a gasp slipped out and its echo bounced off the walls. It was Illiam, standing amidst the shattered glass of a broken windowpane.

His armor was thin, and a long, curved sword hung from his hip. His face was stern and resolved, with his unwavering gaze fixed upon Any. The room was thick with tension as they all geared up for a showdown. It was clear that I had to step in before things got out of hand. But before I could even make a move, Any stepped forward, fists clenched at his sides. In a single fluid motion, Illiam drew his sword and pointed it at him, ready to strike at any moment.

I swallowed, as much as I cherished my brother for stepping up, I didn't think he'd have a chance against my guard.

So, I tried to diffuse the situation. "Illiam?" I said calmly. "What are you doing here?"

"What does it look like? I'm here for you."

I sighed and was about to explain to him that I couldn't go

anywhere without Rio, since our bond was so strong that not being next to him would literally burst me midair, when he rushed at us. He swung the sword at Any and when he ducked, Illiam pulled me behind him. "I'll take her home, and if you want to keep your life, you'll stay put, do you hear me?"

A wave of worry washed over me when I spotted the danger targeting my brother. But then, I caught a mischievous sparkle in his eye. Alas, these men...

"That's a good plan," Any proclaimed, a smirk dancing on his lips. "But let me help you a little, maybe don't tell your enemy about your plan. Keep it a secret—it'll surprise your opponents more that way."

He raised his hand, and this creepy dark power seemed to ooze from it. Without a second thought, I hurled myself in front of Illiam, determined to protect them both. The tension in the room was suffocating, and I knew I had to act quickly to keep things from spiraling out of control. I wasn't going to let them harm each other.

My breathing hitched. "Any, whatever you're planning to do —don't."

Any lowered his hand a little and he looked straight into my eyes as he said, "Lynne, Volt is on his way and he won't hesitate to use his power if he sees him in *your bedroom*. He needs to leave. Now."

"It doesn't matter what skulling *Volt* thinks," I countered. "He has no authority over me—I am not his property even if he's an all mighty whatsoever."

"You have no idea who he is. I'd be careful if I were you."

"But—"

Rio's fierce bark echoed through the room, making me jump in surprise. I spun around to face him, my stomach dropping at the sight of him standing in the doorway, his eyes narrowed and his body tense as he watched Illiam. I knew he was angry, knew where his thoughts were going at and I wanted to object, wanted to explain that there was nothing going on between me and Illiam. But before I could speak, Illiam stepped forward, his own eyes blazing with a fierce determination as he brandished his sword in a clear show of dominance. Oh, for skull's sake...

"Get the fuck out of here or I'll rip your head off in front of everyone," Rio said, the unsettling calmness in his voice crawling beneath my skin.

Everyone looked at Illiam, but he held his ground and Rio stepped forward, clearly out for vengeance.

Any's hand instinctively reached out to grasp Rio's arm. "Volt," he uttered. "Calm down."

"I'll take her with me whether you want it or not," Illiam said, and it was too late.

Rio dashed forward, grabbed him and pushed him against the wall. I covered my mouth, not sure what to do. Had everyone gone crazy?

"The fuck you are," Rio said, pressing his elbow into Illiam's throat. "I should have killed you the last time."

I held onto Rio's shoulder tightly, my grip firm. "Please, don't hurt him," I pleaded.

But it was too late.

Not a flicker of acknowledgment crossed his gaze.

That's when I saw Ebony and Ash looming by the doorway, their twisted grins revealing their sick enjoyment of the whole scene. These people were pure evil, and the realization made my stomach turn.

"Volt," I said again, trying to tear him away from Illiam. "Please, let him go. He's a friend of mine."

"Oh yeah," he sneered, a deep, malicious chuckle escaping his lips. "That's exactly why I can't stand his face."

That skulling bastard! I clenched my fists, staring at the

back of his head as he held Illiam up against the wall. Oh, I wished I had anything to smack against his stupid head.

"Seriously, what's your problem?" I yelled, my voice rising in volume, hoping to steer his anger at me. My last resort. "You really think you can have your way with me, right? Ignore me for years and then suddenly appear and expect to have control over me and whom I'm friends with? I'm not your skulling lap dog and last time I checked there was no leash around my throat!" I spat out the words, almost fuming at Rio's audacity.

Bory nervously patted my shin and whispered, "Lynne, stop it, can't you sense the power that emanates from him? This is no good."

I shook my head fiercely.

I wouldn't back the hell off.

"A leash you say?" Rio's voice sounded calm, and he went utterly still. "I could use a leash indeed. To tie down this bastard here, although tying you down would be more fun."

"Try it," Illiam spat, his face all red now. "And I'll kill you."

Rio chuckled and didn't even get into what he was saying. "Tell me what your queen really wants from her. What is she supposed to do for her once she opens the sigils?"

"I'm not—" Illiam choked, his voice muffled by the tight grip on his throat, "—telling you anything."

"She has to open the gates for her, doesn't she?"

Illiam fell silent and even I knew that Rio had hit a nerve. He had the worst poker face. I made a mental note to never play cards with Illiam.

But he was right, the queen and I wanted to open the Book of Silva.

However, those seven seals standing in our way weren't exactly a walk in the park. If I remained trapped here any longer, there was no way we could crack them open. But the queen didn't want to open the gates, since they were already open, allowing Deathwalkers and Shadowslaves to roam freely in our realm—all courtesy of the Bone Queen. No, the Blood Queen wanted to close the gates.

"Volt. Let us do this," Ash interrupted, his hand firm on Rio's shoulder too. "We can get it out of him. Any can easily question him without trouble."

"Yeah, let's do it," Any said.

He gave me a small nod, silently assuring me that he wouldn't harm Illiam. And when I noticed Rio easing his grip on Illiam, I couldn't help but release a deep sigh of relief. Any gave me a glimmer of hope and I wanted to hug him tight for it.

But as Rio shifted his gaze between us, he suddenly pushed Illiam farther into the wall and snarled, "I can make you talk too."

Illiam let out another strained, gurgling sound, and I was afraid he would be seriously hurt.

"Wait," I pleaded, my voice quivering as I desperately tried to defuse the escalating situation. "Let's talk. I'll reveal what the queen desires, but please, release him."

Rio loosened his grip for good and Illiam crumpled to the ground with a sickening thud. "Fine," he said, and I could have thanked the gods that he was finally listening to reason.

I didn't know what to tell him, though. I couldn't reveal too much information to the enemy, and I knew he would tell his beloved queen everything I told him. But I had to come up with something.

He rolled his shoulders and then turned to Any. "Take that bastard with you and don't be nice to him."

Ebony and Ash cackled with excitement as they grabbed hold of Illiam. They forcefully dragged him out into the dimly lit hallway. In the distance, Ebony's voice reached my ears, echoing through the corridors, "What a sweet boy. I wonder what you taste like but oh, there's someone who knows. Um,

Aria?" Ebony suddenly stopped, her head poking back into view, as she flashed me a grin that stretched from ear to ear. "Wanna tell me?"

"Stop it," Ash growled. "Volt is crazy possessive over her. Don't remind him that they fucked."

Ebony scoffed. "Well, perhaps you could try not screaming it, then?"

I watched Illiam seizing the opportunity of Ebony and Ash's argument to make a break for it, but his hopes were crushed in an instant and I caught my breath. Briz and Isix swooped in from opposite directions, joining the fight and leaving him with no chance to escape. I couldn't bear to see him suffer and with a heavy heart, I shouted, "It's okay, Illiam. Most of the time they're all bark and no bite—"

But before I could finish my sentence, Rio cut me off. "Bory, you're out as well. Now." His voice dripped with anger.

I hesitated for a moment, considering whether I should defy his command, but then an idea hit me. It actually worked out pretty darn well that Bory had to go. Almost too well to be true.

So, I gently scooped up Bory in my arms and carried him towards the door. Crouching down, I let him hop down from my hand. I leaned into him, whispering softly into his ear, "It's fine. Go find the demons. Here," I stuffed a vial of blood under his wings, praying to Stix that Rio didn't see it, "hand it over. They need to block the whole road. Got it?"

Bory looked terrified but nodded bravely before hopping down the stairs.

Closing the door with a resolute click, I turned around to meet Rio's gaze, my eyes blazing with an intensity that could ignite the very air between us.

CHAPTER NINETEEN
LYNNE

"You wanted to have a little chat, huh, darling?" He sauntered over to the window frame, leaning against it casually. A cold shiver tingled through me as his gaze seemed to strip me bare, leaving me feeling vulnerable and exposed.

"You've got some nerve, acting like that," I retorted, my voice laced with a mix of anger and determination. "Try pulling that stunt again, and I swear I'll punch you in the face. Hard."

Rio let out a deep chuckle and approached me. "Well, not to be blunt but if you did that, the only thing becoming hard would be my dick."

I swallowed, unsure of how to respond as a blush spread across my cheeks, turning them as red as a beet. Instead of uttering another word, I lifted my gaze to meet his eyes—wild, untamed, like a predator on the prowl. In that moment, I was suddenly well aware of how much he towered over me and how small I actually was. I knew he could end me with a snap of his fingers. And, against all reason, a part of me found that power undeniably sexy.

"You know, I think *you've got a lot of nerve* bringing your fucking lover here."

"First of all," I said, taking a step back as he approached me, "he's not my lover, second of all, he came on his own because you kidnapped me."

He halted right in front of me, his shoes toe-to-toe with mine.

Taut lines formed across his jaw, and he lifted a large hand only to grip my chin, forcing me to look right into his gleaming sapphire eyes. "But he had you, didn't he? His touch was on you, claiming you for his own. But darling, you're mine. Every inch of you, every breath you take," his voice dropped to a low, dangerous whisper, "belongs to me and only me."

His words took my breath away.

There was no mistaking the accusation in his voice and a nervous flutter filled my stomach. I did sleep with Illiam but only to get over Rio. Something I had never achieved in my life. He leaned into my space, the heat of his body seared against my own, and in a desperate attempt to keep him away I thrust my hand flat against his hard chest.

His eyes narrowed as he glared down at my fingers fisting in his shirt, digging into the fabric and matching his intensity with my own. The air crackled with anticipation, as if a storm was brewing, ready to unleash its fury.

"Do you love him?" he said.

Before I could even muster a snarky response, he closed in on me, trapping me against the wall. His hands landed on either side of my head now, caging me in, his fingers digging into the surface with a force that made me gasp.

"Do. You. Love. Him?"

"Why does it matter?" I shot back. "I'm repeating myself over and over again and I'm sick of it. You went and married someone else, started a whole other life. I think that speaks volumes about your feelings for me, don't you?"

A heavy sigh escaped his lips, his warm breath mixing with mine as he visibly struggled to quell his temper. I caught my breath when he brought his forehead to rest against mine.

"Aria, I was there," his voice dropped to a whisper, "I was there, despite everything. For the hundredth time, I was there."

"You've been lying nonstop, I'm sorry but I can't believe a single word you say."

"Every fucking year I've been there, waiting for you until dawn, asking myself what happened to you and whom I need to punish for it."

I noticed his face tense up as my emotions boiled over. I glanced away but he took my hand from his chest, intertwined my fingers with his and brought it up to his mouth to kiss it.

I stopped breathing for a split second.

This couldn't be true. Could it? He couldn't have been there.

I was there. He wasn't.

That had been my mantra, my guiding belief for years. It was the thread that held together the fragments of my broken heart. But what if it wasn't true all along? What if he wasn't to blame for my pain? What if, against all odds, he had waited for me, just as I had for him?

I shook my head, desperate to push those thoughts away. Allowing those feelings to surface would be my undoing. I would shatter into a thousand irreparable pieces.

Rio grabbed my jaw again and forced my gaze back to his. "Why is it so easy for you to mistrust me? What if both of us were at the cemetery? What if the Blood Queen wanted you to hate me?"

The fury boiled inside me, bubbling like a cauldron set to high heat. Against my better judgment, I hurled back at him with a vehement cry, "But I do trust her, Rio. I've grown and learned so much over these years. I'm not just some naive girl blindly following her lead! She has shown me undeniable proof!"

"Never trust the bloody sisters," he hissed back, eyes ablaze with anger. "And why in the hell would you put your faith in a witch over me? How could you assume I rejected you when I've been fighting just for you? Was everything we shared on Earth just a bloody joke to you?"

His hands cupped my face now, demanding my full attention. But before another word could escape his lips, I found my voice, and I cut in, "It was easy because you never let me in. You made the choice to shut me out whenever you could on Earth, when you took down the gang leaders. When you lied to me. And it hurt, Rio." I fought back the lump in my throat, fully aware that tears must be welling up in my eyes by now. "Do you honestly believe that working behind my back for months on end made it easy for me to trust you? Of course, I thought you had forgotten about me."

A tear streamed down my face and when he caught sight of it his whole demeanor softened.

"I never intended to hurt you," he whispered, brushing away the tears with his thumb.

"Then let me in..."

He took a deep breath and said, "Jamie is my daughter, Slappy fathered her. I adopted her."

My heart sank as soon as I realized it was Cherry's and Slappy's daughter. So, he didn't start a family with another woman. "W-why are you telling me this now? Why not the first time I asked?"

"I needed to know what was going through your mind, and let's not forget that Jamie is my daughter nevertheless. Whether through adoption or biology, she's *my daughter*, and that's a fact. Does this change anything for you now?"

I shook my head. "And what about your wife?"

"That's something you need to find out yourself but this ring," he nodded at his hand. "Is a ring I share with Jamie. I haven't married anyone on Earth, Aria. All I need is you trusting me in this."

I narrowed my eyes, a mixture of confusion and suspicion clouding my expression. I wasn't sure if I understood his words right... each one added another layer of uncertainty to the already tangled web of our past.

"How can I trust you? You've betrayed me before, in different lives. Now you appear in the Underworld like it's just another day. How can I ever be sure of what is real? And that ring... you led me to believe you were married."

"You assumed it," he countered, his tone defensive.

"And you fueled those assumptions with your snarky remarks!"

"Fine, I'm sorry. I may have enjoyed seeing you jealous at times, this way I knew that you still cared for me. I was being selfish. I'm sorry."

"At least one sign of reason... but still, trust needs to be earned."

"I'm trying."

"Try harder."

A hushed stillness settled between us. Our eyes locked in a meaningful exchange that spoke volumes.

"I know I messed up, Aria," he said softly but despite these words I could still detect a hint of something sinister lurking beneath, and my distrust only deepened. "What can I do?"

He pressed a kiss on my forehead. I took a deep breath.

Oh, skull it, Bory was right. I was a moth and he was my flame. Or my rusty nail. "Fine..." I grumbled, cursing my bad taste in men. "Just continue telling me some more truths. Why do you know this world better than I do? How did you enter the Underworld and gain powers like this?"

He hesitated first, as if contemplating whether to answer or not. But then in a hushed tone he replied, "Because this is where I'd always belonged, long before you even existed."

My heart sank as the magnitude of his words set in. So, he had been in the Underworld all these years without me knowing? My mind raced with questions.

"B-But you were on Earth, I watched you at the cemetery each year..."

"I was forced to reincarnate... actually both of us. We met long ago..."

"Forced? By who?"

"There was a curse—argh." He winced and touched his heart, hurt flickering along his features.

I gasped, checking his chest. "Are your panic attacks back?"

"No," he spat out bitterly, his laughter ceasing like a shot. "They never were panic attacks in the first place."

My jaw dropped as dread pooled in my stomach. What was happening?

He cursed and tightened his fists until the veins in his arms bulged beneath his skin. I felt a chill run through me. "Skull, are you alright?"

His face twisted as he let out a groan. "Well, no, I'm obviously not but... but besides that, this happens when I tell you the truth. I'm not supposed to help you in this, there's a dark spell over us that prevents me from opening up about certain parts. Even if I wanted to, I can't. It would knock me out before I could form the words and if I tell you too much, I'll die, which means—"

"—I'll die too." My heart thundered as frustration and suspicion surged through me.

"Do you understand that it's important for you to trust me? To believe me when I tell you that all of this is for you? For us?"

"It's tough to put my trust in you without knowing exactly what's going on here."

"I know. But look, every one of us has to play their parts. There's only one thing you need to remember. Don't you ever think I'd not put you first."

A chill ran through me as I recalled the task I had assigned to Bory and the consequences of my actions. I knew this was a betrayal of trust as well and yet—I couldn't shut out that he was willing to drag me back to face the Bone Court.

"And how is turning me over to the Bone Queen putting me first?"

He released a pained sigh. "I can only say this once—never ask me again." His deep voice was unshakable. "She is listening and I must keep my promise, I have to bring you back. Please, listen to my exact words now. I made sure the Bone Queen is no threat to you."

I narrowed my eyes in confusion.

It felt like he wanted me to understand he would do whatever it took to keep me safe, but he was gravely mistaken. Being near the Bone Queen would certainly be the end of me. And he seemed oblivious to the danger her presence posed. By the Dead, I had no idea why he thought he could protect me from a creature this powerful, even compared to her own sister, she was the most evil I knew and I was never meant to get anywhere near her again. And all the gods be my witnesses: I would do anything to prevent it. Even if just the thought of crossing him hurt me, made me wrench in pain. I just had no choice, he refused to listen. My hands were clenched into whiteknuckled fists as I accepted it.

"Isn't it high time *you* spilled some secrets, darling? What does the Blood Queen want from you?" His chest heaved with pain, the agony still evident in his eyes.

I took a deep breath. "She helped me awaken my magic. Since I was the one who brought the Book of Silva back from damnation, I have to open the seven sigils. But you're wrong about the Blood Queen's intentions. Her sister already opened the gates, which is why your daughter was attacked by Shadowslaves, they most certainly belonged to the Bone Queen."

Rio's fingers played with a stray strand of my hair. "And the Blood Queen offered to close the gates? Why would she do that?"

"She said she's helping Athena and we're to stop her sister. End her rule."

Rio chuckled. "She's working with Athena? I highly doubt that."

"Why's that?"

"Because the Blood Queen wants to free her lover, who's bound to Earth and can't visit her as often as she likes. And it was Athena binding him to Earth, so I'm certain she'd never work with her. But her lover is the number one reason why she wants to open the gates.

Yes, there are cracks in the gates, but they're not open right now. If they were, all humans would be in danger. That's why we have to stop the Blood Queen. You can never open that book for her, Aria."

"But..." I trailed off, unsure of what to say. It all sounded plausible, but how could we know which queen was telling the truth? Right now, it was testimony against testimony.

Another thought struck me, and I asked in a trembling voice, "The Blood Queen told me her sister made me steal Zeus' bones to wake him from the dead. I can't be dragged back to the Bone Court because of that, Rio. She'll force me to bring back the Olympians, and you know Zeus' wrath will destroy us all."

Rio pulled me close, his embrace offering solace. "She won't force you to do anything. Trust me in this. Please. I'd love to tell you why, but I can't, you saw what happens if I try."

My heart swelled at his words, and as he trailed kisses down my neck, I gave in to him. I couldn't resist him. Oh, I wanted to hate him. But I skulling couldn't. Our relationship was so complicated.

Still, something inside me said I needed to trust him. Both queens had good reasons for what they did, and the oracle seemed like our best shot. But Rio was all about getting to the Bone Court as fast as we could. I couldn't let slip about the oracle just yet. I had to wait until the demons blocked our way and we had no choice but to go through the Elysian Fields. That's when he'd finally agree to listen to the oracle. So, I waited, playing the waiting game.

"I'll ask one last time. Have you loved Illiam?" he gently said as he tucked away a white strand of hair that fell into my forehead.

"No, I needed someone to comfort me because I almost died from heartache because of you." I tried to forget the images that I saw in front of my mind now. Him leaving me. Me crying in the middle of the night because I've missed his touches. Missed him.

His fingers moved tenderly through my hair as he pulled me closer, his lips just inches from mine now. "I can't go a single second without craving you."

I let out a shuddering gasp as his lips finally connected with mine. The warmth of his kiss spread through my body like wildfire, consuming my every thought and every breath. I melted into him, into the moment and into his arms, letting him take me away from the pain of the past.

"And I never ceased to feel that way, not for a single heart-beat," he whispered against my lips and kissed me—deeply—

as one of his hands fisted in my hair. "You have no idea what I've done for us. I hope you'll find out but I'm also... scared you'll hate me for it."

I kissed him and a moan escaped my lips when his fingers traced a line of fire down my body. Eagerly he pulled my dress up, the path of his fingers drawing closer to my most intimate places. His head dipped down to capture my lips again and I was lost. My hands clasped around his neck without thought or hesitation. Hell, I missed it when he was mine.

My breath got caught in my throat as he drove his fingers into my panties, and I felt myself tremble with anticipation.

"Tell me, what did you feel when he touched you?" His voice sent a chill down my spine as his fingers continued their tantalizing torture, sending waves of pleasure through my body. He paused and leaned in close to whisper against my ear now, "And what do you feel when I touch you?"

"I..." A soft, guttural sound escaped my lips as a rough hand brushed against my chin, tilting my gaze to meet his. In that moment, I saw my own desperation reflected back at me, a mirror of the wild yearning that consumed me.

I had never felt such a powerful pull before, a force that seemed to draw us inexorably together. I realized our souls had to be linked, there was no other explanation for it. The Fates must have linked us. His fingers traced through the strands of my hair and I knew that we were lost together, wandering in a world that could never hope to contain the intensity of our desires.

"You what?" His voice was low, husky with a hunger that matched my own, and before I could answer, his lips crashed on mine with a possessive hunger. For a moment, time seemed to stop, and nothing else mattered but the devotion and desire that bound us together.

As he pulled one hand out of my panties, his grip tightened

in my hair, holding me close so that our lips kept only inches apart. His breath was hot against my skin, and I shivered with anticipation as he asked me, "Tell me. What did you feel like when you lay in his arms?" His voice was low and demanding, a rumble that sent a thrill through my body.

"Like I was drowning," I whispered, my voice barely audible in the charged silence between us. "Like every breath I took was filled with you, and I couldn't get enough. It was like nothing else mattered but the feel of your hands on my skin, the taste of your lips on mine."

His grip loosened slightly, and I could feel him drawing back, his eyes searching mine for some kind of understanding. When he found what he was searching for, he kissed me again, fierce and wild, a storm of emotion that threatened to engulf us both.

In that moment, there was no past, no future, only the unyielding present. Our bodies were twined together, locked in an embrace that seemed to transcend time and space. And as he held me close, I knew that nothing else would ever matter again.

"I felt like dying from the inside when I couldn't have you," I whispered when he finally pulled away, gasping for air. But he didn't give me another moment to catch my breath because, in an instant, his lips crashed against mine once again. He gripped my hips with both hands, turning into a steel vice as he lifted me up and crushed my legs around his narrow waist. I felt the heat emanating from his body, radiating through our clothes as he pressed his body against mine.

His lips were silky and inviting, his smell like a drug and I felt myself slipping away into him. All the feelings I had kept suppressed surged up within me like a raging storm, and all the touches, the kisses were suddenly not enough. I wanted more—

I needed more—all of him, every part of him, until I was consumed by his love. I wanted everything he had to offer.

"Do you even realize how much you turn me on?" Rio whispered, nuzzling my neck. "Tell me how this makes you feel."

I couldn't help but gasp as an electrifying sensation rippled across my neck at his touch. "You make me feel alive again."

The flames from the flickering torches suddenly extinguish, leaving us bathed in complete darkness. But his lips found mine even in the inky void and he murmured, "You and I are all that matters and no one will ever be able to keep us apart, Aria. We won't allow it."

His assurance as he kissed me passionately made me believe it was true.

"Who wants us apart?" I tried, but then he kissed me again and all reason flew out of the window... how much I wanted this man—no matter what the consequences might be. Skull this shit.

Just then I could feel the hardness of his dick pressing against me and I fisted the shirt of his and growled, "And what about you? What about the women you fucked? You're all possessive but not innocent yourself."

He slowly upended my blouse and a deep growl escaped his throat. "I haven't fucked anyone since you."

I stopped kissing him and just looked at him for several seconds, my eyes blinking. "What?"

He started unwrapping me. "Don't get me wrong. I tried... but only the thought of you made me cum."

With a teasing sway of my hips, I positioned myself to embrace the unmistakable proof of how much he was wanting me. "That problem seemed to have vanished then."

"I wanted you, wanted to fuck you since the day we parted, and I'm not waiting a second longer." With a frenzied passion he finally ripped the blouse from my chest, flinging it to the floor with my trousers.

Impatiently, I tore at his vest until it littered the floor as well. Nothing stood between us now as his scorching gaze swept over my body, as mine swept over his abs, his chiseled body...

"Well," I said, ready to play the same game as him. "How much did you want me?"

"I considered dying to just be with you," he said and we tumbled to the opposite wall, our lips crashing down on each other.

His grip on my hips was so tight I could feel his muscles tensing beneath me. The heat of his body against mine made my skin tingle and I clung to him, unable to control myself. Oh, his heavy breath on my neck sent a shudder of pleasure through me. Then there was the sound of his belt buckle clattering to the floor and in one rough movement, he tore my panties in two like a hungry animal would rip its prey.

"Um, I didn't bring another," I breathed, urgency dripping from every word. "No time to pack."

"I don't fucking care." He slammed into me with a passion that shook me to my core, as if every inch of my body was nothing but his forever and he was claiming it back. His fingers grasped my nipples with relentless hunger, like his touch was a key that unlocked the forgotten parts of me. His lips burned against mine, igniting a flame within me that consumed us both. I felt his desire pulse through me, shaking off the dust of years that had passed without him.

"Fuck, I missed you," he rasped, and his words made me forget what problems we had.

I sighed deeply until I suddenly noticed why he was taking me on *that* wall.

That skulling prick.

I lashed out and punched him in the chest. "You want him to hear us!"

Right behind us was the room where Illiam was being interrogated. Right now.

A wicked smile played on his lips. "Your wetness tells me you like it as much as I do, darling."

He pressed his cock deeper into me and I fought back the urge to moan.

Skull. I did like it.

I bit my lip and met his hungry gaze.

"What's wrong about telling everyone that you're—" another thrust, and we both panted, "—mine."

He rolled his thumb over my clit, hard and fast, increasing the friction between us and I could barely contain the gasp that escaped my lips. Holy hell. I was so lost in this whirlwind of pleasure that my moans escaped uncontrollably as the intensity of my desire for him pushed me to the brink of madness.

Every move he made ignited a fire within me, though deep down, I knew it was all kinds of wrong. Yet, I bit his lip, tugged at his hair, as he pushed me harder against the wall. The intensity grew, and I swear the whole damn town of Catterville could hear us.

My nails dug deep into his back and he growled. Gods, that sound.

I held him close to my core, the buildup becoming more and more intense.

"Claiming me turns you on, doesn't it?" I said, the words barely escaping my lips.

I felt his body shudder beneath me as he fought to regain control, gasping out an affirmation that only fueled my desire.

I dug my nails in even harder, wanting to inflict both pleasure and pain, a heady mix of ecstasy and anguish that only he could provide. He moaned with pleasure as I scratched him, and

I could feel my whole body trembling with need. And then, he brought his lips crashing down on mine once again. Brutal and heavenly at the same time.

"Yes," he breathed into my mouth, his voice rough and ragged. "Fuck, yes."

His tongue was on my neck now, tracing patterns of fire that sent me spinning into a dizzying haze of pleasure. I pressed my hips against him, lost in his embrace, as he continued to pound into me with a relentless passion. His thumb never leaving my core. Never.

And just as I was reaching the peak of my pleasure, his gaze locked with mine.

"Look at me," he commanded, and I felt my body responding to the intensity of his sapphire stare. His eyes were such a dark blue now, I could see my own reflection in them, and I cried out.

His slick fingers firmly gripped my dampened hips, anchoring himself as he quivered against me.

I collapsed against his hot chest, panting for breath, as he held me close.

In that moment, there was nothing but the two of us, lost in a sea of passion.

In that moment I could have cried.

Cried for all the feelings that came over me. Cried for all the time we had missed.

He was here. With me. And yet everything was so wrong. I hung from him like a broken girl.

And I guess I was.

"Could you please stop torturing us all?" I heard Any's voice through the door and both Rio and I froze.

"Oh, by the Stix," I said and wanted to get swallowed up by the ground. "You wanted them *all* to hear, you are... I can't believe you."

He shrugged and let me down. "Had to mark my territory."

I started to straighten my dress. "Yeah, you're very much like a dog indeed. Great. It's gonna be a cold ride without underpants," I tried to joke but I stopped when I met Rio's gaze again.

"No need for underpants. You can sit on me," he said, and I blushed. Actually blushed.

I put on my blouse as Any hammered against the door again. "We paid the innkeeper and readied the horses." He cleared his throat. "We're taking the Blood courtier with us."

"This was a mistake," I stuttered, trying to convince myself that it was smarter to regret the sex but hell, I loved every minute of it.

"No," he said, kissing my forehead. "Not us. Never."

CHAPTER TWENTY
RIO

Aria adamantly refused to ride with me on the same horse, so we got another one and tethered Illiam to Ebony's horse. Bory, as always, sat on Aria's shoulder while Soothie flew above us, his shadow constantly remembering us to treat her well.

I really had to get my jealousy under control because Illiam, that fucker, refused to take his eyes off of Aria and I could have smashed his head each time I noticed. Thank the gods, she did not return his looks, but I stared at her nonetheless. It was for her sake that I agreed on bringing him along. If it were up to me, he would be dead. Just then he looked at me with a burning fire in his eyes, and I could feel the same desperation and outrage swirling inside me. My fists clenched on the reins, and I fought to push past them, eager to break free from his fucking gaze. I could sense his delight in watching me squirm like a hunter tracking its prey and it spurred me on. I had to get away, no matter what it took, to keep him from relishing any further in my misery.

He didn't rescue her as planned but hell, he got under my

skin. "What do you plan to do about him?" Any asked, catching up with me.

He'd already told me that interrogating him didn't help, he didn't slip at all and neither of us wanted to hurt him since Aria had made it clear that we couldn't without hurting her. So, our hands were tied, and I hated it.

I shrugged. "He can't do anything, so we just drag him along."

"You don't seem to take it so well, though."

"He fucked her, how else should I take it, huh?"

Any winced. "He doesn't mean anything to her, you know that."

"And you know I can't help my feelings."

"The curse," Any said and I nodded.

"I had always been possessive, but being back in the Underworld seems to worsen it—I hate that everyone is fucking playing against me."

"Well, you need to get a grip. We all know it didn't take a good turn the last time."

I glanced sideways at him. "Oh, *you* all know? Look where I am. I'm a fucking reaper, retrieving the love of my life for the fucking *Bone Queen*."

"She just has to get all her memories back..." he said, and well, I agreed.

He always brought me back to solid ground. "But we need to be patient. There's a reason we shouldn't remember anything from our past lives, it can destroy us..." he said

"I know. I only had one reincarnation and all the hurt my soul had to endure is killing me each day." I caught a glimpse of the ring on my finger and Jamie instantly filled my mind. When we baptized her, Jamie and I swapped rings from my abuela's collection. I couldn't help but wonder if Jamie had grown enough to wear it on her finger now or if she still kept it as a necklace.

"That's why we need to give her that time. Be patient and stop it with your attitude," Any said.

I sighed. "I will." He was right, so damn right. I'll mess it all up again.

"Don't fall into the same patterns."

"Stop me if I turn dark again," I said, my glance focused on the road—the world a blackened wasteland, a reflection of the burnt-out ruin of my heart. It felt like the universe was taking away everything that I had ever loved, stealing it in a deluge of pain and suffering and although I thought I'd saved it, saved us, I only made it worse.

I could have never thought that love would destroy me one day but the mere thought of losing someone I cared about was enough to push me to the brink. I was close to lashing out. This life on Earth took everything from me and now even the safety of my daughter, the only one I ever had, was threatened by every decision I made.

"I'm here for you," Any said. "I won't let you go dark."

"Kill me before I can make this any worse," I said, half-heartedly joking, and was surprised when he laughed—though it was a bitter laugh.

"I will," he said, and even though he forced himself to smile, there was something in his tone that made me believe it was true.

After hours of riding the cliff's face appeared through the charred trees, growing larger as we rode closer. Inky black clouds churned behind it, swirling up like a giant's stormy brew. There was a hollow, echoing rumble and a sharp crack, like thunder as we neared it and I halted, holding up a hand to signal the others to do the same.

The base of the cliff was dark with a nightly mist that filled the whole plane right before us from the ground up to where we stood— an endless cloud cover shrouding us in even more darkness. Like the last time we passed it, the cliff looked like a mouth ready to swallow us whole, but something was off this time.

My eyes flit over the swirling clouds. Taking a better look, I knew why. Demons were lurking inside the rock and much to my disgust, it seemed like they were setting up a new home right there to nest. A dangerous moment with demons, since it meant they were reproducing and ready to fight their nestlings. If disturbed while nesting they'd promise more than cold-blooded death. This was far from good. Fuck.

"Why the hell are demons nesting here?" Ash muttered as he came into view with Isix and Briz.

Ebony stepped forward. "Damn it, it's very unusual for them to be nesting on these grounds."

Illiam grinned mischievously and I narrowed my eyes in suspicion.

"Do you have something to do with this?" I asked him sharply. "How could I," he said.

Ebony pointing a finger at him. "Don't lie, pretty boy."

He sighed. "How would I be able to summon such an army of creatures? It is strange though, never heard of them nesting in such a busy area."

He was right. He couldn't have summoned this many demons. Fuck. My fingers tightened around the reins until I felt the leather creaking in protest. It left me no other choice but to take another route to the Bone Court.

Unease ran through me, even more so when Aria steered her horse next to me. "I have an idea," she said, and everyone shot her perplexed looks.

Ash scoffed, "Oh, brilliant. As if a girl like you could come up with anything to save us from these demons."

"Oh, please," Aria rolled her eyes dramatically at Ash's comment. "Demons just haven't met a girl as dangerously clever as me before. Now, listen up, I've got a much smarter plan."

"I can't believe you, you're siding with the Bone Court now?" Illiam snorted and Ebony cackled humorously at his expense.

"No need for theatrics," Ebony said, and I think he actually blushed.

Aria didn't so much as look at Illiam and before she turned away from the group, she said to me, "Got a minute?"

Ash and Any exchanged questioning looks, but I just shrugged and followed her. There was something off about Bory, though, and I had a feeling that I wasn't going to like her plan.

As we approached, Bory's grin widened, and even though he stayed put behind her, his gaze was fixed on me. I could feel a sense of unease creeping up my spine. It was like he knew something I didn't, like he was holding all the cards in this twisted game. Odd...

"Okay. What's up?" I asked her as soon as we were out of everyone's earshot.

"Since we have to take the road through the Elysian Fields now... I had an idea. What about we visit the oracle? Both of us have no clue which queen is lying—why don't we go get some words from it?"

I considered her idea for a moment before speaking, my voice barely above a whisper. "The Necromantion?"

"You got it. Instead of wasting time arguing back and forth about who's right or wrong, let's cut to the chase and seek some guidance. The oracle's got the answers we need to pick the right side."

I watched her closely as she sat atop her horse, arms

crossed, and head held high. She didn't need to say it out loud, but I could tell she still believed her side was the right one.

"Since we can't take the route before us, demons and all, this would be an alternative," she added. Bory nodded so exaggeratedly, I thought he might audition for a Shakespearean play. "And the oracle is along the way."

Although there was something off about the way both of them tried to convince me, she was right. There was only one other way to reach the Bone Court, and it led straight through the Necromantion. "Let's try it," I said, the words coming out more confidently than

I felt. Oracles were tricky but maybe it could help her to remember, and we'd be a step further to breaking the fucking curse.

As she edged her horse closer to mine, I could feel the warmth of her thigh against mine.

Instinctively, I leaned in to kiss her, but she pulled back, shaking her head. "Not in front of everyone."

My heart sank and I drew back.

"I don't want to hurt Illiam, or make you think everything is alright. It's not."

I scoffed. "Well, I don't care a bit about him."

"But I do—he's done a lot for me. If you got to know him, you'd realize he's actually not bad. You could be friends."

With a skeptical eyebrow raised, I said, "Listen, I have to admit, I appreciate your good will, but let me burst that bubble real quick: Any guy who's laid eyes on your body won't be getting the "friend" label from me."

She rolled her eyes. "Get your foot out of your own ass and let's ride to the oracle."

"How about you watch that pretty mouth of yours first." She grinned. "Or?"

"By the Hellhounds, could you two please stop flirting? This ride has been nothing but Tartarus for us," Ash yelled.

"Yeah, I think my puppy will cry soon," Ebony snickered, nodding at Illiam behind her.

Aria stiffened up. She glanced at Illiam and rode away from me.

I gritted my teeth. I'm going to murder that brickhead. "Fine.

Let's go find that fucking oracle then."

I wondered why I hadn't come up with this idea myself. Well, it's safe to say that oracles are as bad as witches, but it indeed could be of help. We just had to pray that it said the right words and not lead us astray—and fuck. There was another obstacle to it.

"But we have to pay it and it only takes—"

"—Bloodcoins. I know, I know," Aria finished my sentence as we trotted toward the others. "Lucky for us, I've got loads of it, but we'll have to swing by Cave Town to get our hands on it."

CHAPTER TWENTY-ONE
LYNNE

The wind howled against our faces as we rode at breakneck speed, the ground vibrating with each thundering hoofbeat. I cast a quick look behind me at Rio, his features barely visible in the waning light. My heart was pounding with fear, convinced he'd somehow sniff out my secret. I was holding onto this tiny hope that the oracle would back me up and show everyone how wicked the Bone Queen truly was.

It was a long shot, but hey, it's all I had.

As we made our way through the Underworld, the darkness echoed with the screeches of mysterious creatures and we knew it was time to stop and set up camp. We found a good place in the shadows of a mountain, perfect for Soothie to hide within a cave for the night. I suggested that I sleep with Any instead of Rio, who shot me a sharp look but had to eventually cave in since everyone seemed pleased with that.

I guess no one wanted another scene...

As I took a seat on a log, the scent of roasted meat filled the air. I leaned in towards Illiam, catching his attention from the bustle of activity and conversation around us as the others established our campsite. It was a rare moment for us to speak alone. He pivoted towards me, his features illuminated by the gentle glow of the flickering flames.

"Hi," I said, my eyes drawn to the iron shackles around his wrists and ankles. I winced. Skull it. He had always been willing to go to great lengths for me... and I felt bad for him.

"Hi," he said back, his shoulder dropping as Bory hopped off my back and settled by the fire to warm up his little bum.

"I'm sorry," I said softly, hoping we could get back to the funny conversations. He used to make me laugh so quickly.

"You don't need to apologize," he said, lifting the shackles with a rattle. "You always were honest to me about your feelings. I knew there was never a chance for us."

I sighed and checked on Isix, Briz and Ebony as they fixed our tents, avoiding Illiam's gaze as I had never actually told him about who I used to cry over every night. And now with Rio being one of the Horsemen, it was even more complicated than before.

"Bory lured the demons here," I said once I was sure that no one was paying attention to us.

Illiam's eyebrows rose in surprise. "You?" he said, looking down at my little helper.

Bory grinned widely, his feathers catching the flickering orange light of the campfire. "Yeah, we blocked the passage because the queen is waiting outside Cave Town with an army."

"So, we don't side with them but have to play along, got me?" I said.

Illiam nodded grimly. "I figured it out eventually. I know about the army, and the queen tasked me with finding you and assessing any weaknesses in your group. Soothie will report back to her with any valuable information we uncover."

"Illiam, I'm really sorry. I never wanted to put us in this situation."

He stared into my eyes and for a moment, I felt my heart jump. His touch was warm and inviting, but I couldn't help but worry. Conflicted thoughts raced through my mind, as I felt his hand linger on mine.

"It's complicated, Rio is complicated," I repeated. "But I think we can make him side with us."

"I hope you're right. We need to be careful and stay on guard, regardless of what happens."

Bory cawed, echoing Illiam's sentiment. "I know," I said.

Illiam patted Bory and then turned back to me, fortunately changing the subject, "I think I know a weak point already. Did you know Ash has a crush on Ebony?"

The question jarred me out of my thoughts, and I quirked a brow. "No!"

"It's so obvious, Lynne." He smiled mischievously, and it was clear he was trying to lighten the mood, but the underlying tension was still there between us.

I glanced at Ebony and Ash. Oh, by the Stix. He was right.

I wouldn't have been surprised if hearts had started shooting out of Ash's eyes. Ebony was scolding him angrily, and Ash's cheeks burned. I caught a glimpse of him watching her, his eyes locked on her daring curves.

"Oh, by the Hellhounds. You're right, he totally has a crush on her."

"I don't think she does, though. I noticed when she joked with me, and Ash started frowning. I guess Rio isn't the only one who'd love to kill me. So, we can take this as an advantage. We just have to catch Ebony and Ash is out too. She's his weak point."

"Good observations," I said.

Illiam grinned, and I could tell he liked being a thorn in their side.

"Lynne," he said a split second later. "When we meet the

Blood Queen's army, we'll take off with Soothie, is this all right with you?"

"Yeah I can't set foot in the Bone Court for sure, you know she'll kill me right away. But there's another thing, we'll have to take Rio with us, he's got me tied to him with a bond."

"A bond?" Illiam tilted his head slightly and squinted, as if he was trying to make sense of what I had said.

"Yes, a reaper's bond, I can't move away from him without it taking my breath away. That means we have to take him with us. I hope Soothie can carry us all..."

"Lynne..." Iliam's hazel eyes darted around and then settled on me as if he was looking for an answer but didn't find it. "There is no such thing as a reaper's bond."

I lifted my hand and showed him the squiggly tattoo. "Sure. Look, he bonded me."

"Holy crap," he breathed out, taking my wrist in his hand, the shackles rattling under his touch. "That's not a normal bond."

I felt a chill go down my spine. I already knew this bond between Rio and I was something beyond our control but the look on Illiam's face made me squirm. My hand trembled as I slowly pulled it away from him.

"What is this then?" I asked, dreading the words that were about to follow.

"It's a magical handfasting..."

I closed my eyes, trying to process what the skull he'd just said. Handfasting—an old tradition that I knew—but this couldn't be true. It couldn't.

When I opened my eyes, he said the words that I hoped he wouldn't, "You're married to him."

A wave of anger washed over me. I'd kill that bastard.

"It can't be, he just touched me and—this appeared and no." He can't be serious. All this time I've been digging for information about his wife, and it turns out he was talking about me? "This is enough."

I stood up, but Illiam gripped my wrist in flight and pulled me down next to him again. "Don't. I don't know why he didn't say a thing about it and how the hell this went down, because normally, you have to agree to marry someone, Lynne. This is something I have never seen nor heard of. To marry in the Underworld, you have to give yourself to another soul willingly. It doesn't happen just with a touch since it links your souls forever."

My voice rose with each word, "I have to talk to him, Illiam. He can't just force me to—"

Illiam put a calming hand on my shoulder. "Calm. Down. Lynne. This is bigger than just the two of you. It's a powerful bond that's been made, and we need to be careful. If he can yield magic like that, we shouldn't anger him."

"I don't care!" I cried, tearing away from his touch. He couldn't take this away from me. I didn't want to marry him, and I needed to have a say in this. "I refuse to be tied to someone without my permission. I won't let Rio dictate my life. What was he even thinking?"

"I understand," Illiam whispered, checking our surroundings frantically, "but you have to consider the consequences. You may not like it, but you have to play along until we can reshuffle the cards.

Right now, we are the powerless here, don't forget this."

I clenched my fists, feeling the heat of frustration boil within me. "I won't accept it. I'll find a way to break this bond." The cold crept up my spine and I glanced at Rio over my shoulder. This time, his eyes locked mine and I couldn't shake the feeling that there was so much more going on. So much more that I've missed.

"We'll speak with the queen," Illiam said. "She'll know how to undo this."

I glanced down at the tattoo and wondered if she knew the truth about him. Who he really was. What if she knew it all along? Whenever we practiced, she would mention his name and often used my pain to make me conjure up magic. I touched the strange pattern and felt the smoothness of the ink as my fingers lightly ran along the curves and swirls. The lines were raised slightly from the surface of my skin, giving a pleasant texture to them but the ink was cool, a refreshing sensation compared to the warmth of my own skin. She must have known. What if she really tricked me? What if helping her was another mistake? By the Hellhounds, I had no idea what I was doing. What was wrong and what was right...

I sighed. "I feel like everyone knows more than I do."

In that moment, the light from the flickering fire before us diminished and Ebony emerged, her arms firmly crossed and a smirk of satisfaction playing on her features. "Well, you lovebirds?"

I narrowed my eyes at her and forced a polite smile. "What's up, Ebony?"

"Bedtime, we have no time to stall. So on with you." She playfully jabbed Illiam in the shoulder and he growled in response. As he rose to his full height, his towering figure loomed above her, yet the glint in Ebony's eyes hinted at how much stronger she was than the both of us. That's why she always carried herself with a confidence that suggested she wouldn't hesitate to wield her abilities if need be. As if he had just thought of that too, Illiam took a step back and Ebony grinned pleasingly.

"You're the lucky one, you get to sleep with me tonight," she teased, and Illiam returned a lopsided grin.

"Figured as much. I hope you don't snore."

She tilted her head and said, "Like a slumbering Shadowbeast."

"Why am I not shocked that you can't keep quiet even in the dead of night?" Illiam's eyes shone with amusement, and I noticed the hint of a smile tugging at the corners of Ebony's lips. Despite the playful jibe, she held Illiam's gaze steady and there was a sense of camaraderie between them that seemed to have developed. When exactly did this happen?

"Can I borrow Bory?" Illiam asked me, not taking his gaze off of Ebony.

"Why?" Bory squeaked, startled by the sudden question. "I need your feathers to stuff her mouth."

Ebony's arms crossed defensively over her chest and I couldn't help but chuckle.

"Don't you dare touch me! Not my beautiful feathers!" Bory whooped and hopped on my shoulder. "Everyone's crazy around here, Lynne."

"Tell me about it," I said.

"I know something else you could use to stuff my mouth," she said and I actually choked on my own spit but the smile died quickly on my face since the sound of footsteps on gravel caught my attention. I turned around and saw Rio heading towards us.

Before I could second-guess myself, I stood up, coming face-to-face with him, the banter between Ebony and Illiam fading into the background. With a forced sense of nonchalance, I said goodbye to them and tried to avoid Rio by rushing past him.

But of course, he fell in step beside me, and I refused to make eye contact. Illiam was right, it was smarter to pretend I knew nothing about the marriage, but I also knew that if Rio provoked me, the words would just spill out of me. I just wanted to strangle him. With my bare hands. So, I took a deep breath in and focused on walking.

"Aria," he said. "What's wrong?"

"I'm not talking to you," I said, keeping my gaze firmly on the path. The nerve he had...

"Because?"

On legs that felt like lead, I kept pushing forward until I reached the tent I shared with Any. I wanted to scream at him for all the things he'd done, including kidnapping, lying... forcing me to marry him. But I was a good girl, so I opened the tent and simply said, "You know why."

He probably didn't, considering all the dirt I had on him.

I climbed into the tent and shut it before Rio managed to form a single word. He waited for a few seconds, sighed and finally stormed off.

Once inside, I was startled to find Any already settled down in his sleeping bag.

"Skull," I murmured, reflexively clasping a hand over my collarbone. "You scared me."

"Sorry," Any replied. "Just wanted to rest."

I laid down next to him and Bory tucked himself in next to me.

I pulled the covers up over me, but my mind raced with thoughts of what the oracle would reveal tomorrow. No matter how hard I tried to focus on sleeping, my head was too busy contemplating what could happen. All kinds of possibilities swirled in my head, and to be honest... I just couldn't shake the haunting images of what lay in store for us... for me. Hell, I was freaking married to Rio and he didn't so much as tell me a thing about it. Also, what did it mean that he lived down here long before I did? What if I didn't want to know the truth? What if there was a good reason I couldn't remember anything?

"Any," I said and rolled over, trying to make out where his face was. "What did Rio tell you about who he is? What do you know about him?" I could at least try to get more information.

"These questions are dangerous to ask."

So, he knew about it! "Please give me a hint. You've known him longer than I have."

Any sighed in frustration. "We've been cursed, Lynne. It affects all of us because we share a common fate. There are many more people involved in this besides just Rio and you. Like the Horsemen, entire courts... but what's worse is that I'm not allowed to tell you anything about it. You have to figure out the truth on your own."

"But how am I supposed to do that if no one will tell me anything?"

"You could come to the wrong conclusions and revealing parts of the story can cause consequences."

Wait, so he could actually die too in case he told me anything? I swallowed.

I always thought it was *just* Rio in the line of fire, but after hearing what Any said, it seemed like there might be more involved in this messed-up situation. "Gods, you love almost dying and making deals with witches..."

"Seems to run in the family..." he said, touching my hand.

Out of nowhere, this feeling surged inside me, like a gut instinct telling me I could trust Any, no matter what. Maybe it was all those memories or who knows, but something deep down just screamed that he had my back. Always had.

I had judged him for trying to kill Rio and here we were, in the Underworld, only because of me. I stroked his arm, the familiar gesture comforting against strange tension between us. Somehow, I really wanted to go back to the warmth of the vision I had of us. He made me feel like I was home, something I hadn't experienced before. But, when I opened my eyes and returned to reality, all of it had vanished and I was left with an aching emptiness in my chest again.

"I had a vision the other day, of the two of us. How I met Rio," I said.

Any laughed. "Ah well, that's a nice memory, yeah. No matter in what form I met your soul so far, you're always a wild one, ready to fight."

I felt a wave of curiosity wash over me, as I wondered how many times Any had seen me in other forms, and why he could remember it, while I couldn't recall a thing. It felt strange that he had access to pieces of my past that I could no longer recall.

"Why do you remember what you did in your last reincarnation?" asked Bory.

"It's different with me since I never actually dropped or reincarnated, like you or Rio did, his memories came back after several months of being down here," Any said solemnly. "Yours well... I guess they need longer since it's more... complicated."

I shivered at his words, feeling suddenly that Nana's stories weren't all true. "This sounds encouraging. But how is it possible to never make the drop and exist down here?"

"It's rare," Any said.

The silence that now filled the tent made me feel small and insignificant. I wanted to ask more questions but knew I had already gone too far and I didn't want to hurt him, since he shouldn't help me with this. Not if his words could kill him...

So, I lay on my back, feeling every word he said reverberate in my head, trying to make sense of it all. I felt a heavy weight on my chest and my vision blurred as the realization hit me that everything I had previously been certain of was nothing but skulling wrong. My reality had been completely distorted and I had to rethink every step I had taken. Every year it pulled me back like a magnet, as if it held secrets that only I could uncover. If Rio and I had shared a life before our paths crossed on Earth, could it be that my mysterious attraction towards the cemetery tower was part of a larger purpose? Nothing settled in my mind, yet I felt like a veil was slowly burning away, revealing the truth about my existence—my purpose. And I had to know the truth. No matter what.

"You'll find out," Any said. "You already got a handle on parts of

it."

"That Rio is my husband?" I asked, bitterness dripping from my

voice.

"For one thing."

I grumbled, turning away from him and pulling Bory closer. I closed my eyes, letting his soft feathers bring me comfort for a moment before the realization of what Rio was to me hit me again.

My eyes shot open.

He was my skulling husband.

"Okay. Hold on. One last thing, Any," I said, my hot breath whirling up some feathers before me. "Does everyone know that we're married?"

He hesitated for a moment, as if weighing whether to tell me the truth or keep it hidden.

Then he spoke, and I knew that I hadn't been ready for the answer, "Many have forgotten over the years but most of the old court does yes, this includes the Horsemen, me..."

Skull it. Skull all of it.

CHAPTER TWENTY-TWO
RIO

I was already feeling exhausted from a heated argument between Ebony and Ash before we even departed for Cave Town. Ash was envious of Ebony's connection with Illiam and insisted that I make Illiam ride with Briz instead, causing another argument with Isix and our youngster.

And I couldn't care less about their drama.

So, I left it to Isix to figure out who would be in charge of babysitting Illiam for the rest of our trip, and she chose Briz. The grin on his face was priceless, finally getting some important task to handle. Ebony looked like she was about to burst, but I shut her down with a simple gesture of my hand. It was time for them to handle their issues on their own. Ash has been in love with Ebony for centuries and she liked to play him because she could. Honestly, I think she'd never actually settle down with anyone. She was a free spirit and that's what most men liked about her.

It was going to be a long day's ride, and the thought of that made my stomach churn. Crossing the Underworld wasn't a piece of cake. It was a world with winding passages, bottomless pits, and mighty deities ready to test and challenge anyone who dares to set foot in their domain. They've got their own rule-book, complete with punishments that'll make anyone think twice about crossing their path.

But Aria seemed oblivious, happily telling Ebony, Illiam and Briz about Cave Town—punishing me, no doubt, with her sunny disposition. I tried to keep my focus on the road but her ignoring me hit close to home. She had no idea how much this was hurting me, but I had to give her time.

No matter how hard it was. It was a lot for her stomach. I knew that.

Any rode beside me, trying to make up for Isix and Ash's lack of conversation—but I was too troubled to talk anyway. My mind raced as I tried to envision what lay ahead, that fucking oracle kept gnawing at me. Time was of the essence, and the stakes were too high.

My fear mounted as I pictured what could happen if Aria didn't get to the missing pieces of the puzzle before we crossed paths with the Bone Queen. The mere thought of failure made my skin crawl, and I shuddered at the possible consequences of coming up short. Decades of fighting could all be for nothing in a single moment, and the thought made my heart race even faster. We had come too far to fall short now.

My hands shook as I grasped the reins of my horse, anger flowing through my veins. So, I sped up as we rode through a landscape made up of craggy rocks, deep chasms and valleys of boiling lava. Wisps of smoke drifted up from the depths to our sides with an eerie glow. The air was still but for the occasional wail of a lost soul, or the crack of thunder from the sky above.

We eventually came to a river outlet and our horses plodded slowly through the watery realm, their hooves and mane glimmering in the faint light. Before us, the rivers of the Underworld snaked through the darkness, their waters as black as the night. The raging rapids swirled in a mix of shadows and moonlight while the banks were studded with gnarled trees and craggy rocks.

But then the smell of decay filled the air like a thousand points of rot and I grew perfectly still. Something was up. It was like stepping into a rotted graveyard, a noxious order of death and dying that overpowered any other smell in the air, like a blanket of death that wanted to swallow everything in its wake. It was so strong that it caused my horse to slow its pace, and in turn I held up my hand in a signal for the others to slow down as well.

Fuck. Let's hope it wasn't what I thought it was.

"Do you see what I see?" Any's voice dropped as he stopped right next to me.

"Unfortunately," I said and my gaze flew over a shadowy figure that lay in the center of a smoky river right before us, its eyes glowing with malevolent intent as it stared at us, smirking because we just rode right into its net.

Its skin was the color of pitch and its horns twisted with wickedness. Thick mist swirled around it, sending a chill into the air. Its talons were ready to strike and its teeth shining in the darkness as its mouth stretched into a wide slash.

"Get her out!" I shouted, and out of the corner of my eye I saw Ebony slap Aria's horse on the butt and thank the gods, it rode off, Ebony following behind them with Illiam. Everyone whipped out their weapons, and I knew it was about to go down. What we were facing was no run-of-the-mill Underworld creature, but Tisiphone's fucking pet.

She was one of the three Daughters of the Night, which meant she was up to mischief somewhere around here. She and her sisters were among the most feared in the Underworld. They were old but virginal hags whose skin color was gray, their hair a faint nuance of the wind that could turn into snakes.

I cautiously asked the beast before us, "Where is your mistress?"

It let out a menacing growl, its fur bristling while its eyes never left mine. Then there was a cackle. I glanced up and noticed Tisiphone perched atop a cliff with her feet dangling off the side. Playfully like always.

"Up here, sweetie," she grinned, her gray robe fluttering in the wind as she pinned me down with yellow eyes. My gaze flicked to the poisonous blood that flowed out of them, coating her face.

"Clear our path," I commanded her. "Why should I?"

"Because I'll send you to Tartarus if you don't."

Tisiphone burst out laughing, a sound that filled me with dread. Briz swore next to me, and I signaled him to calm down, I knew it was his first encounter with a high class monster but he had to grow some balls.

"In your current position, that's going to be hard to do," she taunted, "but I've always wanted to spank that pretty ass of yours. I heard it's delicious."

Ash huffed but my eyes narrowed in on Tisiphone. "Before long, I'll be back in my rightful position and will punish you."

She pouted. "Then grant me a wish. You know damn well that nothing comes for free. I can't kill you, I'll give you that. But let me tell you, you're pretty damn vulnerable at the moment, and I can definitely hurt you. Or someone in your group."

Her pet stepped closer to us, growling.

I glared at it until it backed down. She had a point, normally she would have been nothing against me but in my current state...

"My sister," Tisiphone started, her tone suddenly serious. "Is in Tartarus."

"Let me guess," I said with a sigh, noticing Briz wiggling

nervously next to me. "It won't be Alecto because she always hides her machinations well. So how did Megaera end up there? Slept in the wrong bed?"

Tisiphone pursed her lips before answering. "Among other things."

"She fell in love and that love was unfaithful? And she took revenge on the wrong person?" I asked, knowing that I hit the truth. These three have always been troubled sisters and they always had the same issues.

Tisiphone nodded slowly in confirmation. "Typical," I muttered under my breath.

"So, do you want to go on without any losses?" she asked, her eyes glinting dangerously in the faint moonlight. "Even if I can't kill you, someone in your group will get hurt."

She grinned behind me and I knew she was referring to Aria. I hoped they were hiding well enough and gritted my teeth in frustration. Fighting with Tisiphone was too dangerous —we needed our forces for the rest of the ride. Needed all our mana.

"Fine," I replied reluctantly, feeling anger boiling inside. "I'll free her the minute I can but if I see you ever again, Tartarus will be the least of your problems."

Tisiphone smiled triumphantly and nodded at her beast.

"Nyx," she said, and the creature before us curiously inclined its head in response, suddenly giving her the cutest puppy eyes I've ever seen. That fake beast. "Go find some other place to play."

The beast let out a low growl, but there was something strange about it. It turned its gaze behind us, its eyes suddenly carrying a hint of sadness. It seemed to be searching for something, or someone. Aria flashed in my mind, and I couldn't shake the feeling that the beast wanted to find her. But why? It was just a monster and nothing more.

It howled and a sickly stench wafted through the air as it sprang off.

Tisiphone chuckled and stood up, her gray skirt fluttering in the wind. "I hope it was worth it... all of it just for *her*... But despite your threat, we're glad you're back. Things have been... difficult."

"She will always be worth it," I said, noticing Ash and Isix share a look that suggested it wasn't, though I wished I could remind them

that this had been my call to make. I already spent centuries talking with them about my decision and I was so done with it.

"Good luck with that. I've never heard of anyone bypassing the elders' decisions," she said with a smirk. "But there's a first for everything, right?"

Something glistened in her eyes, telling me that she was certain, we'd fail eventually. She turned and her pet flashed its teeth one last time and followed after her, leaving behind only the smoke of the earth that it had stirred up.

As the last traces of light filtered through the skeletons above us, we finally reached the base of some massive mountains. The ground beneath us changed from charred earth to dry, barren sand dunes as we pressed on. I couldn't help but scan the area around us, taking in the scattered bones and rusty armor that littered the landscape.

It was eerily still, except for a faint red glow emanating from deep within the mountain, lighting up underground tunnels that stretched far beyond our line of sight. At some point we unhitched the horses and climbed up the rocky slopes, until we reached a secret cave entrance. It was cleverly concealed in an alcove, surrounded by dense foliage and rocky terrain. Only the faint beam of light peeking through the entrance gave away its location.

Aria's face was a mix of emotions as she spoke up, scanning

our group of people. "We can't just roll up in here with that many people. The Cave Town dwellers might drop dead before we even get a chance to say hello."

"Okay, let's split then," I announced.

"I'll go with Any and you guys just wait here, okay?" she tried, her forehead creased with worry.

"Not a chance," I retorted.

"How about we'll travel in a group of four?" Any suggested. "Better safe than sorry."

I agreed and looked to Ash, Briz, and Isix. "I go with Any, Aria and Ebony. Can you watch that one?" I nodded at Illiam, who was rooted to the spot by Ebony's side, still scowling at me like I was the devil itself.

Isix and Briz nodded in agreement, and Ash rolled his eyes. "Of course, I have to babysit."

"Keep your chin up," I called to Illiam, hoping he would protest, but all I saw was a deep redness spreading across his cheeks. I guessed he wasn't used to being left behind.

"It's going to be quick," Aria said, looking at him over her shoulder and there was this little prick in my heart again. Damn. I wanted to smash that man's head.

With Aria leading the way, we ventured into the cave, the darkness enveloping us like a shroud. Suddenly, a faint hum resonated from the depths, beckoning us forward as we cautiously navigated the rocky terrain.

Slowly but surely, my eyes began to adjust to the dimly lit surroundings, revealing a treacherous path lined with jagged rocks that resembled the sharp fangs of some ancient beast. The musty scent of damp earth filled my nostrils.

In the distance, a cluster of lights flickered like a vibrant constellation, drawing us closer to the glow of slim candles. Arched structures and towering pillars loomed overhead, stalagmites stretching towards us from the ceiling like glittering, icy spears. The weight of centuries past hung heavy in the air, as if the very walls of this place had borne witness to the secrets of generations long gone.

"I've never been here but they really did dig a city into the mountains," I said, stopping right next to Aria.

"Yup," she said, her gaze flying over her former hometown.

I saw Any and Ebony stepping away, suddenly very interested in the dripping stalagmites.

"Aria," I said, touching the small of her back. "How much longer do you plan on ignoring me? This is ridiculous."

She turned her head to meet my gaze, her eyes sparking with a mixture of fury and hurt. "Oh, well that just depends, doesn't it?" she snapped, her words biting like the winter wind. "Perhaps you could have mentioned the fact that you forced me into a marriage before I started to feel like a complete fool!"

I swallowed. "You know..."

A sharp, angry hiss escaped from Aria's lips as she snatched her wrist away from my grasp, displaying the tattoo with an indignant

flourish. "Yes, I know. That's not a bond. That's a skulling handfasting tattoo."

"You're right, it is. But I didn't force you into anything."

"Oh, please. You can't expect me to believe that I willingly married a lying, ruthless whatever you are."

My eyebrows shot up in surprise. "Whatever I am?"

"Yes, I have absolutely no clue *what* you are," she said, her voice laced with suspicion. "But I'll find out. And once I do, I'll decide if I ever want to talk to you again, because I think you did some serious skulling shit."

A wave of sadness washed over me, but I tried not to let it show in my voice. She was right, though. I did fuck up. Big time.

Suddenly, Aria's gaze shifted, fixating on a peculiarly luminous blue blossom nestled amongst the undergrowth. She lowered herself into a crouch, her finger extended towards the flower. I watched her curiously as she whispered, "Oh, skull…"

"What?" I asked.

"No, they can't be serious. Do you see the same flowers as I do?" I followed her line of sight. Blue blossoms. Everywhere.

My heart sank as I realized what that meant. "Oh, for fuck's sake, no."

"What?" Ebony asked, stepping closer.

"Blossom Eve," Aria repeated, swallowing. "Cave Town's most stupid holiday. It's the worst night to sneak around and steal a trunk full of Bloodcoins you could think of."

CHAPTER TWENTY-THREE
LYNNE

"What are you doing?" Rio said.

"Undressing," I muttered as I took off my shoes.

"Is this your way of coping with being back home?"

Any asked with a grim expression on his face.

I threw both of my shoes at him and caught him off guard. Any flailed his arms in a desperate attempt to catch them but they both hit the ground with a loud thud.

"Cave Town dwellers have strange customs, and we can't just walk in on them wearing Blood and Bone Court fashion. So, yes, I'm afraid we all have to be naked. So, if you would go on? It's just skin guys. No big deal."

I sighed deeply and started to undo my corset.

Hell, these dwellers would have a heart attack and drop dead on the spot if we refused to get rid of these clothes, they couldn't even hear the name of our rulers. So, we had to blend in, and by blend in I meant be utterly naked. I had no clue why, but seeing naked people walking down the streets was normal to them. Some wore loincloths, others fur but plenty people preferred to be naked. They'd literally run away screaming when they'd see us in dresses. But naked? All good. I tried to figure them out all my life and never fully got them. So, there was absolutely no time to start understanding them now.

Ebony sighed, rolling her eyes. "I heard these people are nuts but this is just…"

"Stop whining and get undressed," Rio said, unbuttoning his shirt.

"Watch your back the next time you close your eyes," she hissed, her tone laced with threat.

I had to bite my tongue to keep from chuckling. Sometimes, I found myself appreciating her spirit.

I turned to leave Any and Ebony some privacy since it was a little strange to see my brother undress, especially with his awkward movements. His pale skin was red like a beet and he sought cover, hoping to disappear into the shadows, but found no respite. There was no more veil to shield him, no more cloak to obscure him. He stood exposed, the shyness all over him. Maybe it was because he had seen Rio naked? Or maybe he still had a little crush on him?

Well, I knew I said it's only skin but the minute I saw Rio gently lifting the collar to loosen his shirt, I couldn't help but feel a flush of embarrassment as well. Not because of him. Because of me. Because it turned me on. I swallowed and tried to forget the scene that was playing in front of my eyes now. The way he kissed me in Catterville. The way he claimed my body. Claimed me.

As he continued to undress, my pulse quickened, and I just couldn't look away.

"Lynne," Bory hissed, prodding my knee with a jab of his finger. "What the hell are you doing? You can't just stare at him like he's some kind of TV show. Oh, that reminds me of the Bachelor. Ah," he sighed. "Those were good times."

I blinked and tore my gaze away from Rio, feeling a flush of embarrassment burn my cheeks. Skull, why was I acting like such an idiot? But even as I turned away, I couldn't help stealing a quick glance back and almost gasped as I saw his dick.

Hell, I acted like I've never seen him like this.

That's when Rio shot me a sly grin, his eyes sparkling with amusement, fully aware of the naughty ideas that were crossing my mind now. That son of a witch.

I cleared my throat, forcing myself to look away. "Bory," I said, trying to keep my voice steady. "Why don't you go ahead and scout out the route to our cave? We need to get there quickly, without getting sidetracked."

"You're funny," Bory said, pulling my shoes into a dark corner since I forgot to hide them. I tossed him my vest and he stuffed it right in too. "As soon as they see your white hair you're the center of

their attention again, and it's Blossom Eve too. I have a feeling that hiding won't work."

"I know," I hissed, trying to ignore the fact that Rio was naked behind me. Naked. "That's why they can't... um... see us. So go ahead and check which way is the... safest."

"Aye, aye," Bory said and hopped away until I could only see a small blue ball kicking up the dust.

As I undid my blouse, I felt a strange presence behind me, watching me and my knees went weak just at the thought of it.

"By the Stix, this is awkward," Ebony said as I heard her wriggling herself out of her trousers.

I nodded. Most of all it was awkward because I wanted to throw myself at Rio so bad. I didn't care about Ebony. Although her body was a weapon. Those boobs—okay I had to glance away because now it was getting awkward.

"Where can I put this?" Any asked, holding a ball of clothes in his hands.

"In the corner, there," I said, undoing my dress laces. There was a shifting behind me and the minute Ebony and Any started to hide their clothes, Rio touched my waist. He took a step closer, and I could feel the heat radiating off of his body.

"May I help you?" he said, his hot breath caressing my neck. Oh gods...

I nodded since I apparently forgot how to speak.

"Good," he said, his voice so skulling seductive. "Because I need to touch you right now."

With that, he turned me around and pulled the laces and ties out of my dress loops and freed me of my bodice. Then he stripped down my blouse and I suddenly felt pretty self-conscious. Once he loosened the laces of my skirt it fell on the ground and then we just stood there. Utterly naked. The hair on my nape rose as he gently touched the small of my back. I wanted to say something, but Any cleared his throat and Rio stepped away from me.

Thank the gods.

My cheeks burned and I rushed forward, not looking anywhere but the stony street before us.

"Follow me," I said, trailing behind Bory and not thinking about Rio staring at my naked ass.

BORY MET us right before we arrived at the Main Street and told us to enter my cave through Stone Garden. As we hurried over several bridges the chaos below us grew louder. Blossom Eve was in full swing. Although I tried to not look at Rio and the others, I saw Any and Ebony lingering behind, captivated by the enigmatic blue blossoms that seemed to crop up all around us. Thousands of thousands of petals were glowing in the soft blue light of some hidden gems in the rocks, reminding me of times these flowers meant everything to me...

"Beautiful," I heard Ebony whisper, and she was right.

Cave Town was stunning on Blossom Eve but instead of celebrating the beauty that was given to us once a year, cave town dwellers used the day to drink themselves into oblivion.

"What do you guys celebrate on Blossom Eve?" Any asked, his gaze fixed and unblinking, as if he didn't want to miss a single detail.

I ducked under a long hanging stalactite and glanced to Any over my shoulder while the bluish light glittered in his hair like sparkles. "On this night all Cave Town dwellers would come together to celebrate the blue blossoms. They would dance and sing, feast and make merry, as if it were their last day in this world. They believe that the blue flowers have the power to wash away our sins and purify our souls, preparing us for the next journey. It's the only night where kids had to stay in, since over the years Blossom Eve got more dangerous, because some people would lose their mind."

Of course, I always got out and took part in the festival until I found it stupid like hell.

"Too much alcohol?" Ebony asked and stepped over another sea of blue flowers.

"Upon other stuff, yeah," I said.

Cave Town dwellers took everything that could blur their minds on Blossom Eve since they believed it to be their last day of suffering. I stopped believing in this day when I noticed that actually no one was granted salvation. Ever. The few that did die on that day drank too much or ate the wrong things, so they actually died a bad

death. But since people went crazy that night, some wanted to strongly believe that these few people were granted freedom from the Shadow King himself. Such idiots.

"I never knew that the Underworld could look this beautiful," Any said.

He stopped and touched one of the little flowers with his index finger, his lips parted in a silent expression of awe, as if even the slightest sound might shatter the beautiful moment. When he withdrew his finger its tip was coated in a delicate dust that sparkled like a million tiny diamonds.

Rio chuckled and my eyes flicked back to him. "There is always a glimmer of light in the darkness—"

"—and a blossom of beauty in the shadows," I finished, looking at Rio in surprise. "How do you know that saying? Nana said it each year on Blossom Eve."

Rio, Any and Ebony suddenly stared at each other, and I could tell they were each lost in thought. I had no idea what was going on, but whatever it was, it was clearly important to all of them.

"It's an old saying," Rio muttered, almost to himself as if he finally understood the meaning behind it. "But I never associated it with Cave Town."

Ebony pointed at the flowers. "Fits altogether though, in a terribly good way."

Rio nodded and went ahead. Even though I wanted to desperately know what they were talking about, I followed in silence. I figured it had to do with that damned curse.

We hurried through a short tunnel, and I fell into step with Rio. I could feel his body's warmth and the electricity between us and wanted to get rid of it. I wanted to despise him, hate him but I just couldn't. This need I felt whenever he was near me got stronger and right now, I could barely hold myself from touching him again. I guessed Blossom Eve's magic had its hand in this too. I had heard that it intensified people's wishes.

"I can't wait to be with you," he whispered to me, his voice thick with passion, making it all worse again.

My heart thumped in my chest, and I quickly checked to see if Any or Ebony had heard him. But they were too busy marveling to pay attention.

I didn't answer and the silence stretched between us again until I started to see the truth in his eyes. He was stuck in this situation as much as I was. Deep down something in me hoped, just a little flicker—maybe it was just denial or wishful thinking—but I honestly hoped that one day I'd wake up and my life suddenly made sense because right now, my life felt like I had fallen into a deep, deep hole.

One that I'd never be able to climb out of again.

Suddenly, there was a rustle in the shadows behind us. I spun around, but there was nothing there. "Did you hear that too?" I asked Bory, who had been walking a few steps ahead of us.

"No—what?" he replied.

"Probably me," a very familiar voice said.

We whirled around and Marlina slowly came into view, her lips pressed together with a knowing smirk. Like always that woman couldn't be topped with smugness. Oh I didn't miss her at all. "Back again, huh?"

My gaze flicked to Marlina. Her body was draped in garlands of petals, a veil of painted patterns in hues of blue that barely concealed her curves. Spirals etched into her skin flowed like water, while dots resembling raindrops on marble dotted her flesh. Blossom Eve was a sacred night, for in the Underworld, color was a rarity—and the sight of such flowers was truly a gift. On some days, like Storm Day, leaves with the fiery hues of oranges clung to the trees, turning a deep shade of crimson as the day drew to a close. But on Blossom Eve, a strange darkness descended upon Cave Town.

It was different from any other day since a chilling sense of otherworldly energy filled the air. It was odd and kind of fascinating. From out of nowhere, inky tendrils writhed up from the earth, unfurling buds that swelled with a menacing intensity as the clock struck closer to midnight. And when the skulls in the sky began to dim, a bewitching sea of stunning blue blossoms erupted across Cave Town. Just like that.

Once they've bloomed, people of Cave Town picked the flowers and decorated the caves, made clothes, put them in our food, made paint powder and drew beautiful patterns on our bodies just like Marlina had done. It was a sign that everything and nothing was valid that night. No rules for one day, because theoretically tomorrow everything would end.

"We thought you were dead, Lynne," Marlina said, crossing her arms.

As her smoldering gaze landed on Rio, I couldn't help but notice the unmistakable glint of attraction in her eyes. At least she had some sense left in that pretty little head of hers. Instinctively, I reached out and placed a hand on Rio's bicep, staking my claim. Rio immediately caught on and his trademark smirk sent my pulse racing. I took a deep breath, trying to quell the rising heat between us.

Marlina blinked at the sight of my hand but started to play with a strand of hair, pinning Rio down with her gaze. "And who are you?"

"Her hus—

"ky—husky," I finished, fighting the urge to facepalm myself. My Husky? Why in the world would I say something idiotic like that? That's it. I just wasn't meant for social interaction.

Marlina's disapproving expression mirrored the disappointment I had in myself. Even Rio and Any looked at me with a furrowed brow. Oh skull... However, Ebony was the only one who found humor in my blunder. She chuckled and shook her head, as if pleading for divine intervention.

"Erm... I mean his name is Husky, you see, the blue eyes. Like some dogs I saw on Ear... skull. Erm. It doesn't matter. So, I met these three and we want to have fun... on Blossom Eve."

With eyes darting from Ebony to Any then back to Ebony, disbelief etched on Marlina's face. "I forgot about how weird you are... and pardon me for asking but you want to do what? Take part in Blossom Eve? Since when? Like you ever cared about anything around here."

"Well, I've been busy providing for you, Marlina. No time for fun. My money should make life a bit easier for you all today, doesn't it?"

"Your money goes to the orphans," Marlina said sternly. "Nana doesn't give us shit."

I shrugged. "Pity, but think of it this way, I'm taking care of the meals for the kids. Less mouths to feed for you."

Marlina narrowed her eyes. "What a wonderful person you are, indeed. So, I'll see you at the market. If not, I'll alert the others and tell them you're up to something."

"We'll be there," I said, curling my hands into fists. Actually, I wanted to avoid the market with all I got. "I just need to grab something from my cave first."

"Oh," Marlina said, tapping her chin thoughtfully as if she were considering something. "We cleared it out. I don't think you'll find a lot."

My stomach dropped. "You did... what?" I took a step closer, ready to unleash my fury.

"Did you really think that you can just run away with your dragon and we'll ignore it? I mean there was plenty of trash in your cave but there were a few things we could use. Desperate times call for desperate measures... Such a wonderful person like you wouldn't mind, right?"

I clenched my fists, wanting nothing more than to pummel her into the ground but suddenly, Rio's strong arms slipped around my waist and I halted in my tracks. His fingertips danced along my hip bone and the anger that had been boiling inside me vanished. All I could focus on was the fact that he wasn't allowed to trace any lower

—yet his touch sent sparks through me. My rage subsided and got replaced by a deep warmth that spread from my core, coursing through my veins. I swallowed and grabbed his hands to keep them from creeping into dangerous territory and glared at Marlina who watched our every step with an open mouth. "If you've stolen from me, you will regret it."

"We'll see about that," Marlina laughed and scurried across the bridge toward the tunnel behind us, eager to get away from me and hide behind some stronger ones. "I'd hurry, because I'm sure Hugo and Driver would like to know what you're doing here," she shouted. Her voice echoed off the thick stone walls with a sharp clarity, reverberating harshly in the enclosed space.

I sighed. I didn't want to deal with those idiots. So, we had to go.

Quickly.

"Come on," I said and dashed forward, praying they hadn't found my Bloodcoins.

CHAPTER TWENTY-FOUR
RIO

We perched atop the cliff near Aria's cave, listening to her screams echoing through the valley. Ebony had her head on Any's shoulder, while I kept my gaze fixed to the road, lined with a carpet of blue flowers.

"Can't we get her to stop?" Ebony asked, rolling her eyes.

"She'll calm down eventually," Bory said, flinching as we heard an object crash from inside the cave.

"That's it," yelled Aria. "I'm done with this people."

"So, we've come all this way for nothing?" Ebony said, and I shrugged.

"Someone will have the coins we need, so all we can do is get them," I reminded her.

"It's just too much of a hassle," Ebony grumbled. Another crash. I winced at her. "You said that already."

"It still pisses me off." Ebony sighed. "It's getting harder and harder to stay patient, you owe us when this is over."

"I know," I said, and we all fell into a tense silence.

"Oh, oh!" we suddenly heard from Aria. When Bory and I looked at each other, a mixture of surprise and confusion filled us.

"That's unusual," Bory said.

Without a word, I set off to the cave to check what was going on.

Aria's cave was completely torn apart.

As I surveyed it, memories flooded my mind. I remembered how she used to carve shelves into the rock and adorn them with trinkets from the human world, like toothbrushes and small figurines. She had told me all about it. But now, the shelves were empty, stripped of their treasures. All that remained were shattered goods and rocks...

The sight of Aria crouched on the floor, completely naked, took my breath away and I blushed. I had to look away to stop myself from taking her right there.

"What's wrong?" I said, breaking the silence as I stared at the empty shelves for the hundredth time.

"I found a hair!" she screamed, her eyes widening as she stared at the floor. I followed her gaze, and noticed the small crevice in the stone. It seemed like a secret hiding place. A large stone lay next to it, telling us that it's been indeed found by others.

"A hair?" I asked, my curiosity piqued.

A smile stretched across her face as she stood up, holding out a silver, frizzy strand in her hand. "It's Mal's!"

"So, this means what? That he must have the coins? Let's give him a lesson then."

She shook her head. "No, Mal is... was my best friend and I think he rescued the coins for me before they stole all that I had. These skulling idiots. But yeah, let's go to him."

The fury that was just moments ago contorting her face disappeared in a flash and got replaced with an expression of profound sorrow. I felt my heart sink at the sight, unsure of which emotion I should feel more strongly—anger or pity.

So, I stepped closer and stroked her cheek. My sudden

closeness seemed to upset her, because she fell back a few steps until she was leaning against the wall, looking up at me. A vulnerable gaze full of submissiveness. I couldn't help but corner her and leaned in to kiss her neck.

"Rio," she said, and I wasn't sure if it was a plea or a warning.

The closer I got, the more I could feel her warmth against me the more I wanted her, so I kissed her. Her lips were like velvet, inviting me to take them with a passion, and when I pressed my own against them once more I felt a sudden spark, a jolt of electricity that left me lightheaded with desire. I couldn't resist deepening the kiss, exploring every inch of her mouth with my tongue. Holding her close, I took in the softness of her curves against my bare skin, and I knew that I never wanted to let her go again. Aria's arms wrapped around me, and I pulled her close, my hands brushing over her breasts, cupping them and squeezing hard.

"Hell, I want you so much," I whispered against her lips. "Gods... I hate you," she said but kissed me nonetheless.

I could feel her heart racing against mine, and I knew she was just as eager to take it further as I was. We could hear the others talking outside and the thrill that they could enter the cave and spot us, made me want this even more. I wanted to moan when her fingernails slightly scratched down my back but we had to be silent so I bit her lip instead, making her sigh a little. Our kisses were filled with an intensity that made my head spin, and all I wanted was for the moment to last forever.

My hands moved slowly down Aria's waist, exploring every inch until it eventually settled between her legs. She gasped in pleasure as I touched her clit and I felt her press herself against my fingers even harder. Our lips locked again as we stood there, exploring each other's mouths passionately.

But as much as I wanted to fuck her right now, I knew that

this wasn't the time nor the place. With one last lingering kiss, we reluctantly pulled apart and stared into each other's eyes, breathing heavily.

Then she opened her mouth and I thought she'd say something but no, all she did was slap me with full force.

The sting burned on my skin and I looked at her in sheer surprise.

"What the fuck, Aria?" I said, rubbing my cheek.

"Stop seducing me with your stupid eyes and your damned face. Being pretty isn't enough, Rio. I need to understand what's happening. I can't play hubby and wifey or whatever you want to do with me. I need closure and my Bloodcoins." She growled and stomped outside.

I rolled my eyes and went after her. "Well you didn't actually stop me from kissing you, did you?"

"No, because my body is not to be trusted but thank Styx I'm capable of using my brain too," she said and stepped outside to tell the others we had to visit her friend Mal.

I took a minute before I went out, I didn't want the others to see how horny that woman made me. I silently cursed all witches. If only I could tell one fucking thing—it would make anything so much easier.

My wife was stubborn like a mule.

WHEN WE REACHED THE CAVE, its entrance was all dark and moody, framed by furs that were hanging from the walls. Each one was a different shade of earthy browns and deep black, swaying in the breeze like curtains in front of a mysterious doorway. The smell of herbs was so strong, it hit us before we even entered. It was a mix of mustiness and sweetness, like someone had just mowed the lawn or hiked through a damp forest. Aria just straight-up rushed in, no warning or anything, but Ebony and I hung back, feeling a bit more cautious.

"In there?" Ebony said, wrinkling her nose. I nodded. "Looks like it."

"I'll stay out," Any said firmly.

I grabbed them both, my hands gripping the back of their necks. "Stop whining, you guys are Horsemen and this is just a cave. Get in there."

"If only you knew," Bory muttered, taking a deep breath before following Aria.

I straight-up pushed my crew into that cave, lifting up the skins so we could enter. But the second we stepped in, it hit us like a ton of bricks—that sweet and herby aroma mixed with the funky smell of animal hide. It was unique for sure. The walls were lined with thick, luscious furs, all lit up by a flickering candle that cast a warm and cozy glow all around.

In the middle of the cave, Aria was posted up with a man who had long silver dreadlocks and was rocking a leather loin-cloth like it was nothing. He went in for a hug, but Aria wasn't having it and froze, straight-up standing there butt naked. Of course, I was about to protest, but he just rolled his eyes and hugged her anyway. Aria shot me a look that told me everything was okay. So, I tried to relax.

"Mal, let go of me," she said, her voice trembling as she tried to push away her muscular friend.

"Yeah, well," he replied, looking away. "It's been a long time since you've visited my cave, it's always a rush in the court. But... oh, you... brought company?" His hazel eyes swiveled over our troupe, and I could see Ebony tensing up, still not yet at ease in her own skin. When Mal's gaze landed upon Any, his eyes widened in shock and he paused for a moment. I narrowed my eyes at him. This was strange. Did they know each other?

"Mal?" said Aria, nudging him. "What's wrong? Sorry, shouldn't have just brought them along but we—"

"What are *you* doing here?" he cut her off, his eyes still glued on Any, who refused to meet his gaze. I knew Any for many, many years now and he never acted like this before. Something was bothering him about this man. From the blush on his cheeks I could tell he was... excited.

"I don't know what you mean," Any replied stubbornly.

Mal's eyebrows knitted together in a scowl. "You... we know each other, you were at the harvesting festival at the Blood Court—the Dance of the Dead?"

"You must have me confused," Any interjected quickly, his voice rising with an edge of panic that only I seemed to recognize.

He lied. But why?

"No, I'm not," Mal said and the tension between them grew thicker and thicker.

Only then did I fully realize what Mal had said. The Dance of the Dead. Why should Any celebrate the Blood Queen... I glanced sideways at him, and he slowly turned around, trying to act casual as he faced me. I knew he lived in the Blood Court because of their deal on Earth, but he claimed to steer clear of the queen and her rituals. He said he avoided her like the plague. And since Aria didn't have any connection with him either, never saw him there, I thought he was telling the truth.

But then there it was.

A glint in his eyes that told me he hid something from me. I curled my fingers into a fist.

"Okaaaay," Aria chimed in with a nervous laugh, "that was weird but whatever, you might mistake him. He's my brother and there's no way you can know him because his drop was just recently and that's—"She stopped, her finger pointing at me as if she didn't know how to introduce me.

I decided to temporarily ignore Any. I would talk to him in private. Something was going on, and I couldn't afford for him to hide it from me, especially if he's hanging out with the Blood Queen behind my back.

My gaze flicked to Aria and I smirked. "I'm her hus—"

"—hush, hush, *I* want to introduce you," she interrupted, and I couldn't hold back a laugh, she just hated that we're married. Oh, if she only knew how it went down, she wouldn't hate it and tell everyone that she's my wife. "So that's Rio… you know who… ah you know what. We actually don't have the time for such a long story but I'm gonna tell you everything later!" She huffed another nervous laugh. But her hesitation didn't seem to catch his attention, he was still surprised by Any's presence.

"Oh, and these are the Bone Queen's Horsemen," Aria blurted out.

Mal's eyes bulged out. "Horsemen?" he said, as if the mere mention of them sent shivers down his spine.

Aria brushed off his concern with a flick of her hand. "Yeah, but don't sweat it. For now, they're not gonna go crazy or anything. Mal, listen, I'm here because those idiots in Cave Town ransacked my place. Please, please tell me you found my things."

Mal looked at her gravely and shook his head, crushing Aria's hope. "Sorry, I haven't."

Aria's hands balled into fists as she tried to process what this meant. But as Mal looked at her, he couldn't keep up the act any longer and her mouth fell open as she nudged him and said, "Mal! Do you have the coins?"

He chuckled. "Come on. You really think I'd let them loot your cave? I've got them right here."

Aria's body softened as a wave of relief washed over her and Mal broke out into a smile.

"You're such a jerk, you know that?" Aria grinned.

Mal just shrugged. "Hey, you can't blame me for having a little fun. Besides, I knew you'd be worried sick if you thought it was really lost."

"Who wouldn't be?" Aria said, jabbing a finger into his chest. "How many coins did you steal?"

"Two."

"So, it's three..." Aria said. "Fine, I hope you bought better dresses with it."

"I did," Mal grinned and quickly glanced at Any, who still tried hard to ignore him.

I really wanted to know what was going on between them. This was not a chance encounter, and I couldn't help but feel that there was a lot I was missing out on. I made a note to myself to try and corner him when we were alone and get the truth out of him.

Mal disappeared into a side cave then and just a little later he came in with a big chest. He slammed it on the ground in front of us with a loud thud. "Here are your coins."

Aria squealed with delight and swiftly opened it, revealing an overflowing amount of Bloodcoins. Ebony sucked in the air between her teeth at the sight, and I met her gaze.

"Who has *this* many coins?" she whisper-shouted.

I drew my lips into a proud smile. A thief. My thief.

"Mal, there's more than two missing!" she exclaimed in shock, hovering over the chest like it was her baby.

He held his hands up in mock surrender. "I was hungry and didn't know when you'd be back!" Her hands ran over the slightly bloody gold coins and she pulled out a plastic doll from between them, causing me to laugh.

"What's that doll doing there?" I asked and a pang of sadness washed over me.

These were the type of dolls that Jamie enjoyed playing

with. It's funny how much I longed for my human life, for the feeling of having a family. My sisters and brothers... Ebony was right, I really had changed over the years and I like to believe that it made me a better man.

Well, I hoped so. I couldn't have been any worse.

"Oh, Mal, you saved my favorite finding, thank you," she said with a smile.

"Of course, you still play with dolls," Ebony joked.

Aria shot her a glare. "No, I just collect human stuff and liked that one best because we don't have anything nice here."

"One question, darling. Why do you have so many Blood-coins? Ain't it illegal to hoard them and snatch them away from souls?" I mused, voicing my thoughts out loud.

"Sue me," Aria responded sharply and our eyes met in a stormy exchange. "And you're the last person who needs to tell me about morality, Rio."

"Oh... Rio, you say?" Mal's voice purred as he sized me up, his gaze predatory. "Quite the catch. So, he's the one you put yourself in danger for, right?"

"Everyone makes mistakes," Aria interjected, her words weighted with the knowledge of our past.

Ebony leaned in close to me, her breath hot against my ear. "Seems like she's worth the trouble, yeah..." she whispered, and I shot her a glance that quieted her up. They always had their issues with Aria but they never had enough time to get to know her. No one had.

"And where do you plan on taking all these coins?" Mal asked. "To the oracle," I replied, bracing myself for his reaction.

Mal remained impassive. "You'll need most of them to gain entry."

Aria wasted no time in grabbing a bag and filling it with coins. "I know but we're in a tight spot, so we need the oracle. Let's hurry," she declared.

Mal's hand rested on Aria's arm, his voice softening. "But tonight is Blossom Eve, Lynne. You can't walk out without a shot. You can act all against culture and customs but it's bad luck leaving another's home without receiving a drink."

Aria frowned. "I hate Cave Town." She glanced at me as if she wanted to ask if we should take a drink or not.

I shrugged nonchalantly. "A drink won't hurt anyone. But I don't want to be the reason for all of us getting jinxed."

"True, and I really could use a shot," Ebony chimed in with a sigh. "Walking around parched is no fun."

Bory lifted a finger. "Oh, but we really shouldn't drink something that's coming from Mal, no, no, no. This isn't a good idea and I—"

"My vote is for a drink," Any added, drowning Bory out and sealing the deal.

So, Mal walked over to his desk and poured us each a small cup of blue liquor.

Bory, not giving up just yet, shifted uneasily and shot a questioning glance toward Aria. "Are you sure it's a good idea to take anything from him?"

He was right but I was immune to whatever he could put in there, so I quickly shot Ebony a glance, telling her silently that we'd take it. I had to know on which side her so-called friend was on.

"You really should start to live, little bear," Ebony said, taking a full brass cup from Mal's hands and examining it at arm's length. She sniffed it and a small smile formed in the corners of her mouth. "Well, this might be the only thing that can get me through this. Alcohol. My old faithful friend."

"Sounds like a problem to me," Any said to her.

When he reached for the mug Mal offered him, their fingers touched briefly and they exchanged a charged look. I met Aria's questioning gaze. Did Any just tell Mal to be quiet with his eyes?

Mal sighed, returned to his table and filled three more cups before bringing them to Aria and I.

"Bory? Want a drink too?" Mal asked, gesturing to the still frowning furball.

"No way! You're all gonna regret this!"

"Fine," Mal replied with a shrug before pouring himself a drink then holding the cup in the center.

We did the same and chanted: "To Blossom Eve!"

Then we drank the shot in one gulp, but my breath hitched the moment I swallowed, and all I could hear were Aria's damning words ringing in my ears: "Mal, you're a skulling asshole."

CHAPTER TWENTY-FIVE
LYNNE

"No. No. No. Lynne! This is no good. This is horrible."

I could hear Bory scream after us, but my skin felt numb and tingled like I stepped into a beehive. And worse: the

cave suddenly looked pink to me.

"Well, Bory," Mal said, swaying as he tried to put the cup down. He missed and it fell down, the brass clinking on stone. "If you'd like to have some fun too, there is still some Blossom Liquor left."

Bory cried out when he heard what we just drank, and my knees buckled.

Rio held out his hand and supported me from behind. The minute his hand touched me, a fire went through me, and I knew this wasn't good since all I could think about was him and I knew once the alcohol hit, my primal instincts would take over. Blossom Liquor was the strongest alcohol Cave Town had. It was only available on Blossom Eve and was supposed to numb our feelings so that we could do what we truly wanted. It made the souls cherish their last day... It blocked out moral instincts and allowed us to pursue what we really wish for. And hell, I knew what I—deep, deep down

—longed for.

"You... gave us blossom liquor?" Any said, propping himself up on the table, glowering at Mal.

My vision blurred even more but I saw Mal smirking. "Had to make you speak. I've thought about you, you know."

"Fuck," Any said and closed his eyes.

Rio started to caress my back and I turned to look up at him. His eyes were pitch black and I saw shadows swirling inside of them...

"What's with your eyes?" I whispered.

"You know what's with my eyes," he simply said and I shook my head.

"I don't..."

Then he bent down and kissed me, his lips brushing over mine. "You do. Think, Aria. Think..."

"Lynne," Bory said. "We need to go we—"

As the alcohol coursed through my veins, it was as if a switch had been flipped within me. My body moved without the direction of my mind, and in a flash, Mal had taken hold of Any's hand, leading him out of the cave.

"Let's go to the market and dance," he said, and I followed with Rio close behind me.

Then I saw a blur of motion in front of me. Ebony, running and jumping around with youthful energy and suddenly, the air was filled with the sweet smell of the blue blossoms which shimmered and twinkled in the faded light before us.

I heard Bory's heavy sigh and his words rang in my ears, "Yeah, let's just leave the Bloodcoins open here! Great idea! Bory will watch over them, anyway! Right?" I heard him grunt. "Argh! Have fun while I watch the only thing that will solve the skull we're in!"

I mumbled a half-hearted thanks and let Rio pull me down the street.

As we cautiously maneuvered through the caverns, shadows constantly shifted before our eyes and heat rose between us. And then my mind latched onto something else—a lone blue flower. I grabbed it and held out a hand to Rio, stopping him. Smiling, I ran the petals across Rio's hot skin, leaving a sparkly streak on his cheek. "God, you're mesmerizing," he muttered as I smeared the vibrant blue pigment along his body.

He tilted his head back and released a deep growl that reverberated through me. Picking up some flowers from the wall behind him, he traced them up my neck, over my breasts, down my ribs, and over my stomach, his now pitch-black eyes never leaving mine. With his fingertips hovering just above my vagina, a mischievous smile played on his lips. "You belong to me," he whispered, his lips brushing against mine. "Say that you're my wife. Please. Just once. I need to hear it."

"Why?" I breathed, my head spinning like a carousel, trying to take in all the shiny streaks of blue across his ripped body.

The air around us was filled with a mixture of spices and cooking food, but it was strangely mingled with something else—desire. Soon enough I'd have no control of myself anymore. I knew it. It's typical for Blossom Eve. And hell, I wanted him so much. Blossom Eve was the worst that could have happened to me because after this there was no denying anymore that I still deeply loved this man. This way I wasn't able to focus on what really mattered.

He nuzzled the nape of my neck with his nose whilst his fingers lingered on the curves of my ass, staining it in blue as well. "I need to hear it, please."

"I'm yours, I'm your wife," I whispered, each syllable dragging from beneath me, like I had no power to suppress them any longer. My mind feeling foggy and like a void of command.

"It's us against them, Aria," he said.

We took our time, moving at a leisurely pace as if afraid that rushing would ruin the moment. His thumb gently slid under my chin, tilting my face up to meet his gaze. He studied every detail, savoring each inch of my face and I couldn't help but do the same. His eyes, his straight nose, those high cheekbones, and his strong jawline. And those killer eyelashes, oh my gods, they made me melt. His thumb traced circles on my chin, teasingly gentle with each stroke.

"I love you, Aria," he whispered, and something inside me cracked wide open.

"I love you too."

Our eyes met once more in a silent moment of understanding right before he leaned in, his lips finding mine again with a hunger that took my breath away.

It was one of those moments that would define the rest of our lives, the kind that made me realize I had been right all along, and all my fears had come true. He wasn't just some ordinary gang boss or a random man exploring the Underworld. No, he was so much more than that—and I knew it. Deep, deep down I knew who he was. And I wanted to say it, but the longer we kissed, the more my mind turned into a foggy mess. Just as he raised my hip, bringing the tip of his cock to graze my wet entrance, he abruptly stopped.

"No," he said. "I want to dance with you first."

I held him back, my lust thicker than ever since I wanted him inside of me. Now. I yearned to keep him by my side, as close as possible, where no one could separate us. But he held me away from his body, grinning and shaking his head.

"Don't worry, I'm going to fuck you properly, but the longer we wait, the better it will be, darling. I want you to see fireworks," he said and I pouted.

"Trust me."

When we rounded the corner, the cave opened up into a huge market square. Everywhere we looked, there were people milling about, laughing and drinking. There were dozens of stalls set up, selling all kinds of goods, food everyone saved for this day and of course, Blossom Liquor. In the middle of the market there was a stage with several people playing instruments and a woman singing. We hesitantly tried to blend in with the crowd. Everyone's body was smeared with blue paint, many wore dresses made solely of flowers. As we came to a stall that offered flower dresses Rio took a huge blossom scarf.

"Mine," he said and wound the long, wide scarf around my body, skillfully crossing the ends over my chest. He cinched them at my waist, revealing a stunning makeshift dress that clung to my curves.

I quickly grabbed a flower loin cloth and wrapped it around his waist too. Even though I couldn't tell my left from my right, I had to make a point.

The music grew louder and the people around us kissed, danced and lived their last day.

"It's Blossom Night," I said as Rio dragged me into the middle of the dancing crowd. "No one cares about others. What they wear, who they are."

He pressed me against himself as we danced to the rhythm of an ancient song. "I care and if I see your curves any longer I might fuck you right here and now."

"You could," I teased.

"I want my privacy with you," he said. "And don't dare me."

"I love daring you."

Rio grabbed my hand, and before I knew it, I was spinning in dizzying circles to the beat. The music pulsing through my veins, and the rhythm of the beat calling out to me. I closed my eyes and let myself get lost in the moment, swaying to the music, pretending we had no problems at all.

We began to move together, our bodies in perfect harmony with the music and when I opened my eyes I was submerged in a sea of unknown faces—yet all that mattered was us and I guessed it was always like that for me as if my mind was clouded by a stronger force, telling me that all the answers I was searching for had to do with Rio.

His hands roamed my skin as our bodies moved together, a blanket of electricity radiating between us. His breath tickled my neck, sending a wave of icy chill down my spine, enveloping me in a cocoon of pleasure and desire.

The music transitioned to a slower tempo, and I felt him draw me closer. His lips hovered above mine as we swayed to the melody. Our eyes locked for a moment, before he leaned in and whispered softly into my ear. "Now tell me. Who am I, Aria? You know it."

A fire rekindled inside me that had long been dormant, and I felt myself burn in his embrace. His hands moved slowly down my back, setting off tiny sparks that flew through my body and left me trembling with anticipation. I knew that right now, small shadows danced over my heated skin. As the song ended and he pulled away, I opened my eyes and saw his face burning with passion.

As a new song began, the harp's delicate pluck hung in the air, embracing us like a sweet caress. Then, it soared into a whirlwind of notes, whispering through the room like a dream. In that very moment, I absorbed him like a thirsty desert soaked up the rain.

And it was then, as the shadows danced in his eyes again. I swallowed. "I'm afraid to be right."

"Don't be," he said, brushing his lips against mine. "It will all turn out right."

There was a power soaring into him as he kissed me again. "Please let me fuck you," he whispered, and I felt dampness between my legs as a warmth ran through my body. My skin seemed to tingle from head to toe.

I didn't need to answer him, the curve of my lips was enough. I had expected to depart the same way we had come—on foot—but Rio had other plans. Instead, he unceremoniously raised his hands and snapped his fingers, the sound echoing like thunder in the calmness of the harp's music.

Immediately and without warning, the air around us began to swirl and churn, creating a rapidly growing storm cloud of dark black shadows. I looked around, but no one seemed to notice. Everyone still danced and partied.

The smoke then enveloped us, wrapping us in an inky cocoon. I looked up to see his face, but the both of us had already vanished into the darkness. There was no fear inside of me, only an inexplicable sense of anticipation and something so oddly familiar.

"Ah it feels good to be able to do this again," he sighed and I clung to him as we got swept away. A flash of light illuminated the night sky, and I knew that we had been transported into my former cave. Rio snapped again and a huge pile of white furs lay before us, a makeshift bed.

I smiled, feeling a warm rush of affection for him. This was why I hated Blossom Eve. It was primal. Entirely primal. And now I loved every second of it.

I reached out and ran my fingers through his hair, feeling the softness of it against my skin. As I leaned in I pressed my lips to his, relishing the feeling of his mouth against mine. I wrapped my arms around him, pulling him closer. The darkness crawled around me, enveloping me with icy fingers that sent shivers over my body. His shadows loomed and writhed as if alive, brushing against me and leaving trails of electrified static. Oh, I felt every single hair stand up as the chill raced up and down my spine.

"I'm gonna fuck you like you deserve it," he rasped and hell, my body craved it so I grabbed the back of his neck and pulled him towards me.

His hands moved lower, tracing circles and spirals on my bare skin until they cupped my ass.

He lifted me effortlessly, my legs wrapping around him as his arm held me close. Instead of carrying me to the bed, he strode out of my cave, his muscles flexing with each powerful step, igniting a never-ending desire within me. I moaned as I kissed his neck, the heat between us intensifying with each passing moment. Suddenly, I felt a rough stone against my backside and looked around to realize that he had brought me to the outer ledge in front of my cave, using the stones as a makeshift support.

So, I stretched out my arms to both sides. Down below the market still roiled with the hum of activity, a cacophonous clamor that seemed to build and grow with every passing moment. As I hovered above all of them, the people swarmed like ants through the streets, their singing and shouting a chaotic symphony while my stomach clenched with anticipation. I slid my fingertips down the shallow canyon between my breasts and liked the way Rio was looking at me. I felt daring. Rio hummed and seized my wrists, his grip tight. When he pulled my fingers to his mouth, he sucked at them and murmured a single word, "Mine."

I tipped my head back, sighing as he grasped my thigh and lifted my leg, propping my foot up on a stone below me. I crushed my fingers into his biceps, feeling the hard muscle tense and ripple beneath my touch as he lowered his face between my legs, right to my center of pleasure. My fingers traced down his arms until I was gripping his forearms tightly, feeling every contour of his skin as if it were a map leading to some unknown treasure.

"Skull, you're a force of nature," I breathed. "I am," he said and kissed my mound.

I gasped, my breath coming in ragged sobs now. My fingertips trembled as they traced the ridges of the cold stone while the voices of the party faded to a dull whisper.

As he expertly explored my depths, my clit throbbed beneath his tongue and a scream of pleasure bubbled forth from my lips. I clung desperately to the stones, keenly aware that it was him holding me up and saving me from falling down the abyss. I was one inch away from crashing down and hell, I liked the thrill. I liked that he was in charge and held me up, showing me exactly how strong he was.

His tongue moved in and out, the sensations intensifying each time. I felt my muscles tense and my heart race as I started to crest the peak of pleasure. His fingers gripped my thighs hard, as if he had a hard time to holding back from fucking me with his cock and I closed my eyes—let it take me away, my body arching and trembling as I gave myself up to him.

"I missed your taste so much, I could eat you up for years," he said in a dark, rumbling voice and blew a hot stream of breath across my damp folds. My heart raced faster with each passing second and I gripped the back of his head, trying to signal him to finally give me the pressure I wanted. But he only chuckled and the scratch of stubble made me moan again.

"Stop the teasing," I groaned.

"Oh, darling, I won't stop anything, nor will I let you come now." I tore at his hair, wanting to snap something at him but then I felt the wetness of his tongue sweep over my clitoris again and sighed deeply. It circled around my clit as his mouth explored me, his breaths becoming shorter and more ragged.

One of his strong hands secured my back as he moved up my legs to my breast. He stroked over my pebbled nipples and then his fingers swept in under his tongue, sliding into me and feeling me up, each staccato thrust making me jerk and writhe beneath him. Oh, his fingers were thick and strong, and a blend of pain and pleasure cascaded over my body, pushing me closer and closer and closer to the edge of delight then and then—he paused.

He skulling *paused*.

I opened my eyes and saw Rio above me, his towering frame cast in a shadowy silhouette. His cock was as hard as steel as he looked down, his face a mask of sheer desire. I let out a contented sigh at the sight of him, letting my eyes roam over the peaks and valleys of his abs. Gods, he was so handsome. The way his dark hair fell onto his forehead, his stubby beard formed a shadow on his cheeks, how his strong jaw and those deliciously long eyelashes looked...

"Touch me," I said and he smiled as he closed the little space between us again, his hard cock teasingly rubbing against my thigh. I lifted my hips, grinding myself against it. When he bent down, he moaned and kissed me. The heat between us rose as his hands cupped my face and pulled me closer, the tip of his cock at my entrance, teasing me, giving me the faint idea of relief. I tried to push him into me, but Rio refused, shaking his head. I glanced briefly at the barbed wire on his biceps and let out a sigh.

"Oh so wet and wanting..."

"Stop it," I said and grabbed his hair, yanking his face down to me.

His lips crashed down on mine into a furious kiss and my heartbeat went off the scale in a split second. I loosened my grip on his hair and tore my fingernails into his back as my impatience kept growing.

"What do you want?" he said, and I felt him smiling against my neck, as his tongue swirled on my dampened skin.

"You."

"Tell me what you want, darling." The tip of his cock caressed my folds again and I shuddered.

"I want you to love me," I said.

"I do love you," he said and finally pushed his dick inside me. "I've always loved you. You and no one else."

It was then as it hit me...he's always been talking about me all along when he told me about his wife. Like, he never had another girl when we were not together. And damn, it felt so good when he was inside me, moving slow and steady. It was like my mind was screaming that he's my man, my husband.

He moved faster and harder. I grabbed the stone beneath me, ramming my fingernails into the rough stone. I sighed and closed my eyes, but Rio placed a hand around my chin, making me look at him.

"Eyes on me," he demanded. "I want to see you while fucking you. I missed your pretty face, that"—he moaned and pushed even deeper into me—"look on your face when you enjoy me."

I pinned him down with my gaze and once he was pleased with me, he lifted his hand again and squeezed my clit in between his index finger and thumb, rubbing it gently while he slid in and out of me. It felt like igniting a symphony of pure bliss and delight that sent shivers down my spine.

"Now tell me what you need, my queen." He stopped just halted inside of me. A scorching anger filled me up as my desperation for pleasure intensified.

I bucked my hips forcefully, my chest heaving as I sought to press my clit harder against Rio's fingers. His grip tightened painfully around my hip bone, stopping me until I'd tell him exactly what I needed. I growled ferociously, an animalistic sound that rose from the depths of me and echoed around the cave.

"What do you need?" he repeated, shadows dancing in his eyes again.

My sanity fractured like broken glass and every shard was a scream of pleasure inside my head. I had to find my release and fast. A sob of pure desperation tore from my throat as I struggled to find air to swallow and my own sanity began to slip away as he kept on rubbing my clit. I couldn't take it anymore, I couldn't take this prison a moment longer. I had to find the release or I would go mad.

"Fuck me, make me come. Please."

"Say it again," he pinched my clit and I moaned. "Please, make me come, Rio."

His calloused hands burned a trail up my skin as they crept up my legs, gripping onto my thighs and parting them wide. He slid out of me and thrusted into me until he reached my hilt. My legs quivered beneath his touch, trembling with anticipation. His grip tightened as if he wanted to consume me completely, to take away all of my secrets and replace them with his own desires.

He moved faster and harder and I crashed back, my back arching until half of my body hung down, my eyes on the market as my feet clung to him. Part of me anxious that I'd crash down, the other part thrilled as we were both close to climax.

"I have you," he breathed, and a cry of pleasure echoed off the walls. "I'll always have you, darling. Always."

An electricity of pleasure surged through me with each nanosecond that passed, more powerful than I ever thought possible. My core trembled and contracted as the waves of ecstasy rolled in, stronger with each wave until I was overwhelmed. I wanted to cry out in pleasure, yet the knowledge that Rio had complete control over my body sent a thrill of dark desire through me that demanded more.

"Deeper," I said and he gave me what I needed.

Finally, we both exploded in pure bliss, our bodies trembling with pleasure and our minds spinning in pure ecstasy as we moaned and then it happened. I understood.

I hoisted myself up and clung to him as I sobered up. Looking into his eyes I saw the shadows again as we panted and everything cleared up for me. "You never were drugged. The liquor didn't work on you..."

"No," he said, his thumb circling against my back.

He still was inside of me as reality crashed down on me.

I finally understood. I finally let the knowledge sink in. He was...

But this couldn't be true. No. Someone was messing with me.

Anger surged through me and I gripped a stone, before he knew what I was doing I slammed it against his head. He looked at me in shock as he staggered back and pulled me down with him as we both hit the ground. I lashed out again, hitting him but this time he was prepared.

His shadows strengthened and formed a kind of shield. So, I punched at it, but my blows did not hit him.

"Who the hell are you!" I shouted, glad that I was now back to my senses.

"I can't tell you," he yelled back. "You need to say it. All I can tell you is that I love you. That I fucking love you, Aria."

I shook my head, no longer accepting this man's lies. He wasn't Rio, he couldn't be.

As I stood there fighting against this unnatural pull the man had over me, I knew I had to use all the mana that was left in me to break free. I had to go to the oracle. Now. And find the truth but I needed to go without him. He blurred my decisions, and I needed clarity. Once and for all because if I was right... if he was who I thought. Nothing would matter anymore. I closed my eyes, focusing on my inner strength.

"Aria, what are you doing?" He started to move towards me, and I knew I had to act fast.

I opened my eyes and muttered, "Itanos ta e" under my breath and touched him.

"What—" He stretched his arms out, trying to reach me, trying to stop me but I already had summoned the stones behind me into tendrils that crashed down on him. My heart raced as he struggled against them, but I held my ground as they slowly drained my mana. I tried to not use it all, since I may have to do this again. I just hoped it all worked out, but I needed him to stay put now. I needed to find out who was lying to me, who I could trust.

He brought his hand to his chest, scanning his wounds and realizing that there were three claws in his chest that hadn't been there a moment before. But by then it was too late for him to run away, because the tendrils wrapped him up, until he became one with the stone. It wouldn't last long, and yet long enough for me to go to the oracle with Bory. Alone. Without him and his treacherous words.

I wasn't everyone's puppet.

I was tired of always doing what others wanted me to— tired of hiding.

No. I would find out what the heck was going on. All by myself.

CHAPTER TWENTY-SIX
LYNNE

Panting and shivering, I ran straight to Mal's cave and screamed Bory's name. My fingers trembling as I shooed him up from where he slept. The moment he saw me, his little mouth grew into a big O. "What happened—"

I grabbed the bag with the coins. "Run. We have to rush to the oracle. NOW!"

I sprinted off, knowing Bory would be soon on my heels. "What did you do?" Bory screamed behind me.

"It's all a mess. Apparently he... we need to go to the oracle or... or... Skull it!" I shouted in frustration, feeling a wave of vertigo overtake me. Bory was right. Again. I should never have drunk Blossom Liquor. My heart raced and I had to stop, propping myself against a stone wall and trying to take deep breaths.

"He apparently what?" His voice was gentle and calming.

I punched the wall, annoyed with myself for being so weak when it came to him.

"Lynne, you have to tell me what happened. I have no idea how to help you if—" I scooped him up and he let out a tiny squeal as I ran through Cave Town as fast as I could. I was lucky since thanks to Blossom Eve the streets were empty now, everyone was busy in their caves, making love, talking—whatever they wanted to do on their last day in the Underworld. Hell, I was so stupid.

"But what about the spell he holds on you?" Bory said once he was able to breathe more evenly again.

"I know a shortcut and let's just pray it's within reach."

"What shortcut?"

"It's not the first time I've visited the oracle, Bory. That's why I got the idea in the first place."

My heart raced as I hurried down the bridges and stony paths, stepping farther away from the safety of Cave Town. Dread filled me as I came closer to the entrance of the secret oracle, a mere rabbit hole, placed so close and yet so far from where I had grown up.

"What if Rio or the Horsemen find us?" Bory asked me, looking back in fear.

I nodded grimly knowing that if they were to come after us, they would likely take the long way. "Last time I managed to fly relatively far away with Soothie. If I'm right, then the oracle should work out as well."

"And if not?" shivered Bory.

"Then it will knock me out," I said firmly, pushing his worries aside. We both knew that Rio would be able to sense my presence, so we had to get to the entrance before he could track us down.

"I always thought the oracle was farther away," Bory said when I dropped him off in front of the hole.

"That's what a lot of people think, because the actual entrance is much bigger and more convoluted. Actually, the oracle is right next to Cave Town."

"That's odd," Bory commented. "And you want to... use this

entrance here?" He looked into the dark hole and frowned at the sight of the spider webs.

"Yes," I said and climbed in.

As I crawled forward, I noticed moss growing on some of the rocks, providing a subtle hint of color to an otherwise dark environment. The ground beneath me was damp from moisture, but it felt surprisingly warm against my skin. The path became narrower as I crawled along it, my body fitting perfectly into the tight spaces and it suddenly reminded me of when I had to hide in the ventilation shaft, when his schemes all came down and I saw Rio's true nature. Only to find out now that there was so much more...

When I heard water dripping somewhere ahead of me as well as strange chirps and squeaks echoing off every wall, I knew it wouldn't be long until we entered the Necromantion. I trudged forward into the dark maw of the cave, my heart pounding in my chest as I felt the oppressive weight looming in the distance.

"Lynne..." Bory whispered, his voice trembling.

I stopped and picked him up, stroking his back while I slowly stepped into the middle of the cave, right before us the entrance to the Necromantion.

We found ourselves standing in an immense hall that stretched out endlessly before us, its walls vanishing into the inky depths beyond. I couldn't help but gaze in awe at the towering marble columns that rose up from the ground, soaring towards the seemingly endless cavernous ceiling. The columns were so immaculately crafted that they appeared flawless, without even the slightest hint of a seam or blemish.

THE WHOLE SCENE looked as though we had stumbled upon a hidden sanctuary nestled deep within the heart of a cavern. A gasp escaped me when I caught sight of the fierce guardians that stood watch over the entrance. These towering statues, hewn from black stone, seemed to pulsate with an otherworldly glow. Each figure was locked in an eternal battle, their twisted and contorted forms seemingly frozen in time.

As I drew closer, I recognized the two infamous beasts that had been immortalized in stone. The first was Cerberus, the three-headed hound that guarded the gates of the Underworld. The second was the Chimera, a monstrous creature with the head of a lion, body of a goat, and the tail of a serpent. Their fearsome presence was almost overwhelming, and I couldn't help but feel a shiver run down my spine. As we made our way farther to the arch that led us inside of the temple, I could see that the walls were adorned with intricate carvings and frescoes. They depicted scenes from ancient myths and legends from the second dynasty, their colors still vibrant despite the passage of centuries.

I knew them like the back of my hand. Fairytales Nana told us when we were kids about gods that were long dead. The old gods— or rather titans, since there was no such a thing as a god. There was an abundance of revolution in the lives of our titans and now the third dynasty was ruling, led by Athena, Zeus' daughter. She usurped and sent him to Tartarus— punished him for the sins he committed against mankind. Since then, she began to rule over the three worlds and has done so for millennia. It was she who introduced the separation between the worlds, out of protection for the people.

My eyes swept over a picture of her, she stood before the humans, shielding them from Zeus' wrath. The artists painted her as a tall, stately figure with piercing gray eyes and long, dark hair that fell in loose waves around her face. She wore heavy armor, a helmet and a shield on her arm, leading the humans against her vengeful father.

I always loved the stories about Athena but times had changed. The titans don't like to be paid homage anymore, so there are hardly any more paintings about them. Athena stopped the glamour around the titans and ordered the people to stop making an image of their gods, to take a step back, away from the omnipotence of the titans and she succeeded since most of the gods are forgotten by now and only live in stories and fairytales. Although they still exist. All of them.

I made my way to the central chamber, where a deep pit beckoned me closer. I approached its edge cautiously, peering down into its depths. It was like looking into an abyss, a never-ending void filled with an unfathomable darkness.

Altars and offerings surrounded the pit. They were adorned with glittering gems and precious metals. As I stepped inside, the air felt heavy and oppressive, filled with an energy that was palpable.

I closed my eyes and took a deep breath, attempting to focus my thoughts.

"Where is... it?" Bory asked and I put him down.

"I need to contact the oracle first," I said, crouching in front of the pit. I had to beg the oracle to discover the secrets for me, if only for a glimpse of understanding.

I stretched out a finger and let it glide through the dark water in front of me while I unpacked the coins with my other hand, dropping each into the water. At first nothing happened, and I looked at Bory, his gaze fixed on me. When his eyes widened, I quickly looked back and realized that a crystal was coming out of the water. Bory darted back, but I remained rigidly in front of it.

Within seconds, spirits of the dead hovered around us like a swirling miasma, their faces twisted in tormented expressions of pain and regret. Bory squeezed himself against me and I put an arm around him, shielding him.

In hushed tones, I approached them, delicately urging them to call the oracle on my behalf. The hunger for answers consumed me, and I was prepared to go to any lengths to unearth them. "Where did you learn how to do this..." Bory's voice dropped to a whisper.

Well, that's maybe the strangest part of it all. "I... I just know it..."

"This is very old magic, Lynne... you can't... oh no." It was like realization hit over him. I avoided his gaze since I wasn't ready for him to tell me what he just found out about me. I needed some more answers first until I was able to piece back all the puzzles. "Later," I told him. "Please."

I could feel it now—a presence that seemed to thicken the air around me, a hushed whispering calling out from every corner of the temple. I rose to my feet and finally, the massive crystal before us glowed with an ethereal light, pulsing and shifting like a beating heart. I couldn't help but be awestruck by its beauty and power once again. It felt like it was ages ago since I'd seen it... until I felt this age within me too. This old knowledge... Back then I was even more clueless, now I knew it had to do with my former life. With the person I once was.

As I drew closer, the whispers grew louder until words began to form in my mind and yet—they were jumbled and incomprehensible, as though the pieces of the puzzle that were still missing talked to me, begging me to find them.

Taking a deep breath to steady myself, I closed my eyes and when I opened them again... there was the oracle. Clad in flowing white robes and somberly gazing at me with eyes that seemed to pierce straight through me. She flowed over the crystal as if she weighed nothing, was nothing like a spirit herself. Like back then she was unlike any soul I had ever seen before.

Although her face remained obscured by the hood that hung low, concealing her features in a veil of shadows, I caught glimpses of stray strands of hair that escaped the confines of the cloak. It glimmered like spun gold in the scant illumination. It was odd since her presence pressed down on me like an invisible force. But nevertheless, I drew closer. As I stepped forward, my gaze flicked to the oracle's robe. It was covered in strange, glowing symbols and runes, each one pulsing with an other-worldly energy.

"There you are. I expected you to visit me earlier, dear." The oracle spoke in a low, grave voice, and the symbols on the veil began to shift and change, as if responding to their words.

"You did?" I said, trying to breathe away the nervousness resigning within me.

"Yes, but sometimes even my predictions can't be exact," the oracle said, her voice echoing through the dimly-lit chamber. "What do you seek?"

"The truth," I replied, my voice trembling slightly. "I seek to understand the mysteries of the world and my place within it. I want to know who to trust."

The oracle was silent for a moment, her gaze fixed upon me. "The truth is a difficult path to walk," she said. "It requires courage, determination, and a willingness to face the darkest parts of oneself. Are you prepared for what you will find?"

I took a deep breath, steeling myself for the task ahead. "I am," I said. "I am ready to face the truth, whatever it may be."

The oracle nodded slowly, and her hand reached out towards the water beneath her. The symbols on her robe swirled around in a chaotic dance of light and shadow.

"What do you have for me in exchange?"

I took the bag from my shoulders, opened it and showed her

the rest of the coins I got for her. She didn't make a face, but the way her eyes glittered now told me that she loved nothing more than Bloodcoins. Well, who didn't...

Nodding pleasingly, she pointed to the pit in front of her.

"Come here, dear. Step inside and learn about the knowledge of the past," the oracle said. "Seek the truth of those who came before. Listen well, for the secrets of the dead are not easily revealed."

And with that, the oracle began to chant a song, her words weaving a complex tapestry of history and legend. As I hit the water, I felt my body's weight, it was like suddenly I felt every fiber of me.

First my feet, then my chest, buckling under the pressure of the cold and my head started to feel heavy. I think I heard Bory scream my name, but then my eyes slammed shut as the water rushed over me. It plowed through me, a thick liquid wall that sucked away all of the light in the world and then consumed me, eating me up.

CHAPTER TWENTY-SEVEN
LYNNE

Suddenly there was a jolt in my chest, followed by a blinding flash of light that made everything around me blur. For a moment, I felt disoriented, as if I was floating mid-air, even though I knew I just splashed into the pit.

All I saw was black. Nothing but black.

Then colors of red and white whirled back and forth in front of me, a sea of smears that twisted itself into spirals. I wanted to scream but couldn't. Hell, I didn't even know if I had a body or a mouth to scream! I looked around and the panic settled in, so I tried to focus on the swirls, tried to stay patient, tried to not lose my mind.

I breathed in.

Everything was fine... skulling fine. I breathed out.

Just the freaking oracle showing me something. All good.

And then—just like that—my vision changed and just like that, I was thrown into someone else's body, my head helplessly locked in place. I looked around with the stranger's eyes, surveying my new environment. I noticed slender hands adorned in heavy golden bangles that glinted in the sunlight. The person was wearing a white robe with glimmering fibers that sparkled like a million stars. Looking further, I could see a table made of solid gold with plates that shone like the sun. Where was I?

I saw how the body I was in lifted a hand and straightened some hair, showing some more features that reminded me of a girl's body. Strangely, her hair looked like mine... white-blonde. When her gaze slid down and I saw a body that was also very similar to mine, my non-existent heart dropped.

Skull.

That was me, wasn't it?

She raised her head and I saw a scene before me that I had never seen before. I seemed to be stuck in an ancient conference room of some sort? A grand chamber with a high ceiling supported by marble pillars that reached towards the heavens. The room was bathed in a warm, golden light, casting a surreal glow on everything within. My eyes flicked to the table in front of me. It was a massive, circular one made of pure gold with intricately carved designs depicting the various symbols of the several titans I knew of. Around the table were thirteen thrones, with exquisite detailing that showcased the unique characteristics of thirteen deities and the panic in me took over.

I was in the Pantheon. THE Pantheon. This couldn't be. It just couldn't.

I had no right to be in the Pantheon.

I had no right to be in the same room as the gods, I had no—

The girl's gaze shifted and I felt her scratching the skin on her hands with sharp nails. The soft sensation was so familiar that my mind stopped rotating. She was nervous too. When she looked around I noticed various artifacts and relics from the Pantheon scattered about. There were weapons, shields, and armor used by the gods during their battles, as well as various magical items that once belonged to them. My eyes fixed on the walls swept over the several sculptures of various gods and goddesses, depicting their exploits and adventures. The air in the room crackled with energy...

The girl stood on the sidelines and watched as people scurried around and as the seconds passed, even more people filled the room and then, the gods came in. I wanted to suck in the air between my teeth but since I had no control over my body, the girl did it for me. Her heart suddenly crashed against her ribcage and she pressed herself against the wall behind her.

I couldn't believe my eyes.

There they were. The gods of the new generation. Since Athena had overthrown the old gods it was them who ruled over the three worlds. And even though I knew that only few souls ever got the chance to see what I just saw, I was excited, the gods were sacred.

More than sacred. They were the heroes of all stories. In the Underworld, of course, the most important were our rulers, our gods. The Bone and Blood queen and the Shadow King. But there were nine others who ruled over the rest of the world: the water, the earth and the sky.

I never thought I would get to see them.

The sounds grew louder and louder, however, the person I was in looked at her hands again and I noticed her feet starting to wiggle. She had to be really nervous, no wonder if she was invited to the Pantheon. I saw out of the corner of her eye how the seats on the thrones were filling up and up and up. I could literally feel the power emanating from the gods and I was so glad that I wasn't sitting between the rows. Suddenly someone stopped in front of my eyes, blocking my view and touched the girl on the arm. She flinched.

Her eyes flew open and I saw... Nana. My stomach dropped.

What the hell was Nana doing here?

"Honey, what are you looking so shy about," she said, gently stroking her upper arms. I wished I could ask her why she was here and why she still looked the same. She didn't look younger nor older. Not a day. That was beyond creepy. "It's an honor to be invited to the council, smile a little."

The girl folded her arms. "I'd rather be at home, why does Hecate get to be at home?"

"Because she has other things to do," she snarled just the way she used to when she didn't want to continue the conversation. "I wish your mother could see this, Aria."

The girl sighed and I wished the ground to swallow me. This was me? My former self was allowed in the Pantheon?

"Without her sacrifice, this would never have been possible."

Nana nodded. "You're right but just take a look..." she spat. "At the disgrace. It's still too many Zeus supporters, just look at who's sitting among us, who dares to think they are better than us," her voice dropped to a whisper, and I realized that mentioning the dead ruler caused the girl... well cause me to feel uneasy too.

"Nana, please don't bring him up. We can't be sure who still backs the old system and Hecate was right, we should have never come..."

"Look, we must use this chance and—"

"Do you ever stop long enough to listen? I never wanted to come and all these gods make me scared."

"You belong here. You too are divine, just like them." I think my heart stopped.

"I am no god," my former self said. "Like many of us here."

"Silence!" An eerie storm blanketed the room, and everyone's eyes shifted to Athena as she burst through the door, the fabric of her sky-blue dress billowing around her. Some had admiration in their eyes, while others glared at her with contempt, maybe even hatred. I could feel the tensions thick in the air as she scanned the room, the titans, the gods, the divine... I remembered a few stories from Nana and got suspicious. She never just *told* us stories... she taught us the truth. Taught *me* the truth. I had the feeling that maybe nothing I knew was like it seemed. Nothing I believed in was. Nothing.

I remembered when she told us about the new council and that it now consisted of the children of the previous gods. How she made us learn the gods. She always emphasized on the problem that not all descended from Zeus and his siblings, some from other lines, which weren't prominent until Athena took the crown. It was important to her that all the gods were mixed, so now there were also demigods sitting here, gods whose one parent was a human. She wanted to make sure that the gods were more inclined to the humans...

"Thank you for coming," she said, sitting down and then motioned for the others to do the same. Athena's gaze met a stranger's across the table, and this was the moment I wanted to run.

Scream. Run away and vanish forever. This wasn't just any man.

It was Rio.

But he looked different... colder, less engaged with his surroundings. His fingers rippled across the golden table top and shadows formed beneath him like a dark mist.

"Present are the twelve rulers of the three worlds," Athena said, pointing to the gods. "Orpheus, son of Apollo, Triton and Theseus, sons of Poseidon, Plutus, son of Demeter, Phobos, child of Ares, Priapus and Hymenaeus, the children of Aphrodite and Dionysus, Pan, son of Hermes, Helene, my dear sister and daughter of Zeus and—" her gaze now flitted to the Bone Queen and then to the Blood Queen.

I held my breath for a moment.

I knew that all three rulers of the Underworld actually had different names, but no one knew what their true names were.

"The Children of Hades and Persephone: Macaria," she pointed to the Blood Queen and then to the Bone Queen. "Melinoe and last but not least, Zagrios."

I cringed, because it seemed that his nickname was due to his real name... and I never noticed. Never once did I find it weird that his name was so much alike to the name of a god... that's why he always said it was *his* name. Zagrios, but Rio for short. And skull this meant my assumptions were true.

He was Hades' only son. He was the Shadow King.

I wanted to leave. I wanted to run but I couldn't and Athena raised her voice again: "We have chosen freedom for the mortals, yet the consequences are not what we expected. Although we had the best of intentions, people still fear us gods and our actions. To make amends for the mistakes that those before us have made, we must leave our mark on this world and withdraw from it. No more enchantments, curses, enslavements or in general, hurt, should take place, not only in the first and second world, but also in the third— which has been so often neglected. Every one of us must do their part, even the Underworld."

I felt a chill run down my spine as I noticed Rio's intense stare on me, on my former self. The air seemed to be filled with a menacing energy as he continued to study me, his gaze never breaking from mine. He was the Shadow King, and I could feel the potential for destruction in his eyes. I knew that he was capable of anything—and he knew it too. But he was different from the Rio I knew.

I felt the heart of the body I was in beating very strongly and the Blood Queen seemed to notice that as well. Aria didn't see her since she was still locking eyes with Rio but I could. I saw how the Blood Queen smiled and hell, I knew that when that woman smiled, it never meant anything good.

"Since the prophecy that Hecate told us, things have happened that I cannot approve of. You murder as you please down there, when our focus should be on peace!"

Athena grew louder, but that didn't seem to interest Rio, the Blood, or the Bone Queen.

"What prophecy?" asked Orpheus, folding his arms.

"The one that Hades' children have been using to justify their murders since it was told," Helene said.

"I'll repeat the situation again for everyone, including those who seem to have been living under a rock since our last conference," said Athena, sighing. "The prophecy says that once love finds entrance into the Underworld, the three worlds will meet their demise."

"And for that reason, we have agreed that none of the rulers may love," Rio said, shrugging as if love was nothing but a pesky vermin. Who was this man? That was not my Rio.

"For safety, until we know more about it," Athena added. "It had been ages since Hecate had her vision, but we had all decided that no ruler in the Underworld would seek love. For everyone's safety." She looked at the Blood and the Bone Queen and I didn't know why and what the skull had happened but somehow the Bone Queen looked different. Vulnerable and hurt. She had her arms folded, gnawing on her lip, not even looking at her brother or sister.

"Well, I kept my promise," Rio said smugly, and there was a shiver that ran down my spine when I saw the icy glint in his eyes. It seemed like he knew nothing of love. As if he never experienced it in his life ever before and I think he never did. Not to this point. Maybe that's what the oracle wanted to show me that the Rio I know knew love... and this one didn't... this man was the king from Nana's stories.

A calculating, unforgiving man.

Athena slammed her hands on the table hard. "But we also never agreed that the three of you would slaughter one another's partners!"

"Isn't hate the opposite of love?" Rio said, his deep voice rattling through the hall. "I thought that's what we wanted?"

"You fucking asshole!" screamed the Bone Queen, propping herself up on the table. "Only because *you* don't have a heart!"

"What did you expect?" said Helene of Troy and the body I was in startled.

Hell, I knew why. She was the girl that launched a thousand ships. "Of course he's going to kill your mistress, Marcaria. What don't you get about the prophecy? No one of you is allowed to fall in love until we figure it out. No one. You're endangering all of us, so thank you Zagrios, for saving us."

"You're welcome, my sweetness," he said, bowing his head slightly.

Helene's face softened into a smile, but it quickly froze as the Bone Queen fixed her with an icy gaze. But when the queen parted her lips to speak, Athena let out an unearthly screech that made her recoil, stopping whatever she wanted to say in its tracks. I had never seen her so submissive before.

"Stop spreading hatred in the Pantheon as well," Athena hissed at Rio. "And *you*," she focused back on the Bone Queen, "should have been more careful and think twice before lying to us about your secret lover. It's not about us getting a hang of it but more about destroying the worlds!"

The Bone Queen sighed, looking defeated for once. "I had no choice, Athena. Love is not an option, I couldn't just walk away. I fell in love, it just happened."

"Love isn't just thrown in your face. You weren't strong enough to withstand it," she shot back.

"My words," Rio said and I couldn't hold back a cringe. That man wasn't anything like Rio.

"I, on the other hand, need love and to be loved, not like you, you prick!" The Bone Queen screamed at Rio and I could swear I saw a tear streaming down her cheek right before she quickly wiped it away. "And many of you," the Bone Queen looked at everyone in the hall, "know that there is love at first sight. Even you," she jabbed a finger at Rio, "would have done the same if you truly loved someone."

"I wouldn't because I'm not stupid enough to fall for someone in the first place."

"Only because you don't know anything about love," she replied. "But I do. I crave love."

I felt as though I was playing a game without knowing the rules. Everyone in here was so different. Nothing like I'd imagined them. Athena, who I had known to be so sure and powerful, now seemed almost helpless as she argued with the gods.

And them?

Hell, they acted like kids. I always thought they'd be... actually I had no idea what I thought. But not this. I imagined them strong, ethereal... Also, the Bone Queen... I've worked with her for several years, but she never looked this vulnerable, her face was drawn and pale... She no longer looked like a ruler, rather like a scared little girl. Maybe this was the beginning of her vengefulness. The Blood Queen acted as if she didn't care about the conversation, she even casually picked at her nails but her eyes darted around the room nevertheless and I couldn't help but fear that she was planning something sinister. When her gaze lingered on mine, I knew it had to do with me and Rio.

This was the exact moment a dark plan formed in her mind. And I feared I was wrong... I shouldn't have trusted her.

As if Rio had heard my thoughts, his gaze met mine again and my stomach dropped. It was like he saw through me. His beautiful eyes… and then I felt it. The body I was in was going to fall for him too. It was the moment I fell for him for the first time and I wanted to scream.

Have I ever not loved this man?

I loved him when I was human Aria, I even love him now as the girl that stood between the gods. The moment I saw him, I loved him and I still love him. How the hell was this possible? And yet there he sat, speaking of how incapable of loving *he* was… but the way he looked at me right now, spoke different words. He was falling too. I knew this face. I knew him. No matter who he was and what he said. As Rio quickly broke eye contact, the Blood Queen's grin widened and I was sure that she wanted to take revenge and was going to use me for it. Use the girl that Zagrios, Hades' son, was falling for.

I focused on her lips, the way they curved up… and yes. I was a fool once more to trust her. But then my gaze fell on the Bone Queen and I could swear that the hatred she had for Rio right now came alive. Her eyes sparkled and all I could see in them was death. She wanted to kill him.

Why was he even in her corner?

It made no sense, unless… unless he was never really on her side to begin with. I caught my nonexistent breath. He never explicitly stated it. He said he'd have to return me, but he never said he'd agree with her or side with her…

In that exact moment the Blood Queen turned to her sister and whispered something in her ear… their closeness signaled something was amiss. They were sworn enemies, each other's nemesis, so what the hell was happening now?

And then, as if they were reading each other's minds, they both shifted their gaze to me, to Aria. Their icy glares bore into my soul, but my former self was too oblivious to notice, the mind solely fixed on Rio. Back then, I had no idea what was unfolding, what the two queens had plotted in that very moment but now I saw it and the realization hit me like a ton of bricks.

We had been played.

They had played us for fools. Their plan was to make him suffer, for they saw in me the potential to take down *the* Shadow King, to destroy him once and for all. It was like a game of chess, and as always, I was just a pawn, moved around at their will.

Athena spoke up again, her voice echoing throughout the room and tearing me out of my thoughts. "You three have killed too many people in your endless feud, and it undermined your task of rebirth and reincarnation of souls," she said, her face set in a grim expression. "That's why we're voting today. We must take a stand to protect our worlds. I advocate that the three of you be banished to your kingdoms and no one can leave their realm until the prophecy is taken care of."

A heavy silence descended over the room and just when Rio opened his mouth to speak, I felt my body being pulled away. With one final glance, I saw a fierce argument erupting between all the gods.

My sight blurred and the words of Athena echoed in my mind, a relentless refrain:

> *"No offspring of Hades can exit their territory*
> *anymore. And if they dare to fall in love, despite*
> *the sword hanging over all our heads, a curse*
> *will come for them. A curse so dark and deep,*
> *they'll regret not listening to me until the end of*
> *time."*

CHAPTER TWENTY-EIGHT
RIO

I screamed in agony as the pain coursed through my veins, making me tremble and writhe until my body felt like it was about to break. Ash knelt beside me, gripping my hands tightly to provide an anchor if I needed to break away. Isix stood behind him, an expression of disbelief etched into her face while we occupied a dimly lit tunnel.

"This is so messed up," Ash cursed. "Why are you doing this?

Why?"

"Because," I yelled through gritted teeth, still managing to squeeze Ash's fingers in a crushing grip. "I don't want to interrupt her vision. Not even at the cost of all my remaining magic."

Ash rolled his eyes, ready to let loose another retort, when a gasp caused him to look up. Ebony stood in the doorway with wide eyes, her delicate frame tense with worry.

"What's going on?" she asked, her voice barely above a whisper but Ash didn't meet her eyes and I could see that he was embarrassed because she was barely clothed. Well, the perks of Blossom Eve...

"Trip over?" Ash grumbled as another wave of pain ripped through me. Fuck.

"Yeah," Ebony hissed, as Illiam came up behind her. Immediately, a look of hurt swept across Ash's face, and he wasn't prepared for my sudden wave of pain as I tightened my grip on his fingers once more. He screamed and Ebony quickly moved to cover herself with her clothing.

"Why is Illiam free?" I asked through gritted teeth.

Ash replied with a sinister humourless laugh, his lip biting sharply as another wave of pain rocked through me. "You should be asking her," he muttered darkly as his gaze fixed on Ebony once again. "She appeared here all of sudden and started taking off his shackles."

Illiam coughed nervously and both he and Ebony fell silent and I was so sick of all of them. My chest tightened as I yelled, "I don't give a fuck who you fuck, I want—" I cried out again, curling up like an embryo. That bond was no joke. I made it for a reason and that's why I took the pain and will always take it.

Ebony rushed to my side, brushing a strand of hair from my face. "What happened? Tell me!" she demanded.

Ash sighed. "That fool allowed Aria to turn him into a stone, and he used most of his magic to be freed. And now we wait until she finishes her chit chat with the oracle."

Ebony's mouth dropped open. "What, but you have this bond, she can't—"

"That's the thing..." Ash interrupted. "He stretched the bond... with his magic and all the pain that is released because of it is now on him. He takes it all. Like always, because he's fucking stupid."

I shouted back in response, my anger spilling out too quickly to control. I was stupid. I shouldn't have agreed to the Bone Queen, to my fucking sister but at that time I hadn't known who I was. The moment I realized it, when all my memories came back, I could have shouted and cried and retched for years. And I vowed to make her pay. To make both my sisters pay and the gods.

Ebony brushed the sweat from my forehead and signaled Ash to shut up.

"Rio," Eb said, fixing her gaze on me. "Just let her feel it! It's on her, not on you. Once she feels that freaking pain, maybe then she'll stop behaving like—!"

"—the fucking bitch she is!" Ash shouted and I grabbed his fingers, bending them back until he yelped in pain. Ebony tried to stop me, but I wouldn't let her.

"Don't you ever call my wife a bitch again or I swear I—"

"Watch it," Ash growled back, and I gripped his fingers even harder, just a second away from breaking all of them. "I may be your servant but I'm still one of the Horsemen, if you push me too far I'll just walk away and finally do what I want! I'm not bound to you. I'm here because I consider myself your friend. So don't play me."

He winced, but I had no choice and let him go.

All of the Horsemen served me but out of their own free will because I gave them more than anyone would—than anyone could. If they wanted, they could go wherever they wanted to. I made sure of that.

I fixed his gaze with mine. "I'm just telling you to leave my wife out of it."

Ash stood up and stomped away. I knew he had to let go of his anger somehow now and I let him. Ebony took his place and held my hands. I quickly grabbed them and squeezed.

"She's the reason we're in this situation after all but you don't care about anything! Her. Her. Her. It's always her!" yelled Ash, kicking the wall. "She doesn't even deserve you, not one bit of what you did for her. You're fucking Zagrios. Hades' only son. She should worship you."

"Why don't you shut the fuck up," Ebony hissed at Ash. "At least he's not a heartless asshole anymore." She turned back to me and this time her eyes pierced mine. "But… I hate to say it… but Ash is right, at least a bit. She doesn't have a clue, about anything, and she's only making things worse. You lost it, Volt."

I winced. I knew that I risked a lot by forcing us to reincarnate but I had no choice. I had to save her. Maybe it was true what some souls said about me that I was the villain here. Maybe I truly was the villain all along. I did endanger everyone for her. I was selfish and put her over the greater good. The problem was, I'd do it all over again.

"You should snap at the gods who sit in the Pantheon, Ebony. The curse demands that no one speaks of our love, of what had happened. The gods want it all to be forgotten, so she has to figure it out by herself. That's why she can't remember, because they make it as hard as possible for us to be together. But I thought you'd known that," I said.

"Yeah but she makes it so much harder," Ebony grumbled. "All these years we tried to—"

Illiam cleared his throat and we all jerked up. "Maybe you should insist on trust for once and not threaten everyone all the time, maybe she wouldn't run away then—"

"Oh, shut up," Ash and Ebony said as if from one mouth.

"We don't listen to a Blood Courtier," Ash said. "Unless we're fucking them, eh, Eb?"

Ebony glowered at him. Hell, he was so jealous.

I winced at another pain wave. She seriously had to hurry the fuck up. "Where's Any?" I said, trying to diffuse the situation.

"With Mal," Ebony replied, seemingly relieved to have a conversation that wasn't about her fucking Illiam.

"What's he got to do with that one?" Ash cried out in frustration. "Is everyone actually going crazy? That's a Blood Courtier, too, isn't he?"

Ebony tried to answer him, but I grunted out in pain, distracting her again, and she stroked my forehead instead.

"Okay I'll get that girl now," Ash said and stormed off, but Isix and Briz suddenly came running towards us, breathing heavily.

"What now?" Ebony asked.

"The Blood Court. They've amassed an army and barricaded every entry and exit," Briz gasped, the words tumbling out of him.

Illiam was strangely silent amidst our collective shock and my heart sank as the realization dawned on me—they were after her. My wife. To use her to open that damned book to get what they wanted. To get free and kill us and be over the worlds.

"I'll tear him apart," I growled, my agony threatening to consume me. This bastard had the gall to come here and betray—"

"Illiam's not that bright. It was probably her idea," Ebony interrupted, releasing her hold on me. She rose to her feet, her fists balled in fury.

I struggled to crawl towards Illiam, intent on pummeling him into oblivion, but my body refused to obey and I crashed down. I couldn't fight him and the powers that threatened Aria right now. "What did you promise my sister? What is she offering you?" I demanded, my agony mounting with every passing moment. My limbs were unresponsive, the pain nearly unbearable. Aria was slipping away, drifting further out of reach, as though my very essence was being torn apart.

Illiam refused to answer and Ebony huffed out a bitter laugh. "You follow your queen like a good little dog, don't you?"

"Oh, you don't follow yours?" he spat out.

"No, I followed the king," she said and it was then Illiam realized who I was. Flabbergasted, he stared at me.

I rocked forward once more, aching to land a punch on his face— a sad attempt. Noticing that I couldn't even hurt a fly in the state I was in, I crashed down to the floor again. Ebony was right. Aria had betrayed me and joined forces with that fucking, stupid guard. Why wouldn't it become any easier? Just once. Maybe all of this was just a freaking payback for all the shit I've done and because I dragged everyone into it. Into my very own shitload of a life.

I closed my eyes and tried to ignore Ebony's and Ash's fight.

I concentrated, trying to sense Aria's presence instead, finding out where she was.

"She's getting closer," I muttered, my heart pounding with anticipation. "There's got to be a tunnel around here some-where. She didn't go all the way around." I knew she wouldn't be that stupid. She wanted to stay within the range of our bond but since I absorbed her pain, she probably thought she never reached the limit.

"Ash, stay with Volt," Ebony commanded, then looked to Isix and Briz, her eyes full of contempt. "You, guard the entrance up ahead and idiot," she turned to Illiam, her expression softening a little. "We're looking for this..." she swallowed and I was glad she surpassed whatever she wanted to call her. "...for Aria and we have to get her back. Come."

THE MOMENT the pain ebbed away, I knew Aria was close. I sprang to my feet, Ash at my heels, our bond pulsing with urgency. My heart hammered in my chest as we raced up the trail, voices shouting ahead. Then, Aria burst into view, her white hair streaming behind her like a banner. Ebony and Illiam trailed in her wake, calling out frantic warnings.

In that instant, I had a choice—let her charge ahead unchecked, or intervene and rein her in. I took a deep breath, steeling myself for what had to be done. With lightning reflexes, I lunged forward and grasped her arm, halting her in her tracks. The tension between us was so thick that I could have cut it with a knife.

I looked her in the eye, still holding her tight, and said, "You didn't think you'd be able to get away with this, did you?"

She exhaled, her eyes glazed over, and Bory sitting on her shoulder with a sour look on his face.

"How dare you," she spat, struggling to break free of my grasp. "How dare I relieve you of the burden so you can safeguard your plan and troops. My apologies," I retorted sardonically, aware of the spell she had cast to summon the Blood Queen to make sure she was able to catch us with her troops.

Ebony had been right—Illiam was nothing more than moral support. It stung that he was the one she confided in.

Her initial shock had given way to her usual stubbornness, a trait I had always found endearing. "No, how dare you think that I'd run away!" she said and my eyebrows shot up. "I was running to you, not from you. I think I know the truth, Rio. You're the Shadow King," she said without hesitation.

"Yes." I replied, steeling myself for what was to come. "And I'm your wife."

"Yes."

"The Shadow Queen... well... I'm not running anymore, I promise," she spoke softly, her eyes fixated on mine. "But I need to see someone. I have some final questions that need answering and I know you can't answer it for me."

The weight of our silence was crushing, the words we wanted to say and the questions we longed to ask hung between us, unspoken. There was so much I wanted to share with her, to tell her about our love and the happiness we once had, before it all crumbled like shattered glass. We had taken a vow and it became our ruin.

With a deep sigh, I said, "Where do you need to go?"

"To Nana's," she whispered, her voice barely audible as she withdrew her wrist from my grasp, cradling it close to her chest as though it were a precious treasure.

"Why?" I asked, my gaze dropped to the ground, and I lifted my hand slowly to feel the softness of her skin.

I ran my fingers lightly over her cheek, and she closed her eyes in response. "I saw some things... The oracle showed me how we met. How we truly met in the Pantheon and she was there. I wanted to make her explain."

"That would be a good idea if you hadn't unleashed the Blood Court on us," I said, tenderly stroking the back of her head.

Aria opened her eyes again and I could have sworn to see a flicker of guilt. "I didn't know who to trust," she said softly, glancing away from me. "I think I know who's working against us but... I need to ask some more questions, Zagrios."

"You don't wanna tell me that I should have walked on Earth with that name, do you?" I said, trying to grin but it was hard.

"No, that name is awful."

"Hence the nickname."

She smiled sadly as tears began to glitter in her eyes. "Everything I believed in was a lie. You. My life. The queen's involvement in it... I think Nana can give me some more answers."

I pulled her close, wrapping my arms around her. "It's all my fault," I whispered against her earlobe, feeling the guilt of what I had done wash over me. "I wanted you so badly that I dragged you into my mess without a second thought about what it might do to you. I knew there were consequences, but I thought I was excluded because my ego was bigger than my brain."

She didn't answer and we both knew my words were true like never before.

"Go to Nana," I murmured, giving her a gentle nudge away from me. "You deserve the answers, and she'll provide them. But be quick, we need to find a way to escape the troops."

CHAPTER TWENTY-NINE
LYNNE

I raced along the path to Nana's cave, with Bory clinging to my shoulder. Even amidst the vibrant blooms of wildflowers, the silence of the otherwise deserted streets filled me with dread. I had made a mistake placing my trust in the Blood Queen. It was evident now that she had deceived me, just like everyone else and I was so skulling angry.

"Do I have to call you Your Majesty now?" Bory asked, breaking the silence.

I hissed in response. "Bory, if you don't want me to strangle you, shut up."

He continued, undeterred. "And you really think the Bone Queen was crying in your vision, I've never seen her crying once."

"Yes," I answered. "She was devastated and we need to find out why. Something happened in the Underworld and Rio and I are deeply involved. He must have broken the rules Athena declared and now both of us are cursed and we need to find out what the terms are..." I paused for a moment, considering my next words carefully. "They're somehow all in it together—and I know that the sudden influx of Deathwalkers in the Topworld is also connected with this. The worlds have been opened for a purpose."

Bory nodded. "Yeah, something big is happening in the background and it doesn't look good."

"Do you think I can trust Rio?"

Bory scoffed at this. "The Shadow King? Never."

I sighed heavily. Bory had been created by the Bone Queen to monitor me and I suddenly found myself questioning everything I knew about him as well. But Bory was always there for me... I shouldn't have doubts when it comes to him. That's easier said than done since everyone I knew hurt me. Hurt me so much in the past...

As we neared Nana's cave, I asked him one last question: "What do you remember about your creation? What did the Bone Queen tell you?"

"I understand your confusion, but no matter how many times you ask, I still can't remember anything. I may have been created to keep an eye on you, but my loyalty lies with you instead of her, always. You know that, don't you?"

"Yeah, I know, I know. It's not that I don't trust you, it's just maybe we need to rethink everything, we missed a lot over the years and don't you think it's strange that she would send a guard with me? Like I think you should have spied on me. Don't you remember some questions she asked or things she wanted you to keep an eye on specifically?"

Bory tilted his head, contemplating what I said. "She always wanted me to make sure that you don't run with the bones or... wait!" He hopped restlessly on my shoulder. "I should have reported back to her the minute you managed to conjure up some magic or when I see mana transferring from the bones to you!"

"But it never happened..."

"Not until you awakened the Deathwalker on Earth and at

that moment I was completely smitten by you so I would have never betrayed you, Lynne."

"So, she wanted to know if I'm able to do magic... because she knew I was a divine..."

Bory nodded. "I guess, maybe she waited for it. I think it's true that she used you to awaken Zeus and maybe what Rio said about the Blood Queen is true as well. That she wanted you to open the gates so that she could have her lover back..."

"Because both have lost their love... it makes sense," I said. "And once I helped them, they wanted to destroy Rio and me. Gods... We need to figure out who I am, Bory. If what we heard was true, then my parents must've been gods or demigods. That means this power inside me isn't coming from some external sources... I really have strong magic in me."

"It looks like it..."

"I can't believe this. I'm going to kill Any for this."

"It's not his fault, he can't help us either. If he really were part of the Shadow Court, he's cursed as well..."

I stopped right before Nana's cave and braced myself for whatever truth was about to come for me. "We're going to find out about that damned curse."

I pushed away the leather cloth to enter the cave and a wave of guilt swept over me. I had been too trusting. The Bone Queen was leading us toward an even greater danger and yet there I was, blindly following her instructions and retrieving her bones without pause. For what? Food and Bloodcoins. All the while she was laughing at me whenever I sneaked to the surface, thinking that she didn't know what I was doing. And she knew all along, because she and her sister had linked me to their brother, they made sure that we found each other, that we worked against Athena and that we earned her wrath.

I clenched my jaw, and stepped forward into the darkness of Nana's cave.

THE AIR WAS STILL, and the only sound that could be heard was the echoing of my own footsteps.

Suddenly, a voice cut through the darkness and my heart raced, what if I didn't want to know the truth? I stopped dead in my tracks. Well, I guess it's too late for that now. I already found out that I was married to the Shadow King. What's worse than that right?

A dark figure suddenly appeared in front of me, her face hidden in the shadows. "Welcome, child," she said. "I've heard you're back."

My curiosity was strong, but so was my fear. So, I took a step forward and asked, "Nana. Who are you?"

"Tell me your true name first."

I wanted to huff but something said that Nana wasn't suddenly suffering from amnesia. It was a ritual of some sorts. "My true name is Aria and... I'm married to the Shadow King and I'm a divine. Is this true, Nana?" The moment I spoke out the truth, a force drove through me, just like an invisible gush of wind and strange warmth surged through my body. My limbs tingled with a newfound energy and my vision blurred and was filled with a blinding light. Then, as suddenly as it started, the sensation dissipated.

I looked around me, dazed and confused. Slowly, I lifted my hands up to my face and saw that a faint light was glimmering from my fingertips. An indescribable thrill coursed through me —I had gained magical powers. That was magic.

The world around me seemed brighter and more alive than before. Colors were sharper, details were crisper, and I felt an overwhelming sense of possibility that was unlike anything I had ever felt before. Everything seemed surreal in a way that words just couldn't properly explain.

Bory hopped from my shoulder, grasping at my fingers. "Lynne..."

"What is happening, Nana?" I said, my eyes wide in shock.

Nana smiled and stepped towards me. "The more truths you collect the more of your powers return, the more memories you gain... it's part of your journey."

"But what is all of this? I've been with the oracle and it said I'm a divine and you were there too and—"

"Shh," Nana said. "I'm giving you your answers. The time is right, you're safe on your own now but first, hold up time, dear."

"What?" Bory and I said as if from one mouth.

"The Blood Queen's troops are approaching Cave Town, and we need to act quickly. I've given up my powers long ago and now it's your turn. You must find a way to help us. You know the answer deep down, I can feel it."

"But I forgot all about myself, Nana. I don't know anything about my powers I—"

"That's why the divine never reincarnate, but you were forced to. It's your soul protecting you right now, it protects you from remembering too much and too quickly, it can destroy you. Humans forget, they can start over easily, but we don't have that advantage. We have to relearn and remember slowly over time, because reincarnation never was meant for us. But you have to break that pattern now, force the memories you need back now!"

Suddenly I heard Rio calling my name, he was coming for me. The Blood Queen's troops were coming to get me back. To do whatever they wanted me to and I panicked. "Nana! Help me!"

She gripped me by the shoulders, shaking me, her expression grim. "Force your memories!"

"How?"

She gently placed her hands on my chest and I felt my breath catch in my throat. Scenes flashed before my eyes, and a dull ache in my head, like a chainsaw cutting through my brain, filled me with sharp, throbbing pain. I remembered my childhood in Olympia with Any, but my parents were no more than a blur. The secret love affair Rio and I had after we met at the Pantheon... the way he seduced me, the way I feel for him... and then I saw how my dad found out about Rio and me, how I screamed at him, screamed at Any for helping him against me. When Dad forbade me to contact him, he even went so far as to lock me up, but I kept speaking to Rio with the help of my magic. And then our downfall started. Rio stole me from the Olympus. He abducted me and took me to the Underworld to be his wife.

My father exposed us to Athena, and commanded her to bring me back, but it was too late. I already loved Rio with all my heart and since I knew of the old myth, I ate a pomegranate and by eating it, I was bound to the Underworld, bound to Rio. Leaving Athena no choice but to curse us.

Yet, as the images changed in front of me like a tv, a powerful force suddenly came over me, unlocking the secrets to using my magic. I knew what my magic was about... I was able to revive, to create the Undead and bring souls back from the dead.

I was Aria, Goddess of the Moon and Rebirth.

And then I simply flicked my wrist and time stopped. I forced it to do as I said. *Utaria*. Time. *tinaé*. stop.

Without bones.

Without blood.

I was my own anchor. I was the power.

Nana and I faced each other as Bory was frozen in time, looking like a statue.

"Well done," Nana said with relief in her voice. "Now we have a few minutes."

I grabbed a handful of my hair in desperation. "Nana, this is crazy! I thought I was just an ordinary girl from Cave Town who refused to listen to you!"

She let out a laugh. "You've never been ordinary and I tried to lead you to the right path and I think something must have worked out, since you finally found out the truth."

"So, all the stories you told me were to train me?"

Nana nodded. "I knew that the only way to make you understand is to let you free, so I showed you a way out."

"The tower," I said and remembered when she threw me out, when she said to find my own truth in the North. And what I found was the tower. I found Rio.

"Your father is Erebos, your mother Nyx, and you have a sister named Hecate. You are the Goddess of the Moon..."

"...and destined to bring light to the shadows..." I whispered, remembering what Nana had told me time and again.

Nana nodded. "I have always feared that you were meant for him and the Moirai confirmed it once I asked them to see your life thread. That's why I had to send you to the Pantheon. So you could embrace your true calling and start to bring the light into the darkness."

"But what was your role in all this?"

"Take a breath, child, I will explain everything. We have some time and your power is now strong enough to handle it. The more you know about your past life the stronger you will become."

Just like she said, I took a deep breath and decided to shut up and listen for once.

"I was your maid, and when your mother passed away

during the fall of the Olympians, I promised her that I would take care of you, protect you from all the darkness that was surrounding you. So, I gave my life for you."

As I heard these words, my heart raced and my stomach twisted. Nana kept talking, her voice trembling. "Your sister had a vision shortly after you were born that changed the world. We all thought that the new gods would bring balance and harmony, but the prophecy foretold something different. It said:

> *Beware the heart that beats with fiery desire,*
> *For it shall bring down the three worlds with its ire.*
> *When love descends into the Underworld's depths,*
> *Doom shall come with all its fearsome breaths.*
> *Let not love flow in the realm of the dead,*
> *Or face the wrath of the all-consuming dread."*

I let the words sink.

The prophecy seemed clear. Love in the Underworld will destroy the worlds. "So," Nana started again, taking my hand. "It was forbidden for the rulers of the Underworld to love but no one took it seriously. Especially Zagrios who took pleasure in tearing away love from his sisters. He killed all their lovers and turned it into his own cat and mouse game because he believed he couldn't love. Because he never experienced it. The only one he loved was his mother Persephone and you."

"So, the prophecy fulfilled itself," I uttered.

Nana solemnly nodded. "Once love crept into the Underworld, all hell broke loose. The rulers couldn't resist its pull and tried to keep their love hidden from the rest, and killed their siblings' partners as if it were a game. The children of Hades hated each other, and they were constantly mourning, except for the Shadow King.

He was enraged that his lovers were attacked, but he never felt the pain his sisters did. This way, the Underworld became a breeding ground for spies and assassins, until the Blood Queen fell madly in love with one of her female guards. It was true love, stronger than ever before and they managed to hide it for years. But Zagrios caught wind of it, although someone beat him to the punch. The Blood Queen was forced to kill her love, and the Bone Queen wrongly accused Zagrios and brutally murdered twelve people who were linked to him.

It was the Blood Queen who killed her lover, she found out about it years ago, that's why they are on bad terms again. When the Blood Queen lost her beloved, the hatred between them reached new heights. They wanted to hurt their brother like they had been hurt for decades. They went to the Morai, and asked if he would ever find love. And they told them."

"Told them about me..."

Nana nodded. "Yes, you are his soulmate, the one he has long awaited for. His sisters caught wind of your existence and we were summoned to visit the Pantheon. They hatched a sinister plan to bring him down, defying Athena's decree that prohibited them from leaving their kingdoms. With a spell so dark and malevolent, neither you nor the king could have stood a chance against it. They sacrificed everything to cast it, forfeiting their own magic and forever binding themselves to anchors.

The sisters wove a spell that linked you and him inextricably, ensuring that your love would never falter, not even across worlds. But such a powerful spell came with a high price. The Bone Queen lost her beauty and now wanders her castle as a mere skeleton, her skin stretched taut over her bones like morbid parchment. Desperately, she tries to preserve her former appearance by collecting bones, using them as anchors, but it is a futile pursuit."

I swallowed, remembering how often I saw the queen wandering around her castle. Now I understood the dread that followed both sisters. They were exhausted after fighting such a battle over decades...

Nana cleared her throat. "The Blood Queen, on the other hand, has become a monster, craving blood as her sole sustenance and means of using her magic. The sisters' actions have crossed a line that the gods could not forgive. As a result, their power is now drawn from the bones and blood of their victims, who are granted a single wish before their life is taken. Such is the cost of meddling with forces beyond mortal comprehension."

I helped her with that and weaved the bones for her...

"And the curse..." I whispered, not brave enough to end the sentence.

"The Shadow King was cursed to live in misery, alone. His soulmate is destined to die and if both refuse the prophecy will lash out... and the three worlds will become one."

I gasped. "You mean..."

"If the two of you stay together, Athena's curse will crash down on all of us and the prophecy will be fulfilled. The demons will get loose, the humans will die and the gods won't be able to hold back the wrath of the titans since the Bone Queen will be able to free them all once she is on the loose as well. Everyone will be slaughtered."

"But why is no one stopping this?"

"Because he protects you with everything he has. The Shadow King is so madly in love with you that he made the impossible come true just to save you. Everyone tried to kill you."

"What?" My voice was only a croak.

Nana took my hands, squeezing them hard. "Athena found out about your betrayal, and we all came to the conclusion that there's no getting around the fact that you have to die." I staggered back and dashed into a wall.

They all agreed on feeding me to the wolves?

My heart pounded like a drum in my chest, the rapid beats echoing in my ears like a warning bell. Each breath came in quick gasps, my lungs working hard to supply my muscles with the oxygen they needed to fight or flee. Athena was going to kill me.

Everyone wanted me dead.

Nana added: "As always, your kind heart knew no bounds, and you chose to make the ultimate sacrifice. But Zagrios, unable to bear the thought of losing you, lost his mind with grief and lashed out at everyone around him. Even the mere thought of losing you made him rage and thrash like a wild animal."

I blinked several times. Rio had said something about not wanting to lose me again. But hell, I couldn't bear the thought of being the reason for the world's end. The weight of that responsibility was crushing, threatening to drown me. How could I live with that knowledge, knowing that everything and everyone around me was doomed to perish? I didn't want to die but what was it worth living for when there was no one left?

"Despite his efforts to protect you," Nana went on, "Athena eventually caught up with you and just as your soul was about to vanish, Zagrios harnessed the power of his magic and performed a feat that had never been seen before—he reincarnated the both of you on Earth.

"By doing so, he prevented the meddling hands of the gods from influencing your lives. You were new souls, unencumbered by the past, and free to live a life free from the machinations of the divine. Even your life thread had changed, allowing Zagrios and you to live a normal, human life—until today. As long as your souls aren't fully linked with your former lives, you're protected from Athena but there is no denying that the curse is growing stronger by the day. The gates to hell and to the Olympus are opening, inch by inch, until the world as we know it is shrouded by darkness."

Nana let go of my hands and I realized it's a fate worse than death—a fate that I couldn't bear to contemplate. My knees buckled and I tried to steady myself with leaning against the wall. I felt like throwing up...

She continued, wincing, "But then someone brought you back, we don't know who, but someone changed your life thread and cut it off, so you were shot by Rio, the bullet was magically diverted and you came back to the Underworld. I looked for you after your drop and tried to raise you as safely as possible but," suddenly I realized Nana was fighting pain. She cried out and her feet gave way.

My heart raced as I hurried to Nana's side, desperately wanting to help her, but she pushed me away and kept talking. Her voice, usually so gentle and soft, suddenly came out as a hoarse whisper. "Athena had a plan to get rid of you, to end the curse and the prophecy all at once. But her plan backfired and she underestimated Zagrios' power. He'd destroy the worlds for you, little moon. He'd doom everyone over you. Athena didn't factor in his love."

The more seconds passed the weaker she got and I realized what was happening. She was part of the Shadow Court, because she had worked for me. She wasn't allowed to tell me this.

"Nana," I panted and crashed down alongside her, struggling to accept her fate. The tears streamed down my cheeks as I begged her to stop talking. If she'd keep telling me the secrets she'd die and she knew it.

"It's too late," she said softly, touching my cheek with an icy cold hand. "You must take away all his powers. If you die, he'll avenge you with everything he has. Athena tried to take some of his powers but she never fully managed. Go now, because Athena was wrong. If you die, he will seek his vengeance and that's when we are all doomed. You need to find a solution, my little moon. You either need to kill him, weaken him or find another solution."

I sobbed in desperation and looked helplessly at Nana. "Please, stop talking, you're going to die. Please stop..." The tears streamed down my face.

"Child," she said, taking my head in her hands. "The curse is stronger than all of us. If you two keep your love any longer, it will destroy the worlds and there is not a single heart left beating."

I sobbed. "Is there no way to break the curse?"

Nana shook her head, tears streaming down her face too while her thumbs stroked away my tears. She was trembling, her fear palpable in the air. "Sometimes," she croaked. "We have to sacrifice for the greater good. What is one life compared to billions?"

I nodded, leaning into her touch. "How can I strip him of his powers?"

"Find the Omphalos Stone, it can strip any gods magic. Take his magic before you end this," she said, her eyes slowly closing.

"Where?" I cried. "Where can I find the stone?"

"He has it. Hidden in the Shadow Castle. He hid it from everyone, because it's the only thing that can stop him."

My heart squeezed in my chest, and I didn't want to let go. I felt like I did so many things wrong in my past. I treated her wrong. I didn't understand her, the way she taught me. Nana's hands left my face and I desperately clasped them as her head dropped into my lap. She lay motionless before me. I wanted to scream for her to come back to me but before I could act, a Soul

Reaper came looming out of the shadows, its presence driving a chill that penetrated my very soul.

"No!" I shot up, shouting desperately, but the reaper didn't seem to hear me, or he didn't want to.

He simply put a finger on Nana's forehead and she was gone forever.

I sank down to the ground again, my knees buckling beneath me, and let out a strangled cry. I would never be able to ask her to tell her stories again.

As I wept there, the tears streaming down my face, I realized that the pain would never go away. It would always be there, a constant reminder of what I had to do. And no matter how much I begged, pleaded, or prayed, there would be no solace, no peace, no healing until I did what I had to do.

I had to obey Athena.

CHAPTER THIRTY
RIO

When I reached Nana's den, Aria was laying on the floor in a tearful heap. Time was short, so I quickly shouted out to Ash. "Help the Cave Town dwellers! I'll take her to the
Bone Queen."

"Help?" Ash gritted his teeth and his eyebrows nearly hit his forehead.

"Yes, help! We can't leave them behind and Aria would never forgive me if I did."

Ash rolled his eyes in disgust. "I don't care what Aria wants."

Ebony took the lead and Isix followed close behind. "Listen, boss says let's go so let's go!"

"Get Any with you too. I'll meet you back at Shadow Castle. Illiam can go back to his queen or rather, he must because otherwise I'd kick his ass."

Ebony nodded and grabbed Illiam harshly by the arm, who was preparing to put up a fight.

"Where are you taking her?" he said, looking furiously at Aria.

"I have a contract to fulfill first, then we'll return home to Shadow Castle."

"No, we—" Illiam protested, but Briz and Ebony yanked him out of the den without a second thought.

I scooped Aria up in my arms and she buried her face into my chest and cried silently. The noise outside was growing louder and louder as Cave Town inhabitants realized that something was happening.

"Nana," Aria whispered against my chest and I kissed her forehead tenderly.

"I know, we'll pay homage to her soon. But first we have to run and for that we need your knowledge. What's the fastest way to Soothie? You need to let him fly us to the queen."

She pounded against my chest in despair. "Why Rio? Why us?" The noises grew louder.

"Aria! A way out!"

"By her cave," Bory said, hopping from Aria to my shoulder and pointing to the door. "I'll show you."

I ran for my life with her in my arms, praying that nothing would stand in our way.

As I raced through the darkened tunnels, Aria shivered from the cold and I tried to lighten the mood a little. A fool's attempt. "Nothing to complain about, darling? We're going to see the Bone Queen after all."

"Nothing makes sense," she muttered, a spark of fear in her weak voice. "If she wants to kill me, it's the best for everyone to just let her..."

"What did Nana tell you?" I asked, my voice rough.

But Aria was silent, as if she was too scared to speak, stuck in an endless trance now. I was losing her. Again. And I wouldn't let this happen.

"Bory," I said, feeling a sense of dread spreading through my body. "What did the old hag tell her? What happened?"

Bory exhaled deeply and then said, "Well. Whatever, although I have no idea if it's a good idea to tell you anything but what shall I do. I'm only a little bear...so... she knows that you two are cursed. And the only way to break it is that one of you dies."

"No," I said sternly as a fire blazed in my chest. "She's not going to die again. There's another way."

"But there isn't," Bory muttered under his breath. "If she doesn't die, everyone will. The oracle and Nana made it very clear. So, you might call me crazy, but I think this is a mood killer even to Lynne. So, give her time, damn it. She deserves it."

"There is a way," I murmured, feeling the weight of the world on my shoulders. Then I locked eyes with Aria and said fiercely, "We will find a way out of this, if it's the last thing I do."

Bory shook his head sadly and said, "Don't make promises that you can't keep. Seems like you already made lots of those anyway."

I ignored him and was glad when I arrived at Aria's cave. "Where is this way out?"

"Around the corner. Over there." Bory held up a blue feathery wing and showed me a serpentine, stony way that led up to another tunnel. "That's her shortcut to the Dragon's Tread. She loved to sneak out to hunt. Well," a nervous laugh bubbled up in Bory's throat. "Who knew that cave up here would come in handy one day."

His voice trembled as he spoke, and I could hear the fear behind his sarcasm, but I wouldn't let her down. Not again. I made many precautions. This time, I was ahead of all of them.

The darkness was suffocating, pressing in on me from all sides as I tried to make my way out. It would be easier to just vanish through my shadows but since our last little incident I had barely any magic left. So, we had to do it like the mundane. Per foot. As I ran alongside the narrow path, I couldn't see my own hand in front of my face. The walls of the cave seemed to be closing in on me, and I could feel my heart beating faster with each passing moment.

Then, I saw a faint glimmer of light up ahead. It was small, but it was there, and it gave me renewed strength to push on.

I quickened my pace, stumbling over rocks and dodging stalactites as I followed the faint light. As I got closer, the light grew brighter, until I was able to make out the shape of a small opening in the wall. With a surge of energy, I pushed myself through the opening and out into the air. As I took my first deep breaths of fresh air, I felt a sense of relief wash over me.

"So, how do we call for Soothie?"

Bory grinned. "We don't. He's no dog."

I just wanted to snap back at him as he nodded into the air. "Look, your *highness*. There he is. He knows when we need him." I had to give him that. The little bear was brave as fuck and I admired him. He'd do anything for Aria and I loved him for it. I'd just ignore his foul mouth. At least for now.

When the ground shook a thunderous roar filled the air and I tipped my head back to look up. The sky was a blend of burning red, making the skulls look as if they were bleeding, but beneath it, the land was shrouded in an ominous darkness and right before us, a giant dragon descended from the sky. Its wings were like a storm cloud, blocking the red glowing skeletons and casting a long, dark shadow over us.

The dragon's scales glinted in the fading light as he prepared to land. He stretched out his claws and dug them into the earth before us, leaving deep grooves in their wake as it braked towards where I stood. Soothie's gaze seemed to reach into my soul, searching for something hidden deep within me, trying to understand if I meant good or bad for Aria. He was ready to defend her life just like me. I slightly bowed my head and I could see a glint of fire lighten up in his snake-like eyes.

Soothie let out a deafening roar as he prowled closer, wings spread wide. I could feel my heart pounding in my chest, and knew that I had to be ready if things turned sour. But I was also feeling something else—a sense of awe at the majestic creature before me.

"You don't have to burn him right away," Bory said as I heaved myself up with Aria in my arms. I could feel her tense up and I knew she was scared. So, I pulled her onto my lap and secured my feet to both sides on the dragon's back.

"Right now, he helps Lynne but the minute he acts suspicious. Burn him. Or drop him. Whatever suits you," Bory said to Soothie and I wasn't sure if the rumble that went through the dragon's body could be considered a laugh?

"Funny," I said and signaled Soothie that we were secure and ready. "Fly us to the Bone Queen."

Soothie growled, as if he was refusing my request. I was right about him refusing my demands. He'd never work for me.

"Say please," Bory said, his chin held high as he propped himself up on Soothie's head as if he were the captain to his dragon ship.

I rolled my eyes and bit down on my lip, unsure of what to do next. "We don't have time—"

Soothie growled again and this time he even spat a little fire... Reluctantly, I said: "Please, Soothie. Fly us to the Bone Queen." But Soothie still didn't fly.

"What now?" I said, looking around nervously since below us, the Blood Queen's troops seemed to meddle with my men.

Bory tilted his head and looked into one of Soothie's eyes. "He doesn't like the Bone Queen and wants to know why we have to fly to her."

I sighed heavily, trying to think of a way to make this creature understand. "Because the stupid contract I have with her requires to return Aria's soul. So that's what we'll do and then we vanish into the Shadow Castle as free men. Does that sound good enough for you?"

Bory cleared his throat. "He wants to know if you'll leave her with the Bone Queen."

"Never," I said. "She'll walk on her ground for some fucking minutes and once I'm free of her contract and I have my magic back, we'll leave."

Bory tilted his head again, checking on Soothie's other eye and nodded. "Sounds good."

Soothie took off and we bellowed through the sky as we flew higher and higher, the wind screaming past my face and the warmth of his scales radiating through mine and Aria's body. My heart pounded with adrenaline as I clung tightly to the saddle, feeling the immense power of its muscles coursing underneath me. I could barely contain my excitement as we flew through the clouds and towards our destination. The black mountains rushing past me and the bones in the sky growing closer every second that ticked by.

Some time later, Bory folded his puffy arms. "You should be honored to fly with us."

"I am," I said, kissing Aria's forehead again. "Believe me, I am."

We looked ahead for a few minutes, just watching the black mountains pass us when Bory broke the silence again. "What will you do when the Bone Queen strikes? When she attacks her?"

"She can't. The bond I have with Aria connects us both and if she dies, I'd die too and I'm immortal. So, I made Aria immortal too by binding our souls together."

"But, the curse—"

"Like I said. We'll find another way. Sacrificing Aria is no option anymore. It never was and since she can't die, no one will outsmart me."

CHAPTER THIRTY-ONE
RIO

As Soothie descended upon the snow-white forest, the trees seemed to come alive, whispering secrets in their swaying branches. They towered above us, growing ever taller and thicker, their gnarled fingers reaching out like beckoning talons. With a soft thud, we landed on the ground, and I hopped off with Aria still in my arms.

The forest floor was a soft blanket of ash and brittle twigs, which crunched beneath my feet as I stepped forward.

As we made our way deeper into the forest, I couldn't shake the feeling that we were being watched—that hidden eyes were tracking our every move. But I pushed the thought aside, focusing instead on the path ahead, and the mysteries that lay waiting for us in the heart of the woods.

"There we are," I said looking at the castle's looming silhouette scratching against the sky. It was a hulking mass of white marble stone as it stood guard over the surrounding woods. The moat's murky water lapped at its edges with a sinister glow, like a million tiny eyes keeping watch in the night. Though it looked like the castle was draped in snow, it was ash instead. My sister has always loved the color white but ever since Alexis, the guard she loved, was murdered she wanted to drown in white. Even so much that she coated her realm with white ash, making her realm smell like a distinguished barbecue.

"Wanna go with us?" I said, glancing at Bory who still sat on Soothie's head.

"Sure," he said and hopped into the ash. "I won't ever leave her alone with you."

"Fine, but you'll walk on your own. What are you? A kid? All this carrying all the time."

Bory huffed but hopped next to me. "I never liked you," he grumbled. "Thanks for the honesty."

"Nothing to lose here."

As we approached the entrance, Soothie growled so I turned. "It's all right. We won't take long."

"You wait and if anything happens you fly us out of this crappy kingdom, okay?" Bory said.

Soothie nodded and we accelerated our speed, walking up white cobblestones until we came face-to-face with thick iron bars. They looked menacing in their rust and age. I ran my hand along the smooth, cold metal and cringed as I imagined what secrets were hidden within its depths. What else my sister had hidden from me over the years. I knew she hated nothing more than me and seeing me hurt meant everything to her.

It was my fault too. I was mature enough now to give in to this.

But I also knew that I couldn't be in there with Aria looking like that. She needed to appear strong, not broken in her will. I didn't want them to know that they finally got to her. So, I held her tightly in my arms and kissed her earlobe. "Darling, you need to stand up. Please. We're going to show them who we are, we need to appear united..." Not like I kidnapped her... again.

But when I met her eyes, it was like the life had been sucked out of them and it sent a wave of anger through me towards everyone who had done this to her. The Titans. The gods—and even myself. But I wasn't about to give up yet. I tried to appeal to the goddess within her, reminding her of who she was, "You're the moon goddess. You're my Shadow Queen. You bow to no one. Do you hear me?"

She didn't answer but she seemed to take my words in so I continued, "Come on. We have to gain my powers back first and fulfill this fucking contract. Then we can vanish through darkness and shroud them all within."

I could see her struggling as conflicting emotions seemed to bubble up within her. It was going to be a long fight to get back what

was rightfully ours. "Let's not give up."

She finally lifted her gaze and for the first time since I found her broken on the floor, there was some sort of a glint in her eyes again and it made me smile. "There you are."

"You say you have a plan?" she said and slowly the fire grew back and the more the seconds passed the more I knew she was in there. The woman I loved. She came back to me.

"The best."

She swallowed. "I want to make her regret."

I pulled the corners of my mouth up into a smile and I didn't get the chance to reply before she kissed me. My lips parted immediately, wanting to taste and feel her so badly. Kissing her was like air that I needed to breathe and this was the first time I had the feeling she trusted me. Maybe we really had a chance. Maybe I changed enough on Earth to be worthy of change. My hands were on her waist, pulling her closer as we deepened the kiss, our bodies pressed together, our tongues exploring each other's mouths and I knew we were on the right track. The Shadow King and Queen were finally together and we would stay together. No matter what. Fuck the curse. Fuck the gods.

"I love you," I whispered against her lips. She kissed me. "I love you too."

"Could you once think of me, please? Watching you kiss is really awkward for me."

"Could you once stop being a pervert and look away?" I said and smirked as Bory grunted. "You like to watch, just say it."

Bory gasped and I took Aria's hand, grinning.

We went in and were greeted by white walls that were made of marble, everywhere there were long pillars decorated with white fur, white flowers and statues. To both our sides, the turrets and towers stretched up towards the sky, casting long shadows across the ground we walked upon.

We stepped into a grand entrance hall, the air loaded with the scent of wax and ancient stone. The walls were lined with white torches, casting flickering shadows across the marble floor. It was a room of stark beauty, but the heavy wooden door at the far end gave me a sense of unease.

As we approached the center of the hall, I could see that the room was filled with white tapestries and marble furniture. A large fireplace roared at one end of the room, casting a warm glow across the space. But despite the inviting heat, I couldn't shake the feeling that we were intruding on something dangerous.

Our footsteps echoed loudly in the empty space, each step punctuating the silence. I could hear the sound of our breathing and the rustling of our clothing, which seemed to magnify in the stillness of the castle. It was as if the very air held its breath, waiting for something to happen.

My heart pounded in my chest as we approached the two-winged, narrow staircases leading up to the next level. I couldn't help but wonder what secrets lay waiting for us in the darkness above. But with a deep breath, we began to ascend, our eyes fixed on the door at the top of the stairs.

My sister's castle was unlike any I had ever known and as always the silence hung heavy in the air, as if the walls themselves dared not disturb her solitude. And who could blame her? Melinoe was not one for trust, or company and we, my family, had our hands in this. Because of us she kept to herself, with only a handful of trusted souls to keep her company. But she was not defenseless. Her fortress was guarded like the most prized of treasures, every step monitored, every intruder detected.

As we made our way through the halls, I couldn't shake the feeling of being watched. And I was right. Aria's nod indicated that she was there, lurking somewhere in the shadows, her eyes fixed on us with a sinister grin. We had entered her den of vipers, and I knew we would have to tread carefully if we were to come out unscathed.

Mel's castle was a maze of shadowed corridors and dimly lit rooms. As we entered the throne room, the silence was palpable, and I could feel Aria tense beside me. She was a force to be reckoned with, and we both knew it.

But when she spoke, her voice was almost friendly. "Zagrios, you're back with the last soul. Isn't that wonderful? Oh, I've missed you so much!" Her smile was sinister, and I knew better than to trust it.

"I hope just as much as I've missed you, Mel," I replied, my tone laced with sarcasm. "I'm returning the 100th soul." I pointed a finger at Aria, challenging my sister to try anything.

My sister nodded, and I could see her guards lurking in the shadows. She descended the stairs gracefully, her white alabaster dress billowing around her ankles. "Lynne... or should I say Aria? You seem to have gotten a lot of your memories back. Wonderful."

Her pitch-black hair swayed as she spoke.

Aria looked to me, confused, and I wondered if she was having another flashback.

"It's good to have you back," Mel said, trying to reassure her. "And hello, Bory. I haven't seen you in a while either."

I was proud to see Aria's small bear stand tall beside her, unafraid.

But my sister was not done with us yet. "Alright, I won't keep you any longer. Hand her to me, and leave," she said, but I could see the challenge in her eyes. I knew it was a trap.

With a fierce glare, I said. "Fine, take her."

Mel smirked and was about to take hold of Aria when she felt the bond of energy between us, preventing her from claiming her soul. Her expression darkened as she realized she wouldn't be able to have her Bone Thief back. "W-What have you done?"

"Prepared myself," I growled, pulling Aria closer to me, claiming her. "She's mine. Didn't you always say we have to choose our words carefully? Funny because you never paid attention to what I said to you. You wanted me to *bring her back* and I never said I'd *give her soul* to you. So, dearest sister, here she is. Her feet are on your grounds. Our deal is fulfilled."

At that moment, all my powers came back to me and I reveled in it. It was like being enveloped in an electrifying shower. Sparks of power cascaded over my skin. Aria glanced at me with understanding, as though she knew exactly what had happened and how much our situation had changed. And now I could finally breathe freely again. I could tell she could see the shadows that had taken over my body.

The Shadow King was back.

She smiled at me and grabbed my hand as our powers combined. A breeze began to swirl around us and Aria was completely transformed into my Shadow Queen—a black shadow dress hugged her curves now with white lace symbolizing the light that had saved me from my own destruction. Her hair stuck out around her as she took my hand and we became one with our powers.

Mel backed away from us, her eyes filled with terror. I lunged forward and grabbed her by the throat with a strip of dark magic, my beloved shadows curling like fingers around her throat, squeezing. I knew that the gods would soon call for me to be sent back to my realm, but I couldn't leave without making sure she was punished for her misdeeds. The thought of leaving her unpunished weighed heavily on my heart, yet I knew that I could not stay long.

I squeezed her throat until she could no longer breathe and loosened up a bit again. "What are you going to do with the bones you had Aria collect for you?"

She gasped and I saw Aria's eyes light up, they looked like two full moons now—finally my moon princess was back. I waited for eons for this moment. She raised both of her hands and blocked the guards with a white wall as they rushed toward us.

My sister looked at me and gurgled under my grip until she finally began to speak, "Can't you guess whose bones I'm collecting?"

"Zeus," I growled and squeezed harder, watching her eyes light up a little under the pressure.

She laughed bitterly. "I'm still missing one bone, but our sister will help us with the Book of Silva that your mistress dutifully returned like the nice little sheep she is."

Aria wanted to lash forward but I held her back with my free hand. This wasn't our final fight, we had to prepare ourselves first. This was just the beginning.

"So, the two of you are working together against me now?" I noticed the shadows rearing up behind me and Bory gasped.

"Yes, until you are both dead and Zeus is resurrected with

the other Olympians. Just like he deserves. He'll bring back our beloved ones and the two of you will rot as Shadow Slaves just like you deserve," she spat.

My grip was unyielding on her neck as I watched her gasp for air with delight. I clenched tighter and tighter until I could see the veins in my arm bulging as her breaths became shallow and labored. She could only manage to suck in a shallow gasp of air before I released my grip, allowing her a deep, desperate breath. Fucking bitch.

"It's madness that you think that. He never would," I said while she breathed in.

As I watched, her skin slowly began to change into a grayish hue, fading away until her body wasn't capable of holding up her high demand of mana and her true form was revealed. A living skeleton. She had been struggling with her inner demons for far too long.

Something that all of us were suffering from. We were monsters but unlike her, I found a way out, at least I believed in it.

"There is no point in dying and being reborn," Mel rasped. "We're going to end the circle and gain the power we deserve back."

"And Athena doesn't know?" asked Aria.

"How could she, she's so busy keeping her stupid demigods at bay that she doesn't realize what we're doing. We're bringing back the old order, because she sucks at ruling."

"And how are you going to do that?" I asked.

"By screwing with us," Aria said, looking at me. "They don't want me to sacrifice. They're waiting until the curse and the prophecy catch up and the worlds are destroyed to open the gates. They let time work on its own."

"And by making her immortal, you stupid idiot," Mel laughed

bitterly under my pressure. "You helped us, because now no one will ever be able to kill her and the gates are opening up. Each day more gates will and even more demons will return to Earth. It is already overflowing with them. And as soon as we have the last bone of Zeus, we will free the Titans and the Olympians from Tartarus. We will rule again and be able to walk freely in all worlds."

Suddenly, a pain ran through me from the extent of which I had never felt before and Aria cried out too. We both turned and saw Macaria slowly striding into the hall. She twisted her bloodred mouth into a pout and I couldn't believe what I saw.

All of us in one place.

The borders really were vanishing... because if we could walk into each other's kingdoms... this meant that Athena's powers were seizing too.

The world indeed was ending.

Aria and I now stood back to back and I struggled to keep my sister and her guards away from us with my power while Aria had one hand trying to stop Macaria's guards and her. While my sisters had given up their magic in a vain attempt to destroy me, Aria and I were still full of power, her bright moon seeming to even outshine my shadow power. And that was our only advantage.

Macaria held up a hand, trying to use her blood magic against us, but she seemed to be having trouble.

"My dear, Aria, I'm so happy that you finally managed to gain back your powers! And Zagrios," her gaze shifted to me. "We never came to talk to each other ever since... you really outdid yourself with the reincarnation. And all because you are so stubborn that you would do anything, really anything to save that girl. Didn't you say you'd never fall? You'd never be able to love?" She smirked and I knew she loved to be right and hell, she was.

I was utterly stupid to think that love couldn't hurt me. It destroyed me and I destroyed everyone in its wake.

"It's natural to fail, but even stupider to fail twice. So, what does this say about you?"

Macaria's grin widened before she uttered her next words. "Well, I don't know," she said. "But what I do know is that you indeed would go mad for love and you did. You would do anything for Aria, even kill anyone in your way. But have you forgotten about your cute daughter? Didn't you find your way back to the Underworld because of her?"

I gritted my teeth as a wave of guilt washed over me. "What have you done to her?"

"Nothing yet." Macaria grinned. "But since you didn't follow Athena's rules, it's just about time that your daughter dies too."

I gritted my teeth and Mel croaked underneath my grip.

I rose my shadows, ready to flood her body with them but then Macaria spoke up again, distracting me, "You've shot yourself in the foot, because you didn't just take Aria to your heart. You also have a lot of souls on Earth for whom you have a thing these days. All of a sudden our Shadow King is a kind person. Who would have thought that?"

"Everyone can change," Aria said.

"Oh," Mel laughed. "Of course, you're saying that. You're so naive. I actually can't believe you. We knew your powers and that you could revive anything. So, we used you to find Zeus' bones. All these years you've done as you were told and never questioned us. You were under our control, and we manipulated you to do our bidding. Manipulated you to find Rio again and—" she threw her head back and laughed, the sound rippling through the hall. "That you even thought we wouldn't know. I had to stop myself from laughing when you came to my sister and stupidly agreed to return the Book of Silva, an heirloom we needed to destroy you."

Now Macaria took a step closer, and I sensed Aria's mana weakening, her confidence ebbing away as she believed my other sister's lies. "You need to stop acting like a naive girl, dear. Wake up."

"Aria," I interrupted. "Don't listen to them. Whatever they say. You were meant to distrust me and be drawn towards the witches because of the curse. Everyone would feel conflicting emotions in this situation: love and distrust at the same time."

"God, you're such a softie now, it's hilarious to watch!" Macaria laughed mockingly, echoed by Mel. I didn't listen to them and drew Aria to my side, comforting her as well as I could.

"Better a softie than heartless," I said and sent a wave of shadow at her that hit her right at the hip and brought her down to her knees. "I would watch my mouth if I had no powers left."

Hell, I loved to see them hurt.

"But well, I have to thank you, Aria," Macaria said, trying to get up again. "Thanks to you we have the Book of Silva, and you even helped me locate the last Bone from Zeus, while we worked on your magic." She made the gesture of quotation marks as she said "worked on your magic."

"You just used me like a GPS to locate the bone," Aria muttered angrily.

Mel winked, signaling her guards that she's fine.

"And he helped me doing it," she said and suddenly Illiam emerged from the back, his head hung low as he tried not to look at us. I could tell he was hurt but my sympathy was low. I always hated that prick.

"Illiam?" Aria whimpered, and her magic subsided, the guards slowly formed up and set about charging at us.

"Aria," I said. "Come. You're stronger than this. Come on. Your shield!"

Aria tried to concentrate, but the betrayal of Illiam seemed to weigh heavily on her mind. Her hands trembled as she tried to hold her magic up. I forgot that she was out of practice and how exhausting such a mana concentration could be.

"Thanks to sweet Illiam, I knew what you were talking about in your sleep, and let me tell you, it was a lot." Macaria grinned and when Mel laughed too, that was enough for me.

Aria gasped in disbelief. "Illiam, I can't believe you would do this," she said.

"I'm so sorry," he replied, voice shaking. "But there is more to it, we—"

Before he could finish his sentence, a red-hot blast of energy shot from Mel's hands like a lightning bolt and hit Illiam's chest. He screamed out in agony as streams of blood poured from his eyes, nose, and mouth. The ground beneath him turned crimson and he continued to gurgle despite the lack of air in his lungs. That's when something shifted on Macaria's face and I narrowed my eyes at her. She didn't want to hurt that guard. He meant something to her too.

"Okay, now you overstepped. I can't hold up that fucking façade anymore. Eat this, bitch sister," Macaria said and stopped concentrating her powers on Aria and shot it all at Mel.

Aria's screams pierced the air like a siren, her shield trembling and echoing with every blow. Knowing there was no time to spare, I lunged forward and scooped up Bory. I tried to ignore Macaria and tightly grasped Aria around her waist, sprinting towards a swirling vortex of shadows I created. We were thrown inside, quickly embraced by the solid walls of my Shadow Castle. The throne room. Despite my harbor, a picture wouldn't leave me.

It was just a second, but I saw that Macaria had helped us.

She attacked Mel's guards... making way for us to vanish. Was she on our side?

"ALL GUARDS UP!" I commanded with a powerful thunder, my voice shaking the walls around us. "NOW! Protect the Shadow Castle with all you have! Not a single soul shall pass the walls, not even the gods themselves!"

The guards didn't so much as blink when they noticed that their king was back.

They simply nodded in agreement, standing tall in unison and running to defend our home with ferocity.

CHAPTER THIRTY-TWO
LYNNE

My head was starting to spin as I remembered more and more of my past.

I didn't tell Rio but when I had passed out in his arms, a vivid memory materialized before my eyes. It was the haunting image of my father, standing tall, flanked by the Blood Queen and Any. My father was the queen's lover... and it was the day they had exposed the forbidden depths of my relationship with Zagrios.

That night, they dropped a bombshell on me: the gods found out what we did, and their wrath was burning hotter than the sun. I never saw it coming, never thought my life would get tangled up in their drama. But to make things even worse, Zagrios swept me away to the Underworld, not giving a damn about what anyone said or the consequences. It was like a twisted version of Hades snatching Rio's mother Persephone all over again, history repeating itself in the worst possible way.

Everyone was hell-bent on tearing us apart and the prophecy loomed over us like a dark cloud—dictating our fates.

But our love was a force to be reckoned with, a blazing inferno that defied all odds.

Despite the spells, the reincarnation—we always found our way back to each other.

Our love wouldn't be extinguished, no matter how fiercely they fought against it.

But as all the weight came crashing down on me, I felt my world shatter into a million irreparable fragments. I lost my grip on control, my legs giving way beneath me, and I crumpled to the floor in our former bedroom.

"Don't leave my side," he said, going down with me and desperately trying to calm me down. He let me cry against his chest and when he cupped my head, he looked at me intently. "I can't lose you a third time."

He didn't say it out loud but we both knew it was only a matter of time until the Bone Queen or Athena figured out how to break in and come for us. We had to find an answer quickly. I loved my life and when Nana told me that there simply was no way out, I panicked. I needed a way out. Maybe it was because I've never truly lived. I always had to die for the sake of the gods. Over and over again.

Rio leaned into me. "You're mine, and I will never lose you again, do you hear me?"

I could feel my heart racing, but I couldn't bring myself to answer him. I couldn't promise him that. "We never know what tomorrow brings," I said and tried to breathe evenly. "Life can change within seconds."

"We weren't made to just accept our destiny, Aria. Sometimes we have to make our fates instead. Fuck the prophecy. Fuck the gods."

He kissed me and I let him consume me once more. That's exactly what I loved about Rio. He knew no boundaries. Not even the sky was the limit for him.

Our breathing grew more ragged and desperate as our kisses intensified, our hands grasped onto each other, desperately aware that at any second, some powerful force could swoop in and snatch away our stolen moments together once more.

"Maybe you should have let them take me," I said in between kisses, the tears streaming down my face.

He lifted his gaze and realization hit me. He was scared.

Despite his tough exterior, fear gripped his heart. For me.

It was the first time I realized that he'd do anything just to keep me alive and this scared me even more.

I broke free of his embrace. "It would've been easier to just let me go. What's one life among billions, Rio?" My words trembled with a mix of resignation and anguish, the weight of sacrifice heavy upon me.

His grip tightened around my head, his gaze piercing into the depths of my soul. "No," he uttered with determination. "I would shroud the entire world in darkness to save you."

"That's the damn problem, Rio..." I sobbed, tears streaming down my face like a relentless downpour now.

In that moment, fragments of Nana's stories collided in my mind once again and I just wished it would stop. That all these memories would vanish. I just wanted to be Lynne, the Bone Thief, and nothing else. Becoming Aria again was the last thing I desired.

I didn't want any of it, not even for a second.

But little did I know, the haunting tale of the shattered mind of the Shadow King was like a cruel twist of fate. I never imagined I could be the reason behind it all—the reason for his descent into darkness. The weight of that truth settled heavily upon me, a burden I couldn't ignore. The Shadow King went dark because of me.

He skulling *vanished* because of me!

When our eyes locked again, I saw a whirlwind of shadows

battling within his gaze and in that haunting moment, I glimpsed the reflection of my surrender in his eyes. It transported me back to that one day, where we stood together on the balcony, my flowing white dress twirling around me. I had told him that I wanted to end my life, to surrender to all of them. His sisters. Athena. The gods. To end that curse. But before he could react, I chugged down poison Athena gave me, and that's when he lost it.

He simply refused to let me die and gave all of his magic to catch my soul in flight and force us to reincarnate instead. Only to find me as a human again.

"I can't lose you, Aria. I just can't," he confessed. "I would have died instead of you. But I can't. I'm immortal but I can't exist without you."

Rio's hands shook uncontrollably as he desperately reached out towards me, pulling me into him once more. As his words still hung in the air, his lips seized mine once more, igniting that fiery passion that consumed us both since day one. In that moment, we surrendered to the overwhelming intensity of our love, entwined in a passionate embrace that spoke volumes of our unbreakable bond.

"I know," I whispered, my trembling voice betraying the ache in my heart, as I clumsily brushed aside the strands of hair that obscured his forehead. "I know. But sometimes to love means to sacrifice," I managed to say through tear-filled eyes, desperately kissing him.

"Aria, I—"

His voice trailed off, his lips still touching mine but then, in an instant, a golden glow enveloped his mouth. I tried to tell myself that everything was okay, that it was just my imagination playing tricks on me. But the shimmer on his lips wouldn't go away. It was like a cold hand gripping my heart, squeezing it tightly. I've seen this before. Back then when we kissed in the park.

"Rio, your lips," I stammered, my words tumbling out in a breathless whisper.

His eyes widened as realization hit him as well.

It's the moment the Blood Queen finally used the essence of our first kiss.

"Say something, Rio. Please," I pleaded, my hands gripping his arms as if trying to anchor him to reality.

But he remained motionless, caught in a moment of paralysis.

The air seemed to crackle with tension, suffocating me, as if a heavy weight pressed down on my chest, making it hard to breathe. Time seemed to slow into a crawl while the world faded into insignificance.

"Rio?" My throat closed up.

He didn't respond. Instead, a ripple of dark energy radiated out of him.

"What... is... happening?"

He croaked and my heart sank into my stomach as my tears kept racing down my cheeks. He was immortal. He couldn't die... he couldn't, right?

This wasn't happening.

"Rio, I'm sorry this is my fault. I—" I should have told him about the kiss. Why didn't I tell him?

His eyes rolled back, disappearing into the depths of his skull as he fell over. I tried to hold his body up with all my might, but I couldn't, and he crumpled onto the floor. A guttural scream tore from my throat, reverberating with sheer horror, as the doors burst open, unleashing a torrent of guards into the room with Any in tow.

"What happened?" Any shouted, pushing past the guards to get to Rio's body.

"He's dying!" The words escaped my lips, carrying the weight of my shattered heart.

Any bent over Rio's body, gently shoving me away.

I curled up into a tight ball next to them, my eyes glued to the horrifying scene unfolding right before me. "H-he," I stumbled over my words, swaying gently back and forth, desperately clinging to my sanity, "he can't d-die... right, Any? Right? H-He's the Shadow King..."

As Any remained silent, my heart leaped in my chest.

I watched him bending over Rio, listening for a heartbeat, checking for signs of life.

"Any?" I croaked, my voice barely audible.

"Please, just give me a moment," he said, placing his hand flat on Rio's chest and closing his eyes.

I fought to control my breathing, silently praying to every deity I could think of. Please. Please save him. He can't die. He can't.

Any drew out a long breath, focusing back on me. "Okay. He's alive—but he's been put to sleep by a powerful spell."

I crashed against the wall behind me, releasing a deep breath. Thank Stix. Thank *fucking* Stix.

In that moment, Ash charged into the room, frantically taking Rio in. He stared at me, his nostrils flaring. "What have you done?"

I opened my mouth to reply but all that escaped were choked sobs. "I... I... oh gods—"

He was right. This was because of me. I haven't told anyone about the kiss and now Rio was... what was he?

"Brace yourself," Any ordered while the guards checked on Rio. "Why?" I said.

Any winced and pulled me up. "Because we're about to leave." My heart plummeted into my gut all over again as I suddenly noticed the lurking shadows in every nook of Rio's bedroom. Had they been there all along, hiding in plain sight? In a blink, the shadows vanished, leaving an unsettling void in their wake. I gripped Any's hands tightly as the shadows seemed to deepen and twist. Something was moving within them. Someone was moving. Someone has been watching us.

Any pulled me closer.

I couldn't quite make out who it was at first, but as the darkness shifted, a figure began to take shape and I realized the Blood Queen has been waiting for us in the shadows, casting her evil spell on Rio. When I let out another piercing scream the Horsemen were ready to fight, holding up their swords and shielding Rio, Any and me from the queen.

She laughed and I noticed that Mal appeared behind her as well, his expression full of guilt.

"Mal..." I whispered in full shock.

"Oh, dear," said the queen, wiping the dirt off her dress like she just came for tea. "Your show at my sister's was extraordinary and I'm still sorry you felt like you had to run away from me but well, I did side with my sister for a bit, so... I forgive you."

Ash, on the other hand, was not holding back. "Get out of here, you witch!" he shouted, charging towards her with all his might. But the queen simply snapped her fingers and Ash froze in place, unable to move a muscle. Ebony screeched to a halt, and before she could run towards the queen as well, she and all the Horsemen were frozen too."

I gasped.

"Stop overreacting," the queen said. "They were getting on my nerves and it won't last long anyway. My mana is very low, so, where were we?" She scratched her hair. "Ah, yes of course. So, it may be unpleasant to see Rio like this, but we had to take away his powers. Enough is enough."

Her gaze shifted past me, and I caught sight of Isix and Briz.

They must have placed Rio on the bed while we were talking. They stood next to him, frozen as well.

"After all," the queen continued, and I turned back to her, "we're running out of time. We must set things right, once and for all and you have to help us."

"But..." I struggled to find my voice, still clutching onto Any as if releasing him would shatter me once more, "why did you put Rio to sleep? Why?"

"Isn't it obvious?" she scoffed, rolling her eyes. "He's lost his sanity, girl. He'd sacrifice anyone, and we can't afford the world to crumble. It's too late to close the gates now and..."

"What?" My voice got caught in my throat. "Why is it too late?"

"Because they're wide open. I fear my sister has succeeded in the meantime. But I have a gift for you," the queen snapped, conjuring a swirling red smoke from her hand. Within its embrace, the Book of Silva materialized, snatched by her deft grip. "Open it, you're strong enough now. At least that's what I've learned from your little power demonstration earlier and then we must take matters into our own hands. It's up to us women, to save the world once more. So, let the sleeping beauty rest while we rectify the wrongs. When he wakes up, all will be fine again. Wonderful, isn't it?"

She winked at me as if all of this was nothing but a joke to her.

I swallowed, attempting to process the queen's words. This was crazy. Abhorrently crazy.

"B-But why should I trust you?" My gaze shifted to Any, Mal, and the frozen Horsemen. "Why should I trust any of you?"

"You simply have to," Any assured, his hand rubbing soothing circles on my back. "We're out of time. It's now or never."

The room fell into an uneasy silence, leaving me unsure of how to respond. Sensing my inner turmoil, Mal spoke up, "Lynne, listen, I know we have much to explain, but please, believe us. We're all fighting for the same cause. Look, the Blood Queen and Illiam used you to locate the bone, yes, but once we had the place, she ordered *us*," he pointed at Any and back to himself, "to steal Zeus' last bone. That's why we vanished on Blossom Eve. We secured it in a safe location, preventing the Bone Queen from awakening the Titans. So, no one was working with the Bone Queen, ever."

I took a deep breath, anger boiling up inside of me. "So, you're just telling me to trust all of you? Don't you think I've been punched enough in my life already? Everyone I trusted betrayed me. Even you," I said, my voice trembling and my eyes all watery again.

Mal stepped forward, his gaze intent on mine. "The Blood Queen is our only chance, unless you want everyone to die."

"Aw, you're the best," the queen said.

But Mal ignored her and added, "If we keep on waiting, your friends on Earth, Bory, Any, I, everyone would die. Except you and Rio and a few more gods maybe. Don't you think life would be very boring someday?"

I gulped. That's not what I wanted. I wanted everyone to live... I wanted—

"Rio did an amazing job in saving you, yes," Mal continued. "But he forgot about anyone else. You will live on forever now but what about us, Aria?"

It was the first time he said my true name and it hit me in the core.

Tears welled up in my eyes, and my voice trembled as I spoke, barely audible above a whisper, "I don't want you to die..."

The queen cleared her throat. "I admit, I've tried to kill you *and* Rio. I may have wanted to overthrow him at times, but then..." she lowered her gaze and I saw something honest in her eyes, "I fell in love with your father, and he wasn't exactly delighted with what I did to you, so I tried to become a better person and... we're working on fixing everything ever since and let me tell you, it's anything but easy. When you guys reincarnated, I wanted to strangle Rio."

I looked to Any. "And where's our *father* now?"

He made a face, driving a hand through his white-ish hair. "He was cursed by Athena for falling in love with the Bone Queen. He walks between worlds now and is not allowed to stay anywhere for more than a month. He's currently on Earth."

The Bone Queen scoffed. "As you can see. The curse hurt every one of us. But since Zagrios refused to work together, we simply had no choice but to find a way to take him out. We tried a lot over the past decades, but Zagrios stood in our way. He always managed to destroy our plans and work against us. He never knew what love was and once he had it, he got obsessed."

I glanced toward Rio, my fingernails tearing into Any's skin all the while I watched him sleep.

"Only you could stop him," Any interjected. "It wasn't easy to come up with the plan, since you guys vanished to Earth and we had to wait until we could bring you back to the Underworld again... and when you visited Rio on Storm Day, father and I made sure that you lost a bone and had to beg the Blood Queen to save you. That's how we came up with the idea of the essence of a first kiss. And when you kissed him on Earth, the power of your bond was so strong that it allowed us to finally knock him out. It was our last resort, Lynne. This way, we brought the book back, the powerful spell, and we made sure that Rio found his way back as well..."

"The Shadowslave? You murdered Jamie?" The words

lodged in my throat, choking me with disbelief at what my so-called brother

was confessing.

"It was me, yes," the queen admitted without remorse. "We expected him to follow you back to the Underworld, but he refused because of this human girl. So, we had to expedite matters."

"I can't believe you," I whispered, my voice trembling with a mix of anger and horror.

"Oh, spare me your naïveté," the queen sneered. "The girl is merely collateral. Sacrifices must be made for victory."

Disgust twisted within me, and I turned to Any, my voice quivering with betrayal. "How can you of all people be this deeply involved in all of this? You incarnated with me, didn't you?"

"Not really... it was father," he replied, and my stomach plummeted. "Father somehow found a way to bring me to Earth as well... It's a complicated story, and I promise to explain it all to you later. But, Aria, trust me when I say that my purpose is to protect you. I have never done anything else but be here for you."

I was at a loss for words.

It was all too overwhelming, too much to process.

"Sorry for keeping you in the dark, but you know... the curse. We weren't allowed to tell you what had happened," Mal said, sensing that I was at a loss for words. "None of us wanted to risk our lives, especially when everything relied on you regaining your memories. But damn, I tried to help you. But you're as stubborn as Hades himself!"

At that moment, Bory jumped onto my lap, seeking comfort, but I couldn't even muster the strength to stroke him. I felt paralyzed.

Then the queen approached me with slow, deliberate steps,

holding the book out for me. "You need to return to the Topworld, but first touch the book," she commanded.

"Topworld? Why?" I interrupted, my patience waning.

"We must find the Omphalos Stone. Rio has hidden it," Mal explained.

"To strip him of his powers?" I questioned, but the Blood Queen shook her head.

"No, it's a misconception that the Omphalos Stone can steal magic. It's actually a way to summon the gods in the Pantheon. But time is of the essence. With the gates open, countless humans are being slain, and we can't handle all the souls down here. Our world will collapse if we can't tend to them properly. So, we must act swift-

ly. By using the Omphalos Stone to call upon the gods, we can negotiate with Athena. It's high time she intervened."

"B-but according to Nana, it should be in the Shadow Castle," I remarked.

Any shook his head. "No, Rio hid it in Chicago. We have to search for it there."

"Touch the book, Aria! Open it!" the queen exclaimed, suddenly standing before me with eyes as red as blood.

My heart thumped against my temples, the weight of responsibility crushing down upon me.

"Touch it," Mal and Any said in unison, their urgency palpable.

My thoughts raced, searching for answers, but all I found were more questions. I stood there, frozen in indecision, my heart torn between trust and doubt.

"It's on you, Aria. You must right the wrongs you've, that we've caused," the queen said.

I raised my trembling finger, touching the book, willing it to open. And just like that, the world around me plunged into darkness.

All I could hear was Nana's voice, echoing across time and
space:

> "There is always a glimmer of light in the dark-
> ness and a blossom of beauty in the
> shadows."

THANK YOU FOR READING!

Thank you so much for reading and taking a chance on this series. If you enjoyed The Bone Weaver's Curse, please leave a review on Amazon and/or Goodreads and don't forget to follow me on Amazon, Instagram and TikTok so you'll be notified for every new release, giveaway or preorder!

Want more of the Bone Thief Saga?

COME JOIN my newsletter or Facebook Group and win bookish swag, special editions and more! I have a contest every quarter! You'll find all links here: www.heleendavies.com

The Bone Thief Saga

The Bone Thief's Tale

The Bone Weaver's Curse

The Bone God's Wrath *(coming Winter 2023)*

ACKNOWLEDGMENTS

As I sit here, penning the final words of this book, I am overwhelmed with gratitude for the many individuals who have supported me throughout this incredible journey. Writing a book is no small feat, and I couldn't have done it alone.

First and foremost, I want to express my deepest appreciation to my readers. Your support, encouragement, and feedback have been the driving force behind all of it. Your enthusiasm for my work has kept me inspired and motivated to bring this book to life.

Thanks a million to my beta readers, Karen, Gretchen, Saya and Sarah and Christina. Your keen eyes and insightful feedback have shaped this book into its best possible form. Your meticulous attention to detail and constructive criticism have pushed me to grow as a writer, and I'm so grateful for your dedication to this series!

I want to acknowledge the incredible team at pixel farm. From the cover to the map design, your passion and expertise have helped bring this book to the hands of readers worldwide. I am immensely grateful for your hard work and commitment to excellence.

Also, a big shoutout to everyone who supported my Kickstarter project. You made the special edition and the audiobook for book one possible and I appreciate you all so much.

To my family and friends, thank you for your unwavering support and understanding during this writing process. Your belief in my talent and your patience with my occasional bouts of writer's block have been a constant source of strength. Your love and encouragement have sustained me through the ups and downs of this creative journey.

I want to express my gratitude to the countless authors, both past and present, whose words have inspired and influenced my own writing. Your stories have ignited my imagination and fueled my passion for storytelling. Thank you for sharing your craft with the world.

Lastly, I want to thank all the nameless faces—strangers who have offered kind words, fellow writers who have provided valuable advice, and anyone who has contributed in any way to the creation of this book. Your collective impact may seem small, but it is immeasurable in its significance. Every word of encouragement, every shared resource, and every gesture of support has made a difference. In conclusion, writing this book has been a labor of love, and I am humbled and grateful to everyone who has been a part of it. Your contributions, whether big or small, have shaped this work and made it possible. I hope that my words will touch your hearts, ignite

your imaginations, and leave a lasting impact.

Thank you, dear readers and supporters, for joining me on this extraordinary adventure.

Love
Heleen

ABOUT THE AUTHOR

Heleen Davies is a teacher with a passion for writing and creating different worlds. She writes Fantasy Romance, set in magical worlds with fierce heroines and broody, morally gray heroes you'll fall in love with. Heleen is a mother to a little girl and a Golden Retriever, lives in the mountains in Europe and usually sticks her nose in all kinds of books. Find her on TikTok, Instagram, Twitter and Facebook! Also, how about you join my reader's group on Facebook:

Sketch of Rio and Lynne
by Surya Baswara

For updates about upcoming releases, please visit her website www.heleendavies.com/fantasy and sign up for the newsletter to get access to free short stories within the Bone Thief Saga universe or join her Facebookgroup here.